WOMAN

ON THE

VERGE

OTHER TITLES BY KIM HOOPER

Ways the World Could End
All the Acorns on the Forest Floor
No Hiding in Boise
People Who Knew Me
Cherry Blossoms
Tiny

WOMAN ON THE VERGE

A Novel

KIM HOOPER

LAKE UNION
PUBLISHING

Published by Lake Union Publishing, Seattle

www.apub.com

Amazon, the Amazon logo, and Lake Union Publishing are trademarks of Amazon. com, Inc., or its affiliates.

EU product safety contact:
Amazon Media EU S. à r.l.
38, avenue John F. Kennedy, L-1855 Luxembourg
amazonpublishing-gpsr@amazon.com

ISBN-13: 9781662526381 (paperback)
ISBN-13: 9781662526398 (digital)

Cover design by Jarrod Taylor
Cover Image © Mariia aiiraM / Shutterstock

Printed in the United States of America

For my dad.
I miss you every single day,
but I'm glad you won't be reading the sex scenes in this
book.

Part 1

Chapter 1

NICOLE

"Mommy? Mommy? Mommy?"

I read somewhere that mothers are summoned by their small children once every three minutes. I have two small children, and they are rarely in sync, so I am summoned far more often. At least once every sixty seconds, I'd guess.

The one summoning me was Grace, my three-year-old. Her sister, Olivia (we call her Liv), is two. They are adorable, real-life versions of Cindy Lou Who from *How the Grinch Stole Christmas*, which is a reference I can pull quickly because they watch that movie year round. On a daily basis, I kiss as many inches of their tiny bodies as I can. I would die for them. I would. And I just might because I think they are trying to kill me.

"Mommy?"

I did not respond right away. An article I read online suggested that I've trained Grace to whine like this because I've been too reactive and responsive to her. It's my fault, essentially. It's always the mother's fault.

"Mommy?"

Before having the girls, I craved this title—*Mommy*. It took nearly two years for me to get pregnant with Grace. (I assumed it would take as long the second time, but lo and behold, it happened right away.

This is why the girls are only sixteen months apart.) Now that I have the title, I realize that I'd completely romanticized motherhood. I had no idea what it entailed, not the day-to-day nitty-gritty of it. How can anyone really know?

"Mommy?"

I started to break out in a sweat so intense I wanted to peel off my skin. Google says I may be going through perimenopause, a full-blown life transition, à la puberty, that should probably not coincide with raising toddlers.

"Mommy?"

I gave in: "What is it, sweetie?"

"Can we go to the park today?" Grace asked.

"Park!" Liv shrieked. She is her sister's parrot, ensuring that I always hear everything at least twice.

"Sure."

It was a Tuesday morning, and I was a mother taking her children to the park.

I never thought this would be my life.

I used to work as a graphic designer at an ad agency—creating logos and brochures touting the benefits of a poison that people (women, mostly) inject into their faces to get rid of age-revealing wrinkles. It wasn't the most meaningful work, but I rationalized that at least I was doing something loosely connected to my college degree. I went to the Rhode Island School of Design for photography, but I took enough graphic design classes to be dangerous. People at RISD thought I was talented, "going places." I don't think suburban Orange County is what they had in mind.

At the agency, I was in charge of photo shoots—positioning models at various angles to capture the beauty of their frozen faces. My artsy friends at RISD would call me a sellout if they knew, so it's probably good that I lost touch with all of them by the time I entered my thirties.

I was determined to stay full time at work even when I had kids, and I did, for a while. After my maternity leave with Grace, I went back to work, which meant she was in day care nine hours a day. I knew I was supposed to feel an immense amount of guilt about this, but I loved going back to work. I missed her—the soft warmth of her skin against mine, her goofy toothless smile, her gleeful babbles, the sound of her little hands slapping at the hardwood floor as she learned to scoot and crawl. But I missed myself too. Working felt like returning to that self. I savored the luxury of eating sandwiches with two hands while in a seated position, something that had not happened since I'd become a mother. I could hear my own thoughts, and remembered that I liked them. And I liked having an identity beyond my child. I liked feeling competent. A more evolved person may not need a job to give them a sense of self-worth, but I believe it will become clear that I am not an evolved person.

I got pregnant with Liv while still breastfeeding Grace (I was one of those idiots who didn't think this was possible). I attempted to repeat the same series of events—take maternity leave, enroll baby in day care, return to work. But it quickly became apparent that working fifty hours per week with two babies—"two under two!"—was not going to be sustainable. The cesspool that is day care meant that one or both girls were sick nearly every week. I'd get a call from the day care to come retrieve the feverish child, which led to abandoning my to-do list for the remainder of the day (and sometimes the next day) to play nurse. Kyle and I never formally discussed that this responsibility would be mine. It seemed like the natural choice because his paycheck was larger than mine, and, well, wasn't caretaking a fundamental maternal duty? The day care thought so—they'd called me, after all, even though they had Kyle's number too. Kyle thought so, judging by the fact that he never offered to play nurse. And if I'm honest, I thought so too. As progressive as I think I am, I have absorbed all the messages about what a mother should be. I have taken them as gospel.

On the illness front, Liv was especially problematic because every cold became an ear infection that caused her to scream-cry in agony through the nights. This meant I wasn't sleeping because, per gospel, the mother is the one who gets up with the children. In a state of severe deprivation on many levels, I had a middle-of-the-night panic attack, the first of my life, accompanied by a sudden understanding of what mothers meant when they said they had no choice but to leave the workforce entirely or dramatically reduce their hours.

"I think I should go freelance," I told Kyle.

We were both up past midnight, sitting next to each other in bed with our trusty laptops, attempting to finish work that had spilled over from the day. It was almost unfathomable that there had been a time when we were college sweethearts who couldn't keep our hands off each other, who felt a physical ache when separated for a handful of hours. Were those even the same people?

I presented my case, telling him that about a third of the people at the agency were freelancers. Sure, they sacrificed the benefits of company-paid health care and retirement plans, but they could work flex schedules on their terms.

"Okay," he said, still typing away. When he finally looked up, he added, "We're lucky. We have options."

But that was just it—I didn't feel like I had an option at all. I *had* to quit my full-time job. I *had* to "dial back." Kyle wasn't going to do it. He was still "going places" with his career.

"I just can't do it anymore," I said.

"Okay. Let's crunch the numbers and figure it out."

That's my husband for you—always the pragmatist.

My boss, Michelle Kwan ("like the figure skater," she'd tell everyone upon meeting them), a woman with no kids, was supportive of me going freelance, but I sensed disappointment, like maybe she was thinking *Another one bites the dust*. I told her I'd come back full time when the girls were a little older, and she said, "Of course," not unkindly, but with a tinge of pity. I promised myself I would prove her wrong. I was not abandoning my career; I was simply taking a scenic detour. She would see.

I worked about thirty hours a week, which covered the cost of day care and left us with about $1,000 extra each month. It wasn't as much as I was bringing home before, but it was fine. The crunched numbers satisfied Kyle, and I was feeling like maybe I could do the elusive thing of having it all. Then, a few months ago, Michelle called me into her office and said the agency had lost the poison-in-the-face client and needed to make some "staffing adjustments."

"We need to prioritize the full-time employees, make sure they have enough billable hours on other accounts," she said. "I'm sure you understand."

I didn't understand, not at first. She must have seen the blank look on my face because she added, "We don't need any freelance help. For now."

When I told Kyle, he said, "Well, we can take the girls out of day care until you find something else. That will mean we won't see much of a dent financially."

Ever the pragmatist.

So that's how I got the title "stay-at-home mom" affixed to me, following me around like a piece of toilet paper stuck to the bottom of a shoe.

∼

It took us thirty-five minutes before we were ready to leave the house. Grace wants me to do either everything for her or nothing at all. I never know which is right in any given moment. If I attempt to help her with her shoes, she screams, "I can do it myself!" If I do not offer assistance, as I didn't on this particular day, she yells that her socks "don't work" with the urgency of someone witnessing the arrival of a colossal asteroid from outer space. Liv is easier, for now. She just puts her feet in my lap helplessly.

I don't know why the "terrible twos" are a thing. Two is easy. Three threatens to annihilate me. So many mothers lament the passage of

7

time. They say "Time is a thief" and "They grow up so fast." When I look at baby photos, I understand what these mothers are saying, but some days, I cannot wait for the girls to be older so they can tend to their own shoes and socks (and teeth, for the love of god). Their independence will be synonymous with my own. People say things get easier by kindergarten. On really bad days, I fantasize about going into a coma until then. There's probably a company on the dark web that offers this type of thing—VoluntaryComa.com or something. I have no idea how to access the dark web.

Grace insisted on stuffing her backpack full with trinkets and treasures necessary for our outing. These included a doll-size teacup, a fistful of Paw Patrol Band-Aids, and two baby dolls that had been touched with so many filthy fingers that their plastic skin had turned an odd shade of gray. Liv contributed the torso of a Barbie to the backpack, and Grace did not object.

Grace hung her backpack on the handle of her toy stroller, then put the dolls in the stroller. There was not enough room for both of them, as I warned her there would not be, but she was determined to make them fit. She grunted and whined, and I offered to help, but she said "No" and swatted my hand away. I decided it did not qualify as hitting, though Kyle would have disagreed. He thinks the girls need more discipline. I don't disagree, but discipline involves an ongoing cycle of reprimanding and redirecting, which would require a reserve of energy I do not have.

I closed my eyes. I told myself to breathe. I pretended to be a yogi, someone enlightened. But I couldn't get a full breath into my lungs, just fast, shallow ones. It's like I'm in a perpetual state of hyperventilating. There are many times I wonder if I should smoke weed. Or take edibles. Instagram keeps serving me ads for a THC-infused sparkling beverage. There are so many options for dissociating these days.

When I opened my eyes, Grace had made the dolls fit, one sitting on the other's lap, their legs weirdly bent and contorted in a way that did not bother her at all.

"Ready?" I asked with a smile that any adult would identify as fake, forced. The girls are not that sophisticated yet. They take upturned lips for what they look like.

"Ready," Grace confirmed.

"Ready," Liv repeated.

"Can we say bye to Daddy?" Grace asked.

I sighed again.

"He might be on a call, but we can check."

We went to his office. Kyle is a sales representative for a pharmaceutical company. He has always worked from home (in between on-site meetings with customers). Before, when I went into an office every day and the girls went to day care, he worked at the kitchen island, on the living room couch, anywhere he pleased. Now, he's holed up in the guest-room-turned-office, hiding from the chaos that is his family.

I pressed my ear to the door and heard nothing. It's usually obvious from several rooms away if he's on a call because his voice is unnaturally loud.

"Go ahead, sweetie," I told Grace.

She clasped the doorknob with both her tiny hands, still chubby with dimples instead of knuckles, and my heart swelled with so much affection for her that I thought I could cry. There is nothing like the emotional whiplash of motherhood.

She opened the door and walked in, Liv toddling behind her. I brought up the rear, which was strategic. If I walk in first in these instances, Kyle gives me a look of annoyance before transforming his face for the girls' benefit. If the girls walk in first, there is no opportunity to give me the Look.

"Daddy!" Grace said.

"Daddy!" Liv repeated.

Grace climbed into his lap, and Liv wrapped her arms around his legs.

He had his wireless earbuds in, ready and waiting for his next call. He is the most successful sales rep in Southern California. I'm proud of him, I am. From the moment I met him, he wanted to be exactly who he is now. He works hard. He takes his role as primary provider seriously. I just wish his accomplishments didn't make my own impossible.

When Grace was an infant, Kyle looked at me breastfeeding her and said, "Look at you—you're made for this." He was clearly oblivious to the fact that she had nearly torn off my nipple the first time she latched, which then led me to hire a lactation consultant to coach me through breastfeeding with "the wound" (her words). I appreciated his obliviousness because I wanted him—and everyone—to think I was blissfully bonding with my baby without complication (and certainly without "wounds"). I made the mistake of taking his comment— "You're made for this"—as a compliment. I made the mistake of feeling a surge of smug pride. It's only now that I wonder if the remark was an assignment for me, an unconscious way of letting himself off the hook.

"You girls getting ready for a nap?" Kyle asked them.

It was nowhere near nap time.

I'm never sure how ignorant Kyle actually is. Sometimes, I think he says and does things purposefully to remind me of his incompetence, to reconfirm my assignment. The other day, Grace asked him to move her new dollhouse from the living room to the kitchen, and he picked it up by its roof, which led to the whole thing dismantling, hours of my engineering work undone. He looked at me like *Oh shucks* and said he would rebuild it. And I believe he would have. In his own time. But I knew the girls would whine until it was fixed, and I'd nag Kyle, and Kyle would be annoyed with me for nagging him, and I'd be annoyed with myself for being the Nag. So I just did it myself that night after putting the girls to sleep. When Kyle saw it reassembled the next morning, he kissed me on the cheek and said, "Supermom to the rescue!"

"We're going to the park!" Grace told him.

"That sounds fun," he said.

Does he really think it sounds fun? Maybe he does. Maybe I'm the weird one for failing to find the joy. Whenever I talk to him about my fatigue, my boredom, my discontent, he says things like "It's not as bad as all that, is it?" or "Babe, come on—you got this." But I don't got this. Resentments are bubbling up like hot lava through cracks of black earth.

"Daddy has to make a call," he told the girls, looking back at his computer, clicking through his email with one hand.

I ushered them out of the room and closed the door behind us. Then we went to the garage, and I spent five minutes trying to convince Grace to sit in the double stroller with her sister instead of pushing her babies in the toy stroller.

"I can attach the toy stroller to the back of the big stroller, okay?"

Tears sprang from her eyes with alarming force, which then made tears spring from Liv's eyes with alarming force.

"But I want to push my babies," Grace cried, collapsing onto her knees like an actor in a Shakespearean tragedy.

"It will take us forever to get to the park that way," I told her. This was the truth. Toddlers do not walk anywhere with purpose. They are like village drunks, wandering haphazardly.

"But I want to!"

My skin began to prickle with an oncoming flash of heat.

"Okay, then no park," I said, my voice sterner, bordering on shouting.

This caused more tears from both of them.

"Girls, let's take a deep breath, okay?"

They did not listen. They continued to fuss and whine. I fanned myself with my hands, overheated by rage or hormonal mayhem.

"If you want to go to the park, both of you need to sit in the stroller, okay? We can play with the baby dolls when we get to the park."

Their crying slowly began to subside. My body cooled. I began to feel victorious.

"Fine," Grace said, arms crossed over her chest.

I lifted each of them into the stroller, the muscles in my back angry. *I'm sorry,* I often tell my body, this body I don't recognize as my own some days. *I am a mother now. I must sacrifice you for them.* I imagine my back is not happy about this, so it continues to bring me pain.

"Here we go," I told the girls.

And off we went.

~

When the girls were babies, I surprised myself by relishing the all-consuming love for them. They were so helpless and fragile. Their neediness infused me with purpose and pride. As they've grown, the all-consuming love has felt parasitic, as if they are sucking me dry of all life-giving force. Now their neediness infuses me with panic.

"Mommy, did you bring snacks?" Grace asked.

We had made it just twenty feet past our driveway.

"Of course," I said.

"Snacks!" Liv yelled.

I do not travel anywhere without snacks—goldfish crackers, graham crackers, saltine crackers, so many crackers.

I placed a graham cracker on each of their trays and braced myself for the whining. Is it normal to fear one's own offspring, to approach them like they are live grenades? There are two options: detonate successfully or be blown to smithereens.

Liv began nibbling at her cracker, but Grace said, "I don't want this."

Liv has been a good eater so far, but Grace is never pleased. I saw a meme on Instagram the other day—*The best way to ruin a toddler's day: ask them what they want for lunch, then make that.*

"Gracie, you love graham crackers," I told her, then immediately chastised myself for wasting these words. It's laughable, my ongoing loyalty to logic. "We just bought these the other day, remember?"

I braced myself for more whining. It's no wonder my neck is always sore—most hours of the day, my shoulders remain up near my ears in tense anticipation.

"No," she said, throwing it on the sidewalk. Liv then did the same, though I knew she was enjoying her graham cracker. She is going to be a sheep, I fear, the girl who copies whatever her friends are doing. I will have to worry about her smoking pot and piercing body parts and exposing her midriff.

I briefly considered making the cracker throwing a learning moment, lifting the girls out of the stroller and telling them to pick up the now-broken crackers. But as I said, my back is perpetually sore, and I simply did not care enough. I picked up the broken crackers myself, stuffed them into the pocket of my jacket, which has become a repository for all kinds of crumbs and other debris. My failure to give them consequences means the girls will grow up to be spoiled, awful people, and I will be to blame. Kyle will shake his head at me in disappointment. Like I said, it's always the mother's fault.

"You're a bad mom," Grace said, as if reading my mind.

This had no effect on me. I've heard it hundreds of times. I knew that five minutes later, she would tell me I'm the best mom ever, and that would have no effect on me either. The whiplash has a numbing effect. The only way to manage the wildly varied emotions of small children is to have none yourself.

I rewarded the girls' behavior by offering an assortment of other snack options, holding them out like a magician fanning a deck of cards.

Grace selected the goldfish crackers and Liv selected a graham cracker (of course), and we went on our way.

"Where are we going?" Grace asked.

Sometimes I feel like I live in an insane asylum and I'm not sure if I'm the patient or the doctor.

"To the park, remember?" I said, trying to sound cheerful.

When I first became a stay-at-home mom, I went at it full force, as I would a new ad campaign. I was a bit manic, putting my graphic design skills to work to create a color-coded schedule for the girls. I thought I would become That Mom, the one who has a Pinterest board and knows all the latest educational apps and sneaks spinach into smoothies. That lasted about three days. Then I began to feel like a pent-up racehorse. Texting with old coworkers or checking the news headlines on my phone became equivalent to my daily trot around the stable.

I miss work. I miss clear-cut productivity, the gratification of task completion. Motherhood is never complete. There are no encouraging performance reviews, no pats on the back. I miss excelling at something. I miss confidence.

Jill texted the other day to say she got promoted. Jill is one of my good (and only) friends. Before motherhood, I had more friends. As an introvert, I've always had a small social battery. There's only so much I can give outward before I am completely depleted. Now, all my "give outward" energy goes to the girls; there is nothing left for anyone else, myself and Kyle included.

Jill's friendship persisted because our work offices were next to each other and we saw each other every day. Minimal-effort relationships are the only ones a mother can be expected to sustain. Now that I'm home, Jill has stayed in touch via text strings that she always initiates. We will see how long that lasts. Anyway, she's a copywriter at the ad agency, not in competition with me, so I shouldn't have been agitated by news of her promotion, but I was. Jill and her husband, Matt, are childless—or child-*free*, as people are saying now. Of course she got promoted. I know it's not fair to hate her, but life is not fair, is it?

Whenever I share my sorrows with Jill, who probably gives herself pedicures while listening to me, she says, "Nic, it's just temporary, remember?" The work hiatus, she means. Except, is it ever really temporary for women? A couple of years back, the agency hired a woman named Beth who was returning to the workforce now that her children were in elementary school. She was only forty-two, but she seemed like a grandmother. Before they could fire her, she quit. Curiosity led me to look her up on LinkedIn, to see if she found a job elsewhere, but her profile was completely gone. Poof.

It took an embarrassingly long time to update my résumé, and then I resolved to send it out to one company every day until I landed a new freelance gig. I didn't think it would take long. I have experience!

I have contacts! But I haven't even landed an interview. Nobody wants to hire a part-time mother, I guess. There are full-time positions listed, but I can't imagine starting somewhere new. I would need to bring my A game for at least six months to earn respect, and the reality is that I'd be ducking out early to pick up a sick kid by week two. "It's tough out there," Jill told me. Not that she would know. After a month of nothing happening, I told Kyle, "This job search is a lot to juggle with the girls." To which he said, simply, "Okay." There was no pressure from him because he thought the arrangement with me home and the girls out of day care was just fine. The finances were manageable, and we weren't dealing with cesspool viruses. "I'll get back to it," I told him. "I'm just going to take a short break."

I'm still on that break.

"Mommy?" Grace called from the stroller.

"Mommy?" Liv echoed.

"Yes?"

"You're the best mommy ever," Grace announced.

Right on cue.

⁓

When we got to the park, it was almost ten thirty, which I have come to consider "close to lunchtime." Such optimism is a survival strategy.

There was the usual group of moms huddled together, some bouncing babies in their arms, others yelling commands at small children of various ages: "Micah, gentle hands. GENTLE HANDS." There were no dads—there rarely are during the week. The husbands come out on the weekends, likely forced by their exhausted wives. They do not congregate. They sit on the outskirts staring at their phones. I've often thought that would make a great exhibition—photos of fathers at a playground versus mothers at a playground.

I sat on a bench across the playground from the group of moms. They are Professional Moms, moms who would never put their kids in day care in order to work, moms who make leprechaun traps on Saint Patrick's Day and buy organic-cotton onesies and never do screen time. They are made to mother. They make me feel woefully inadequate.

Somehow, despite being harried (I assume) stay-at-home moms, they all look fit and fashionable. At least one of them must be a social media influencer. Most wear expensive-brand athleisure—the labels visible and making me feel like the nerd I was in high school all over again. Some wear trendy high-waisted jeans that look to be tailor made for their bodies, accentuating tiny waists and perfectly shaped asses. Since I became a stay-at-home mom, my daily uniform is a gray hoodie and a pair of sweatpants from Walmart. I look like someone about to rob a liquor store. And I have not figured out how to incorporate exercise into this new life—perhaps I should ask these Pilates-bodied women their secrets—so the fanny pack of fat I've had since the girls were born has grown in size. The other day, Grace poked my stomach and asked if I was having another baby.

I gave the Professional Moms a smile that didn't show teeth and said a silent prayer that Grace would not shout "PENIS" at anyone. She has become obsessed with the word and is known to incorporate it into random verbal bursts: "DOGGIE PENIS POO-POO HEAD!" I still have a note in my day planner to ask her pediatrician if this is some form of toddler Tourette's.

In a rare moment of idyllic sisterhood, Grace and Liv played in the sandbox with their dolls. There was no whining. Grace showed Liv how to rock the baby doll in her arms, and Liv watched intently, her little mouth agape in wonderment at her big sister's wisdom. These moments, when they are utterly delightful, are my sustenance.

"Mommy, let's play ice cream shop!" Grace yelled, jumping up from the sandbox.

I hate playing ice cream shop. Whenever we play ice cream shop, time slows. I cannot explain this phenomenon, but it is true. Nobody tells you about the boredom of parenthood. I don't know if withholding this information is an act of kindness or cruelty.

"Why don't you keep playing together for a bit?"

"Noooooo," Grace protested. "Ice cream shop!"

She came to me, grabbed my arm with a force that would be considered harassment in any other context, and tried to pull me from the bench. They really do think my body belongs to them.

"Ice cream!" Liv shouted.

I gave in. For the next twenty minutes, we played ice cream shop, which involved Grace and Liv saying "Ice cream for sale, ice cream for sale" while I crouched down to their level and pretended to be a customer. I'm going to need knee replacements by the time I'm forty-five, which will cost a fortune. Maybe they'll give me a two-for-one.

"Mommy, you need to order," Grace said, stomping her foot.

One of the hardest parts of motherhood, at least for me, is the expectation to be both childlike (while playing make-believe, for example) and authoritative. I do not know how to strike this precarious balance.

"What flavors do you have?" I asked.

Grace rattled off a list of flavors, most nonsensical, like "unicorn rainbow." I ordered chocolate and handed my invisible money to Liv, her face alight with joy at this responsibility. I could not help but pinch her cheeks and say, "You are the cutest ice-cream-shop worker there ever was."

We repeated the ordering-and-paying process about three hundred times. Sometimes I ordered the "wrong" flavor, and Grace became unreasonably upset. "Not *strawberry*, Mom," she said, as if I was the crazy one. It's worth noting that Grace called me Mom before she ever called me Mommy or Mama. She incorporated the latter terms upon realizing that they were more endearing and would serve her better in negotiations.

In the beginning of my stay-at-home-ness, the mind-numbing pretend play used to make me feel like I had fire ants crawling all over my skin. I was going through a kind of withdrawal from regular life. Now there are no fire ants. I've imagined the parts of my brain that would have lit up with activity on an MRI before having gone dark. There was a news segment a while back about a power outage at a New York playhouse. It was empty, pitch black inside, and I thought, *That's my frontal lobe.*

I looked at my watch. Almost eleven. I recently told Kyle that I wanted to write a book titled *Killing Time: A Memoir.* I couldn't read his expression, but I think it was one of confusion. I really did consider it, as a project to buoy me. I would include anecdotes along with photos of the mundanity of life. It would be marketed as the first book created completely with an iPhone—using the camera and Notes app. For a few days, I took some photos at the park, tapped some thoughts into my phone. Then I got tired of being interrupted every twenty seconds and gave up on the endeavor.

Grace left the "ice cream shop" and went to play in one of the plastic tunnels, Liv following after her.

"Mommy, come here," Grace said with a mischievous smile, her face peering out of one of the round windows in the tunnel.

I was fairly certain she was going to have a booger on the tip of her finger and would place it in my palm and ask me to dispose of it. I went to her anyway.

Surprisingly, she did not hold out a booger-adorned finger. Instead, she said, "I have a secret" and motioned for me to lean in.

At bedtime, the girls and I do this—whisper into each other's ears. I say, "I love you to the moon and back, forever and ever," and they say it back to me. It's one of those moments that compensates for so many others.

I leaned in, her breath hot on the side of my face. "Mommy," she whispered. "You. Are. A. Penis."

She erupted into giggles.

"Grace," I said. I try not to give the penis talk much attention. "Five more minutes, okay?"

I set the alarm on my phone. I am attempting to train the girls to respond to the sound of the alarm. I am attempting to turn them into Pomeranians.

"Okay," she said, though I knew it wouldn't be okay when the five minutes were up.

∿

"Oh, sweetie, what happened?" Kyle said. He was giving Grace the exact reaction she wanted, rewarding the tears that rolled down her cheeks with his attention. Of course, Liv saw the attention Grace was getting and then also started to cry. Their ability to create tears spontaneously fascinates me. In good moments, I silver-line the meltdowns by envisioning one of the girls—probably Grace—winning an Oscar. She will thank me in her acceptance speech. She will buy me a house in Malibu.

"Mommy said we had to leave the playground," Grace whined, falling dramatically into Kyle's open arms. Liv pressed herself against Grace's back, and Kyle included her in his embrace too.

"What a bummer," he said.

"Mommy is mean," Grace said.

"Mommy is not mean," Kyle said, and I wondered if that was the best he could do. He went back to looking at his computer.

"Mommy is so mean that she is now going to make you girls lunch," I said.

I went to the kitchen, the pitter-patter of four little feet behind me.

"What are you making me?" Grace asked. Like *Chop-chop, servant.*

"Grilled cheese?" I asked.

She scrunched her nose.

"Gracie want yogurt," she said with a baby voice. "Livy, you want yogurt too?"

Liv nodded.

Grace has been doing this a lot—talking (and crying) like a baby. The only thing worse than a three-year-old is a three-year-old pretending to be an infant.

"You had yogurt for breakfast," I told them.

There was that pesky logic again.

"Gracie and Livy want yogurt," she said again, her request followed by a dramatic "Waaaa."

Predictably, Livy added her own "Waaaa."

"Fine, whatever," I said.

They climbed into their seats at the table, and I gave them each a yogurt cup. I propped up the iPad between them so they could watch strange videos of Asian parents playing pranks on their children, or car tires rolling over containers of Play-Doh.

I considered calling my boss, or former boss, to beg for work. I'd had a Zoom call with her a couple of weeks earlier to "check in." (That was the subject line of the meeting invite. I'd thought she might have a project for me, but no.) The call happened to be an hour after Liv had scratched my nose with one of her hadn't-been-trimmed-in-weeks nails. My boss leaned into the screen and said, "Are you . . . *bleeding?*" I was, in fact, bleeding.

There are more injuries involved in parenting than I anticipated, most sustained while the girls are walking the fine line between abuse and play. Last week, Grace said, "MOM, BE A DRUM!" and then proceeded to pound on me. Yesterday, I was bent over Liv, feigning fascination with an ant, and she looked up abruptly and hit me in the face with her extremely dense skull. I saw stars.

∽

I called to Kyle: "Babe, can you watch the girls for a half hour this afternoon?"

Babe. A relic. A remnant of years past. My continued use of it is representative of our collective denial about our present.

"Mommy, mommy, mommy," Grace said.

The girls are ruthless and blatant in their attempts to prevent me from having, or sharing, a complete thought. Most of the time, my brain feels like it's in a car with a teenager learning to drive stick shift. Start, stop, start, stop.

"What?" Kyle asked.

"Mommmmmmmy!" Grace said, louder.

"Mommmmmmmy!" Liv said.

I shouted: "Can you watch the girls for a half hour this afternoon so I can call Michelle Kwan?"

He said, "Ummm," which meant no. "I have a few calls later, but let me see what I can—"

"Never mind," I snapped.

I could have turned this into a fight—it is one of my superpowers—but that would have ended with Kyle saying I needed to work on my anger issues.

"Mommy, I don't like this flavor," Grace said.

I did the only thing I knew how to do—I got her another yogurt.

~

When the girls finished their yogurt and crackers (yes, more crackers), they got out of their chairs and climbed onto the bench seat on the other side of the kitchen table. Grace turned onto her stomach, both hands stuffed underneath her, touching herself. Yes, like that. Then Liv did the same.

According to Google, it's normal. Do toddlers have orgasms? I've wanted to google this but am too afraid of what kind of list such a search would put me on. I envision the FBI showing up at my house, confiscating our computers. In any case, orgasms or not, the girls are undoubtedly pleasured, and I resent this. They are both more sexually satisfied than I am.

"Girls, are you tired?" I asked them.

They usually touch themselves when they are tired. They must get this from their father.

Grace did not look up but said, "Five more minutes" as she writhed around.

I busied myself with the dishes, not knowing if I should discourage them. I don't want to be *Catholic* about this type of thing. I don't think they're going to go blind, for god's sake. But I don't want to be too lenient either, so lenient that they start doing it in public, flopping down in the middle of Target, rubbing against playground equipment.

I've never told Kyle about the girls doing this. He would be appalled. It's been weeks since we've had sex, Kyle and me. Eight weeks, maybe. Meaning it's accurate to say we haven't had sex in *months*. There are times he touches me—a casual squeeze of my forearm, a tap on the butt—and I shudder. What a terrible thing, to recoil from touch. But it's not just touch, pure and simple. I can't help but feel it as a demand, a preface, a precursor to requests to come when the girls go to bed.

"Girls, come on," I said after a few more minutes. They were both all sweaty. When they looked up, their cheeks were red.

"Five more minutes."

"You already said that, Grace."

She rolled around a little more, then sat up. Liv kept going for a few seconds, but upon realizing that Grace had stopped, she did too.

"Fine," Grace said.

"You ready to go for a car nap?"

Neither of my girls is a great sleeper. They have never gone gentle into that good night. They share a room, so they do the whole bedtime routine together, a routine that I have always managed, even when I was working full time. It started innocently enough—I was breastfeeding, so I would do a top-off and then put the girls down. Now that they're older, Kyle could step in, but he doesn't, and I haven't pressed it. He works a lot; he's tired. Plus, I'm better at it than he would be.

The girls take approximately two hours to brush their teeth, then want to read seven hundred books. Kyle would never survive this. When they finally get into bed, I close the door knowing one of them (usually Grace) will summon me back at least twice: *Mommy, I don't like that shadow on the wall.* Or, *Mommy, my pajamas feel weird.* Some nights, I feel a wave of nausea come over me upon hearing the whines. It's visceral, motherhood.

By the time I go to bed, after a cup of tea or a glass of wine or both, I am still tense with anticipation of the girls calling for me. This is when Kyle reaches for me, pulling me into his side. I used to just give him what he wanted, even though I'd been touched all day and I was tired of giving. "The male ego is a fragile thing," my stepmom told me once. Lately, though, I reach into my bag of cliché excuses, a bag every mother must carry around (along with the snacks), and use one of them. *I'm so tired. I have a headache. I have a particularly bad period.* When I do this, he sighs, likely bothered by both the rejection and my lack of creativity in delivering it, and I know I'll be to blame if he ever cheats on me.

It's not that I'm turned off from sex completely. It's just sex in this context. The context of Wife, Mother, Servant. I have found myself daydreaming of sex with men besides Kyle on many occasions. There's a cashier at Trader Joe's, for example, a young man who can't be more than twenty-five years old, who I think about fucking in a back room of the store. There's that dad I used to see at day care drop-off, the one who knew the name of his daughter's baby doll, the one who asked the teacher if his daughter was doing better at nap time. He wasn't particularly hot in a conventional way. He was balding. He wore orange Crocs sometimes. But he was so *attentive.* I was convinced he'd make me come with just his tongue.

The fantasies remind me that I'm still in there—Nicole, the person I was before I became Wife, Mother, Servant. They, the fantasies, are what sustain me.

~

The girls sleep through the night, mostly—there *is*, apparently, rest for the wicked. Sometimes I wake up between 2 a.m. and 3 a.m., the insomniac's witching hour, and then one of them calls for me, as if they know I'm stirring, as if we are still physically connected, tethered in the way we were when they were inside me. It's as magical as it is terrifying, much like motherhood itself.

No matter what time they go to bed, no matter if they wake up in the middle of the night, they are up for the day at five thirty in the morning. Most parents cope with this type of insanity by keeping their eyes on the prize of nap time. Grace, however, will not nap. Or not in a bed, at least. As an infant, she would only sleep in a swing turned on at top speed. We had to change the batteries in the thing every week—those fat D batteries that you never have just lying around. When she grew out of the swing, we tried to get her to sleep in her crib, but she wasn't having it. She required motion. We resorted to putting her in the car and driving around aimlessly. The Car Nap was born.

Liv would probably nap on her own, in her bed, but I can't successfully separate them, so she comes on the drive too. When the girls were in day care, I only had to do the Car Nap on weekends, which was fine. Now I have to do it every day. I haven't told many people about the Car Nap because they say things like "You still do that?" As if I am a terrible parent. The truth is it's the only reliably quiet time of my day. So yes, I still fucking do it.

"I don't want a car nap," Grace said, her whine extra high pitched because she was in desperate need of the very thing she did not want.

Liv did not attempt to put her distress into words; she just started crying.

"How about we go to another park after?" I said.

Grace jutted out her bottom lip and said, "Fine."

Liv stopped crying.

"Hold me," Liv said, reaching up, her little hands clenching and releasing.

She gave me all her weight when I lifted her. My back ached, but in that moment, the ache was offset by the oxytocin that came with holding her. She was tired. She trusted me completely. I've come to consider this trust my performance review—I am doing okay because my daughters hold on to me as if I am everything in the world.

~

In the middle of the day, the freeway is mostly quiet, and it's possible to drive seventy miles per hour without hitting the brakes once during the Car Nap. On this day, I looked over my shoulder to see both girls asleep, lulled by the white noise of the freeway. I exhaled, then resumed the audiobook I'd been listening to, this one a memoir by a woman who left her husband of ten years to be in a relationship—a *throuple*, they call it—with two women. I tend to gravitate toward memoirs of people whose lives have completely imploded in some way.

I lost the plot of what I was listening to the moment I drove underneath the overpass connecting the 5 freeway to the 73 toll road. About a month before, during the Car Nap, this section of the freeway was at a standstill, which led to various whispered curses flying from my mouth. As the traffic inched along, I saw police cars on the overpass, next to a tan minivan parked on the shoulder with the driver's side door open. The southbound side of the freeway was completely closed, empty of cars. When I got closer, I saw why—a white sheet draped over what I'd later learn was the body of a woman who had jumped to her death. I couldn't—and still can't—drive by that overpass without thinking of her. She was thirty-seven. Her name wasn't published. I thought of that minivan, wondered if she had kids, if she was a stay-at-home mother.

I looked back at the girls again. Still sleeping, open mouthed, doe-like eyelashes fluttering, fleetingly angelic. Nothing has ever made me so choked up as marveling at the innocence of my daughters. Is this why we have children, to reconnect with the purity we lose to the world?

I shut off the audiobook because I couldn't focus, and turned to my next recurrent thought process: leaving Kyle. It's actually more like daydreaming than thinking. There's a rosy glow to the visions—me as an empowered single mother in a cozy townhouse, utterly exhausted by "doing it all," but in a kind of romantic way. Life, after all, would not be logistically easier if I left Kyle. I would be truly alone, as opposed to just *feeling* alone. Maybe that would be better, though. As it is, he's *there*, so I can't help but expect more from him. If he wasn't there, the burden of expectation would be gone.

In my visions, the girls and I would bond, cuddling on the couch together after our long days. It would be very *Gilmore Girls*. I would cherish our time together more because there would be less of it. Kyle and I would agree to fifty-fifty custody because we are decent, fair-minded people. We would commit to always putting the girls first. With my sudden influx of free time, I would have the opportunity to relax, to work, to have coherent thoughts, to read a goddamn book, to do yoga and banish my fanny pack of fat. And I would have the opportunity to miss the girls. Every mother should experience the complex luxury of missing her children from time to time.

On this day, I enumerated grievances in my mind. I thought of how, while I'm making dinner, Kyle watches reruns of that tasteless show with the comedian who makes jokes about YouTube videos. I thought about how he complains when I do meatless Mondays. I thought of how when I ask him to make dinner, he does something like salmon with a cream sauce, even though I've mentioned how I feel about combining fish and dairy. I thought of how he goes for early runs without asking for permission. I would ask for his permission if I wanted to go for a run because I would consider the impact of my absence, how it would give him the responsibility of getting the girls up for the day. He never seems to consider the impact of his absence. I thought of how he hates when I use lube for sex, even though I tell him I need it because of dryness related to the probable perimenopause. I thought of how he never asks what that's like for me—to lose my youth, to have that lovely rug pulled out from under me. I thought of his stupid coed softball team and how he kept right on playing after the girls were born. I thought of how his leisure is a given and mine is gone. I thought of how we are always jockeying for position. I thought of how I never win. I thought of how we are not partners; we are adversaries.

Just as I concluded that this was the definition of *irreconcilable differences*, a cry came from the back seat. I could feel my blood pressure rising. Sometimes I wonder how close I am to a stroke.

"Mommy?" Grace whined.

It was too soon for her to wake up. I usually get a full hour of quiet. I didn't respond, in hopes she'd fall back asleep.

"Mommy?" she said, louder this time.

I shushed her, gripping the steering wheel tighter in anticipation of her waking Liv.

"It's not time to wake up, sweetie," I whispered.

She shrieked and thrashed as if she were a caged animal in need of escape.

"I don't want these," she said, pushing against the straps of her car seat.

In the rearview mirror, I saw Liv's eyes blink open. She appeared confused before her face scrunched into a look of utter despair. She began wailing as Grace attempted to get out of her car seat. She'd done this before, a Houdini-like maneuver that caused me to summon a yell from deep in my core, something that could only be described as a roar.

"Grace, no. We're on the freeway," I said/roared. I did my best to sound calm. Three-year-olds are no different from people on ledges.

"I want *out!*" she said, kicking the back of the seat.

Liv wailed louder.

I had no choice but to get off the freeway, to relinquish my hour of peace.

But then I decided I did have a choice.

I decided that I would go home and I would tell Kyle to watch the girls for a half hour while I . . . did something. Or nothing. In silence. And if he hesitated, just the slightest bit, I would tell him it was over. I imagined the conversation:

It's over, Kyle.

What's over?

This. Us. It's bullshit. I'm done.

What are you even talking about?

He would probably say that last part with a little laugh meant to poke fun at my hysterics. Then he would hammer the nail in his coffin by telling me to calm down.

My heart pounded as I drove through our neighborhood, wondering if he'd want to keep the house, or if we'd sell it and split the proceeds. Would I stay in this neighborhood? If not, where would I go? How would our divorce affect the girls? Were there therapists for toddlers?

"Where are we going?" Grace asked.

"Home," I said.

"But I want ice cream."

"Ask Daddy when we get home. He can take you."

They had no response to this. They were intrigued. I had never said this before.

I pulled into the driveway, my heart still racing. I knew Kyle could see us pulling in from his office window, but he wouldn't come out. He probably didn't even realize that we were back sooner than we should have been.

When I unbuckled Grace, she squirmed away from my attempts to hold her and ran toward the house, likely curious to encounter this mysterious version of her father who was going to take her for ice cream in the middle of a workday. Liv, still tired, was dead weight in my arms, nuzzling into my neck.

I followed after Grace, and once inside, I heard Kyle's voice: "You guys are back!"

"Mommy said you'd take us for ice cream," Grace announced.

Liv raised her head from my shoulder to see the reaction.

"Oh, she did?"

Kyle's eyes were on me, his eyebrows raised, asking for my consent. In many ways, I am his mother too. I nodded.

"Well, okay then," he said with a smile. "That works out anyway because Mommy may need to call Grandma Merry."

Merry—short for Meredith—is my stepmom. I hardly ever talk to her and didn't know why I would need to now.

Liv squirmed in my arms. "Down," she said.

I put her down, and she and Grace went into the kitchen to pack their backpack for the ice cream excursion.

"Merry called," Kyle said once the girls were gone. "She said she tried your cell and you didn't pick up."

His eyes looked concerned. I sat on the guest bed next to his desk. When I checked my phone, there was a missed call from Merry. It must have come in while I was roaring on the freeway.

"She said something's wrong with your dad."

"What do you mean?" I asked.

He shrugged. "I don't know. She said he's acting weird. Memory issues or something. I told her you'd call."

"Okay," I said. "You're taking the girls now?"

He stood from his chair. "I'll take them."

He looked at his watch, one of those sporty watches that counts your daily steps. Kyle has the brain space to consider his daily steps. I can't fathom this.

"I need to be back in an hour for a call," he said.

"Okay. That works. You know I can't stand to talk to Merry for more than twenty minutes."

This was once one of our bonding things—talking about how draining my stepmother could be. I'd just dangled this bait in front of him, welcomed him to take it, to partner with me again.

Instead, he just said, "Nic, she's not that bad."

This was the day I marked as the beginning of everything that would come.

This was the day that would serve as the dividing line between before and after.

Chapter 2

KATRINA

The bartender brings a whiskey for Katrina (her second) and a beer for Elijah (his first). That's his name—Elijah. Moments ago, he sat next to her at the bar. She would like to think he was seeking her company, but the truth is that the seat next to her was the only one open. They have just exchanged names. He is one of the most handsome men Katrina has ever seen. Not regular-guy handsome, but might-be-a-Calvin-Klein-model handsome. He has big brown eyes, irises like melted chocolate, and curly brown hair in a bun on top of his head. His eyelashes are outrageously long. Women pay stupid amounts of money for extensions that make their lashes look like his.

"So are you from around here?" he asks, before taking a sip of his beer.

Her hands are in her lap, and she fiddles with her wedding ring. Should she take it off? The thought of it gives her a thrill. She could pretend, just for tonight, to be single and spontaneous and alive. On nights other than this night, she is married and boring and dead inside.

"I'm not," she says.

She knows he is from around here because he mentioned, when introducing himself, that this bar is his usual spot.

"I've been in town for a couple weekends. Visiting family," she says.

His smile makes her think of the word *genial*. What a strange word—*genial*. One letter away from *genital*.

"Where you from?" he asks.

She does it. She slips off her wedding ring and drops it in the inner pocket of her purse. Then she brings her hands to the bar. If she's not mistaken, he glances at the all-important finger.

"Los Angeles," she says.

"And what do you do in Los Angeles?"

What do people do in Los Angeles?

"I work for a production company."

"Fancy," he says.

That's what she was going for—*fancy*.

"And you live around here?" she asks.

"I do. My apartment's just a few blocks away."

Is it just her, or did he say that with a certain twinkle in his eye? Would he invite her back to his apartment? She wouldn't go if he did, but it would be nice to be asked.

"And what do you do?"

She hates that question, but he asked it first, so the reciprocation is only natural. She remembers hearing somewhere that nobody asks that question in Europe. Ask a European what they do, and they will likely list their daily activities and hobbies. Only in America is your career equivalent to who you are.

He takes a long pull on his beer. It's already halfway gone. She is nursing her drink because she is a lightweight, especially when it comes to whiskey. She doesn't drink it at home, ever. There is the occasional glass of wine from a $9.99 zinfandel purchased at Trader Joe's. That is her life.

"I'm a paralegal for now, hoping to be a civil rights attorney," he says. "I just took the bar, actually."

"Well," she says. "Fancy."

He raises an eyebrow.

"I'm impressed," she adds.

"That's premature. We don't know if I passed yet."

We. As if they are already an item.

He finishes his beer. Within three seconds of his placing his empty glass on the bar, the bartender is there to collect it and ask if he wants another. He does.

"How long till you get the results?"

"A couple months," he says.

She keeps staring at his lips, then scolding herself for staring. She can't help but wonder what it would be like to kiss him. She really has no business wondering this. It's just that he's nothing like the other guys she's been with before, bland white guys with sandy-blond hair and light eyes and aspirations for a 401(k) and a house in suburbia.

"You seem young to take the bar," she says, fishing for his age. It's obvious he's younger than her, but she's not sure by how much.

"I like to describe myself as a former twentysomething," he says with a smile. That smile, those dimples.

"We're all former twentysomethings," she says.

"Well, I just graduated from that decade a few days ago."

Katrina thinks of the twenties as "late adolescence," a time for mistakes and self-absorption and aimless wandering. The fact that he's already taken the bar exam means he must be far more mature than she was at his age.

"You can't be much older than me," he says.

She feels his thigh pressing against hers. Or maybe it's not pressing. Maybe it's just there. But it wasn't there a few minutes ago.

"That's a sly way of finding out my age," she says.

"I thought so."

"I'm thirty-five."

He nods. There is no eyebrow raising or other facial reaction to suggest he is in any way uncomfortable with her being "an older woman." After all, they're just flirting. It's not like he's assessing her as marriage material.

"You were still in junior high when I graduated from high school," she says.

He laughs.

The truth is really much worse. She's forty. He was still in junior high when she graduated from *college*.

"I've always had a thing for older women," he says.

This one comment makes it clear that the interest is mutual, which is shocking. He is so far out of her league, but he doesn't seem to realize or care. She could blame it on the booze, but he's only had two beers. To be clear, it's not that she's horribly unpleasant to look at. On a good day, she might even be described as pretty. But on most days, she would be described as average.

She finishes her whiskey and places the empty glass next to his empty pint glass.

"So, Kit Kat," he says.

"Kit Kat? You've already bestowed me with a nickname?"

"Too soon?"

She wants to say *Too unnecessary because I'll never see you again.* But she decides to enjoy the moment instead, to pretend that it's not unnecessary, that they are at the beginning of something. How fun to be at the beginning of something. For so long, she has felt at the end of everything.

"It's cute," she says.

"Should we get one more?" he asks.

Her head is pleasantly fuzzy, her skin warm and tingly. She is at the stage of drunkenness when the world seems kind and possibilities are endless. If she has one more, she will cross the line into drunken despair or, worse, puking. No woman her age should cross that line.

"I think I'm done for the night," she says.

"Done drinking or done talking to me?"

"I assumed the two went together."

"They don't have to."

There is that twinkle in his eye again. *My apartment's just a few blocks away.*

~

Katrina has never personally known a woman who has had an affair. Or rather, she's never known a woman who has *admitted* to having an affair. Not that this thing with Elijah is—or would be, if she let it happen—an *affair*. It would be—if she let it happen, which she won't—a one-night stand. A dalliance. A blip on an otherwise uneventful radar. But still, she's never known a woman who has confided in her about a blip.

She remembers listening to one of the marriage podcasts she subscribes to—because her marriage is at a point in which podcasts are needed to salvage it—and the guest, a prominent psychologist, said that about half of people have an affair at some point during their marriage. Half! One out of two. That means either Katrina or her husband is likely to cheat. She wonders if her husband has already had an affair. She can't imagine he could manage the logistics of it. He is terrible with texting.

On that same podcast, the psychologist said that men and women have affairs in equal numbers. It's just that women are more secretive about it. After all, it's more shameful for a woman to stray. There are scarlet letter *A*s for women. For men, cheating scandals are very ho hum. A good percentage of the world's leaders are adulterers, and most people can't be bothered to care. Those poor men can't be blamed for their biology—they are made to spread their seed, they are governed by their base instincts. Poor men and their ambitious penises.

When Katrina was in high school, it was well known that the history teacher, Mr. Adams, cheated on his wife with the English teacher, Ms. Pressley. Some of the kids started calling her "Ms. Press Me," which didn't make a ton of sense, but the gist was that Ms. Pressley was a slutty home-wrecker. She ended up leaving the school—by force or of her own accord, it was never clear. Mr. Adams stayed. He seemed disheveled and didn't wear his wedding ring for a few weeks, but then it was back. The students were left to assume that he had been properly reproached by his wife and would now be better behaved.

What if Katrina did go back to Elijah's apartment? Maybe they would just make out like teenagers. She deserved a little fun, didn't she? Even if they had sex, was that so awful? She might return to her husband a better wife if she had some excitement for once.

She scours her mental Rolodex of friends and acquaintances, wondering which ones would be most likely to have a one-night stand like the one she is considering having. It reminds her of when they learned in high school that one in five people has herpes and she and her four friends all looked at each other, trying to decipher which one of them it would be. The consensus was that it would be Kristen. They arrived at this consensus behind Kristen's back, of course.

Truthfully, she can't imagine any of the women she knows having one-night stands. It's not that they seem blissful in their marriages; it's just that they are so *busy*. When would they have time to sneak off to a bar and meet their own Elijah? They are all mothers. They have bedtime routines to manage. They spend most waking hours in faded black leggings. A few weeks ago, she never would have been able to imagine herself in this scenario either. It's a unique circumstance, a circumstance not accessible to most women she knows. For better or worse.

～

"Where would you want to go . . . to keep talking?" she asks him.

There is a twinkle in her own eye now, she can feel it. His smile conveys mischief. They are in on this together.

"You're welcome to come to my place. It's a short walk."

"Just a few blocks," she says. "You mentioned that."

"Just a few blocks."

"It would be nice to get out of this noisy bar."

"It is very noisy."

"Okay then, let's go," Katrina says.

She takes out her wallet, and he places his hand on her hand, which sends a jolt through her system. She didn't think she was capable of feeling such jolts anymore. It's as if his hands are those paddles paramedics use to revive the nearly dead.

"Let me," he says, taking out his wallet. He leaves cash on the bar top.

"You don't have to do that."

"My mother would have my head if I didn't."

Before she can think up a quip about him being a mama's boy, he says, "Come on," then takes her hand and leads her out of the bar.

The night air is cold, but his hand is warm. She tries to picture what her husband would think if he were walking down the street and saw her with this gorgeous man, leaning into his side, holding his hand. He wouldn't believe it. He would blink his eyes in disbelief. Because it is, truly, unbelievable. When she wakes up tomorrow, she will doubt her memory. She will question what really happened. This night, the magic of it, will seem like a fever dream.

"It's right here," he says, pointing to a high-rise, the reflection of the Hilton logo from the hotel next door shining in his eyes.

This is her chance to say *You know what, I've really enjoyed talking to you, but I think this is where I'll say goodbye.*

She considers it. She doesn't owe him anything. She knows that. But does she owe herself something? She tries to think of the last time she did something *for her*, the last time she embarked on any action that was not in service to another human being. There was that massage last month. She'd had to ask the woman to ease up on the pressure. She was sore for days after.

He must sense her hesitation because he says, "I promise I'm not a serial killer."

She laughs.

"That sounds like something a serial killer would say."

He laughs.

"If you don't want to come up, it's totally fi—"

She puts a finger to his lips, a bold move that surprises him, judging by the way his eyebrows shoot up to his forehead. It surprises her too. She likes this version of herself, this confident, knows-what-she-wants version. The psychologist on that podcast said women have affairs not because they fall in love with someone else, but because they fall in love with who they are when they are with someone else.

Not that this is an affair.

"I want to come up," she says.

"Okay then."

He takes her hand again, and they walk through the double glass doors into his building.

Chapter 3

NICOLE

One of the parenting books I read a while back—and I've read many—mentioned that parents who come from divorce are likely to feel intense emotions when their own children are at the age they were when their parents separated. This might explain why I feel as if I'm cracking up most days, why I ruminate on that woman who jumped off the overpass, why I want to make Kyle my punching bag.

I didn't come from divorce. But when I was three—Grace's age now—my mother died. A car wreck. It's tragic, objectively, but I have a hard time believing this event is to blame for any of my current state of mind. But then I think of how Grace and Liv would be affected if I died today. They would be shattered. Their current brains would be overcome with grief, and it stands to reason that this would affect them as they grew older, even if actual memories of me faded.

Google says that experiential memories go back to 4.7 years of age. I have no idea how this can be so precise, but there it is. Sometimes I think I remember my mother's voice, but I could be imagining it. "Did she used to sing to me?" I asked my dad once. He said he thought so, but didn't seem sure.

I've seen so many photos of her, and I've hoped they will trigger something, but they just . . . don't. I look just like her—"spitting image," my dad says. He's said I have her laugh too. He saved some of her clothes and shoes, gave them to me when I was in high school. They didn't fit. I'm taller than she was, and I have bigger feet.

Years ago, I tried to look up her name online. I don't know what I was searching for—details of the accident, an obituary? She existed before the internet, though. So now it's like she didn't exist at all. My dad says things like "I don't like to talk about that time," and I've tried to be respectful of that. He's said she loved me. He's said she was very smart—*brainy* was the term he used. I know so little else.

My dad raised me on his own until he met Merry. He toted me around to school and appointments and birthday parties and activities. He was dreadfully forgetful, in accordance with the trope of the bumbling father, but he was there. He was reliable in the ways that mattered. I was nine when he introduced me to Merry. Apparently, they'd been dating for a year before that. He married her when I was ten. I didn't have any of the usual kid angst about acquiring a stepmom because there was no competing loyalty with my real mom. In fact, I was a bit excited to have a woman around. She ushered me through puberty and did her best to advise me about boys. She ran the household while my dad worked, took over all the tasks my dad had previously done for me. They seemed to have a peaceful agreement when it came to traditional gender roles. She is, for all intents and purposes, my mom. But I've never called her that. I've called her what my dad calls her—"Merry." We don't have the best relationship now, but it's not the worst either. She can be rather exhausting, which is why I always dread calling her.

～

I waited a few minutes after Kyle left to take the girls for ice cream before calling. She picked up right away and came out with it:

"Something is wrong with your father."

Merry has a flair for the dramatic. This is one reason why she's exhausting.

"What's going on?"

"I don't know, Nicole," she said, exasperated. "His memory is shot. I had to pick him up at the golf course today because he couldn't find his car keys. Then when we got home, we found them in his golf bag."

Both Merry and my dad are in their late sixties. My dad has been forgetful for as long as I can remember. Kyle is similarly forgetful. Men get to be this way because their wives perform all the executive functioning for the family. Must be nice.

"Okay? Is that it? He forgot his keys were in his golf bag?"

She sighed. "It's not just that. I told him we have to start getting things ready for our taxes—he always does our taxes—and he said he couldn't remember how to *do* them. He went to Costco the other day and brought home a bag of avocados, a tray of blueberries, and a bunch of bananas, which is exactly what he had bought just two days before. What am I going to do with all this *produce*?"

I immediately began to consider that my dad could have early-onset Alzheimer's, then realized that it wouldn't be considered early onset. It never ceases to shock me that my dad and Merry are *elderly*, that they receive Social Security benefits and take blood pressure medication and have a will. My grandma, my dad's mother, had Alzheimer's. Or I guess it was classified as dementia. I don't know what the difference is. But I'm guessing whatever it was has some genetic component.

"Have you taken him to the doctor?" I asked Merry.

"Not yet. You know how your dad is with doctors."

I didn't know how my dad was with doctors. How is a daughter supposed to know such a thing?

"He won't go?"

"He doesn't think he needs to. Because he doesn't remember what he forgets."

"What?"

She sighed again. "He doesn't realize how forgetful he is. I'm the one who has to suffer the reality of it."

I rolled my eyes. Merry is the type of woman who gets all females accused of being histrionic.

"It sounds like he needs to go to the doc—"

"And his walking! My god. We went to Walgreens the other day, and he was stumbling like a drunk person. I was embarrassed to be seen with him."

I had been pacing the length of the kitchen up to this point of the conversation. When she mentioned his trouble walking, I sat on a stool at the island.

"His walking?" I asked.

My mind started racing then. My first thought: brain tumor.

"He's completely unsteady on his feet," she said, still exasperated.

"How long has he been like this?"

"I don't know. A few weeks?" she said. "He said he thinks he hit his head while retrieving a golf ball."

"What?"

"He said he thinks he hit his head—"

"Mer, I heard you. What do you mean he hit his head?"

"Well, I guess one of his balls went in someone's yard and he hopped the fence—"

"Dad hopped a fence?"

My dad has always been in good shape, but I had a hard time picturing this.

"I wasn't there, so I don't know. This is what he said, although now he doesn't remember saying it."

"And he fell?"

"Apparently."

"And he hit his head?"

"I wasn't there, Nicole. But it stands to reason."

"And now he's having memory issues and trouble walking?"

"Yes."

"When was this fall?"

"I have no idea. He has no idea."

Now it was my turn to sigh.

"You need to see a doctor. Is Dad there now? I'll tell him."

"He's upstairs. Hold on."

It sounded like she yelled directly into the phone: "Rob! Nicole's on the phone."

I heard the click of a new line. They still use landline phones—archaic and charming.

"Nikki!" my dad boomed. He is the only person who calls me Nikki.

"Hey, Dad," I said. "How you doing?"

"Well, I'm great." He sounded jovial, as usual. My dad has always served as a counterbalance to Merry, who thinks life is just one inconvenience and disappointment after another (ironic, considering her name).

"Merry said you went golfing today?"

"Not today. She mistakenly thinks I golf every day when I do not."

This has been the Fight of their marriage—my dad's golf and Merry's disdain for my dad's golf. I have encouraged Merry to get a hobby of her own, but I think her favorite hobby is complaining about my dad. If she were to get another hobby, there would be less mental energy for the primary hobby.

"Rob, you did go golfing today," Merry said, irritated.

"What are you doing on the phone, Mer?" It was as if he had no idea she had been there. It took me a second to realize he really *did* have no idea.

"I've been talking to Nicole, and she wanted to talk to you, so I told you to pick up the phone," Merry explained.

"No you didn't. I just called her myself."

It was then that I realized how serious things were.

"Rob, that's not what happened," Merry said, getting upset. "And you *did* play golf today! Remember I had to pick you up because you lost your keys?"

"What?" he said.

"Nicole, do you see what I mean?" Merry shouted. She was nearing hysteria.

"Guys, I need you both to be quiet," I said.

"This is just absurd, Nicole. It is *untenable*," Merry went on.

"Mer. Stop," I said.

She sighed for the hundredth time in five minutes and then went quiet. My dad made little grunts before quieting himself.

"Why don't I come up for a visit?"

The last time I'd seen them was Christmas. They'd come to see us, showing up with too many gifts. I had a hard time remembering the last time I had gone up to see them. Was it before Grace was born?

"A visit?" Merry asked.

"Yeah. I could come up, see how things are there." I tried to sound casual. I didn't want to alert my dad to my concerns about a brain tumor. He would order me to stay home, to stop being silly.

"It would be nice to see you," Dad said. He was back to being jovial, perhaps having forgotten the tension of a moment earlier.

"It's been a long time," I said.

"Would you bring the girls?" Merry asked.

I thought about it. Flying up there would be too expensive. I'd have to drive. I pictured seven hours in the car with them. I wasn't confident I wouldn't kill them or myself along the way, so I said, "I don't think so. I'll just come for a couple days. Kyle can watch them."

The words felt strange in my mouth: *Kyle can watch them.*

Kyle had watched the girls once overnight before, when I had to attend a photo shoot for work in Los Angeles that didn't end until nearly midnight. I stayed at a hotel and then drove home early the next morning. Kyle insisted everything had been fine without me, but he looked wrecked, the bags under his eyes assuring me that I wasn't the only one who found it difficult to be the primary parent.

"Kyle can watch them?" Merry asked.

She made no attempt to hide her surprise. I've never complained to Merry about Kyle, never let on that I am in any way disgruntled. She is a bottomless pit when it comes to her hunger for this type of gossip, and I've refused to feed her. But a part of me felt validated to hear her surprise, to know that she saw me as the one carrying the weight of everything alone.

"Yes, he's quite capable," I said, though I wasn't at all sure of this. "He is their father, after all."

Merry is from a generation that does not understand the expectations of modern fatherhood. Modern fathers also do not seem to understand the expectations.

"We'd love to see you, Nikki," Dad said.

"Okay, I'll talk to Kyle and let you know when I'll come. But soon, okay?"

"Thank you, Nic," Merry said, her voice suddenly saccharine. "Tell Kyle and the girls we send our love."

I told her I would right as I heard the garage door open, Kyle and the girls back from the quickest trip to the ice cream shop ever recorded by man.

~

As I packed my small suitcase, I felt something like a thrill, akin to the thrill I felt when packing for my first big trip with Kyle—to Las Vegas of all places. I met Kyle my sophomore year of college in a very typical way. We were both at a bar in downtown Providence. I was attending RISD, fancying myself a renowned photographer in the making. He was at Brown, fancying himself rich and successful by any means possible. Over those first drinks, he told me how he'd grown up poor, how he got a scholarship to Brown, how he was determined to make a good life for himself. He was very handsome, could have passed for Keanu Reeves's blue-eyed brother, but I was most attracted to his drive. He had a seriousness about him, a maturity. Most of the guys I knew at

RISD smoked weed and laughed at the concept of a five-year plan. My dad had always told me to find a guy with a five-year plan. Kyle had a ten-year one.

When we turned twenty-one, Kyle wanted to go to Vegas. It was something he'd just always wanted to do, he said. I knew it wouldn't be my scene, but I wanted to be a cool girlfriend, so we went. I felt besieged the entire time—too many sounds, too many sights—but Kyle was like a kid at Disneyland, so I held my breath for the weekend and put a smile on my face. (As a side note: no one tells you that, in terms of overstimulation, every day is Vegas when you're a mother.)

I suppose I am partially to blame for our marital problems. We were so young when we met. Our brains weren't even fully developed. I did what so many women do—in the absence of my own identity, I accommodated his. How can he be expected to understand my needs when I spent years pretending I didn't have any?

Now, what felt like three hundred years after that Vegas trip, I was packing to leave Kyle (and the offspring I had created with him) to visit my elderly dad and stepmom in Daly City, just outside San Francisco. I felt that flutter of excitement that comes with embarking on something new. It wasn't the place that was new—I'd lived there, after all—but the freedom. A plane ticket, even for just myself, was too much money to rationalize, but I was looking forward to the drive, pondering taking the long route, along the coast, just to enjoy extra time to myself.

It was Friday afternoon, a few days after I'd talked to my dad and Merry. I was waiting for Kyle to officially finish his workday before I could get on the road. The girls were basket cases, not taking well to the idea of me leaving them. "Daddy doesn't know how to do anything," Grace moaned, which was a sound objection. Liv wailed, flopping her little body onto the floor while I packed. It was like they were in competition to show me which one of them was in more distress. I'd be lying if I said the whole show didn't flatter my ego.

"You two will be fine. I'll be back Sunday night. That's in two days," I said.

I hugged them, their bodies side by side, my arms wrapped around them. When I let go, they were caricatures of sad people, their little mouths downturned, their eyes somehow larger than usual, cheeks tear streaked. My stomach clenched, and I briefly considered canceling my trip, but decided this was as good for them as it was for me. As one of my recent parenting books reminded me, I am modeling motherhood for them. If they decide to become mothers, I want them to know it's okay if they have lives and desires and needs separate from those of their children.

I zipped my suitcase and took it to the front door. Grace and Liv followed me, Grace stepping on my heels, Liv grasping onto my pant leg.

"You all packed?" Kyle asked.

"I think so."

I'm sure he didn't love the idea of me being out of town, but when aging parents and medical issues are involved, one must, for lack of a better term, suck it up. This must be in a marital handbook somewhere.

He looked at his watch. "You better get going, or you'll be driving till midnight."

I sighed, feigning apprehension, when really I could not wait to get out that door and into my car and on the road. The anticipation of freedom was making me all buzzy inside. I tried to control myself, to hide my ecstasy.

"I'll text you when I get there," I told him.

He nodded.

"Noooooooooo," Grace said, and Liv joined in.

They each attached themselves to a leg with palpable desperation. I knelt down and pulled the three of us into another embrace, our faces smashed together.

I gave them each sloppy kisses on the cheeks and said, "I love you, you little boogers."

That made them laugh. When in doubt, say *boogers*.

"I'm not a booger. Liv is a booger," Grace said.

"Grace is booger," Liv said.

They were howling with happiness, which was my cue to leave.

"Drive safe," Kyle said.

"I will."

I blew the requisite kisses, and then I was out the door.

Free.

~

Daly City is somewhere people live when they can't afford San Francisco. It's only twenty minutes from downtown, just south of the Outer Mission. When I was a kid, I felt like a loser for living there. My dad probably could have afforded to live in San Francisco proper—he was a reputable dentist, and Merry managed his busy practice, before they sold the business and retired—but they always said they liked being on the outskirts, away from the "hullaballoo." They shelled out for me to go to a private high school near Golden Gate Park, so all my friends were rich and brilliant and gave me a complex that I carry with me to this day.

It took me eight hours to get up there. When I pulled up to the house, Merry was standing by the front door, waiting.

"You made it," she said.

I gave her a hug. Hugs with Merry have always been awkward. She is not the affectionate type. I've always longed for the mothers from sitcoms who embrace their children with ferocity, mothers who say things like "You're my favorite human," things I say to Grace and Liv all the time. It would be easy to assume that Merry just never felt it was appropriate for a stepmom to say those sitcom-mom things, but I think the truth is that she doesn't have it in her. She never had her own kids, for reasons I've never investigated. One time she mentioned, randomly, "I'm not a touchy person. My parents were German."

"I made it," I said.

"Who's there?" my dad called from upstairs.

"It's Nicole, Rob," Merry said.

She looked at me and shook her head. "I just told him that you would be here soon."

The house was warm because Merry is always cold and sets the thermostat at seventy-seven at all times. Unlike mine, her perimenopause days are long behind her.

"I've got your room ready for you upstairs," she said, as if she were a hotel manager.

She insisted on taking my suitcase, and I followed her up the stairs and to my old bedroom, which was painted and turned into a guest room about five seconds after I left for college.

She set my suitcase on top of the queen-size bed and said, "This will do, right?"

"Mer, of course it will do. It was my bedroom for eighteen years."

"I guess that's true, isn't it?"

"It is."

I found it hard to remember what it had been like as my room. I'd had artwork and Polaroid photos taped or tacked to the walls. It was very *me*. Or the me I used to be. I thought of the face Kyle would make if I came home and insisted on covering every inch of the walls with visual inspiration. He would have me committed.

"Dad's in bed?" I asked.

"He is," she said. "Just to warn you, he's even worse at night."

I followed her to their bedroom. The TV was on, an infomercial for a food processor that was described as "revolutionary." My dad was sitting up against the headboard in his boxer shorts and a T-shirt, his legs stretched out in front of him. He looked like he'd lost weight.

"Hey, Pops," I said.

He turned, and there was shock on his face when he saw me.

"Nikki! What are you doing here?"

Merry sighed loudly behind me.

"I decided to come visit, remember?"

"You did? Are you pulling my leg? Is this a surprise?"

"I guess it's a surprise for you," I said, forcing a laugh.

He swung his legs over the side of the bed and stood.

"Well, let me give my girl a hug."

That's when he took a step in my direction, and I saw immediately that something was very wrong. He looked like someone walking on the deck of a boat in rough waters.

He teetered from one foot to the other with each step, his gait unstable and staggering. I looked to Merry, my mouth agape, tears coming at just the sight of him. She looked at me like *See, I told you.*

When he finally made his way to me, he wrapped his arms around me with the strength and tightness that Merry never gave me. He was warm and solid, and I buried my face into his shoulder, drying my eyes on his shirt. I didn't want him to see me upset.

"Daddy, what's wrong with your legs?" I asked him.

"Oh, I don't know. My balance is off."

"I think we need to take you to the doctor."

"Don't worry about me, Nikki. I'll get better."

"But we don't even know what's *wrong* with you," I said.

Though I knew. I was sure I knew. The words kept flashing in my head—*Brain. Tumor.*

He hugged me tighter. "Let's talk in the morning, okay? It's late."

I nodded. I felt so much like a little girl in that moment, a little girl being told by her all-knowing father that she needed to get some sleep.

I kissed his cheek and then walked back to my room, Merry behind me.

"Why haven't you taken him to the hospital?" I asked her. I tried to temper my tone, but couldn't help but sound accusatory.

She looked flabbergasted.

"He doesn't think anything is wrong! You saw him!"

"But something *is* seriously wrong," I said.

She looked like she was going to cry. That's when it occurred to me that she wasn't taking him to the doctor because she knew something was seriously wrong, and she didn't want to know that, not for sure.

"It's okay," I said. "I know it's hard."

She stared past me. "My father, he had Alzheimer's. It was just . . . awful."
I had vague memories of when her father had been sick. I was a teenager at the time, completely self-absorbed. A wave of guilt washed over me as I considered how Merry had continued caring for me during that time, keeping me blind to whatever horrors she was encountering.

I put my hand on her arm.

"I don't think it's Alzheimer's," I said. "It's something else."

"What do you think it is?" she asked me. Her voice was small, and suddenly, of the two of us, she was the child.

"I don't know. I'll take him to the hospital at UCSF tomorrow. I have an old friend who works there. Remember Prisha Patel from high school? She's a doctor there. Anyway, I'll figure it out. *We'll* figure it out, okay?"

Her eyes were big and scared.

"I can go with you," she said. "To the hospital."

I could tell she didn't want to, though. She seemed terror stricken at the prospect.

"Let me handle it for you, okay?"

She looked past me again, then found my eyes with hers.

"Okay," she said finally.

"Dad's right, though. We should all get some sleep."

With that, she turned and went back down the hallway to their bedroom. I didn't bother washing my face or brushing my teeth. I just stripped down to my underwear, put on a sweatshirt, and lay down, staring at the ceiling. When I got immediately overheated, I took off the sweatshirt and just lay bare chested, beads of sweat dotting my breasts.

I texted Kyle.

Sorry, forgot to text you when I got here. I'm here

While I waited for a response, I sent a message to Prisha on Facebook, asking her what to do about my dad, then swiped through photos of the girls on my phone. Thousands of photos, thousands of moments when I thought *I just have to capture this*, thousands of reminders of motherhood's magic. As eager as I was for time away from them, I already missed them. Or maybe *miss* isn't the right word. It's more that it felt wrong that they were not near me, a troubling discordance.

Prisha responded before Kyle did, suggested I bring my dad in through the ER at UCSF.

> The teaching hospitals leave no stone unturned. They'll likely admit him, given the symptoms.

I sighed. That would be my day tomorrow—the ER.

Ten minutes later, Kyle still hadn't responded. He was probably already asleep, exhausted after enduring the battle that is the Bedtime Routine. Grace had started doing something I called the Wet Noodle at bedtime, where she let her entire body go limp and refused to assist me with putting on her pajamas. It was like trying to dress a corpse. I thought of Liv throwing her usual tantrum when presented with a toothbrush. I thought of them requesting "one more book" ad infinitum. Kyle was normally in the other room, "wrapping up some work," during these shenanigans. He must have heard the pandemonium, but didn't step in to help. Was it all white noise to him? Was he that confident I had it handled? It was awful of me, but I hoped the girls were giving him an especially hard time. I hoped they would call for him thirty-seven times during the night, asking him to fix the blankets. You might think that realizing what a terrible person I am would have kept me up all night. But no. Somehow, I fell asleep and didn't wake up until nine the next morning.

Chapter 4

KATRINA

As Elijah puts the key into the door of his apartment, Katrina expects one of two things: a trendy bachelor pad designed to impress women, or a messy bachelor pad designed to impress no one. Instead, he welcomes her into a space that could only be described as warm. It's lived in, but tastefully. Her eyes go right to an unlit candle on the coffee table. It's not just for decoration—the wax is sunken in. She tries to picture this gorgeous man at home by himself, lighting a candle, and she has to suppress a giggle.

"My humble abode," he says, stretching his arms out to the side.

His arms are incredibly long, like his legs. He is all limbs.

"It's . . . nice," she says, meaning it.

He laughs. "I can't tell if you're being sarcastic."

"Most people can't," she says. "But this time I'm not. Promise."

The furniture looks like it's from Pottery Barn. Does this thirty-year-old man shop at Pottery Barn? There is a bookcase. She's too far from it to scan the titles. There is a framed photo on one of the shelves, but she can't see that either. The kitchen is directly off the living area. There are dirty dishes in the sink, so he is, in fact, human. A half-full bottle of red wine is corked on the counter. Did he share it with someone else? Is she one of many women he brings back to his place?

"I don't ever do this," he says, as if reading her mind, a terrifying prospect.

"This?" she asks, coy.

"I don't ever invite women back to my apartment," he says. "Actually, I hardly ever meet women at bars, at least not ones worth talking to."

She squints her eyes at him. "I find that hard to believe."

He shrugs. "I'm picky, I guess."

"Well, I never do this either."

Now he squints at her. "I find *that* hard to believe."

She barks a laugh. Does he think she's someone who prowls for men? A bona fide cougar?

"I didn't mean it like that," he says, again clairvoyant. "I just meant you're beautiful, so I'm sure all kinds of men want to talk to you."

Is she blushing? Jesus, when was the last time she *blushed*? And when was the last time someone called her *beautiful*? Everything in her wants to talk him out of his opinion: *Oh, stop; beautiful is a bit of an overstatement.* But she refrains. Confidence is sexy, according to all the internet articles.

"You want to sit?" he asks.

They sit on the couch, their thighs touching the way they were at the bar. She doesn't want another drink, but when he asks if she wants a glass of wine, she says yes just so she can hold the glass and have something to do.

For a while, they stick to their plan of just talking. They act as if they are just two people who met for conversational purposes. This charade is thrilling in a way, a sort of foreplay.

"How long have you lived here?" she asks, taking in more of the space. There's a door cracked open across from the kitchen. The bathroom, she presumes. There's another door, also cracked open, beyond that one. The bedroom.

"About a year. I was living with my mom before that."

"I'm not sure you should be admitting that to me."

He laughs. "I don't have any shame. It's the best way to save money. And my mom is pretty cool."

Definitely a mama's boy. It's more endearing than cringeworthy.

They each sip their wine. She's wondering what's going to happen next. What does she *want* to happen next? When it comes to considering her desires, she's rusty.

"I find it hard to believe you don't have a girlfriend," she says. "I mean, you have candles."

He laughs again. He makes her feel like a comedienne. A sexy comedienne.

"I happen to like candles," he says. "Who doesn't appreciate some good ambiance?"

"Wait . . . you're not gay, are you?"

"Come on now. A straight dude can be into ambiance."

"I don't know. I've never met such a guy."

"You're missing out, then."

He's right about that.

"Anyway," he says. "I did have a girlfriend. We broke it off last year."

"Who ended it?"

"You go right for the jugular, don't you?"

"I don't like to waste my time."

"It was mutual," he says.

She rolls her eyes. "Of course it was."

"What? It *was* mutual. She took a residency in Illinois. Different paths, that's all."

"Residency?"

"She wants to be a pediatrician."

"Of course she does."

Even his girlfriends sound saintlike.

"What about you? You don't have a boyfriend?" he asks.

She shakes her head. "Nope."

She's not lying. She doesn't have a boyfriend. She has a husband.

"And with the last one, was there something wrong with you or something wrong with him?" he asks.

She thinks of her husband, who, right about now, is probably lying in bed in his holey briefs, watching *SportsCenter*.

"Definitely something wrong with him," she says.

"Because there's nothing wrong with you."

"Obviously."

She sets her glass on the coffee table. She decides she's just going to go for it. She's going to kiss this man who is basically a stranger because he seems kind and not like a serial killer. And he is beautiful.

"I have a question," she says, turning to him on the couch.

"I hope I have an answer."

She leans in toward him. "Can I kiss you?"

He smiles, possibly the widest smile she's seen from him tonight. His teeth are bright white in the dim lighting. He sets his glass on the coffee table next to hers.

"You're in luck," he says. "I do have an answer."

She tries to appear seductive even though she feels completely terrified. That voice inside is pestering her: *What are you doing? What are you doing? What are you doing?*

"And?"

"You may kiss me," he says. "In fact, I would very much enjoy that."

She wills her face to move closer to his, and just as their lips are about to touch, she closes her eyes. She is dizzy, from the drinks or from the exhilaration, she isn't sure which.

His lips are even better to kiss than she'd imagined. They are, dare she say, *pillowy*. She has never kissed pillowy lips before. In college, she and her roommate Jessie kissed once, just for shits and giggles, and Jessie's lips were somewhat pillowy, but nothing like Elijah's.

Their tongues touch and then slip inside each other's mouths. Suddenly, everything *down there* comes alive. She has long mistaken dormancy for death.

Soon, she is on top of him on the couch, straddling his middle. His hands slip under her shirt, touch her bare skin. There are instantaneous goose bumps. When was the last time she got instantaneous goose bumps?

"Do you want to go to the bedroom?" he asks.

She knows if they go to the bedroom, they will sleep together. She will officially be an adulteress. She will have this secret to keep from her husband. She will have to live with the guilt. Will there be guilt? In this moment, after two whiskeys and a glass of wine, she does not anticipate any guilt.

"Yes," she says.

They do that thing that lovers do in movies—they stumble to the bedroom, he walking backward, she falling into his front, their feet tripping over each other. They attempt to keep their mouths attached as they go, their teeth bumping. They laugh. When they get to his bed, they fall back. The room is small, with just space for his bed—a queen—and a dresser and nightstand (with a candle).

She unbuttons her own pants and then his. Soon they are naked except for their underwear, these thin layers of clothing all that remain between her and someone she never thought she'd be. He is hard against her, and large. Well, larger than her husband, who she's always assumed is about average. She's only slept with three men in her whole life. Her sample size is small.

She shimmies out of her completely unsexy cotton underwear and tugs on the waistband of his boxers. Soon his boxers are on the floor next to her unsexy cotton panties, and she is staring at him in all his naked glory. If she were to tell a friend about him, she would use the word Adonis. She would say he looked like he was carved from clay.

But she won't tell friends about him because she absolutely cannot tell anyone about this.

She finds herself kissing his chest and then moving downward. She can remember the last time she gave a blow job—on her husband's birthday, terribly cliché—but she can't remember the last time she *wanted* to. She wants to now. She wants. Now.

He moans, and she feels more successful than she has in ages. When his body starts to twitch, she knows he's close. He pushes her off him and says, "Your turn." Then he moves his lips down her body and starts licking her there. It feels so good she *giggles*. She's always thought she isn't an oral sex type of person. With her husband, it has always felt like he let a goldfish loose in her labia. For a few moments, she is so consumed with pleasure that she forgets that this part of her body was made for any other function besides this. She forgets that children have come from this vagina. *Her children!* She has temporarily forgotten their existence, a glorious but horrifying amnesia. Thought of them threatens to take her out of this unprecedented moment, but then Elijah does something with his tongue, and she is right back where she wants to be.

"Oh my god," she says, because she is truly astonished.

She pulls on the curls of his hair, and he lifts his face, a dopey smile on it.

"Can you get inside me already?" she says.

He laughs and reaches into his nightstand. She'd forgotten about this step—the condom! *They still make those things?* she thinks irrationally.

He is inside her no more than three seconds before she decides this is, by far, the best sex of her life. She wraps her legs around him as he rocks into her. She comes once, then twice. He flips over so she is on top, and then she comes a *third* time. He comes with her that third time—simultaneous orgasms, something she previously thought mythical. When anyone mentioned having them, she always thought they were lying.

She rolls off him, and they are lying side by side, sweaty, breathing heavily.

"That was good," he says, removing the condom.

"Um, yes," she says. "It was."

"Really good."

She pushes up onto an elbow, looks at him. "It was, right? I mean, is it always that good? For you, I mean?"

He laughs. "That was particularly good."

"Right."

She lies flat again.

"You okay?" he asks. She can hear the smile in his voice.

"Very much okay."

He sits up, reaches for the comforter that they've kicked to the end of the bed, and pulls it up over their naked bodies. Then he turns on his side and wraps an arm around her middle.

"Would you be mad if I was a typical man and fell asleep?" he asks.

She sits up, his arm still on her middle.

"No, no. But I should go," she says, lifting his arm.

His closed eyes blink open.

"What? Really?"

She didn't anticipate that he'd want her to stay.

He kisses her thigh.

"Stay," he says.

"I can't."

But technically, she can. Her husband is not expecting her home until tomorrow.

"Please?" he says.

"Wow, you've really perfected that puppy-dog thing."

"Is it working?" he asks.

Her body wants to stay. That much is clear. Her mind doesn't know what it wants. Her mind doesn't know *how* to want, period. Her mind has operated in accordance with *should*s for years now.

"Okay," she says. "I'll stay."

He nuzzles into her neck, says, "That's what I like to hear."

Then he falls asleep with his head on her chest, his fingers interlocked with hers, and she worries he wants more from this than she can possibly give.

Chapter 5

NICOLE

When I woke up at nine o'clock in the morning, later than I'd ever woken up since becoming a mother, I checked my phone, and there was a text from Kyle:

Glad you made it safe.

Whenever he puts periods on the ends of text messages, it feels like an assault. The text was timestamped at 5:18 a.m., which must have been when the girls woke him up. I felt a mixture of sympathy and delighted amusement about this.

He hadn't texted to ask about my dad, which bothered me. I'd given him the general rundown of my dad's symptoms and figured he'd be as invested in the medical mystery as I was. The girls must have had him distracted; he could not mentally multitask like I could.

I'm worried about my dad. Taking him to the ER today.

I am not above adding my own passive-aggressive periods to text messages.

I headed downstairs and found my dad and Merry in the kitchen, having their morning coffee. Merry had the crossword in front of her, and my dad had the newspaper, both wearing reading glasses that they probably got in a multipack from Costco. It all looked so normal that I forgot anything was wrong.

"Good morning," I said, with more energy than I'd had in months (years, maybe) due to the uninterrupted nine hours of sleep.

"Good morning, dear," Merry said.

"Nikki, what are you doing here?" my dad asked, genuinely dumbstruck. It was the genuineness of it that made my heart contract. His memory, at least his short-term memory, seemed to be really and truly gone.

"I got in last night, Dad," I said.

"You did?"

He didn't seem bothered by his forgetfulness, more in awe of it, like *Golly, would you look at that?*

"You were tired," I said, making excuses for him because it seemed like the kindest thing I could do.

"You're going to the doctor today," Merry said to him.

"The doctor? For what?"

I reminded him of the memory issues, the walking issues. He seemed upset, but then quickly moved on:

"You want some eggs?" he asked, starting to stand from his chair.

Merry and I went to him, told him to please sit.

"I can make my own eggs, Dad," I said. "You just relax."

My phone buzzed with a text. Kyle.

The ER? I hope everything is OK.

Wasn't it obvious that things were not okay at all? I decided to change the subject and focus on what I really needed from him—care of the girls.

Did you brush Grace's molars really well?

I asked this not only because my father was a dentist and it's ingrained in me to care about such things, but also because Grace has hypoplasia, which means her teeth enamel is weak and she is prone to cavities. The dentist asked if she'd been sick a lot as a baby, as that can be related to the development of this particular dental calamity. She was in day care, so of course she was sick a lot as a baby. As I spiraled into feeling guilty about this, the dentist, who must have seen the worry on my face, said, "Oh, Mama, don't feel bad." My dad said the same—"Don't feel bad, Nic." But I did. And I still do. Grace has already had two cavities, one the dentist described as "craterous." She will need either a crown or a root canal once she's old enough to, as the dentist put it, "withstand the procedure."

Kyle responded:

Yes.

It would have made me feel better if he'd elaborated—and he must have known this—but he did not. I fantasized about him praising me: *I really had no idea how intense this teeth-brushing thing is! All those cheese puffs really do get stuck in there, don't they? I always thought you were overreacting, but no! Thank you for caring for our daughters' teeth up to this point! I am forever in your debt!!*

Then I laughed at myself.

"Maybe I should come to the hospital," Merry said to me.

"The hospital?" my dad said.

"Merry, just let me take him. We'll be fine."

"Make sure you tell the doctors about how he fell and possibly hit his head," she said, talking about him as if he weren't right next to her.

"Huh?" my dad said.

I beat three eggs in a bowl and then poured them into the hot, oiled pan.

"I will."

"Who hit his head?" my dad asked.

"You did, Rob."

Merry was turning all her concern and fear into frustration—a magic trick of self-preservation.

"I did?" he said. "When?"

She stood up and took her breakfast dishes and mug to the sink, muttering something under her breath.

"Mer, why don't you go . . . do something?" I said.

I tried to think of something to suggest she do, but struggled to come up with anything she enjoyed. She read books. She browsed atrocities on the internet. She gardened occasionally.

"You're sure I shouldn't come?" she asked.

"Just stay here. Try to take it easy. If he's admitted, you'll be at the hospital all the time."

"You think they'll admit him?" she asked me, her eyes pleading with me to be omniscient.

"I don't know, but probably."

"Who's going to the hospital?" my dad asked from the table.

"Don't worry about it, Dad."

Merry looked hesitant. I don't think she wanted to go with us. I think she just didn't trust me to do things correctly. It occurred to me that Kyle must feel toward me how I feel toward my stepmother, and this was deeply unsettling.

"Okay," she said, finally, as if after serious thought. Then: "I'm going to take a shower."

"That sounds great."

With that, she went upstairs, and I went to the table for my dad's dishes.

"Dad, I'm parked right out front, okay? I'm going to drive you to the doctor."

I didn't want to say *hospital* or *ER* because I figured that would freak him out. I resolved to talk to him the way I would talk to Grace and Liv.

"The doctor?" he said.

"Yes."

He was perplexed, but he didn't resist when I encouraged him to stand. I hooked his elbow into mine, and we made our way to the front door. He put more of his weight into me than I expected him to, admitting with his body that he needed me probably more than he wanted to. He had at least sixty pounds on me, and I worried what would happen if we both went down.

"You okay?" I said to him, but also to myself.

"Yep," he said, still with joy in his voice.

It took about fifteen minutes for us to shuffle to the car, but once I helped lower him into the passenger's seat and buckled him, I exhaled with relief.

"Thanks for driving me," he said when we were on our way.

"No problem. I'll take any opportunity to hang out with you."

A few minutes later, he said it again: "Thanks for driving me."

I repeated what I'd said before, and it was clear he had no recollection of it.

"Traffic's pretty light for a Monday," he said.

"Dad, it's Saturday."

"It is?"

"It is."

"Are you just going to park your car at the airport?" he asked.

I tried to make sense of what he was saying but could not.

"At the airport?"

"Yeah, are you just parking your car there? Or wait, are you just dropping me off at the airport? I can't remember if you're going with us to Maui."

Up until I left home for college, we did an annual trip to Maui, the three of us. He and Merry still went. The last time they'd gone was six months earlier.

"We're not going to Maui, Dad."

I felt my heart seize, as if in preparation for shattering.

"We're not?" he asked. "Then why are we going to the airport?"

"We're not going to the airport," I said. "We're going to the doctor, remember?"

I knew he didn't remember, but I said it anyway. It seemed respectful, like alerting him to the fact that we'd discussed this already.

"Oh, right," he said, playing along.

A few minutes after that: "Hey, thanks for driving me."

~

He was confused when we pulled into the parking lot for the UCSF Emergency Department. He was confused when we checked in, me explaining his symptoms to the intake person while a nurse took his vitals.

"I'm going to get a wheelchair," the nurse said, immediately noticing that he was a fall risk.

We helped him lower into the wheelchair, and he had the most clueless smile on his face.

I wheeled him to the triage room. A resident assessed him and said they'd run a CT scan.

"Even if things look normal," he said, "it's likely we'll admit him."

His symptoms were that strange, I guessed, that worrisome. I texted Merry, gave her the update. She sent a frown-face emoji, which was odd—I didn't think she knew how to use emojis. I tried to assure her:

This is good news. They'll get to the bottom of it

From the triage room, they took us to another room, got my dad into a hospital gown, and had him sit in a bed. I sat in a chair next to him, and they pulled a curtain closed behind us. On the other side of the curtain, a woman moaned and talked to whoever was with her in another language. I couldn't understand what she was saying at all, but I understood her pain and desperation all too well.

"Is Mom still in the waiting room?" my dad asked.

"Mom?"

He just looked at me expectantly.

"Merry?" I said. "She's not here."

He gave me a half smile and squinted his eyes. "You're pulling my leg."

"I'm not. She stayed home, remember?"

He shook his head in disbelief at himself and his failing brain. They took him for his CT scan, and when he returned, he promptly fell asleep.

~

Over the course of the next several hours, various people came to take blood—so much blood—and check his vitals. Between proddings, he slept while I scrolled through more photos of the girls and perused Instagram, looking at photos of other people's fun weekends, cursing their apparent bliss. Kyle hadn't texted to check in. Merry had texted to check in too many times.

An internal medicine resident who looked to be about nineteen years old seemed to be the person who knew the most about what was going on. He said the CT scan hadn't shown anything unusual and that they were waiting for some preliminary blood test results. He was cute in a Doogie Howser sort of way. The only thing that assured me that he was, in fact, not a teenager was the bald spot on top of his head. I was bored enough to google his name—Dr. Joshua Belton. There was nothing interesting, not even a birth date to confirm his age. I looked to see if he had a profile on Instagram. He did not. Or if he did, it was under a secret name. Millennials call these finsta accounts, short for "fake Instagram." I tried to imagine his, tried to picture him making a sexy face next to the handle @drfeelgood. This entertained me for about two minutes.

A nurse came by with a plastic container that she called a urinal and hooked it onto the side of my dad's bed.

"When he wakes up, have him give a sample," she said.

She didn't give me any instructions beyond that, so when my dad woke up, I told him he had to pee into the container. It did seem designed for such a thing, had a long, curved neck on it. Still, if I hadn't known better, I would have thought it was meant to hold juice on camping trips.

I helped him sit up and scoot to the edge of the bed, his hospital gown opening in the back so I could see the crack of his butt. I turned away because I knew he wouldn't want me to see that. But then, as if forgetting I was there at all, he took out his penis and placed it in the neck of the container right in front of me. It was floppy and small, and I thought I was going to burst out crying. I didn't cry, though. Motherhood has made me quite adept at suppressing my own emotions to service the needs of others.

When he was done, I took the container from him and set it on the tray next to his bed. It sat there for a half hour before the nurse came to retrieve it. How much pee did this poor woman transport on a daily basis?

It was nearing three o'clock when Dr. Doogie Howser Joshua Belton returned to do a cognitive assessment.

"Okay, Rob," he said to my dad. "I'm going to do some tests to see how your brain is doing."

"All right," Dad said, sounding up for the challenge.

"First, I want you to name as many words as you can that start with the letter *F*."

"That's easy," Dad said, sitting up straight and confident. "*Fart. Fuck* . . . Can I say *fuck*?"

Dr. Belton and I laughed.

"That's my dad for you," I said.

"Any others?" Dr. Belton asked him.

"*Farm*," he said. Then he stopped. I guessed he forgot what he was supposed to be doing and was too confused to ask.

When Dr. Belton was sure they'd reached the end of that exercise, he moved on:

"Okay, now I'm going to give you five words to remember, and then I'll ask you to say them back to me in a few minutes. Here they are: *elephant, flower, red, door, pencil.* Got it?"

My dad laughed a little, which is what we do in my family when we're uncomfortable. I was fairly certain he had already forgotten the words.

"Do you know what hospital you're at?"

Dad looked at me, as if hoping I would give him a hint or whisper the answer to him, as if we were two kids in chemistry class.

"I'm not sure," he said.

"Do you know what county?"

He thought hard about this. It pained me how hard he thought.

"Daly County," he said finally. Which is not a county. Daly *City*, where he lives, is in San Mateo County. But we were at UCSF in San Francisco (which, incidentally, is both a city and a county).

Dr. Belton looked at me with his baby face, and I shrugged. Up until this point, my dad hadn't said much, had been pleasant and easygoing and not obviously demented. I could tell that Dr. Belton was just then realizing how serious things were.

"We're actually at the UCSF hospital, in San Francisco," he said to my dad.

"We are?" my dad asked.

Dr. Belton nodded and moved along. "Do you know what month it is?"

My dad looked up at the ceiling. "September?"

"Close," Dr. Belton said, with a good-natured smile. "It's March."

My dad snapped his fingers, like *Almost had it.*

"Who do you live with, Rob?" Dr. Belton asked.

"My wife, Meredith, and my dog," he said.

Dr. Belton looked at me to validate this, and I said, "Dad, you don't have a dog."

Their last dog was Ruby, and she had died at least ten years earlier.

"Of course I have a dog!"

"Dad, Ruby died a long time ago."

"Go get Mer. She'll tell you. Where is she?"

"She's at home, Dad."

"No, she was just here!"

This was the first time I had seen him become agitated. I reached for his hand, held it in mine. He calmed.

Dr. Belton asked him to count backward from one hundred by sevens. He did okay at first, though it took him longer than it should have to come up with the right answers—ninety-three, eighty-six, seventy-nine. When he got to the sixties, he seemed to completely forget what he was doing. He threw up his hands with a laugh. I'd never seen him so embarrassed.

Dr. Belton showed him an illustration of a clock and asked him to recreate a drawing of it. My dad drew the circle, but got tripped up when attempting to draw the hands of the clock at six and two. He had the concentrated look of someone presented with quantum physics. Then that went away, and he just appeared utterly lost. The same happened when Dr. Belton showed him a drawing of a cube and asked him to recreate it. After a few minutes of trying, there were just disconnected lines on the paper.

"Okay, Rob," Dr. Belton said. "Now, do you remember those five words I gave you a few minutes ago?"

I could tell by the look on my dad's face that he didn't even remember that Dr. Belton had given him five words. He scrambled, spitting out random words in a hurry:

"*Paper? Bird? Plane?*" he tried.

Dr. Belton shook his head.

Elephant, flower, red, door, pencil, I thought to myself. I had to confirm my own sanity.

"So?" I asked, as Dr. Belton made notes.

He looked up at me.

"We're going to admit him."

"They're admitting me?" Dad asked.

Dr. Belton and I both ignored him.

"What do you think is going on?" I asked.

Dr. Belton sighed. "It could be any number of things, from a nutritional deficiency to an autoimmune issue to . . . We just don't know yet."

Then he left, saying someone would be back soon to bring us upstairs.

"Okay, Dad, we're going to figure this out."

"I'm tired," he said. "I've been here all day."

I squeezed in next to him in bed, snuggled into his side, feeling like a little kid again.

"I know," I said. "I've been here all day too."

He shifted in bed to look at me and said, "You have?"

~

Once they admitted him, I assumed he'd have his own room, but he didn't. There was a curtain divider, with an older man on the other side who had a Filipino translator and, from what I could gather, a problem with his liver.

I texted Merry, told her they were getting my dad settled.

Merry: They must have some idea what's wrong with him.

They don't.

My phone buzzed with an incoming call—Merry.

"Let me talk with the doctors," she said.

"They're not here. They have other patients. They do rounds."

"Well, how long are we supposed to accept their inconclusiveness?"

"As long as we need to. They have to do their thing. We are not doctors."

"Should I come there?"

"I'll stay until he gets some dinner. It's probably best if you rest tonight and start fresh tomorrow. He's tired anyway."

"Is that Mer?" my dad asked from his bed.

I nodded. "You want to talk to her?"

He extended his arms out for the phone, and I gave it to him. They talked about practicalities, which is what they've always excelled at. There was discussion of Merry bringing him his pajama pants and some tortilla chips. He also told her to make sure Medicare was "springing for all this." When he gave the phone back to me, Merry was no longer on the line, which was just as well.

I sat at his bedside, waiting for them to bring his dinner. He fell asleep. A notification from Facebook popped up on my phone, a message from Prisha, my high school friend who had told me to bring my dad to the ER. Actually, calling her a friend might be going a bit far. We were acquaintances. Her parents did not condone her having friends because she was always supposed to be studying (which I guess paid off, considering she is now a doctor).

Hey. Just wanted to see how things were going with your dad . . . and how you're holding up. I get off my shift at 6 if you want to get food or a drink or something. I'm sure you've had a long day.

I debated responding and telling her that she was the only person in my life to check in on me. But I decided that sounded rather pitiful and instead wrote:

I definitely need a drink. Tell me where to meet you

She suggested a bar in Union Square, a few miles from the hospital, and I told her I'd be there. Then I texted Kyle because even though I was irritated with him, I missed the girls, and he was my only direct line to them.

How are things there?

He responded almost immediately.

Fine. How are things there?

I was already exhausted by this text exchange. Kyle has never been good with texting, and I have never been good at accepting this.

Ok. My dad was admitted to the hospital. They don't seem to know what's going on. We'll see what all the testing turns up. What did you guys do today?

He responded with one word:

Park.

I could have turned this into a fight by making a snarky comment like *Thank you for the detailed account.* But instead, I didn't respond at all, which I knew wouldn't have any kind of effect on him but still felt satisfying.

They brought my dad the most depressing-looking dinner I'd ever seen—a rubbery piece of chicken, mashed potatoes that appeared gray, an iceberg lettuce salad, and a cookie in plastic wrap.

"How long did you say I had to be here?" he said.

"Not much longer," I told him. For all I knew, he thought he'd already been there a week.

"But I have to stay the night?"

"Yes," I said. "You want to watch TV?"

I handed him the remote, found a preseason baseball game on, and watched his eyes lock onto the screen. My dad has always loved watching baseball. He didn't seem interested in his dinner, understandably, but he appeared content. I felt for the first time that day that I could leave his side.

"Dad, I'm going to head out, but I'll come by tomorrow, okay?"

"I'm staying here tonight?" he asked.

"Yes."

I gave him a kiss on the cheek and told him I loved him.

"Love ya, Nikki," he said. Just like he's always said.

~

The bar was a quintessential hole-in-the-wall, and the inside was made to look like a speakeasy. Prisha was already there, sitting on one of the stools at the bar, a martini in front of her. She had the same long, black, shiny hair she'd had in high school, cascading down her back to her waistline. She was wearing a black pantsuit with a plunging neckline, a lacy camisole beneath. She looked so stylish while I looked like a frumpy housewife in my black stretchy pants and an oversize sweater with obvious pilling.

She must have seen me coming out of the corner of her eye because she turned and said, "Nicole Larson."

I didn't correct her, didn't tell her that my last name is now Sanchez, that I completely abandoned my ancestral roots and co-opted my husband's Mexican identity (well, half-Mexican—his dad is from Guadalajara, his mom from Ohio). It feels like a form of cultural appropriation—me, a Sanchez, with my sandy-blond hair, blue-green eyes, pale skin, and bare-minimum knowledge of the Spanish language. I should have kept my maiden name. Or at the very least, I shouldn't have felt such glee upon taking Kyle's. Most women seem to feel this glee at officially being possessed, updating their names on Facebook within two hours of their ceremonies. Everyone should just keep their damn names, or hyphenate, or come up with a brand-new name. The brand-new name could be based on one's occupation or hobby, like in the old days—Blacksmith, Tailor, and so on. Kyle and I could be the Bickerers—Kyle and Nicole Bickerer.

Anyway, I didn't correct Prisha. I kind of liked that I was still Nicole Larson to her.

"Sit, sit," she said, moving her purse from the stool next to her. I complied. I was grateful she didn't require a hug. Like I said, we weren't really *friends*. We just ran in the same circle of overachievers. I must be the biggest failure of the bunch.

"This place is perfect for my mood," I told her.

"Dark and dingy?" she said.

"Exactly."

She raised her hand to flag down the bartender, a skinny guy with a septum piercing. He tossed a cocktail napkin in front of me.

"Vodka tonic, please," I said.

She took a sip of her martini and ate one of three olives off her toothpick.

"How's your dad?" she asked.

I shrugged. "I don't know. Out of it."

"So it's like he's not even there anymore? Like, mentally?"

I thought of him saying "Love ya, Nikki" and said, "He's there . . . just in one-minute increments."

"And he repeats things? Seems confused?"

"Yeah. It's like *Groundhog Day*. Or *Groundhog Minute*, I guess."

She shook her head. "And it's just you taking care of things? You don't have siblings, right?"

"Just me."

This was the first time I'd really felt the weight of being an only child. I always knew this time would come. Living in fear of it was part of the reason I wanted Grace to have a sibling. Liv was my assurance that Grace wouldn't have to bear the same weight in the future.

"That's hard," Prisha said.

If I remembered correctly, Prisha had a whole assortment of siblings, at least four of them.

"It is."

She took a long sip of her martini. "The symptoms are really bizarre."

I laughed. "It's kind of nice to hear you, a doctor, say that."

The bartender brought my drink, and I took a sip.

"I should probably know this, but what kind of doctor are you?" I asked her.

She smiled. "I'm hurt you haven't kept up with my medical career."

I haven't even kept up with my own career, I wanted to say. But I wasn't ready to confess my failures.

"I'm a perinatologist," she said.

I wasn't sure exactly what that was, which must have been obvious on my face, because she explained, "I handle high-risk pregnancies."

"Oh, wow, that sounds intense."

"It can be. I see a lot of tragedies and a lot of miracles."

Her face showed zero emotion about this.

When it became evident that I didn't know what to say, she jumped in:

"I should probably know this, but what kind of work do you do?"

For a second, I thought about lying. I thought about telling her I was a successful photographer and that I was going to have a gallery show in San Francisco next year. But we were Facebook friends. The truth was right there in my profile, which she must not have visited recently because . . . why would she?

"I'm on a bit of a work hiatus at the moment," I said. "I was a freelance graphic designer at this ad agency. They had some cutbacks. Anyway, it's temporary."

Now it was her turn to not know what to say.

I started to get hot. Any kind of discomfort or stress seemed to trigger the flashes. I was sure she could see the sheen of sweat on my face. She had the most beautiful skin with a perfect matte finish to it. We were the same age, but she looked to be in her hormonal prime.

We each took sips of our drinks. I was already buzzed, probably because I hadn't eaten anything but a granola bar since breakfast.

"Are you married?" I blurted out.

She wasn't wearing a ring, and my curiosity got the best of me.

"Hell no," she said. I took that to mean she was divorced, as most people are not passionately opposed to marriage until they've been in one. But she said, "I don't see myself ever having time for all that."

"All that?"

"A husband, a picket fence, the kids."

She uncrossed and recrossed her legs. As she shifted in her seat, I caught a whiff of her perfume. She smelled good. I couldn't remember the last time I'd spritzed myself with perfume.

"You?" she asked.

Again, I was tempted to lie, to tell her I was unmarried and childless. And again, I thought of how Facebook would betray me.

"I have the husband and the kids. No picket fence."

"Ah well, you know what they say—can't have it all."

She didn't ask me anything about Kyle or the girls, and I was fine with that. We chatted about various friends from high school, and when we finished our drinks, she asked if I wanted to stay for another.

"I have to get going," I said. "My stepmom wants me there for dinner."

The words had already left my mouth before I realized how embarrassingly juvenile they sounded.

I tapped my phone to check the time—just before seven—and sure enough, there was a text from Merry saying she was making halibut.

I stood, but Prisha didn't. She was staying for that second drink. Her night was still young.

"Keep me posted on things with your dad," she said as she beckoned the bartender. "If you're up here again, text me."

"I will, thanks."

I left feeling sad, not just about my dad but also about Prisha's carefree life and my lack of one. I wanted to have an "It's not fair" tantrum as wildly irrational as the ones Grace and Liv had. But instead, I walked calmly to my car, and then I drove to Dad and Merry's house to eat halibut. Before I went to bed, though, after failing to restrain myself from texting Kyle a reminder about the teeth brushing, I went on Amazon and bought myself a thirty-dollar bottle of Vera Wang perfume.

Chapter 6

Katrina

In the movies, people wake up in the bed of someone they barely know after a one-night stand and express shock: *What have I done?* Katrina does not do this. First of all, she doesn't *wake up*. She's been awake all night, contemplating the strangeness of being in bed with this man. She is also not appalled. What she feels is bemused pride.

A smile comes to his face before he even opens his eyes. It's as if he has become conscious of her presence before visually confirming it, and this consciousness brings him joy. It feels good to be the source of someone's joy.

"Good morning, beautiful," he says as he opens his eyes.

She watches him watching her come into focus. His smile gets wider. He evidently has no regrets about their night together. Either he has one-night stands all the time, or he doesn't think this is a one-night stand.

"Good morning, handsome," she says.

He really is so handsome. She wonders if here, in this bed, with the morning light streaming in across her face (likely highlighting the wrinkles that seem to multiply by the day), he will realize that she is not on par with him, attractiveness-wise.

He reaches over, puts his hand on her bare stomach, seemingly oblivious to its folds and flaws. Are they going to have sex *again*? She wasn't anticipating that, was thinking they would say their awkward goodbyes and go back to their regular lives.

"How did you sleep?" he asks.

He's sweet. In another life, she would have heart eyes while imagining their future together. But she has this life, and her future is spoken for. The heart-eyes days are behind her.

"I slept fine," she tells him. May as well keep the lies going.

"That's good," he says, sliding closer to her in bed. He kisses her forehead, then her nose, then her lips. She wants to giggle at the preposterousness of this. She wishes there was someone filming the whole thing so she could have evidence of it happening.

He rolls on top of her, takes her hands in his, and holds them up above her head. As sweet as he is, he also knows how to take charge. It surprised her last night, the way he *handled* her. She wonders how many women he's slept with. Judging by his skill, she guesses dozens.

"You are so hot," he says, kissing her neck, a spot that triggers full-body goose bumps.

His lips travel down her body until they are at her inner thighs, and then his tongue is inside her and she writhes around. When she moans, she wonders for a split second who is making those sounds. She is both embarrassed and impressed upon realizing it's her. She didn't know she had it in her. With her husband, any moaning is manufactured, produced in attempts to hurry things along. She didn't know that moans could occur naturally, involuntarily.

Their sex is slow, with less urgency than the night before. He is both gentle and direct. After this, she doesn't know how she can go back to the old kind of sex, the rushed and forced and unfeeling kind. It's possible he has ruined her. Or resurrected her. Is there a difference?

He doesn't leap out of bed after they are done. He lies next to her, catching his breath, his skin hot and sticky against hers. He strokes her face with one of his fingers.

"You want to go to breakfast?" he asks.

Breakfast? What thirty-year-old man wants to take his one-night stand to breakfast?

He must see the surprise on her face because he says, "What? You just wanted to thank me for my services and run?"

Kind of, she thinks.

"No, no," she assures him, unsure what to say.

"Then join me for breakfast," he says. "After all, we burned a lot of calories."

She hesitates. Sitting with him at a dark bar and then going back to his apartment is one thing. Going out with him in broad daylight is another. There is little chance someone she knows would see her, but *what if?*

"There's this cute little French bistro nearby," he says.

What thirty-year-old man uses the word *cute?*

"Okay," she says, figuring *What the hell?* She is starving, after all.

He gets out of bed, and she watches him walk to the bathroom, admiring his body, his musculature. Adonis, indeed. She hears the shower go on, and he comes back to stand naked in the bathroom doorway.

"Join me?" he says.

In the shower? she thinks. The desire to giggle returns. She hasn't showered with a man for any reason other than efficiency since her early twenties. Even then, she remembers thinking it was impractical. There is nothing romantic about togetherness in the shower. If anything, it causes resentment because someone always has to shiver away from the hot-water stream.

"Come on," he says.

Again she thinks *What the hell?* The last twelve hours have been about completely abandoning everything she thought she knew of herself.

Thankfully, Elijah has one of those showerheads that's on the ceiling, so they don't have to jockey for position in the stream of water. Instead, it feels like they are caught in a tropical rainstorm together, which is sort of lovely. He soaps up her body, rubs his hands all over her. She does the same to him. If she thinks about this moment too hard, she will burst out laughing at the absurdity of it. Last week, if someone had told her that she would be standing in a shower with a gorgeous man she'd met at a bar, she would have gone into hysterics.

When they get out, he wraps her in a plush towel, and she can't help but wonder if he would always be like this. If they were actually in a relationship—which they will never be—would he be this attentive? Unlikely. It's easy to be the ideal guy when the woman you've just slept with is about to drive home to a faraway city.

She dresses in her clothes from the night before, both aghast at and delighted with herself, a forty-year-old woman doing the walk of shame. She wraps her wet hair into a bun and asks Elijah if she can borrow a hat—something she can hide under to help ease her anxieties about someone she knows seeing her. He gives her an A's baseball cap and tells her she looks adorable in it. *Who is this guy?*

The bistro is a short walk from his apartment. She feels paranoid, exposed in the sunlight. She's thankful when they get a table on the back patio.

"I want everything," she tells him as they peruse the menu.

"Everything?" he asks.

She nods. This is who Katrina is—a hungry, greedy woman driven by her base instincts.

"Let's get everything, then," he says, not missing a beat.

They settle on three things—pancakes, eggs benedict, and a scramble. They will share, which seems too intimate for people who will soon part ways and never see each other again, but she really does want to try each of the dishes. And what Katrina wants, Katrina gets.

After the waitress comes and goes, Elijah sits back in his chair.

"So," he says, a mischievous grin on his face, "I've been thinking."

"Oh god, that doesn't sound good."

He laughs.

"You should stay a few days with me," he says.

She's both flattered and panicked.

"I can't," she says. "I've got so much going on, and—"

"Okay, just one more day, then. Play hooky."

"So you *do* have a mischievous side," she says.

"Of course."

"I was beginning to think you were some kind of saint."

He furrows his brows. "Why's that?"

"You're just so . . . *nice.*"

He unfurrows his brows, laughs. "You say that like it's a bad thing."

"It's very strange," she says.

"You don't have a lot of nice men in your life?"

She considers this. "I find most men to be very egocentric."

He nods. "They are. We're socialized that way, told to be tough, hide emotion, win no matter what."

"I thought you were a lawyer. You sound like a shrink."

He laughs again. "A wannabe lawyer. Not a shrink. But I was raised by a sociology professor."

"Your dad is a sociology professor?"

"Ah, see, you just revealed hidden bias, assuming *professor* equals male," he says. "What if I had said *sociology teacher*? Would you assume female?"

She rolls her eyes, hiding her shame behind annoyance with his pedantry. "So your *mother* is a sociology professor?"

He taps his nose with his index finger.

"Well, please thank her for raising you to be a nice gentleman."

"I will," he says. "She'll appreciate that."

"I can see it now: 'Hey, Mom, this woman I had a one-night stand with said you're a good parent.'"

"I was kind of hoping this wasn't just a one-night stand."

She sighs, her fear realized. Leave it to her to find the one hopeless-romantic man in existence at a phase of her life when she wants nothing to do with hopeless romance.

He leans forward, elbows on the table, and looks into her eyes. She wants desperately to look away but wills herself to hold his gaze.

"I mean, if that's what you want, that's okay," he says, "but that's not really my style."

"Oh," she says, dumbly. Then: "What's your style?"

"I've honestly never had a one-night stand," he says.

She is shocked.

"You haven't?"

He shakes his head. "Like I said, not my style."

"But I told you I was from out of town," she says, aware she sounds like she is pleading a case.

"I know. I guess I'm not scared off by a little distance between us."

Christ, what have I gotten myself into?

"You don't even know me," she says. Because, really, he doesn't.

"I get a good vibe. It can't just be me who felt a connection, right?"

He looks so earnest. It's the eyes—those eyes! She has never met someone so sincere, so forthright, so honest. Yes, she barely knows him, but she can say that with confidence.

"It's not just you," she says.

It's true. She does feel a connection. But she is older than him, arguably wiser. For all they know, this "connection" is just lust. They are awash in dopamine, stupid from it.

"Okay then," he says.

The waitress brings their food, places the three plates on the table in front of them.

"This looks delicious," Katrina says.

They take their first forkfuls, the sharing of entrées not nearly as awkward as she thought it would be. She feels comfortable with him in a way that's hard to explain, almost as if she's known him before, like they are old childhood friends who have reunited.

"I love a woman who can eat," he says.

"So do I."

They don't talk much while they eat. When they've made a significant dent, he puts down his fork and wipes his mouth with his napkin, then says, "I just realized your car is still parked at the bar."

"Shit," she says, imagining the ticket stuck under a windshield wiper. There are all sorts of parking rules in this city.

"I'll walk there with you. If there's a ticket, I insist on paying it."

She sits back in her chair, hands on her full belly.

"Seriously, you are too nice," she says. "But you don't need to pay my ticket."

"I want to," he says. "I'll consider it the price to pay for the pleasure of your company."

"Okay, that just makes me sound like a hooker."

He laughs again, this one big and hearty.

"You crack me up, Kat," he says.

Kat.

~

He pays their bill, and they walk past his apartment to the bar. Her car is the lone one in the lot, and amazingly, there is no ticket affixed to the window.

"It's a miracle," she says.

"I wouldn't say that." He points to the sign explaining the parking rules. "You abided by the rules, that's all."

"My abiding by the rules is a miracle."

She fumbles around in her purse for her keys. She would be lying if she said she didn't feel sad saying goodbye to him. She has felt better, more alive, in the past twelve hours than she has in the past few years.

"I'm really sad to see you go," he says.

"I am too." A truth amid so many lies.

"I still think you should play hooky from your regular life."

She smiles. "I can't."

"Well, if you change your mind, here's my number," he says, handing her a blue Post-it.

She recalls a stack of blue Post-its on his kitchen counter at his apartment and says, "Did you really write your number on this and have it in your pocket to give to me?"

He nods. "I did."

"You're an old soul."

"So I've been told," he says.

"Well, thanks," she says, holding the Post-it.

Maybe she'll enter the number in her phone, under the name E. It could be fun just to have it there, to confirm his existence and reinvigorate herself with the memory of their dalliance. It would be like a little bump of cocaine to her system, not that she's ever done a little bump of cocaine. She's always been a good girl. Until now, at least.

"It would make me feel better if we saw each other again," he says. "I really don't know if I can live with myself for having a one-night stand."

"We had sex this morning, so technically it was more than one night."

"You're killing me."

"I'm sorry." Another truth.

He goes to her, pulls her body close to his, and she feels that jolt of desire again. He wraps his arms around her so tightly, and she feels suddenly like crying—not a few tears, but surging sobs of both sadness and gratitude. He has given her life. He will never know this, not fully, but he has.

They pull apart, and he takes her face in both his hands and kisses her.

"Goodbye, Ms. Katrina," he says, his farewell words, the false name, reminding her that he doesn't really know her at all.

"Goodbye, Elijah."

She gets in her car, despite everything in her body telling her not to. As silly as it is, she misses him before she even puts the key in the ignition.

Chapter 7

NICOLE

When I got home Sunday evening, the girls were naked in the kitchen, and there were several open containers of Play-Doh on the floor. I'd bought a twenty-pack from Walmart, and it appeared Kyle had given them all twenty, thinking that more containers would equate to more time they would be entertained on their own. I was already annoyed.

"Mommy!" they screamed when they saw me. That moment was probably the closest I'll ever get to feeling like Mick Jagger taking the stage at a concert.

Their little naked bodies jumped up and down as I crouched next to them. Their hair smelled sweet, a familiar scent. After a moment, it clicked:

"Do you have yogurt in your hair?"

"Yogurt!" Liv shouted.

Just as I was about to ask where Daddy was, Kyle appeared in the kitchen wearing his softball shirt, the dumb team name—Bat Intentions—across the chest.

"There you are," he said. "I'm sorry to have to run, but my team will have to forfeit if I don't get there."

Well, hello to you too! My drive was great, thanks for asking. It only took me seven hours, and I've had to pee for the last two, meaning I'll probably get a UTI. Nobody knows what's wrong with my dad, thanks for asking again. I'm so sorry I forgot about your stupid fucking softball game.

"Have the girls eaten?" I asked.

It was almost six. They usually eat around five.

"Not yet," he said. "I'm sorry."

He gave me a slapdash kiss on the cheek, grabbed his cleats and his stupid bat bag, and was out the door.

"Mommy, mommy, mommy," Grace said, still hopping up and down.

"Just a minute, sweeties. I have to go potty."

They followed me to the bathroom, their hands on my arms, my legs, whatever they could grab to reassure themselves of my presence. I was abruptly back to real life, a life in which my body is rarely not touched and I am rarely alone on the toilet.

Grace instructed me not to flush and then analyzed my pee like a chemist in a lab.

"Why is it so yellow?" she asked.

"I'm dehydrated," I said, and immediately regretted the word choice. Predictably, she asked me what that meant, and I had to spend three minutes explaining it. I can't help but wonder if there are mothers out there who relish these learning opportunities. There probably are. They are the ones who are teaching their preschoolers Mandarin.

"What do you girls want for dinner?" I asked. The moment the question left my mouth, I wanted to take it back. Was I expecting them to come to a consensus like civilized human beings?

Grace yelled, "Pizza!" and Liv yelled, "Pasta!"

"Okay, what did you have last night?"

"Chips!" Grace said.

"Chips?"

"Chips!"

I sighed. When I looked in the pantry, the bag of potato chips was indeed gone. I, like many mothers, have an almost photographic memory of the contents of my pantry. There is a ticker always running in my brain, tracking food inventory.

"Let's do pasta," I told them. I tried to use my authoritative voice, hoped they wouldn't pick up on my fear.

"I don't want pasta," Grace whined.

It was already six thirty, meaning I needed them to eat quickly and get in the damn bath. With the yogurt in their hair and the pasta sauce about to be on their faces, we couldn't skip the bath. Bedtime is supposed to be seven thirty, but I knew we wouldn't make it that night. I resolved to get as close as possible, for my own sanity.

"Here, watch YouTube," I said, thrusting the iPad at Grace.

She calmed immediately. The iPad is the new pacifier.

I started to text Kyle:

You could have at least fed them and started the bath.

I didn't send it. Delete, delete, delete.

There was no point. I could already imagine the back-and-forth:

Me: You could have at least fed them and started the bath.

Kyle: You didn't tell me to do that.

Me: I shouldn't have to tell you. You know the routine.

Kyle: When you're not here, I have my own routine.

Me: Okay, but you knew I was coming back.

Kyle: I actually thought you'd be back by five, which is why I wasn't anticipating being late to my game.

～

"Mommy, is me done?" Grace asked after taking exactly one bite of her penne.

Thankfully, Liv was shoveling noodles into her face. If she followed in her sister's footsteps, she wouldn't start becoming a total pain in the ass about eating until her third birthday.

"No, Grace, you have to eat all your noodles."

She collapsed, moaning, as if I'd just told her I'd systematically removed the heads of all her dolls, which seemed like it would be incredibly gratifying in that moment.

"How much do I have to eat?" she whined.

"All. Of. The. Noodles."

"Nooooooo."

"Grace, seriously. Mommy is really tired. Eat your noodles or no dessert."

This led to more sobbing. I did my best to ignore it, which has always been Kyle's advice: "You just have to ignore it." It was advice we'd both been applying to our marriage.

I turned up the volume on the YouTube video—this one featuring a girl slowly unboxing a dollhouse—and poured myself a glass of wine. I texted Merry, told her I was home safe.

I wish you could have stayed. How am I going to deal with this alone?

I drank my wine like it was juice. I didn't need this guilt trip from her. We'd talked about this, about how Kyle works, about how I have the girls. It had crossed my mind that I could bring the girls up there with

91

me, stay indefinitely. But I was sure I would end up institutionalized in those circumstances.

You're not dealing with this alone. I'm here for you, even if I'm not physically there every day. Okay?

She sent a kissy-face emoji, and that was that.

～

When Merry and I had visited the hospital earlier that day, there were still no answers. My dad seemed content, though confused as ever. Every few minutes, he was surprised to realize he was in the hospital. They were waiting to attempt a lumbar puncture. Apparently, they had attempted the night before and could not get the needle in or something. They were quite sure they would be successful the second time, had called in the Spinal Tap Big Guns.

"That test may give us more information," the neurologist, a young Chinese woman, said. According to her badge, her name was Charlene Lee. She couldn't have been more than five feet tall, swimming in her pale-green scrubs.

"What do you think is wrong with him?" Merry asked.

I looked at my dad, who was smiling absently, seemingly unbothered by us talking about him as if he wasn't there. Merry sat next to him on the hospital bed, held his hand. They'd never been a physically affectionate couple, even in their early days (from what I can remember, at least). It was strange to see Merry cling to him.

"The list of possibilities is long," Dr. Lee said. "Cognitive decline in a subacute period is very concerning, especially for someone who is fairly young and healthy."

Only in a hospital setting is a sixty-eight-year-old man considered "fairly young."

"We're looking for vitamin deficiencies, infections, toxins, seizures, autoimmune issues, tumors," she said.

"Tumors?" Merry asked. She seemed alarmed. How had she not considered tumors?

Dr. Lee nodded.

"We've sent a paraneoplastic syndrome panel to the Mayo Clinic. Those results take a week."

Merry said, "A week?"

I said, "A para . . . what?"

"Paraneoplastic syndrome. It's when the antibodies in the body go to fight a tumor somewhere else and mistakenly attack cells in the nervous system. And yes, it's a very specialized test, so it takes a few days."

Merry sighed her displeasure.

"What about his fall?" she asked.

It took a moment for the doctor to recall what she was talking about.

"With the golf ball?" Dr. Lee asked.

Merry nodded.

"That doesn't have anything to do with what's going on. A red herring, as we say."

"A red herring," Merry echoed.

"And the other tests haven't shown anything?"

"The CT scan showed some calcification around his basal ganglia. It's a little unusual in the location and pattern, but I can't say it's related to anything yet. His scan is normal for his age. There were no signs of Alzheimer's."

"Thank god," Merry said.

"There are all kinds of dementias, though," Dr. Lee said with a warning tone. "Dementia is as heterogeneous as cancer."

"Is there a test for that?" I asked.

"We did the EEG. It didn't show any seizure activity, but it did show encephalopathy."

"What's that?" I asked.

"Slowing of the brain."

Merry and I nodded. At this point, my dad had fallen asleep.

"We saw in his records that he had an MRI done about a month ago. Is that right?"

Merry and I looked at each other. She said, "He did?"

Dr. Lee consulted her notes and said, "Yes. You didn't know?"

Merry said, "No. I wonder if he did that after the fall."

"And didn't tell you?" I asked.

She shrugged. "He wouldn't have wanted me to worry."

"In any case, that MRI didn't show a brain tumor or stroke. It was basically normal," the doctor said. "We may run another for comparison depending on what the lumbar puncture shows."

"What are you looking for with that?"

"Inflammatory cells. Signs of infection."

We nodded. There are a lot of nodding and a lot of crying in hospitals.

"There are some incredibly rare neurodegenerative diseases that we're checking for, just to cover all bases," she said.

Merry let out another one of her sighs. I felt the need to counteract her negativity, so I said, "We really appreciate that you're so thorough."

"Of course," Dr. Lee said with a tight smile. "I'm hoping we'll have more information for you tomorrow."

She left, likely to explain complex medical terms to other families who would either nod or cry.

~

By the time I got the girls bathed and brushed their teeth and put on their pajamas, it was just after eight. I told them we only had time for one book, but Grace insisted on two, and I didn't have the energy to negotiate or fight. I sang my usual song—"You Are My Sunshine"—and then closed the door. I stood in the hallway, waiting for one of them to summon me, every muscle in my body tense. *Mommy?* Often, I hear it in my head and think it's real—an auditory hallucination. Isn't that a sign of posttraumatic stress disorder? Is there such a thing as present traumatic stress disorder?

Anyway, they didn't call for me. Sometimes I think they can tell when I'm hovering at the edge of a precipice. Sometimes I think they know not to push.

I unpacked, took a shower, and got into bed just as I heard the garage door open. Kyle was home.

"Did you win?" I asked when he came into the bedroom, still wearing his cleats, clomping around on the wood floor.

I didn't really care if he'd won, but it was a question asked out of habit. Before we had kids, I cared if his team won—or, I cared that he cared. Just like he cared to take off his cleats before clomping around on the wood floor. We have devolved, mutually.

"We won," he said, sitting on the bed to take off his cleats.

His hair was slick with sweat, his shirt damp from exertion. There was a time I would have considered this manly and sexy; now it's just gross.

"You get any hits?" I asked, again out of habit.

"Not tonight."

He stood and went to the bathroom to shower—thank god.

When he came back, wearing his boxers and nothing else, he got into bed next to me and put his arm around me.

"You tired?" he asked. This was code for "Can we have sex?"

"Yeah," I said, which was code for "No."

He removed his arm from me and lay flat, staring at the ceiling. I did the same.

"I think my dad is going to die," I said.

There were so many things he could have said to make me feel loved:

God, honey, I'm so sorry.

You must be so scared.

Let's talk about what the doctors told you.

Instead, he sighed in the defeated-yet-annoyed way Merry sighs, and said, "You don't know that."

A hot flash took over my body, sweat coating my chest and back in a matter of seconds. I threw the covers off.

"It would be nice if you didn't seem irritated by my concerns," I said.

I always speak more freely in the midst of the hot flashes. It's like I'm too agitated to contain myself.

"I'm not irritated," he said, again with a sigh.

I tried to take a deep breath because everything on social media talks about how deep breathing is the way to inner peace. I wasn't successful. It felt like my lungs were the size of hummingbird eggs.

"Have the doctors given you answers yet?"

His tone was careful, similar to the tone I use with the girls when they are on the verge of a tantrum.

"No," I said.

"So see, there's no reason to think he's going to die."

"Okay, but he might. Can you just go with me on this for half a second?"

"I just don't want you getting carried away again."

"Again?"

"Huh?"

"You said carried away 'again.' Do you see me as someone who is often getting carried away?"

Now that the hot flash had passed, my body was chilled with the cooling sweat left behind.

"Nic, do we have to do this now?"

"Oh, I'm sorry. Did you have a long weekend caring for your offspring?"

"Nic . . ."

"I was in the hospital with my dad who has no short-term memory and can't walk."

"Are we in a competition?"

"We shouldn't be. Do you think your stress is in any way comparable to mine?"

"Can we talk about this tomorrow?"

"Why? Am I getting 'carried away'?" I used air quotes then.

"Nic . . ."

"Fine. We can talk tomorrow. But you should mentally prepare yourself for the fact that I might need to go back up there this weekend. So hire a babysitter or something if you can't handle two days on your own."

He didn't respond, just rolled away from me in bed and switched off the light.

Then I said the thing that I'd promised myself I wouldn't say, because I knew it was petty and sure to aggravate him:

"Grace told me you didn't brush their teeth."

She had, in fact, told me that.

He didn't respond, which just made me feel like a petulant child.

Instead of falling asleep, I lay flat with my arms crossed over my chest, contemplating if it's possible for two people who have children together not to despise each other on a somewhat regular basis. As with any tragedy, nobody thinks it'll happen to them—all wedding vows are laced with naivete and arrogance, all newlyweds convinced their love will be different. But then there are the embarrassingly common stressors of kids and jobs and money. Then you must swallow your pride and admit that what you thought could survive anything may not survive the predictable struggles of an ordinary life.

~

The next morning, Kyle didn't say anything to me, and I didn't say anything to him. I was waiting for him to apologize, and he was probably doing the same. Or maybe he wasn't thinking about me at all. Maybe he was just focused on starting his workday. In any case, the girls made it impossible for me to get too emotionally invested in our marital standoff because they were particularly unruly, likely punishing me for my forty-eight hours of absence from their lives.

"Girls! Stop it!" I yelled in my Mom-means-business voice.

Grace had taken a stuffed unicorn from Liv, and Liv was losing her mind. They did not even register my voice. To them, Mom never means business. Mom is a joke.

"Girls!" I tried again. Still, nothing.

Kyle closed the door to his office, separating himself from the chaos, as usual.

I didn't feel like fighting about breakfast, so I gave the girls bowls of Lucky Charms. The little burst of text on the box—"11 g. whole grains per serving!"—assuaged my maternal guilt. When I was pregnant with Grace, I envisioned myself as a mother who baked granola. I was committed to avoiding sugar, to serving muffins sweetened with bananas instead of cupcakes on birthdays. I was adamant about breastfeeding both girls, turned up my nose at formula. Now I let them eat the stale McDonald's french fries they find in the crevices of their car seats.

I've decided I want to be done with maternal guilt, once and for all. Do fathers ever feel guilty about what they feed their children? How often do they even feed their children? I want to buy myself a gold bracelet engraved with "WWMD" for "What would men do?" I want to stare at it every time I am consumed with self-hatred about how I raise my children.

"I don't want milk in mine," Grace said, always adept at finding a problem with anything placed in front of her.

"Grace, you have to eat your cereal with milk."

"I don't want milk! I want it dry!"

"Then it's basically just a sugary snack. The milk has protein and calcium."

As if she gave a shit about protein and calcium.

People say you should talk to your kids as equals. They say it's a sign of respect and encourages maturity. I haven't seen evidence of this being a good strategy. It seems like it would be more effective to talk to them like the immature cave people that they are: *You eat cereal with milk. You do now.*

"I don't want milk either," Liv said.

I was torn between praising her for using a complete sentence and chastising both of them for their disobedience.

"Eat your cereal. With the milk," I said, employing my cave-people strategy.

Liv cooperated.

My phone buzzed with a text from Merry:

Just got to the hospital. The doctor wants to talk to us later about all the results.

Grace started whining about the milk again, so I gave her the iPad. That quieted her, and she began to just pick out the marshmallows from the cereal, which I supposed was better than nothing. Or not.

Ok. What time?

I don't know. You know how these doctors are. They come when they please.

Ok. Then just call me when it's time

She sent me a thumbs-up emoji.

How's Dad?

The same. He says hello.

Tell him I love him

She sent me another thumbs-up emoji.

I took the girls to the park after breakfast because Kyle's voice was booming on his calls and it was making me want to punch a wall. It's also possible that his voice was at its normally loud volume but my resentment had made me more sensitive to it. This is all to say that I needed to get out of the house.

There was one other mom at the park, wearing a sweatshirt that said I RUN A TIGHT SHIPWRECK. I liked her until I saw her perfectly coiffed little girls, about the same age as mine, dressed in matching pink dresses. Shipwreck, my ass. Her girls ran over to her for a snack of "cheese" puffs made out of chickpeas. Up close I could see that the ends of their hair were most definitely curled. I tried to imagine Grace and Liv sitting still for such a procedure. It would never happen. Someone would end up with a third-degree burn.

"Your daughters have beautiful hair," I said.

Sometimes, I try to play nice. Even though I have nothing in common with them, I want them to accept me. It's complicated.

"Oh, thank you," she said, beaming with pride.

"My daughters won't let me come near them with a brush."

Which was obvious. Grace's hair almost always resembles Gary Busey's in that infamous mug shot. The last time I took her for a haircut, they charged me an extra twenty-five dollars for "the severity of her tangles." Liv, thankfully, has shorter, wispier hair with less potential for dishevelment.

"Well, we have a rule that we don't compromise health or hygiene," the shipwreck-my-ass mother said.

Health or hygiene? Was beautifully done hair hygienic? Was she calling me unhygienic? Kyle did sometimes refer to Grace's hair as a vermin's nest.

"Rules? What are those?"

I was being sarcastic, but she didn't laugh. It wasn't until I became a mom that I realized how many people are not My People. There was another mom a few weeks before this who I'd talked with about the popularity of unicorns, and she'd said, "Have you read that *How to Catch a Unicorn* book? I bought it because it's a *New York Times* bestseller, but *the language*! I had to return it." When I inquired about the offensive language, she whispered, "*Fart*. The book has the word *fart*," and I knew we could never, ever, ever be friends.

My phone rang, and for once I was grateful for that because it gave me an excuse to turn away from this obnoxious woman. My relief was temporary because I saw the call was from Merry.

"The doctor is here," she said.

I checked to make sure the girls were happily playing—they were—and walked to a nearby bench. I knew I'd need to sit for this, no matter the news.

"So we've got all the results in," the doctor began. I assumed it was Dr. Lee.

Merry interrupted: "Can you hear that, Nicole? I have you on speakerphone."

"Is that Nikki?" I heard my dad ask.

"Yes, Mer, I can hear. Hi, Dad. Go ahead, Doctor. Sorry."

"We didn't see any inflammatory cells with the lumbar puncture. No infection. No malignancy. All the biomarkers for autoimmune issues were negative. The paraneoplastic syndrome panel is still pending, but we did a CT scan of his chest and didn't see any tumors. The blood work is negative for any other issues."

I wasn't sure if this was good news or bad news. Her tone screamed bad news, but to me it just sounded like they were still uncertain.

Until . . .

"So we did a repeat MRI, and that showed significant changes from the last one that was done."

She began to explain the changes in what sounded like a different language. I would have asked her to slow down, but it sounded like she was on her way to the important information, a train barreling down a rickety track.

"Considering those changes, along with the EEG showing irritability in the frontal area, and his unsteady gait and subacute cognitive decline, we think it's a degenerative process called CJD."

She paused, thinking we must have questions, but I had no idea what she was really saying.

"What do I have?" Dad blurted out.

"It's one of the extremely rare neurodegenerative conditions I mentioned yesterday. It's a prion disease."

I'd heard of prion diseases before.

"Like mad cow disease?" I asked.

"Sort of, but this isn't something from meat or anything. It just . . . happens. Sometimes prion proteins in the brain misfold, similar to how healthy cells turn cancerous. We don't know why."

"And it's definitely this?"

"The confirmatory test of the spinal fluid will take a couple weeks, but we are reasonably certain."

She paused again.

"Can I drive?" Dad asked.

"I'm sorry, but you really shouldn't be driving," the doctor said.

"Wait, what is it called?" I asked.

"I need to be able to drive," Dad said.

"Rob, hold on," Merry told him. "We need to get all the information."

"It's CJD," the doctor said, addressing my question. Then she said what CJD stood for, but again, it sounded like a foreign language.

I quickly googled CJD, and as I tapped on the first result, my entire world changed.

CJD.

Creutzfeldt-Jakob disease.

Human prion disease.

Rapidly progressive.

Invariably fatal.

Death within one year.

One case per million population.

Merry, who quite clearly hadn't googled, said, "What are our treatment options?"

The doctor said, "I'm sorry, Mrs. Larson, but there's no treatment."

"No treatment?" She sounded personally offended. "What do you mean no treatment?"

"I'm sorry, Mrs. Larson. There are no known treatments for this."

"What about golf? Can I play golf?" Dad asked.

Nobody answered him. It was silent. I checked my phone to make sure the call hadn't dropped. It hadn't.

I remembered with a start that I had children and they were here at the playground. I looked up, half expecting them to be gone, kidnapped. Already I had come to see tragedy everywhere. But there they were, Grace playing with the perfectly coiffed girls and Liv sitting by herself, playing with something she had likely found on the ground. I figured if it was anything dangerous, the annoying mom would come fetch me.

"Can he come home, then?" Merry finally asked.

"Yes," the doctor said. "I have some recommendations for hospice care and—"

"We don't need that right now, thank you," Merry said. I could picture her waving off Dr. Lee, her hands swatting at the air.

My dad didn't say anything. I wondered if the word *hospice* had registered with him at all. Perhaps it had for a split second, and then it was gone. Perhaps that was a blessing.

"Nicole, I have to go," Merry said abruptly.

"Mer, wait. We should talk—"

She hung up. I texted her immediately.

Call me.

She responded:

I need to get him out of this place. Will call when we are home.

I had a hard time picturing Merry as capable of handling the logistics of signing him out of the hospital and getting him to the car. My dad was the one who handled all that life stuff.

Are you ok?

Such a stupid question, in retrospect.

Of course I'm not OK. They've given up on him.

I started typing a response that included an explanation of why they weren't "giving up." I started to tell her that this was a terrible disease. Then I deleted all that and just wrote:

I love you. Call me later

I heard the shipwreck mom call to her girls that it was time to leave, and of course they came right to her like well-trained poodles. She gave me a wave-from-a-distance, and then they piled into their Range Rover. I walked back to the playground. Grace was pouting because her "friends" had left. Liv was still playing with something on the ground.

"Look what me found, Mommy," she said, her eyes full of wonder.

It was some kind of purple plastic object. She put it in her mouth.

"Okay, Liv, let's not put weird things from the ground in our mouths."

I went to take it from her, and that's when I realized it was a tampon applicator. I instinctively threw it into the bushes with a yelp.

"What, Mommy? What happened?" Grace asked, intrigued by my horror.

"Nothing. Let's go. We have to go home."

I resolved to make Liv rinse with mouthwash and then scrub her hands until they were red. Then I would chastise myself for not being a better mother. Could Liv get a disease from a tampon applicator? How would I explain her having oral herpes to Kyle?

"I want toy," Liv cried.

"What did you throw in the bushes?" Grace asked, starting to wander over there to investigate.

"Girls. Seriously. Mommy's going to lose it."

Grace climbed into the bushes, and Liv increased the volume of her crying. I felt my body getting hot, boiling from the inside. That's when it happened. I closed my eyes and opened my mouth, and out came the most primal scream of my life, matched in intensity only by the sounds I'd emitted during labor. It was long, requiring every last bit of oxygen in my lungs. I was sure the shipwreck mom, now a block or two away, could hear me.

When I stopped, my heart still pounding in my chest, I fell to my knees on the ground and opened my eyes, and the girls were staring at me, dumbstruck and afraid.

Grace blinked hard. "Mommy?"

"We need to go home," I said, finger combing strands of now-damp hair behind my ears.

Neither of them protested. Apparently, the quickest way to get children to behave is to become mentally unhinged and scare the shit out of them.

They were silent in their double stroller for the entirety of the walk home. I wondered if they'd fallen asleep, but when I checked, they were both wide awake, bug eyed, looking at me as if I were a complete stranger.

"I'm sorry I yelled," I said.

They both just nodded. It was possible I'd broken them and they would forever cower in my presence.

I made a vow to myself to hold it together over the next few days. I would have to do that impossible thing that every mother must do—forget myself completely, tend to them as if I had none of my own concerns.

When we got home, Kyle was in the kitchen getting himself a snack. If he were wired like me, or like any mother, he would have simultaneously made the girls lunch. Women are masters of efficiency, always considering how many birds they can kill with one measly stone. Men are accustomed to having all the stones in the world and none of the birds.

The girls played quietly with their baby dolls, and I could tell Kyle was temporarily impressed with my control over them. If he'd known what had inspired their good behavior, if he'd heard my outburst, he would have been horrified: *Do you think the neighbors heard you? Did anyone see you?*

"We heard from the doctor," I said, standing close to him at the island, speaking softly.

The girls don't see their grandparents enough to be very close to them, but I wasn't prepared to talk to them about death as a concept. Grace, in particular, would have three thousand questions, and I worried I might die in the process of attempting to answer them.

He continued spreading peanut butter on a slice of bread and said, "Uh-huh?"

"My dad is dying."

I really wanted to say "I was right" or "I knew it," but I managed to be mature for once.

He paused his peanut butter spreading and set the knife down.

"Are you serious?" he said.

"It would be pretty messed up if I wasn't."

I told him the name of the disease. He said, "Man, that sucks," which sounds like something a surfer would say in response to less-than-great waves, but that's just the extent of Kyle's language for unhappy events. At least he didn't say "Bummer." He looked appropriately upset. I have never seen Kyle cry, so I didn't expect tears. He's always had a civil relationship with my dad, but they aren't, like, *pals*. They don't play fantasy football together or talk politics or whatever else fathers and their sons-in-law are supposed to do. Kyle isn't even close to his own dad, so there's no way he can fully understand my devastation.

"I'll go up there again on Friday," I told him.

He resumed making his sandwich. "Yeah, okay. God, I'm sorry, babe."

"Do you want me to call a sitter to help with the girls?"

"Don't worry about the girls. Or me. Okay?"

"Are you sure?"

"We'll be fine."

"Okay. I'll leave the sitter's number," I said. "Just in case."

He put an arm around my shoulders, pulled me into his side. It felt stiff and awkward. We just aren't that type of couple, which begs the question of what type of couple we are. Our relationship was founded on physical attraction, buoyed by the hormones of youth, as most college relationships are. We became more attached as we went through all the steps of young adulthood together, side by side. Marriage was one of those steps. There was no reason *not* to get married, as far as we knew. I can't even say that getting married was a mistake. We have made a good life for ourselves, for our family. We do not share tender embraces and offer each other shoulders to cry on, but we have a nice house and two beautiful kids and a loose plan for retirement. The fact that Kyle has the emotional depth of a rain puddle didn't bother me until after I had kids, when I needed tender embraces and a shoulder to cry on more than ever before.

"I've gotta get back to work, but we can talk more later," he said.

He gave my shoulder a squeeze, another unusual gesture for us, then took his sandwich to his office and shut the door.

～

Once he was gone, I started crying right there in the kitchen, while the girls continued their miracle of playing quietly. Had I ever cried in their presence? These tears did not care who was there, who needed me. These tears were resolute. I wasn't sure if they were about my dad or my marriage or both. Perhaps they were about everything I should have cried about for years, but didn't. Whatever the case, the dam had broken. I was grieving and it was awful, and it would probably be that way for a long time to come.

Chapter 8

KATRINA

Katrina drives away from Elijah feeling immediate pangs of regret and longing. At the end of the street, she looks in her rearview mirror, and he is still standing there, at the place they said their goodbyes, hands jammed into the pockets of his jeans. She holds a breath in her chest. It occupies every nook and cranny of her lungs. When she releases it, she doesn't feel relief or peace; she feels empty, deflated. She is not only driving back to her regular life today; she is leaving behind the possibility of a better one.

~

It's after midnight when she finally gets home. The house is quiet. Everyone is in bed. She makes herself a cup of chamomile, hoping it will relax her enough that she can sleep. She is simultaneously exhausted and wired. She goes to the living room, sits on the couch. It's nice—sitting alone, in the quiet. She can't remember the last time she's done this. When would she have time to just *sit*?

She finds his number in her phone, under E. She smiles like a giddy schoolgirl just looking at it. She shakes her head in disbelief at herself.

When she was at his apartment, she saw mail on his kitchen counter, made a note of his last name: Baker. It would be prudent to know his last name in case he did show serial killer tendencies, after all. And as importantly, she foresaw her desire to google him, to comfort herself with whatever images of him were on the internet for all the world to see.

Google reveals more Elijah Bakers than she expected, the most prominent being an English actor. When she scrolls through images, she sees several photos of the actor, along with an older musician and a Baptist preacher. A few clicks in, she finds him, a headshot on LinkedIn. His profile is sparse and doesn't offer any information she doesn't already know, but she appreciates the photo, saves it to her phone.

She opens the Instagram app, hoping for more. Elijah doesn't seem like the type to have much of a social media presence, but he is a millennial, and she assumes an Instagram profile, at the very least, is required of millennials. When she types in his name, she is confronted with a plethora of Elijah Bakers. Most are easy to dismiss just based on the little circular image alone—he's not a white guy, he's not a super-dark-skinned Black guy, he's not a twelve-year-old, he's not a bikini-clad woman (this one makes no sense). There is one profile picture that is a lighthouse, and she wonders if that's him. When she taps it, the profile is private, though. All she can see is that the account has only three posts, sixteen followers, and twenty-seven followees.

She takes the last sip of her tea, sets the mug on the coffee table, briefly wonders why it's called a coffee table and not a tea table. She's slightly delirious. It's nearly one o'clock at this point, and she should go to bed.

She wants to text him. She could ask him for a photo, a keepsake of sorts. She wishes she'd given him her number so he could be the one responsible for reaching out. As it is, it's up to her, and she's told herself explicitly that she won't. What would be the point? It would only prolong that overwhelming melancholy she felt while driving away from him, wouldn't it?

She closes her eyes, strokes her soft belly, pretending her hand is his. She remembers doing this as a teenager, kissing the back of her own hand, imagining her skin to be the lips of her crush. Her hand slides beneath the waistband of her pants. She has to keep her eyes closed because if she sees herself doing this, she will feel too foolish to continue. And she wants to continue.

That word blares in her mind, like a neon sign—MASTURBATE. Such an ugly, blunt word for such a delicate thing. It sounds more like a word for beating something into submission—eggs, dough. What she is doing is not that. What she is doing is sweet and sensual, a little desperate maybe. Her fingers are nothing like Elijah's long, thin fingers, but the imagination is a powerful thing.

Within minutes, she makes herself orgasm, something she hasn't done since she was a teenager alone in her twin-size bed, hormones instructing her to do things that her brain didn't understand. She opens her eyes, satisfied, pleasantly surprised. *Well, look at you,* she thinks to herself with more than a little bit of pride. She didn't know she could still do that, hasn't felt compelled to even try in years.

Then, with that surge of empowerment to blame, she picks up her phone and just does it:

Hi. It's me. Katrina.

She doesn't expect a response because it's one in the morning. But just as she stands to take her mug to the kitchen, she sees three dots on the screen. She stops, heart hammering away in her chest.

Him: You have no idea how happy I am right now

She sits exactly where she is, right there on the wood floor, because her head is light and fizzy and she might faint. She doesn't know what to say and is thankful when he writes more:

I was hoping you'd text. I probably shouldn't admit this, but I was staying up to see if you would

She sets her mug on the floor next to her, holds the phone in both hands, staring at it as if it is the Hope Diamond.

Oh god, I'm sorry to keep you up so late

Him: Do not apologize. Please. How was the drive?

Uneventful. Home safe and sound. Kind of wish I was still there

Just as she's wincing, chastising herself for her cheesy admission, he puts her at ease with his own.

I wish you were still here too. I keep thinking about you.

Me too

Him: I know this week is busy for you . . . Can you come next weekend? Or I'll come there

She tries to picture Elijah in her house. It's as ludicrous as imagining a circus elephant sitting in a chair at the kitchen table.

I don't know . . .

She does know. Or she's supposed to know. She's supposed to say *No, absolutely not.* But she does not say that. She lets Elijah know, with a single ellipsis, that she is considering it, or at least *considering* considering it.

Him: I'll take that as a maybe

She has the stupidest smile on her face, the kind of smile that will make her cheeks hurt if held too long.

I should really go to bed . . .

Him: OK. I hope you have sweet dreams, Kit Kat.

The stupid smile remains.

You too

He adds a heart emoji, and she sends one back. It is shamefully teenage, and the person she was two days ago would feign barfing at this type of thing. Something has happened to her, and while her rational brain tells her it's quite catastrophic, her reckless heart, still hammering away, has a different opinion.

~

The next day, in the midst of her regular-life duties, the stupid smile remains on her face, and her husband says, "You're in a good mood" with a tone of relief and hope. She has not been in a "good mood" in a while.

"I am, actually," she tells him.

When she got into bed the night before, he was sound asleep, definitely not kept up with worry about her getting home safe and sound.

"I thought you'd be tired."

She shrugs, as if she's a person who has a very take-it-or-leave-it approach to sleep (she has never, ever been this person).

"I am tired, but it's okay."

He looks suspicious, as he should. Suspicious of the mood, skeptical of its duration. He wouldn't suspect her of having a lover.

Is that the correct term for Elijah? A *lover*? She likes it. It feels very French. In any case, her husband has never had a good imagination, and picturing her with a lover would require a good deal of imagination. Practically speaking, it would seem outrageous to him. When would she have the time?

~

She texts Elijah throughout the day, which makes the grind of her life much more tolerable, less soul crushing. Maybe this has been the answer to the drudgery—a lover. She likes going through the motions with this secret in her head. It's similar to how she felt when she was newly pregnant, when she was walking around with a private dream growing inside her.

At the grocery store, instead of dragging her feet up and down the aisles, she nearly skips. While emptying the dishwasher, she starts humming to herself. *Humming!* She is more patient and forgiving toward the world, the type of woman who lets out a genuine laugh when someone steps on the heel of her shoe: *Oh, whoops, no worries!*

By the end of the day, she has decided that she deserves this kind of joy. She has *earned* this kind of joy.

I was thinking . . . maybe I will come see you next weekend

She could swing it. It would be fun to see Elijah one more time. This time she would be less dazed and confused, more assured. This time she would not be a woman tiptoeing into infidelity; she would be a woman launching herself into it, arms open, eyes wild.

He responds to her text with a GIF of Carlton from *The Fresh Prince of Bel-Air* doing his happy dance, which prompts her to reply:

You're too young to know that show

Him: Nah. Everyone knows that show. It's a mac-and-cheese show

A mac-and-cheese show?

Him: A comfort food type show

Ha

Him: I like how you say "ha" when something is funny

Ha

This banter has made the day go by quickly. It has made her children seem more delightful than they usually are. It has made errands less burdensome. It is a salve, this banter. She is already addicted to it, the rush of seeing his name appear, the anticipation, the giddiness.

Returning to the topic of her visiting him again, he says:

I can't wait

Me neither

Him: How is it only Monday?

I don't know, but at least it's the end of Monday. You've made it much better than Mondays usually are

She wants to hear his voice, to see him, to confirm the reality of him. But it's not feasible to have a phone call, let alone FaceTime. There is always another human being near her. Texting, for now, will have to do.

I can't wait to hold you

I can't wait to kiss you

Their sappy messages go on like this until she tells him she has to go to sleep. She is in bed texting, daring her husband to say something. He just stares at his own phone, looking at sports scores like the stereotypical husband he is, until he falls asleep, the phone on his chest, rising and falling with his breath. If he ever finds out about Elijah, she hopes he blames his own obliviousness. He won't, of course, but he should.

"Good night," she whispers to him, though she doubts he can hear her. He is the type of person who enters a deep sleep approximately four seconds after closing his eyes.

He doesn't respond, as expected. He's on his back, meaning he'll be snoring soon. She gently pushes him, and he rolls onto his side with a grunt. Perhaps if he gave her the courtesy of a *good night*, if their communication involved something more substantial than grunts, she would feel more guilt about Elijah. As it is, she feels no guilt. She feels only exhilaration.

Chapter 9

NICOLE

It was just before midnight when I got to my dad and Merry's house Friday evening. Merry had left a key under the doormat, and I let myself in quietly, not wanting to wake them, but then discovered Merry was still awake, sitting on the couch in the living room, watching something with a laugh track on TV.

"Hey, Mer," I said, not wanting to startle her. She was startled anyway.

"Oh god, Nicole, you scared me."

She put her hand to her heart.

"You're still up?"

She was fully dressed in linen pants and a wool sweater.

"I can't sleep. Your father has these muscle spasms. It's like someone shocks him with a cattle prod. He hit me in the face last night."

I'd seen the spasms in the hospital. Whenever he'd fall asleep, his arms would start to twitch. Sometimes one of them would float upward and stick straight up in the air.

"I'm sorry." I sat next to her on the couch. "How is he today?"

She shrugged. "The same. I'm worried about him on the stairs. His walking has gotten so much worse just in the last week."

I'd read online about this—the rapid decline. He would need a wheelchair in the near future. I had no idea how to procure a wheelchair.

"I was thinking on the drive up that we should move him to the guest room down here," I said.

"The guest room?" She sounded appalled, like I'd just suggested we eat raw sewage for breakfast.

"It's not safe for him to be going up and down the stairs. You just said that."

"That room is so stuffy."

I put my hand on her shoulder.

"And there's no TV in there!"

"Mer, I know none of this is pleasant, but we have to consider what's safest for him, right?"

She shifted so my hand dropped from her shoulder, then stood.

"Can we talk about this tomorrow? I am exhausted."

"Yeah, sure. Of course."

I was already sensing that she wouldn't want to talk about this tomorrow, though. She wouldn't want to talk about this at all. I would have to be the one to make decisions, to force them if necessary.

She walked toward the staircase.

"Your old room is made up for you," she said over her shoulder.

"Okay, thanks."

She clung to the banister as she took the steps. I couldn't remember if she'd done that the last time I was there. It was as if my dad's diagnosis had made us feel vulnerable to tragedy in a way we'd never been before. For the rest of our lives, we would be watching our steps and clinging to banisters.

∽

I took a Benadryl so I'd sleep, knowing I'd need my energy in the days ahead. When I woke up, it was nearly eight—not as life-changing as nine, but still "sleeping in" according to any mother of small children.

I didn't hear my dad and Merry downstairs, so I walked to their bedroom, feeling suddenly like the little girl I once was, on her way to cuddle with her dad and watch cartoons.

Merry was in their bathroom, applying cream to her face and neck. She does not go outside these days without several layers of protection from the cancer-causing sun. I was about to ask her where my dad was when I turned and saw that he was still in bed, sound asleep, flat on his back, snoring.

"He's tired," she said. "I'm sure he doesn't sleep well with all that flailing around."

I sat on the bed next to him.

"I'm going to make coffee. You coming down?" she asked.

"I'll wait for him to get up."

"Okay. He'll need help on the stairs."

"I know, Mer."

She went on her way, and I lay next to him, my head on the edge of his pillow. He seemed so peaceful. Did he have any idea he was dying?

His eyes fluttered, and I said, "Hi, Daddy."

He blinked several times. I repeated myself: "Hi, Daddy."

Slowly, he turned his head. When he saw me there next to him, he smiled.

"Nikki Bear," he said. It's something he used to call me when I was little.

"How did you sleep?" I asked.

"Okay," he said. "When do I get to leave the hospital?"

"Dad, we're not at the hospital. We're at home."

He looked around him, bewildered. "Oh," he said. "I guess we are."

"But you *were* in the hospital."

"I was?"

"Don't worry about it," I said.

"Where's Ruby?" he asked, patting alongside him where the dog used to sleep. That dog was always at his side.

"Dad, Ruby died a long time ago."

He sighed, and I could almost see him start to forget the conversation we'd just had.

"Do you have school today?" he asked.

"School?"

"Is Mom taking you?"

"Dad, there's no school today. I'm visiting you from Orange County."

"Orange County?"

"Yes. That's where I live."

I rested my head on his chest, his solid, safe-place-to-fall chest.

"Nikki, life sucks sometimes," he said, apropos of nothing.

It was the most sensible thing he'd said since the beginning of this mess.

I felt the telltale tingle in my nose that always precedes tears. My vision blurred. I swallowed back the sadness, wiped my eyes. My grief would confuse my dad. He didn't understand that there was anything to grieve.

"It does suck," I said.

"But I guess it makes you appreciate the good times."

I lifted my head and looked into his eyes. He was still there, my dad. He was still him, at least for short moments.

"Why don't I drive us to get doughnuts?" he asked.

Just like that, he was gone.

"Dad, no driving."

He groaned.

"If you can count backward from one hundred by sevens, maybe you can drive," I said.

"Oh, Nikki, that's too hard."

He laughed, so I laughed, both of us pretending he was joking, bonded by our mutual denial.

"Do you want me to help you get up?" I asked.

My dad has never been one to ask for help. Frankly, I have no memories of him needing help up until that moment. Merry did a lot to keep the household running, but she always seemed stressed, always operating in a state of mild overwhelm. My dad embodied strength and calm. He neutralized her anxieties. If I imagined our three-person family as a house, he was the load-bearing wall, that unassuming beam responsible for keeping everything from caving in on itself.

He didn't answer my question, so I took it upon myself to get out of bed and go around to his side. He didn't protest as I pulled his arms to help him sit up. I put his slippers on his feet and then helped him stand. He was wobbly and tipped into me, quickly overwhelming me with his weight. I was able to set him straight. He had a crooked smile on his face. He seemed both embarrassed and amused.

"We need to get you a cane," I said, adding that to my mental list.

I helped him walk to the staircase. He was okay once he got going, but the steps presented a significant challenge.

"We'll just go slow," I told him.

And we did. We took one step at a time, pausing on the landing of each one to assess our next move. In just a week's time, he'd gone from walking strangely to barely walking. There was no way he could continue sleeping upstairs. He had to be in the downstairs bedroom.

When we got to the bottom, I'd broken out in a sweat. I walked him to the kitchen table, and when he sat, he said, "Ahhhhh," as if he'd just settled into a lounge chair at a resort pool in Maui.

Merry brought two mugs of coffee—one for me, one for him—along with a plate of toast with butter and jam. I watched my dad's hand shake as it reached out for a piece of toast. He was able to get it himself, no problem, but at the rate things were going, I didn't think that would be true next week.

"Do you want one of those smoothies in the plastic bottles?" Merry asked him.

He nodded, so she brought it to him. He took one sip and said, "This has a funny taste" and put it down. Merry looked put out, as if she'd made the smoothie herself as opposed to buying it at the store.

I bit into a piece of toast and then decided we had to get down to business.

"Okay, so, plan for today," I said, clapping my hands together like a motivational speaker and then immediately hating myself.

Merry sat across from me, holding her mug of coffee with two hands.

"Dad, I think we need to get you set up downstairs in the bedroom," I said.

"Downstairs?" he said.

Merry interjected: "Nicole, do you really think—"

"Yes, I really think it's necessary. Dad, I'll set up a TV in there. You won't have to deal with the stairs anymore."

It occurred to me that I was using the tone of voice I use with the girls when trying to make something sound fun that isn't fun: *Look at these colorful floss picks we got! Aren't you excited to brush your teeth tonight?*

(Yes, I'm back to the teeth brushing.)

"The bed in there is a queen," Merry said. "That's not going to work."

"Mer, I think Dad can fit in a queen bed."

"What about me?" she asked. "I'll be sleeping with him, won't I?"

I hadn't thought about that.

"You two can't fit in a queen bed?"

"Nicole, with the spasms, I need as much space as I can get."

"Spasms?" my dad asked.

We both looked at him. He truly had no idea what was happening to his body.

"This is delicious!" he blurted out suddenly, in reference to the smoothie.

"Did the funny taste go away?" Merry asked him.

"What funny taste? These are delicious!"

Merry and I looked at each other. Her eyes were pleading with me—for what, I don't know.

"Okay," I said, returning to the previous topic, "how about I disassemble the king bed and move it downstairs?"

I thought Merry would say something like "Don't be silly, we'll make do with the queen." You know, like a normal person.

Instead, she said, "You can *do* that?" as if reassembling the bed was akin to lifting a car off the ground.

"I think I can figure it out."

If there's one thing motherhood has taught me, it's that I can figure shit out.

She set down her mug, crossed her arms over her chest, and sighed. "Well, I guess that would be fine."

"Nikki?" Dad said.

"Yeah?"

"Where's my juice box? I think your phone ate my juice box."

I didn't dare look at Merry, couldn't handle her pleading eyes again. "I don't know, Dad. I'll find it."

I finished my piece of toast and told them I was going to get started on the bed situation. If this was anything like building an Ikea bookcase for the girls' room, I was in for a long day.

∼

Five minutes in, I realized that despite my bravado, I would need help. The mattresses were too heavy and awkward for me to maneuver alone, especially on the stairs, so I had to convince Merry to ask Jim to come over. Jim and Alice have lived next door for as long as I can remember. Jim is a big lumberjack of a man. (Though he's not an actual lumberjack—he's a high school English teacher. Or he used to be. He's retired.) He's in his sixties, but looks fiftysomething. Merry reports that he lifts weights in their garage and goes for daily jogs. Alice is a psychologist who still works, which baffles Merry: *They must have more than enough money.* They have a daughter in her thirties who teaches at a fancy university in England—Oxford or Cambridge, I can never remember which.

When Jim came over, with Alice in tow, it was immediately obvious that Merry had not told them anything about my dad's health issues. They seemed alarmed when he attempted to stand from the couch to greet them. (It was a failed attempt. He sat back down before he was fully upright.) Merry did nothing to address their alarm, so I took it upon myself to explain when I got them in the other room.

"He was just diagnosed?" Alice said.

Neither of them had heard of Creutzfeldt-Jakob disease. I don't imagine I'll run into many people in my life who have.

"Yes. On Monday, actually. It's a really rapid decline, from what I've read."

"Is there a doctor treating him?" Jim asked.

I shook my head. "I don't think there's any treatment to be done. We'll have hospice . . . when Merry's ready for that."

"Hospice. My god," Alice said.

Both their faces were long and drawn. I hate pity.

"You'll need help, dear," Alice said. "Soon."

"I'm starting with getting him set up downstairs. One thing at a time, right?"

They nodded in sync.

"Do you want me to look into some options for help?" Alice asked.

"Sure, that would be great."

She turned to Jim, and they had a mini conference about some friend of theirs named Suzanne who had a great caregiver for her husband, who had Parkinson's. I busied myself with pulling the sheets off the mattress and folding them.

"So what's the plan with these beds?" Jim asked. He seemed excited to have a task, to be helpful in a real, tangible way.

I told him about the mattress exchange, and he nodded his understanding, then said, "Let's do it." I was grateful for his enthusiasm because I had exactly none.

Alice took on a supervisory role, coaching us down the stairs with the king mattress. Merry just sat on the couch with my dad, turned away from the commotion, as if she couldn't bear to see her life literally being turned upside down.

We leaned the king mattress against the wall in the downstairs bedroom, then brought the queen mattress upstairs. Jim was sweating at that point, which made me feel bad.

"Thank you," I said when we'd gotten the queen mattress upstairs.

"What's next?" Jim asked, noticeably out of breath. Even though he's quite obviously a healthy man, he's still elderly. I didn't need a heart attack on my conscience.

"Your part is done." I put my hands in prayer position to express my gratitude.

"We have to build the beds, right?" he asked.

"I can do that," I said. "I have my dad's drill and everything."

He swiped his hand at the air, waving off my agenda.

"I'll build the beds," he said.

"No, really, you don't need to do that."

"He's very good at this type of thing," Alice said. "Come, I'll make you some tea at my place."

"I can at least be an assistant," I said.

"It's a one-person job, and I insist on being that person," Jim said.

"There's no point arguing with him, hon," Alice said.

That was that.

Alice and I walked downstairs.

"Mer, I'm taking Nicole to have a cup of tea. You want to come?"

My dad couldn't be left alone, though. He would likely try to walk somewhere and fall.

"I'll stay here with Rob. Thanks, though."

"You don't mind if I steal Nicole away?" she asked, as if I were a minor in need of permission.

"Go right ahead," Merry said.

∼

125

Jim and Alice's house is a Victorian meant for San Francisco proper. When we went inside, it looked the same as I remembered from childhood. It smelled the same, too—cinnamon and vanilla. Alice was always baking something.

We sat at the kitchen table, and she poured two cups of tea from a kettle on the stove. She was the type to always have a kettle of tea at the ready. She brought a little cup of sugar cubes too. Alice was someone with little cups of sugar cubes.

"I have to say I'm in a bit of shock about your father," she said.

"I am too."

I dropped one of the cubes in my tea, watched it dissolve.

"Merry told me your father had taken a fall . . . Is that what started all this?"

I remembered what the doctor had said: *A red herring, as we say.*

"No, not related. Just a coincidence."

"I just didn't know his symptoms were so serious."

"They weren't really until very recently."

She shook her head.

"How is Merry doing with it?" she asked.

"I think she's in a bit of denial."

"Denial can have very protective qualities. Our psyches can only handle so much."

I nodded.

"I guess I feel like we don't have time for denial. We have to start making arrangements and things."

I immediately regretted using that word—*arrangements.* As if we were already talking about his funeral.

"He will need significant care," she said.

"I know." She didn't need to keep hammering this home.

"I'll talk to Merry."

I thanked her, then took a sip of my tea. It tasted strongly caffeinated. Alice reached across the table and held one of my hands in hers.

"You need to take care of yourself, okay? I know you have two little ones. Coming up here, that's a drive."

This was a common refrain on social media—*All you mamas out there, you need to take care of yourselves. Put on your oxygen mask first, remember? You got this.* Of course, most of these messages were put out there by celebrities and influencers who probably have three nannies on staff. I don't know how the rest of us common folk are supposed to take care of ourselves when so many human beings rely on us to take care of them. That saying "It takes a village" implies there is a village readily available. But where is the village? Did I miss the registration email?

"I'll do my best," I said.

"You need to."

Her eyes were serious. I got a glimpse of what she was like as a psychologist with her patients.

"And I'm always here to talk if you need to."

"Thanks, Alice. I appreciate it."

~

When we finished our tea, we went back to the house. Jim was nearly done setting up the king bed downstairs. When I told Merry this, she said, "And what about the TV?"

"I'll figure that out," I told her, though I had little confidence in my technology skills. I don't rely on Kyle for much, but he is in charge of all things audiovisual.

"I can help with the TV," Jim called from the bedroom.

"Thanks for eavesdropping," I called back.

"What's happening with the TV?" my poor dad asked.

I was about to text Kyle to check up on the girls when my phone buzzed with an incoming text. It was Prisha. We had messaged a few times since the previous visit. She'd known I was headed to the Bay Area again.

Hey. Was just thinking of you. Wanna meet for a drink? I'm off at 5

My first thought was to decline the invitation. I wasn't sure it would make me feel better to see beautiful, unencumbered Prisha again. But then I thought of what Alice had said about taking care of myself. Maybe I needed some Prisha energy in my life. Besides, Merry was irritating me.

Hi. Yes. Would love that. Same place?

Yep. See you then

I spent the rest of the day pretending to assist Jim (I was really just watching him while scrolling on my phone) while Alice sat and chatted with Merry and my dad. Kyle and I exchanged a few texts, basically confirming each other's existence and nothing more. Alice picked up sandwiches for lunch, and we all ate together at the kitchen table. When my dad was sitting, not attempting to walk, it was easy to believe things weren't that bad. He didn't participate much in the conversation, but he had a pleasant smile on his face. He just seemed quiet and tired. He started to doze off and then went to nap on the couch when we were done.

After lunch, we finished with the beds, and Jim set up the TV. I made a run to Trader Joe's for Merry, where I felt assaulted by the peppy cashiers: "How's your day going? Any fun plans?" They really need a "sad line" for people who are dealing with terrible life circumstances or just having a particularly awful day. In this line, the cashiers would be reverentially silent.

By the time I unloaded the groceries, I was exhausted and very much in need of alcohol. I told Merry I was going to meet Prisha. I told her not to wait up, that we might be out late. I wanted the option to wander the city and feel carefree again. Alice said, "Have fun," and Merry said, "Please don't drink and drive. I can't handle more stress."

~

I had packed a form-fitting black dress this trip, figuring I didn't want to be in leggings and an old sweater again if I met up with Prisha. My hair is usually a sloppy topknot situation, so I decided to blow it dry and wear it long. I used Merry's round brush for as much curl at the ends as my hair would allow. I swept some blush onto my cheeks and swiped my eyelashes with two coats of mascara. I felt, dare I say, *pretty*.

The bar was busier than the last time we'd come. There was a large group of people who appeared to be celebrating someone's birthday (there were party hats). I took a seat at the bar and ordered a whiskey straight, which is not something I ever order, but I wanted the burn. Some people drink whiskey recreationally. It's their drink of choice. For me, whiskey is for when life feels unbearable. And I was quite sure life was becoming unbearable.

I'd winced my way through half the glass when I got a text from Prisha:

I'm so sorry. I'm not going to be able to make it

Doctors can say this type of thing and people just accept it.

Oh, bummer. Ok.

Her: Are you there already?

Yes

Her: Ugh, I'm so sorry. We've got a complicated delivery situation . . . I'm sorry. Have a drink for me?

Already on it

She sent me a clinking-glasses emoji.

I was mildly disappointed, but it was fine. Prisha had done me the kindness of giving me a reason to leave the house. Now that I'd left (and downed half a glass of whiskey), I didn't actually need *her*. I settled in, trying to remember the last time I'd sat at a bar alone. Had I *ever* sat at a bar alone? In my younger years, I'd traveled in packs. And then I was married.

"You want another?" the bartender asked.

It was a different bartender than the last time. Every inch of visible skin on his arms was tattooed.

I assessed my empty glass and said, "Why not?"

He nodded distractedly and traveled to the other end of the bar.

I felt someone behind my chair, grazing my back, and I was mildly annoyed with the intrusion into my personal space.

"Sorry," the person said. A man.

He sat next to me, and I groaned to myself. I didn't want to talk to a stranger. At the very least, we'd have to exchange polite greetings, as our elbows would be in close proximity.

The bartender threw a napkin in front of the man, and they had a short discussion of the IPAs on tap. The man ordered one of them. The bartender brought it, and the man took a sip. I didn't want to look at him directly because I thought that might be inviting conversation I didn't want. But he *sounded* handsome. His voice was deep.

"It is packed tonight," he said.

Was he saying it to me? There was a woman in the seat on the other side of him, but her back was to him. She was laughing hysterically at the woman facing her. They were both wearing party hats.

I dared to look at him. He *was* handsome.

"It is packed," I said.

He looked at me then. It was our first eye contact. His eyes were the kind people get lost in, little Bermuda Triangles.

"It's not usually like this."

"I've only been once," I said.

"This is my usual spot, and if it was always like this, it would not be my usual spot."

We laughed.

He wore a white button-down shirt, a stark contrast with his darker skin. I decided, right then, that I would flirt with him. I would pretend to be a single, childless woman, a woman like Prisha.

"I'm Elijah," he said, sticking out his hand at an awkward angle. I shook it at just as awkward an angle.

When I was a kid, playing pretend with the neighborhood kids, I always gave myself this one somewhat-exotic name. I hated my own name. Nicole. It was so boring, so common. I wanted a name that an interesting, important, gorgeous woman would have.

"I'm Katrina," I said.

I especially liked that it came with a cute nickname—Kat.

When he smiled, there were dimples.

"You can call me Kat."

Part 2

Chapter 10

NICOLE

I am parked in front of Elijah's apartment building. Or rather, *Katrina* is parked in front of Elijah's apartment building. It's outlandish, I know, creating this other person. It's really no different from Grace prancing around the house calling herself Elsa and singing "Let It Go" at the top of her lungs. There are probably deep psychological problems afoot, "Katrina" being an attempt to compartmentalize my indiscretions, separate myself from the reality of what I'm doing. Yesterday, while lying in my childhood bed, unable to sleep, I googled my little heart out: *split personality disorder, identity disorder, types of personality disorders, nervous breakdown,* and *am I crazy?* What I've concluded is that no label fits perfectly, but yes, I am probably crazy. That word every woman hates to have applied to her may just be appropriate for me. Someday, when people find out what an awful person I am, they will come up with a new term named after me—Nicole syndrome. This will be a syndrome that makes mothers of small children with less-than-stellar husbands lose their wits and abandon their lives in times of crisis.

Just as I have the past two weekends, I drove up to Daly City yesterday. I spent today with my dad and Merry. Things continue to go downhill at an alarming rate. My dad cannot walk unassisted now. We have a hospice company involved. They are bringing a wheelchair to the house on Monday. Dad spends most of his time at the kitchen table, listening to music and "reading" the paper—in quotes because he mostly just stares at the pages, brows furrowed. Merry has a small whiteboard on the table in front of him with basic information on it—the date, the day of the week, any plans for the day. I asked him if it bothered him that he couldn't remember these things on his own, and he said, "Nah, all that's going to come back when I get better."

It's easy to be lulled by his overconfidence, to sink into the deliciousness of denial. Merry gives him these little cognition quizzes every now and then—"I'm going to give you a number to remember, okay?" She hasn't given up hope. Before I left today, she gave him the number ten—"a nice, easy number," she told him, placing the ball on the tee for him to hit out of the park. A moment later, she said, "Now what was that number?" and he said, "Thirty."

My dad has always exuded warmth, but he's especially sweet and kind now, almost childlike. When I gave him a hug this morning, he said, "Why don't they do hugging in the hospital? It feels so nice." It sounded like something Grace would say. I told him I agreed, then went to another room so he wouldn't see me cry. When we ate lunch today, Bob Dylan's "Knockin' on Heaven's Door" came on, a gut punch that made me think Apple really is all-knowing, and my dad just hummed along with a dopey smile on his face. Merry told a couple of his golf buddies what was going on, and they've been visiting every day since. *Randy and Al coming over*—that was on the whiteboard this morning, and Dad said, "Why are they coming by?"

Merry said, "Because they know you're sick and they care about you."

He said, "They're acting like I'm gonna croak."

Sometimes I think he does know he's going to die. On some level, at least. Maybe his memory loss is a blessing, the disease protecting him from the reality of its awfulness. Perhaps it is not a terrible fate that causes humans to suffer, but our ability to ponder it.

～

As much as I think it's ridiculous that I am here, in front of Elijah's apartment building, I also cannot wait to go in, to enter this other world, to be Katrina. I told Merry that I was meeting up with Prisha again. The last time, when I went home with Elijah, I'd texted Merry to say I was staying at Prisha's place in the city, that I would stop by to see them in the morning before heading home. "I'll probably go to Prisha's place again," I told her before heading out today. Prisha has become my alibi.

I knock at his door just once, and he opens it, as if he's been standing directly on the other side, staring through the peephole.

"It's you," he says.

I've been hoping he won't be as attractive as he was in my mind, but he is. I half expect him to see me and decide that this is all a bad idea, but his smile doesn't falter. There is no discernible disappointment.

He wraps his arms around me, and that's it—I have left everything behind, and I am Katrina. He has such strong arms, the arms of someone who goes to the gym religiously (which I have learned he does, thanks to our text conversations, which are most definitely out of control to the tune of hundreds of messages a day). He holds me so tight that he lifts me off the ground, my black ballet flats dangling from my toes. I'm not a small woman (five foot nine), but he is six foot three and makes me feel tiny, petite. I have never felt petite before. Kyle is exactly my height; I've never been able to look up to him.

When he puts me down, he kisses me, long and hard. Any second thoughts I had about coming here vaporize. He pulls me into the apartment and kicks the door closed behind us. We stumble to the bedroom, yanking at each other's clothes.

"You have no idea how much I've been thinking about this," he says.

"I think I do."

We are breathless.

The sex is less tentative than last time, more decisive and forceful. We've been storing up desire for a week. We are desperate.

It is over in a matter of minutes, but I can't say this disappoints me. Nothing is sexier than a man who can't restrain himself.

"Sorry," he says, burying his face into the pillow in dramatized shame.

"Why?"

"I didn't last long," he says, voice muffled by the pillow.

"I still finished." I did, easily and without question.

He lifts his head, kisses my thigh.

"I know," he says. "I can feel it when you do."

I asked Kyle once if he could feel when I orgasmed because it seemed impossible that he couldn't. It would be like sleeping through an earthquake. He said no, though. It offended me in a way I couldn't articulate then. I can now, though. I was hurt that he couldn't feel something so overpowering to me, that we were in such separate experiences. I suppose that could summarize much of our marriage lately.

"I wanted you to come twice," he says.

I pat him on the head, playfully. "Aw, young lad, you will have another chance."

~

He does, in fact, have another chance. Not more than an hour later, we have sex again, this time slower. At one point during it, I think of Sting, the rock star, waxing poetic about tantric sex. I used to think sex as "spiritual act" was woo-woo bullshit, but now I'm reconsidering.

When we are done, he falls asleep, and I watch him, his lips barely parted, his eyelids twitching in the midst of a dream. An hour later, the sun sets, and I'm ravenous, as if I haven't eaten in days. I rest my head on his bare chest, hoping he'll stir. He does.

"Hey," he says, groggy.

"Hey."

"You're hungry, aren't you?"

"It's like you can read my mind," I say.

He stares right into my eyes and says, "Maybe I can."

Of course, if he could, he would not be as enamored with me as he is—an adulteress with two small children.

"Or maybe you just heard my stomach growling."

He laughs, sits up against the headboard.

"Wanna order in?" he asks. "You can try my favorite Chinese place. If you don't like it, we'll have to end things."

"Wow, you have intense feelings about Chinese food."

"It's objectively the best in the city, so anyone who doesn't agree it's good cannot be trusted."

"You shouldn't have told me that. Now I could just lie to you and say I love it so you think I'm trustworthy."

Which I'm not, clearly.

"I don't think you're that conniving."

He has no idea. The longer the lying goes on, the more it's getting to me. I've let him care for me more than he should. He's getting attached to me—or to Katrina. My self-serving deceit could hurt this kind man if I'm not careful.

He reaches for his phone on the nightstand, and while he's busy ordering, I get out of bed and go to my purse. I check my own phone. No messages. I keep feeling paranoid that there will be some emergency back home and I'll be too busy having sex with my lover to properly respond. How could I live with myself then? I'm not even sure how I'm living with myself now.

I text Kyle:

Hi. Give the girls a goodnight kiss for me.

He responds right away, probably because he's doing what I do and scrolling on his phone in search of dopamine hits that make parenting a little easier.

Ok.

"Done," Elijah says, referring to the Chinese-food order.

"That was fast."

"I know what I like," he says.

He comes up behind me, nuzzles—nuzzles!—into the back of my neck, his breath hot. I drop my phone in my purse.

"You do know what you like," I say.

"Let's go sit at the kitchen table like respectable adults. I have a good bottle of wine."

"Respectable adults? I didn't know you were into role-playing."

"Ha ha. Speak for yourself, woman."

I follow him to the kitchen, wrapped in a throw blanket from his bed. His kitchen is small, but there is a round table with two chairs. I sit in one, knees pulled to my chest, while he pours our wine.

"Try this," he says, handing me a glass.

I take a sip.

"Mmm," I say.

"Like liquefied jam, right?"

"Exactly."

"I'm glad you like it. We would have had to break up if you didn't."

"You have a lot of conditions," I say. "And 'break up' implies we are in some kind of relationship."

I throw in a teasing laugh for good measure, though I really am increasingly concerned about our differing expectations.

"Aren't we?" he says, confirming my fears.

I take a long sip of wine. "Elijah, I'm not exactly looking for a relationship."

"And yet you came up here to see me."

"Well, you are very good looking."

"And 'nice,' right?" he says, air quoting the *nice*.

"Right."

He takes his own long sip of wine. "Can I ask why you're not looking for a relationship?"

"Because relationships are terrible."

His eyes go wide. "I think you must be more damaged than I thought."

I laugh. "Aren't we all more damaged than we thought?"

"Touché."

He sits across from me, sets his glass on the table, and crosses his arms over his chest.

"Seriously," he says, "what's up with you and relationships?"

"I'm a very complicated person, Elijah."

"I like complicated people. I am one myself."

"I beg to differ. You seem to be a very simple person, and I mean that in the best way possible."

"You don't know me well yet," he says, grinning.

"And you don't know me well yet either."

"I think we can agree there is something good between us, yes?"

I roll my eyes. "I believe the amount of sex we've had in a short amount of time can attest to that."

"And I know I've told you this already, but I haven't really felt this kind of connection before."

You're only thirty, I want to say. Really, though, I haven't felt this kind of connection either, but I can't disclose that. If I do, that means we are admitting that we have something special, something unique, something promising. I am in no position to have something special, unique, or promising.

"It could all be chemical, you know," I say.

He doesn't seem deterred. "So you don't believe in soulmates?"

Now my eyes go wide. *Soulmates?*

"No," I say, "I do not believe in soulmates."

I do not need this poor man to believe I am his soulmate. I most certainly am not.

He nods. "Interesting."

"Interesting?"

"I guess I'm the romantic of the two of us," he says.

"I guess you are."

His phone, on the table next to him, lights up with a text. He glances at it.

"Food's ready," he says.

He stands, goes to the kitchen counter to retrieve a set of keys from an empty fruit bowl.

"You cool staying here? It's right down the street, so I won't be long."

"Sure, that's fine," I say.

He gives me a kiss on the cheek and leaves.

I am alone in his apartment. He trusts me to be alone in his apartment. It's baffling. I look around for a camera. Everyone has cameras now, don't they? I don't see anything, so I take it upon myself to snoop. He doesn't have much—as I said, he seems to be a rather simple person. His bookshelves are full, mostly with nonfiction books about various topics—global warming, racism, feminism (yes, feminism). There is a framed photo of him with an older woman who must be his mother. They have the same nose, the same smile. She is white. He mentioned that in one of his texts, said he often dates strong white women and maybe that's because he was raised by a strong white woman. I'd teased him about having an Oedipus complex.

There's nothing of interest in his medicine cabinet, no antidepressants or herpes antivirals or whatever else. He has dental floss and toothpaste and mouthwash. That's it. He doesn't even have face wash, which is shocking considering how beautiful his skin is.

In the bedroom, there's only space for his bed, a small dresser, and his nightstand. I open the drawer, find the roll of condoms we are depleting. There are two left. There's a phone charger, earplugs, a book on meditation.

I wonder if Elijah has ever committed a sin before I came along—a real sin, I mean. Then again, if a man sleeps with a married woman, is he saddled with a derogatory term? Women sleeping with married men are called mistresses. Is there a male equivalent? I don't think so. Patriarchal society may look at men sleeping with married women as *smart*—enjoying the milk without buying the cow, so to speak. Elijah seems to want the cow, though. I am, rightfully, the cow.

I hear the door open and rush back to the kitchen. He can tell I've just come from his bedroom, though. I'm sure I look caught.

"Snooping?" he says.

"Guilty."

"Find anything interesting?"

"No. You're incredibly boring."

"Guilty," he says.

He sets the plastic bags of food on the counter, begins unpacking the Styrofoam containers.

"Can I help with anything?" I ask.

"You can finish your glass of wine so I can pour you another."

I comply, taking my seat at the table.

"I don't understand why you're single," I say. I've been thinking it and figure I may as well just come out with my thoughts. I have nothing to lose. This can be an experiment in radical authenticity.

"You sound like my mother," he says.

"It really doesn't make sense. There must be something drastically wrong with you that I haven't discovered yet."

"I'm sure there are lots of things wrong with me."

He takes scoops from each container and puts them on a plate, then brings it to me. Then he makes his own plate and sits at the table.

"Your last relationship—with the pediatrician—ended last year?"

"Good memory. And yes. About a year ago."

"And you were together a long time?"

"Couple years."

I'm not sure why I'm asking all this, why I'm getting to know him better. Maybe I'm hoping I'll lose interest if I learn more about him. *A crush is just a lack of information*—I saw that meme making the rounds on Instagram recently. But there is also the risk I'll fall for him more.

"And nobody since?"

"Just you," he says.

"Hmm."

"That bothers you?"

"Just hard to believe. No sex for a year?"

"Until you," he says. Then: "What about you?"

I take a bite. "This is really good," I say.

"I know. And I'm glad you agree. But don't change the subject."

"I don't want to talk about me," I say.

"You are a tough nut to crack, aren't you?"

"Did you just call me a nut?"

We laugh, and he doesn't press further, and we enjoy the food, and it feels strangely *normal*, like we do this all the time. It's how I felt at the breakfast place last weekend. If I was someone who believed in past lives, I would wonder if we'd been lovers in another era. But I am not someone who believes in much of anything.

"The woman in the photo with you," I say. "Is that your mother?"

"So you *were* snooping?" he says. "Yes, that's her."

"You're close?"

He nods. "We are."

"And your father?"

Just as I'm formulating an assumption that his father abandoned the family, as fathers are permitted to do in a way mothers never are, he says, "He died," and I feel like a horrible (or more horrible) person.

"Oh," I say. "I'm sorry."

He doesn't seem particularly emotional about it.

"He died before I turned one," he says. "He was a firefighter."

"So you never knew him," I say, thinking of my mother.

He shrugs. "No. Which I know is terrible, but it's hard to miss what I didn't know."

"True," I say, tempted to share my own story. I decide against it, still unsure how much of a bond I want to develop.

"Any siblings?"

He shakes his head. "Just me."

Same as me, I think. We have a surprising amount in common.

144

"An only child, that's why you're so mature," I say.

"Am I mature?"

"For a thirty-year-old man? Yes."

"My mom would be happy to hear you say that."

I finally take a bite of my egg roll.

"I told my mom about you," he says.

"Oh god."

"I talk to her every day, so it came up," he says. "Naturally."

"You really are a mama's boy."

"Guilty."

"I guess if it was just the two of you, it makes sense."

"We are talking an awful lot about me," he says.

"I know. It's great."

"Katrina, Katrina, you are an enigma," he says with an amused shake of the head.

"That sounds like a song lyric."

He attempts to sing it, and his voice cracks. I have found his first flaw: he cannot carry a tune.

"I told my mom you were funny," he says.

I put my hands over my ears.

"La la la, I don't want to know what you told your mom about me."

"Okay, fine. We can talk about something lame instead. What are your favorite movies?"

~

When we are done with dinner, we have sex again—Katrina is a freaking animal—and then we sleep. Or he does. I am wide awake again, staring at the ceiling wondering what the hell I'm doing. I'll leave in the morning, go visit with Merry and Dad again, then head back home to reality. This time—this time!—will be my final goodbye with Elijah. It has to be. I can't keep this going. Or can I? No. I can't. I will tell him I'm serious this time. I will tell him not to text me. I will delete him from my phone. I will return to my regular life and sustain myself with the memories. Maybe I'll buy a vibrator and pair that with those memories. Yes, that will be enough. It will have to be. He'll be disappointed. And he's such a sweet guy. And so handsome. And funny. And kind. But no. This is it. The last time.

Chapter 11

Rose

September 16, 1984

Dear Diary,

Ha. Dear Diary. Look at me, acting like an eleven-year-old schoolgirl. I didn't even keep a diary when I *was* an eleven-year-old schoolgirl. It never occurred to me to keep a diary until just now, at age twenty-eight. They say necessity is the mother of invention, but I think motherhood is the necessity of invention. My thoughts have to go somewhere.

Nicole is sleeping. Her daily nap is the only time I have to myself. A year ago, she would sleep two or three hours at a stretch. Now it's just forty-five minutes or so. By the time she turns four, she may not nap at all. What then? She's already started refusing naps some days. When she does sleep, like today, I can't fully relax or engage in anything because I'm never sure when she'll wake up. If my attention is a flock of seagulls, half the flock is busy waiting for her to cry. I keep telling them, "Silly birds, come back to me. Let us focus on something together that has nothing to do with her," but they don't listen.

I told Rob that we need to hire a babysitter soon, someone who can look after her a couple of hours a day. He said, "I know, sweetheart. We will. Money is just tight until the practice is up and running." His beloved dental practice, his lifelong dream, coming to fruition. Has he forgotten that I have dreams too?

Maybe this diary is to help me get reacquainted with my dreams. I will write in it when I need a break from working on my dissertation. Well, that's what I'm calling it. I'm fooling myself, playing pretend just like Baby and her dolls. I am not in a doctoral program and likely never will be. I was supposed to be. That was *my* dream—to get my PhD in history, to be a professor at a university—an Ivy, my secret aspiration. I had always assumed my life would be one of acquiring, discussing, and sharing knowledge with brilliant peers and eager students. Alas, I have tripped and fallen into this conventional life, and I spend all my time with a toddler.

If I'd kept a diary when I'd met Rob, I would have written things like:

He loves my brain.
He supports my studies.
He is truly progressive.
He is my ideal man.
Sigh.

The pregnancy wasn't expected. My inclination was to end it, to realize my power in this post-*Roe v. Wade* era. Rob seemed truly sad when I mentioned my intention. He can be so sentimental. "Maybe it's meant to be," he'd said. "We'd be great parents," he'd said. *Parents.* I remember when he said that word and I felt decades older, instantly.

He made it sound so romantic, though. I started having second thoughts, started wondering if maybe I should keep the baby. Rob loved me, unambiguously. I loved him, more than I had any other man before him. I'd never really thought about motherhood, except that I'd assumed (like most women) it would happen at some point, but after I settled into a career, after I lived a little more.

"I always thought you liked surprises." He'd said that too.

While I was still debating what to do, he proposed, placing a diamond upon that all-important finger. I'd never smiled so big in my life. It was the strangest thing. I kept covering my mouth, out of embarrassment or shame. I knew, logically, that this glee was a product of social conditioning. Society has taught all of us women to want the ring, to crave the title of *wife*, to passively wait until some man declares us worthy. I knew, logically, that this was all nonsense. And still I said yes. And I wore a white dress on our wedding day, to boot!

I don't always know who I am anymore.

At least I didn't take Rob's last name. Seemingly, I am still capable of some selfhood. Thank god. None of my friends understood. Mother certainly didn't. "I like my name," I said. "I don't understand why we have to give up things to get married." Men don't take their wives' names because that would be emasculating. It would represent his identity being folded into his wife's, a partial obliteration of his self, a loss of power.

For women, this loss is not problematic. It is normal. Obliteration of self is just "how things are."

Rob was fine with me keeping my name. "It's yours," he said. "Who am I to take it from you?" If he'd shown any doubt, I would have called the whole thing off. I would have ended the pregnancy. But he said the exact right thing.

Nicole has his last name, which seemed completely appropriate at the time we were filling out the birth certificate. It was the day after she made her grand entrance, and I was awash in oxytocin, in love not only with her but also with my vision of Rob and me sharing the responsibility for this beautiful human we'd created. I pictured a truly equitable arrangement.

I was so naive.

In her book *Of Woman Born: Motherhood as Experience and Institution*, Adrienne Rich pointed out that *mothering* is a verb, implying an ongoing relationship with unending care for children. Not surprisingly, *fathering* is not a verb in our social lexicon.

Fact: Men are among the 3 to 5 percent of male mammals who contribute anything at all to their children postinsemination.

So I guess I should be grateful. I may be starving for a baguette, but at least I have these crumbs.

To be fair, Rob does more than most fathers. I hear other mothers talk about their husbands who have never touched a diaper. Rob changes diapers, when he's home. He's just not home much. Because of *the practice*. But he adores Nicole, calls her Nikki Bear, grits his teeth when he just looks at her, as if he is restraining himself from acting upon his playful threat to eat her up. I watch the muscles of his jaws clench when he does this and think he might adore her more than I do. His enthusiasm for her is boundless and so seemingly natural. Then again, he doesn't have to spend every hour of the day with her. If I had some time to myself, to my work, I would have more enthusiasm too. A few weeks ago, I told Rob that mothering is hard for me. He said, "You make it look so easy, though. You are a wonderful mother!" Then he kissed me. He is a sweet man. I am just not a sweet wife.

In any case, despite her father's adoration of her, Nicole should have my last name. Fournier. So beautiful, so French, so much more "me" than Larson. She grew inside me, and now, even with her outside me, we are still so attached. Anyone peering into our lives would say that she is my everything.

I think of my identity, my personhood, as a giant pie. Before Nicole, there were so many slices—reader, researcher, lover, swimmer, dancer, friend-haver. Now the pie is mostly her, with a tiny sliver left of me.

This diary is dedicated to the tiny sliver.

Nicole's calling for me. Must go for now.

Chapter 12

Nicole

"Mommmmm, can you push me on the swing?" Grace calls.

We are at a park (again), and I have just sat at a picnic table, hoping for a few minutes of quiet while the girls play. So much for that.

I'm back to being the aggravated, bitter person that I am accustomed to being. When Elijah and I parted ways yesterday, I was very clear. I told him I couldn't see him again, despite everything in my body resisting this declaration. Ending it felt like a betrayal of self more than a betrayal of him. He was disappointed—"I'm gonna miss you, Kit Kat"—and in denial: "Maybe you'll change your mind in a couple days." I let him (and myself) hope for that when I said, "Maybe." But at the first red light I came to after driving away, I deleted him from my phone (his number and all our messages), because that's the right thing to do, because I have to focus on my dying father and my needy children and my troubled marriage.

Now that I'm at the park, being summoned, I regret deleting him. I crave his messages, crave the boost they gave me. Last week, there was nothing the girls could do to bring me down. Did they want me to diaper and rediaper their dolls for hours? Sure! Did they require a completely different breakfast? No problem! Their whining was like white noise, barely audible over the chirping birds in my head.

How am I supposed to get through my days now?

"Mommmmmm," Grace calls again.

Liv is playing with the wood chips on the ground under the swing set, throwing them up in the air like confetti. A piece hits a little boy near her, and the boy's mom looks at me like *Are you going to do something about this?*

"Liv, honey, let's not throw that around," I say in a singsong voice, doing my best impression of the meditation teachers in the Calm app that I've used exactly once.

The mom takes her little boy to the other side of the park, not wanting to expose him to my heathens. I give the middle finger to her back because it feels good. I am tragically juvenile.

I put Liv in the bucket swing, which is right next to the swing Grace is in, a tiny miracle that may keep me from a nervous breakdown (for today, at least). I push Grace with one arm and Liv with the other. The rhythm is meditative until they both tell me they want to go higher. Because nothing is ever good enough. Last week, when I had Elijah to look forward to, I shrieked with glee along with them while I pushed. I said things like "You're going to go to the moon!" Not today. We are all trapped on Earth today.

An email notification dings on my phone:

New test results available in your health chart

It's my dad's test result, the one we've been waiting on to confirm if he actually has this one-in-a-million disease. I registered my dad's medical account to my email, told Merry I would handle all of that. In the two weeks since the doctor told us they were quite certain of a prion disease, Merry and I have flirted with the idea that the doctors are wrong. It has felt good to flirt.

"Girls, just a sec," I say, ceasing my swing-pushing.

When I open the email, there is a report in front of me. I scan it.

Likelihood of prion disease: > 98%

There are other things, medical terms that mean nothing to me: T-tau protein (CSF), 14-3-3 protein (CSF), RT-QuIC (CSF). At the bottom, it says:

The NPDPSC is able to offer a no-cost autopsy for this patient.

We are already discussing autopsies.

I google NPDPSC because I don't know what that is. National Prion Disease Pathology Surveillance Center.

"Mommmm, higher!" Grace demands.

"Grace, just a sec."

The familiar rush of heat moves through my body. I push up the sleeves of the sweatshirt I'm wearing, wanting to take it off completely, to stand there braless and bare, throwing wood chips with reckless abandon, to the horror of all bystanders.

"Mommmm, I'm almost stopped," Grace says.

"Kick your legs. You have legs!"

The heat within is so intense I think I might pass out. Then it fades, and a gust of wind cools the sweat on my body, making me suddenly cold. I push down the sleeves of my sweatshirt and curse the fact that I cannot trust something as simple as my bodily thermostat. Nothing in this life is reliable.

"I can't kick!"

She is about to melt down, so I shove her as hard as I can. There is an immediate rush, a release. Then I panic as I picture her flying out of the swing, landing past the wood chips on the hard cement. She shrieks, and I can't tell if it's fear or delight, they sound so similar.

"Mom, that was higher than ever," she says. It's delight.

"Higher, higher," Liv says.

I shove her too. This is all I can do right now—shove them, direct the currents of fear and grief and rage running through my body into my arms, into these damn swings.

$\sim$

Thankfully, they both succumb to the Car Nap after our park outing. I drive around confused by a beeping noise until I realize, a half hour in, that the beeping noise is alerting me to put on my seat belt. I have never forgotten my seat belt before. It is as automatic as breathing. Am I going to stop breathing too? Is this what happens when the psyche is taxed, emitting smoke like an overheated appliance? Sometimes, on dark days (today being one of those days), I hum the tune to that Sugar Ray song, "Fly," but in my head, the lyrics are "I just wanna die." I don't actually want to die. I don't need to call a suicide hotline. I'm just exhausted. In a rut or a funk or whatever. Another Instagram meme making the rounds: *My autopsy report: This woman was just very tired.*

$\sim$

The girls sleep a full hour—another one of the sanity-saving tiny miracles that all mothers need. When we get home, it's about three o'clock, and Kyle is still working, so I tell the girls we're going to play with chalk on the driveway. This will kill about seven minutes, and then it'll be on to another activity.

"Hey," Kyle says, coming outside, squinting in the light like a bear emerging from a cave after a long hibernation. He stretches his arms over his head.

"Taking a break?" I ask.

"Yeah. It's been a hell of a day."

I try to muster a sympathetic look, but I probably just look constipated.

"Daddy, do chalk with us!" Grace says.

155

"I'm just taking a short break, girls, then back to work for a couple hours."

Grace pouts for thirty seconds, then snaps back to her cheerful self upon realizing that Kyle does not care about her pouting. Sometimes I think he's an emotionally empty asshole, and other times I think he's doing parenting way better than me.

Things have been weird between Kyle and me ever since my fling with Elijah. Things have been weird between us for a while, but now I've lost any and all interest in pretending that they aren't weird. I can't even look Kyle in the eye. I've never been a good liar, for one. If Kyle and I take a moment to really look at each other, will he see my deceit? Maybe he should see it so we can talk about the bigger issues we keep avoiding. The crux of my angst is that Elijah has heightened my awareness of the chasm between Kyle and me. It's not that Kyle no longer makes me feel like Elijah does; it's that he *never* made me feel that way. I chose Kyle because I didn't think it was *possible* to feel that way.

~

I got home around ten last night, and Kyle was still up, which could only mean one thing—he wanted sex. I took my time in the bathroom, brushing my teeth with more care than I ever have, washing my face with the slow, circular motions they demonstrate with lotions and potions on infomercials. I put on my rattiest sweatpants and a T-shirt with pit stains. I couldn't fathom having sex with him. I'd had sex with Elijah that morning.

Predictably, Kyle rolled toward me and put his hand under my disgusting T-shirt. I froze, body stiff and awkward. He didn't seem to notice, just kept going forth with his own carnal wish list, a determined bull in a china shop. He kissed my neck, and I stared at the ceiling, wide eyed. Soon, he was pressing his body on top of mine, whispering in my ear that he missed me, still apparently oblivious to the fact that I was completely still, unresponsive to his advances.

When he started to pull off my sweatpants, I said the thing women say too often:

"I'm sorry."

He kept kissing my neck, said, "Hmm?"

"I'm sorry," I said again. "I'm so tired from the drive, and—"

He sighed heavily and rolled off me. The man whispering sweet nothings was gone; a rejected ego took his place.

"I'm sorry," I said again.

Turned away from me, he muttered, "Whatever" like a sullen teenager.

The people pleaser in me wanted to make a litany of promises—*we'll have sex tomorrow, we'll set a schedule, we'll plan date nights.* But those promises would just be more lies, so I said nothing, promised nothing. This morning, we didn't talk about it. But I have noticed he's having a hard time looking me in the eye too.

~

The girls are pleasantly busy with their chalk. Grace is showing Liv how to draw a heart, and I praise their cooperation: "Such sweet sisters, you two!"

Kyle watches. He doesn't usually come hang with us during his workday, even just for a few minutes. Maybe he does want to talk about last night, or wants to say something, but can't formulate the words. Much of our marriage has involved me waiting for him to formulate words.

"What's for dinner?" he asks.

"You already hungry?" I nearly offer him a snack, as I would the girls.

He shrugs. "Just curious."

"Lasagna."

"You know I love your lasagna."

He probably considers this statement a peace offering. I decide to try for some intimacy, some connection beyond our future food consumption:

"I got my dad's test result," I say. "He does have it."

Kyle looks confused. "Test result?"

"Remember how I said they were doing a confirmatory test?"

"Oh, right," he says, though I can tell he doesn't remember.

"Yeah. It's confirmed."

He nods. "Okay, well, you expected that, right?"

"I guess I was hoping for a mistake or a miracle."

"Yeah. I'm sorry, babe."

He stands, as if ready to depart from the emotional breakdown he expects me to have. I think about Elijah. I am sure he would put his arm around me. He would hold me. He would let me cry without making me feel stupid about it. He would say, "Let's get a babysitter so we can go out and talk." He would never be a bull in a china shop in bed.

"Wait," I say in a small voice.

He's taken one step toward the door. He stops. Turns to me, waiting for further instruction. Why isn't it natural for him to comfort me? Why does he need instruction?

"Can you just, like, hug me?" I ask him.

I feel stupid asking. Every woman's fantasy is never having to ask—for help, for affection, for tenderness, for gratitude. I wouldn't have to ask Elijah.

"Sure, yeah," he says. He looks surprised by the request. I've never asked him this before.

He puts his arms around me, and I close my eyes to try to conjure the feeling of safety and love I feel with Elijah. It's just not there, though. Hugging my husband is like hugging a tree trunk. He pulls away after just a few seconds and looks at me like *Did I do okay?* and I want to cry. My dad is definitely dying, and my marriage is too.

"Daddy!" Liv says, running over to him, holding something in her hand. She waves it in front of his face as he kneels to receive her.

"Look what me found!"

He takes it from her, squints. It looks like one of the pretend credit cards that came with Grace's toy cash register.

"What is this, Livvy?" he says, perplexed.

"What is it?" Grace asks, coming over to investigate.

"It looks like a key card for a hotel," he says.

I glance down and see that's exactly what it is, "Hilton" printed in red letters.

"Where did you get that?" I ask her, though I know exactly where she got it: the park. She has become quite the scavenger.

"Mommy's bag," she says, pointing to my purse sitting on the garage floor.

"Liv, tell the truth," I say. "Did you find that at the park?"

"No," she says, eyes big and blameless. This morning, I put what little hair she has into two fountains on top of her head. She is, indisputably, darling.

"She's been picking up things at the park," I say to Kyle. I do not mention the tampon applicator. I will never mention the tampon applicator.

"Well, good find," he says to Liv, handing it back to her. She looks quite pleased with herself. They both love their father's praise. It is doled out sparingly and, therefore, coveted.

"Can I have it?" Grace says, already taking the card from her sister.

Liv starts crying.

Right on cue, Kyle says, "Okay, I'm going to head back inside."

It takes me ten minutes to get the girls calm again. I tell them nobody gets the hotel card until they can agree to take turns. They agree to take turns, then promptly lose interest in it and request that I draw hearts with them on the driveway. I comply. I press so hard with the red stick of chalk that it's nothing but a nub by the time we're done.

~

159

When the lasagna is done, I put pizzas in the oven for the girls and set a timer for ten minutes. The girls are running circles around the kitchen island. For some reason, they have taken off their clothes. I suppose this is fine because they do need a bath tonight. Kyle is sitting at the dinner table, looking at something on his phone, waiting to be served. Every now and then, he says, "Girls!" when they get too loud. It quiets them for twenty seconds, and then they return to their usual volume.

"Mom, come sit on the floor," Grace says. She has mischief in her eyes.

"Girls, don't bug your mom," Kyle says, not looking up from his phone.

"Mom, please?" Grace says, her little hands clasped together, begging.

I go to the rug and sit on it. Sometimes complying with their wishes is easier than a back-and-forth discussion about why I am not complying with their wishes. *You bring it on yourself.* Kyle's said that before. He rejects their demands frequently and easily. Sometimes I think I comply to compensate for his refusals.

"Okay, I'm sitting," I say.

Grace turns around and starts walking backward into me, her bare butt headed straight for my face. She's already giggling.

"Grace, what are you doing?" I ask.

Liv starts copying her, so there are now two bare butts coming for me. Liv's is adorably dimpled.

When Grace's heels touch my legs, she crouches so she's almost sitting in my lap but not quite.

"Pretend you're a toilet," she says to me.

"Grace, come on," I say, starting to press myself up.

She starts making farting noises and the girls erupt in hysterics.

This is probably something they saw on YouTube. So it's probably my fault. I should limit their screen time or police what they watch more closely. I deserve to be a toilet.

~

When the timer on my phone dings, I go to turn it off and see a text message. It's from a number I don't recognize, most likely spam. It's not enough that there are spam calls. Now there are spam texts, alerting me to ways I can save on loans that I don't have, or encouraging me to share my home address so I can receive a special gift.

Hey. I'm sorry, I know you said not to text. I just can't stop thinking about you. Don't hate me.

It takes me a while to exit my "spam text" mindset and realize that this is Elijah. Unlike me, he has not deleted all our messages. I am still in his phone. For some reason, I didn't consider that he would reach out to me.

"Mom, I'm huuungry," Grace says, snapping me back to reality.

I put down the phone.

"I'm bringing your pizza now," I say, taking the pizzas out of the oven.

I am instantly lifted, soaring. I dance my way to the kitchen table.

"Pizza? I don't want pizza," Grace whines.

I don't even care, though. Let her whine.

I bring two plates of lasagna for Kyle and me, and say, "Let's go around and say what we're grateful for."

I only do this on days when I'm in a good mood, when I'm capable of considering gratitude.

"I'm grateful that Mom is a toilet," Grace says.

I laugh right along with her and Liv. Kyle looks at us like we're all insane. Maybe we are. I am, for sure.

~

I savor the text throughout the rest of the night. It carries me through bath time, teeth brushing, pajama changing, book reading, and lullaby singing. I am longing to respond and also not sure about responding.

If I respond, it will escalate. Do I want it to escalate? The irresponsible, selfish part of me does. Should I honor that part? It's been so neglected.

I close the door to the girls' bedroom and tiptoe to the staircase, deciding I will go to the living room, curl up on the couch with a cup of tea, and engage in a text messaging extravaganza with Elijah. But as I step onto the first stair, I hear Kyle:

"Hey," he says.

He's in bed. I can see light from the TV dancing across the walls.

"Did you need something?" I ask, peering into our room, hands pressed into opposite sides of the doorframe.

He turns off the TV.

"You coming to bed?"

"I was thinking I'd watch TV in the other room," I say. "It's been a hell of a day."

He doesn't seem to notice that I've co-opted his phrase from earlier.

"Why don't you come here?" he says, patting the bed next to him.

I'm anxious to tend to my phone, to respond to Elijah. I'm humming with nervous, excited energy. I must look like I'm on uppers.

"I feel like I need some alone time after today," I say.

He sighs. "Okay, can't say I didn't try."

His voice is dripping with self-pity, and I am overcome with wrath.

"This isn't about you," I say.

"What?"

"I'm going through a really hard time, and you're just mad I don't want to have sex with you. This isn't about you."

He looks surprised by the vigor and venom in my voice.

"I miss you, Nic. You act like that's some terrible offense to you."

"You miss my body, which you want on your terms, when it's convenient for you. I'm tired of it."

My limbs tingle with adrenaline or a coming hot flash. Kyle puts up both hands, like a cop trying to calm down an erratic, angry meth head.

"Whoa now," he says.

"Don't do that," I say. "Don't act like I'm crazy."

"I didn't say you were crazy," he says, slow and measured. It's how I talk with the girls when they are, in fact, crazy.

"Don't patronize me," I say, abandoning my post in the doorway and going toward him.

He puts up his hands again and says those maddening words: "Nic, calm down."

I break out in a sweat as I get right in his face and say, "Don't say that to me."

He leans back against the headboard of the bed, away from me. It is the only time in our twenty-year relationship that I've seen him afraid of me.

"I don't know what you want from me," he says, shaking his head.

I want to feel loved when you hug me, I think.

I collapse onto the bed, face first. I wait for him to put a hand on me, to stroke my back like I stroke the girls' backs when they lose their shit. He does not put a hand on me.

"Nic, tell me how to help," he says. "If you need alone time tonight, have some alone time."

I want your company to soothe me, but it doesn't, I think.

I lift my face from the bed and stand.

"What if this doesn't get better?" I ask him.

I am already thinking ahead to filing for divorce. Now is not the time. I'll have to wait until after my dad dies.

I can't believe my dad is going to die.

"It will get better," he says. Then again: "It will."

That's the thing with Kyle—he cannot sit in the darkness with me. He insists on only tilting his head to the light.

~

In the past couple of years of resentment building, I've been questioning the institution of marriage as a whole, thinking it unreasonable that we're meant to choose a person when we are only a quarter of the way

through our lives and remain bonded to that person *forever*—eating the
same meals, watching the same TV shows, listening to the same music,
sharing the same bed and sleep habits, aligning on financial values and
sex drives and energy levels. To top it all off, there are the children, little
grenades, each of them. Each baby is an explosion in a marriage, but
you are supposed to carry on as usual, holding hands as you navigate
the ruins and rebuild.

~

Some months ago, I tried talking to my work friend Jill about it:

"Think about your best friend in high school, or your college
roommate. Could you live with them forever? It's normal to grow out
of relationships, is it not?"

"What are you saying, exactly?" she asked. "Do you want to get
divorced?"

"I don't know. It seems like that should be the norm, doesn't it?"

I went on to declare that "till death do us part" really only benefits
husbands, citing an article that said women's health and well-being
improves after divorce while men's tanks. I ranted and raved about how
our society praises relationship masochism, applauding couples who
stay together for decades, calling women's self-sacrifice "commitment"
and their suffering "loyalty."

Jill just listened. When she was sure I was done, when I allowed
for a second of silence, she said, "Nic, a lot of couples go through
hard times."

"Right," I said. "Because marriage is fucking hard."

She was silent, so I returned to my rant: "If we have to do marriage,
we should have to renew the contract annually, like home insurance."

"Would you renew your contract with Kyle?" she asked me.

"I don't know. I can't commit to any contracts right now. I have two
small children," I said. "Would you renew your contract with Matt?"

"I would."

I groaned. "That's because you don't have kids. It's easy to like your spouse when you don't create humans with them."

She laughed. "Would you date Kyle if you were to meet him today?"

I thought about it. "I don't know," I said, though the more honest answer was no. Kyle wasn't interesting to me anymore. His ambition had been attractive when we were younger, when we were college kids with no money and big dreams. Now, though, he was someone who worked hard and was well paid. We had a good life by anyone's standards, and I wanted, desperately, for that to be enough. But it just wasn't.

"Really?"

"I don't know if I'd date any man again," I said.

"Switching teams?"

"I wish I could. I just can't be attracted to vagina."

"Are you attracted to penis?"

I gagged. "Good point."

"Nic, I really just think you're super stressed right now," she said. "It's a phase."

~

Later that day, I asked Kyle the question Jill had asked me:

"If you met me today, would you want to date me?"

I hoped the question would foster a larger conversation about the very foundation and purpose of our marriage. I fantasized about us being an evolved couple who could have these Big Talks and raw confessions and maybe agree to "consciously uncouple" if that was best for our individual paths, namaste.

"If I met you today?" he said. "Sure."

Sure. As if I'd just asked him if he could pick up dishwasher detergent pods at the store.

I waited for him to ask the same question of me, but he didn't. Because he's just not that curious. He doesn't like to pick at things. He doesn't crave the kind of intimacy that I do, an intimacy that involves knowing the deepest, darkest parts of each other. I didn't crave that intimacy until I became a mother, until I became aware of the deep, dark parts of myself that I needed to have witnessed and pardoned. This is my problem with marriage: it's predicated on two people never changing. I had the very best intentions, but I've failed. I've changed.

~

I curl up on the couch, cover my legs with Grace's pink unicorn blanket. I read and reread Elijah's texts. I realize any psychologist worth her salt would make note of how I've manifested—the latest trendy word—this lovely Elijah distraction right when my life is falling apart. I could have turned to booze or prescription pills for a pleasant release from reality, but no, that would be too conventional. So instead, I've become dependent on the saga of Katrina and Elijah. I like to think the fact that I have insight into what I'm doing means I'm not crazy.

Hey you

He texts back immediately:

Omg, way to leave a guy hanging. I really thought you were pissed

Maybe I was. But I've forgiven you

Him: I seriously can't stop thinking about you

I am burdened with this same problem

Him: You can't stop thinking about you?

Ha ha

166

Him: I don't know if I can accept not seeing you again

I'm not sure if I can accept it either

Him: Remind me again why we can't just keep doing what we're doing?

You have no idea, I want to say.
So many reasons, I want to say.

Maybe we can . . .

He sends a party-hat emoji.

Him: I've worn you down already?

I regretted ending things immediately after I did it

Him: So it's not just me feeling this thing?

It's not just you

Him: I know you're hesitant. It's long distance and everything. We can be mellow. I just want to see you

Maybe I can come back up this weekend

I wasn't planning to, had told Merry and my dad that I'd be back in a couple of weeks. But I have every right and reason to change my mind.

Him: You serious?

It would be cruel if I wasn't

He sends a musical-note emoji.

Him: Music to my ears

We text until nearly midnight. The crushing fatigue I've felt all day vanishes. When I tell him I have to go to bed, it's not because I'm tired but because I know the girls will be up early and *then* I'll be tired.

Him: Alright then, night-night Kit Kat

We send each other kissy-face emojis, and I head back to the bedroom with a stupid smile on my face. Kyle is sleeping deeply enough to snore. I get under the covers and stare at the ceiling, heart slamming in my chest. I rehearse what I'll say to Kyle:

I want to tell Merry about the official diagnosis in person. I feel like I should be there every weekend, for a while at least.

～

I'm still wide awake at two, then three. I don't care, though. Even if the girls call for me at five, I'll have a smile on my face.

Chapter 13

ROSE

September 21, 1984

Dear Diary,

Last night, after putting Nicole to bed, I told Rob that I was on edge, that I felt cooped up being home with her all the time. His response: "Take her out more! She'd love that!" He keeps saying, "It will get better," but I'm not sure if *it* is motherhood or *it* is my attitude. I presume he thinks it's me that's the problem, not motherhood itself.

Maybe he's right.

He wanted to have sex this morning before leaving for work. He was abuzz with excited energy at the prospect of putting the final coats of paint on the walls of his practice. He expected me to be abuzz by proxy. I was not abuzz. I was exhausted. Nicole called for me at two o'clock in the morning. She has these nightmares sometimes. Or that's what she says. Sometimes I think she just inherited my insomnia and wants company. In any case, it took me an hour to get her back to sleep. Then it took an hour after that for me to get back to sleep. Then it was an hour after that when Rob started kissing my neck.

In *The Sexual Responsibility of Women*, published in 1957, Maxine Davis encouraged wives to shoulder the burden of "sexual adaptation."

In *The Total Woman*, published in 1974, Marabel Morgan advised wives to greet their husbands at the front door naked, Saran Wrapped like leftover meatloaf.

Wives are not supposed to rebuff their husbands.

And rebuff is exactly what I did.

I love that word, *rebuff*. To check, repel, refuse, drive away.

He was frustrated. He said he wished I could join him in his enthusiasm about "the future." *The future* meaning his practice. He has assumed that his future is my future. Society calls this kind of merging beautiful. I find it unjust at best, suffocating at worst.

"I know you're having a hard time lately," he said. "Things will get better."

That tired promise, as familiar as it is vague.

He just left for the day, and Nicole is not yet awake (a minor miracle). I should stop writing, take this time to do the dishes. The dishwasher is broken (again), so I'm back to wearing rubber gloves and handwashing like a 1950s housewife. Rob has left his clothes on the floor (again), so I must decide whether to just leave them there or pick them up (as he must assume I will and as I usually do).

In 1889, a magazine offered a prize to the spinster who could provide the best answer to this question: Why are you still single? The magazine never picked a winner, but this one's my favorite:

"I find it more delightful to tread on the verge of freedom and captivity, than to allow the snarer to cast around me the matrimonial lasso."

Ah yes, the matrimonial lasso.

I will leave the clothes where they are. A small rebellion.

When Nicole wakes up, we'll go to the library. Rob is right—I need to get out of the house more or I'll go insane. I was thinking the other day about Sylvia Plath, about how she taped herself shut into her kitchen, sealing all the cracks, then rested her head on the drop-down door of her oven, turned on the gas, and went to eternal sleep while her children were waking from their nightly slumber upstairs. It is not so hard for me to understand her choice now. She went over the brink. That is all.

I do what I can to avoid the brink.

At the library, I can do research for my little project, my faux dissertation. There's a children's area with toy blocks and books and whatnot. It'll entertain Nicole for a half hour, max, but I'll take it. Oh, how I long for the days of eight-hour stretches of time to be with my thoughts. I have not come to terms with the fact that those stretches will not happen again. Or not any time soon, anyway. By the time those kinds of hours are available to me, when Nicole is older, it's likely I will have lost the attention span and brain cells necessary to work.

I don't have a title for my project yet. It's about the history of marriage and motherhood. I have always found comfort in history, in the way it enables us to contextualize our own lives, to understand ourselves in a grander picture. Nothing about the present is that surprising when you consider the past.

If you look at the historical record, the most culturally preferred form of marriage—and the type of marriage referred to most often in the first five books of the Old Testament—was actually of one man to several women. Some societies also practiced polyandry, where one woman married several men.

Modern marriage, with one man and one woman pledging their lives to each other, is quite strange, historically speaking. The original purpose of this type of marriage was not to ensure that children had a dedicated mother and father but to acquire advantageous in-laws and expand the family labor force. Women were deemed property, passed from one male caretaker to another—father to husband—as a business arrangement between families.

A quote from Sir William Blackstone's eighteenth-century *Commentaries on the Laws of England*:

"By marriage, the husband and wife are one person in law: that is, the very being or legal existence of the woman is suspended during the marriage, or at least is incorporated and consolidated into that of the husband; under whose wing, protection and cover, she performs everything."

The woman is suspended.

She performs everything, but controls nothing.

Seems about right.

Just a handful of years ago, most states had "head and master" laws giving special decision-making rights to husbands. In these laws, *rape* was defined as a man having forcible intercourse with a woman other than his wife. In other words, forcible intercourse with his wife was just fine in the eyes of the law.

Before 1973, a woman couldn't serve on a jury.

Before 1974—just a decade ago—a woman couldn't apply for a credit card (and before the 1960s, she couldn't open a bank account).

Before 1978, she could be legally fired for being pregnant.

Considering history, it's hard to blame today's men for their sense of entitlement. It has been passed down through generations, imprinted on their DNA. And it's hard to blame women for their subservience, also ingrained.

I cannot hate Rob. I hate The System. I hate the unspoken rules. Rob and I have never had an actual conversation about who takes care of Nicole, who cooks, who cleans. It's assumed to be me. I am not faultless. I have done nothing to counter the assumption. I am in The System as well.

In *The Second Sex*, published in 1949, Simone de Beauvoir wrote that equality between the sexes could only be achieved if the institution of marriage was eradicated. She described marriage as slavery for half of humankind. In *The Feminine Mystique*, published in 1963, Betty Friedan expressed similar thoughts, comparing the life of an American housewife to being trapped in cage.

Why did I get married?

I see why Rob wanted to marry. The role of husband is a grand one. A husband is the king of the household. He is doted on by a self-sacrificing wife.

Marriage is like an ongoing ego stroke for men. What is in it for women? A sense of security? The satisfaction of fulfilling one's prescribed life's purpose?

I fear I fell for a marketing ploy. The institution of female subjugation was repackaged as a fairy tale, and I fell for it.

I love Rob. I do. I just feel . . . stuck. Trapped in a squirrel cage.

I hope things are different for Nicole. I hope her generation sees through the marketing ploy.

Anyway, all this is going into my dissertation. I suppose the best dissertations attempt to clarify or articulate something for the betterment of academic society (or, if one is ambitious or arrogant enough, society at large). Perhaps all I'm doing is clarifying and articulating something for myself. I can accept that. I have done so little for myself in the past three years.

Also in *The Feminine Mystique*, Friedan writes of the daily grind of a wife and mother who is afraid to ask herself a single haunting question: Is this all?

I am not afraid to ask the question. I ask it all the time.

Is this all?

Is this all?

Is this all?

I have been having this fantasy lately about attending a PhD program.

The other night, I dared to mention it to Rob.

"It would just be four or five years. We can have a nanny to help with Nicole. It'll be good for her to see her mother do this."

His eyes bugged out as I was talking. I could see the entirety of the irises, surrounded by white. He wasn't angry. He was flummoxed. He had no idea what to do with this desire of mine.

"Sweetheart, I want you to be happy, but I don't think it's the right time. Maybe we can discuss it again when Nikki's older, when the practice is more established?"

I couldn't muster up a response, but the disappointment on my face must have been obvious.

"You could start back part time when Nikki goes to elementary school," he added.

Elementary school felt like a hundred years away.

The thing is, I could apply. Just to see. Rob doesn't have to know. I've always kept some cash from Mother in an envelope, my just-in-case fund. I can pay any application fees from that fund.

Princeton.

Yale.

Harvard.

Brown.

Cornell.

University of Pennsylvania.

I was at the top of my class in undergrad. I have the grades.

Of course, what if I get in?

I wouldn't go. Couldn't go. Rob spelled out the reasons why.

But maybe the high of an acceptance letter would sustain me for months to come. Years, even. Maybe I just need to know what's possible, even if I remain in my usual life.

It makes me happy to think about.

Elizabeth Cady Stanton, in a letter to a male cousin in 1855: "Did it ever enter into the mind of man that woman too had an inalienable right to life, liberty, and the pursuit of her individual happiness?"

No. I do not think this ever has entered into the mind of man.

It would be fun to do this just for me. It would infuse me with pride and confidence. It would remind me of my separateness.

I might just do it.

Another small rebellion.

Chapter 14

Nicole

My dad met Kyle for the first time when he came out to see me during that sophomore year of college. He loved to visit, to see the seasons. He'd been born and raised in California, had never considered living elsewhere. When I told him I was going to Rhode Island, he was befuddled. "*Rhode Island?*" he'd said, as if I'd announced I was headed to Mars. He came to accept it, though, and then said he was going to visit once a season. I was an emotional disaster my freshman year, and those visits from him made me feel less like I was floating in space. Just knowing he was coming, even if it was weeks away, tethered me.

"Dad, I want you to meet my boyfriend," I told him when he arrived. Kyle and I had been dating only a month, but it felt like something that could be long term, something I wanted my dad to approve of.

He raised his eyebrows, appropriately suspicious of any male I was spending time with.

"He's a good guy," I said.

"We'll see about that."

We met Kyle at a TGI Fridays, which was considered high end by most of the college kids. We got a booth, my dad and I sitting together, Kyle across from us, as if we were interrogating him together. We were, I guess.

My dad asked him questions, made jokes. Kyle was awkward and nervous. I kept reaching under the table to tap his knee reassuringly.

"Where do you see yourself in five years?"

"Dad!" I said, play hitting him.

Kyle didn't miss a beat, though. Like I said, Kyle was someone with a ten-year plan.

"In five years, I should be done with my MBA and entering the workforce."

My dad nodded, satisfied.

On the drive back to my apartment that night, my dad said, "He's smart, that's for sure."

"He is," I said.

"He treats you well?"

I wasn't sure what to make of this question. What did it mean to be treated well? We were twenty years old. We were starry eyed about the future and having a lot of sex.

"You gotta make sure you're on the same page with things," my dad said. "You gotta support each other's dreams."

"Dad, we're not getting married yet," I said with a laugh, though I had already started thinking of Kyle as my future husband.

"Okay, okay," he said. "I'm just saying."

"He's a good guy, promise."

"I trust you, Nikki Bear," he said. "And if he's ever not, you just call me. I got guns."

He kissed each of his biceps, and I laughed. I'm quite sure that the hardest I've laughed in my life was with my dad.

Kyle got into UCLA for business school, and I decided to move with him. One of my professors had hooked me up with an internship with her famous photographer friend in New York City. She was one of the people who thought I was a "natural talent" who was "going places." When I turned it down, she looked me dead in the eye and said, "I can't believe you're choosing to become another woman following a man." I never talked to her again.

It was an easy decision to follow Kyle, though. We were two years into our relationship and enamored with each other in the way only young people are. Besides, I wanted to get back to California. Harsh winters were not for me, and I missed being close to my dad and Merry.

In LA, we moved into a crappy apartment with walls so thin we could hear our neighbors, a fortysomething married couple, fighting. We were astonished by the vitriol of their words, made a promise to each other that we would never be them. We talked about getting married, agreeing that we would wait until he finished school, got a job, and saved a certain amount of money. That amount was $50,000, which seemed like an impossible sum to my young ears. He assured me we would get there. "It'll just take time. We have time," he said.

While he was in business school, I held a variety of fairly meaningless jobs. The coolest one was working as a tour guide at LACMA—the Los Angeles County Museum of Art. I had plenty of time to do my photography—mostly nature stuff. I'd drive out to Joshua Tree before Instagram made it famous and take photos of the rocks. I'd go to the beach and photograph the waves, the surfers. Out loud, I said I didn't really want to rely on photography for income. I wanted it to be fun, never obligatory. Secretly, though, of course I hoped to make it big. I hung some prints in local mom-and-pop restaurants, sold a few. I had a couple of photos published in travel magazines. I created a website to showcase my work, pretended not to care that there were only a dozen visitors to the site per week. I paid the hosting fee on that site until shortly after Grace was born. I didn't make an active choice to let go of the site. I simply forgot to update the credit card information to pay the renewal fee. Some months into new motherhood, I typed in the website address and got an error message. The thought of making phone calls to resolve this seemed like entirely too much. I took photos of Grace—thousands of photos—but those days of spending hours in nature, snapping away without time pressure, felt like another life in a galaxy far, far away.

～

After business school, Kyle got a job with a prestigious pharmaceutical company based in Thousand Oaks, a suburb of LA. Within a year of being there, he was already getting awards and bonuses as one of their most successful sales representatives. He was ecstatic, and I was ecstatic for him. It felt like this thing we had planned for so long was finally happening. And in the last year of our twenties, our bank account crossed the $50,000 mark, and he proposed on a beach walk, pulling the ring out of the pocket of his board shorts and then getting down on one knee. His hands were shaking, and I said, "Why are you so nervous, silly?" He said he wasn't sure if I would say yes, and I was shocked that he had any doubt. "Yes!" I said over and over again as we kissed and strangers clapped for us as they walked by.

I can't say I thought much about what I wanted in a husband or if Kyle checked those boxes. I loved him. He loved me. Marriage was a romantic notion, this idea of us continuing to grow together—buying a house, having kids, accumulating all the components of the American dream. This was what we'd been instructed to desire. We didn't know to want anything else. Even now, I'm not sure Kyle would want anything else. He's happy enough, aside from the less-than-active sex life. It's me that's the problem.

In those early days, I liked being married. I liked the ring on my finger that alerted anyone near me that I had successfully achieved this life event. I liked saying *husband* and *wife*. I would call Kyle at work sometimes just to say "Hi, husband, it's your wife." I bought an apron with polka dots and a Betty Crocker cookbook. I had dinner ready when he got home from work.

I got my first ad-agency job via Kyle's boss's wife, who was a creative director looking for graphic design talent. Before long, Kyle and I were two business professionals with a promising future. There was never a doubt we wanted kids, but Kyle wanted a house first, so we worked and saved for a down payment. He got a job offer in Orange County, at another prestigious pharmaceutical company, the one he still works for. We moved there, finally bought a house. I was ready to try for a baby, but he wanted to wait until he was established enough to "take paternity leave in good conscience."

When we finally started trying, we had no luck for a year, at which point the doctors gave me a diagnosis of "unexplained infertility." It was during the sadness of this time that I realized that Kyle and I hadn't been through anything truly difficult before. In response to my sadness, the likes of which he'd never seen before, he worked more. I remember having passing thoughts about whether or not we would make it through this. Then, a year later, I got pregnant, and any doubts I'd had were replaced with all the plans and preparations for parenthood.

~

My dad is in a wheelchair now. It's a clunky, heavy old thing with a wonky wheel. The hospice company dropped it off along with a pack of adult diapers.

"He needs diapers now?" I say to Merry, just above a whisper because my dad, who is fast becoming an invalid, is sitting just a few feet away at the kitchen table.

"Not quite yet, but I think we're getting close."

The depressions under Merry's eyes look deeper, darker. It is as if she has aged ten years just since last week.

When my dad reaches for his coffee mug, his hand is shaky. It's obvious that it takes a good deal of concentration for him to move his fingers around the mug's handle. I wonder when he'll no longer be able to grip it himself, when he'll need a sippy cup like his granddaughters do.

"How's your oatmeal, Dad?" I ask him, as if it's any other day, as if Merry and I aren't over here talking about when he'll become incontinent.

"Good!" He remains upbeat, chipper even.

He glances at the whiteboard in front of him. It says, *Nicole is here today.* When I woke up this morning, I drew a heart on it and wrote, "I love you, Dad."

"Hey, it says here that Nicole is here today." He looks up, sees me. The gears of his brain lock into place for a moment. "And there you are!"

"Here I am," I say.

"When did you get here?"

He's asked me this three times already.

"It's Saturday morning," I say, reminding him, though it says it right there on the board. "I got in last night."

"From Rhode Island?"

"Rob, she hasn't lived in Rhode Island in years," Merry snaps. It's irrational to snap. We both know he's not trying to be difficult. She's just had it.

"I drove up from Orange County, where I live with Kyle and the girls."

"Yes! Right!" He says it as if we are playing charades and he has just guessed what I've been miming.

"How's your car running?" he asks, which is his way of inquiring about my general well-being.

"Good, Dad, good."

He eats a few more bites of oatmeal and then sits back in his wheelchair with a satisfied sigh.

"That sun feels good, doesn't it?" he says, closing his eyes as beams of light come through the window, streaking his face.

Merry starts clearing the table.

"He's been sleeping a lot more," she says. "He's really only awake for about an hour for meals, then back to bed."

Sure enough, a few seconds later, his head is hanging, lolling about above his chest.

Merry starts cleaning the dishes. I hold a towel, ready to dry.

"Sometimes I just let him sleep right there like that. I don't know how I can keep helping him in and out of bed, in and out of the wheelchair."

She puts a hand to her lower back, rubs.

I say, "I can help, for today at least."

"And then there's tomorrow and the next day and the next," she says with a sigh.

I keep wondering if I should bring the girls up with me and just stay indefinitely, compromise my own sanity for the good of the group. It's that or convince Merry to get daily professional help, soon.

∽

I wheel Dad to the downstairs bedroom as he sleeps with his chin on his chest. I park the wheelchair at the side of his bed and rub his shoulders in an attempt to rouse him. I massage his bald head, as if a genie will appear to grant me my wish to make all of this not real.

"Okay, Dad, time to get into bed."

Merry sighs. "He won't be able to help much."

"Is it nighttime?" Dad asks.

"No, Dad. Just time for a nap."

He doesn't protest. He puts his hands on the armrests of the wheelchair to push himself up. But once again, Merry is right—he can't help much.

"Alice said there's some kind of belt we can get to help pull him up," Merry says. "I need to ask the hospice people about that."

"A belt?" Dad says. "I have lots of belts."

"Not that kind of belt, Rob," Merry says.

I put both arms around his middle, help him stand. He is wobbly, but he is upright. Merry stands back, supervises, looking slightly nervous. I have no idea how she's been doing this by herself, even if just for a few days.

"Okay, Dad, the bed is just right here."

All he has to do is turn his body ninety degrees and fall back. But shuffling his feet to turn that ninety degrees takes a painfully long time.

"All right, now fall back," I tell him when he's aligned properly with the bed.

He looks at me like Grace and Liv look at me, his eyes saying, *Am I going to be okay? Am I doing this right?*

"You're okay, Dad," I tell him.

He falls back onto the bed. I help him swing his legs up and pull the comforter over his body so just his head is showing.

"You comfy?" I ask him.

"I am."

His eyes start to glaze over with fatigue.

"Can I get in next to you?" I ask him.

He's already asleep. I get in anyway, my body curled up next to his.

"I'll leave you two," Merry whispers and closes the door behind her.

I listen to my dad's breaths, feel the warmth and solidity of his body. Tears come when I remember the impermanence of these things. I dry my cheeks with the edge of the pillowcase.

"I'm going to miss you," I whisper.

He doesn't respond, but I like to think he hears me anyway.

～

I nod off for a bit and am awakened by my phone buzzing with a text message.

Can't wait to see you

Elijah. If I didn't have him to look forward to, I would likely wither away alongside my dad.

I can't wait to see you too. Will be there around 5

He sends back a GIF of people cheering.

$$\sim$$

Merry is sitting on the couch in the living room, clipping her toenails, when I emerge. I sit next to her. She doesn't look up from what she's doing.

"I've been too busy to even clip my toenails," she says.

I find this hard to believe, but am willing to indulge her misery. I know a thing or two about raging pity parties.

"I need to clip your father's too. They're getting so long."

"I can do that," I tell her. "When he wakes up."

She keeps clipping.

"Can I book you a massage today? I can stay at the house with Dad."

She looks up. "That's sweet of you, Nic, but I can't imagine how I'd be able to enjoy a *massage*."

She says it like I've suggested she go skydiving.

"I just want to make sure you're getting out, taking care of yourself," I tell her.

"I don't see how that's possible."

"Can the hospice people come more often?"

As it is, a nurse comes by once a week for about a half hour to check his vitals. And random aides drop off supplies that Merry complains she could get cheaper on Amazon. Prisha had warned me that hospice isn't really that involved until the very end, when death is imminent, which I like to think, childishly and foolishly, is far, far, far away.

"Maybe we need to look into a caregiver, someone who could stay here and help," I say. "Jim and Alice seemed to think that was a good idea."

Merry looks disgusted with this suggestion, as I thought she might be.

185

"I don't want anyone in my home."

Well, I don't want my dad to die, I want to say.

We can't always get what we want, I want to say.

"Okay" is what I actually say.

~

When my dad wakes up, I trim his toenails while he's still lying in bed. I'd never noticed it before, but his feet are somewhat feminine—long, lean, with nicely shaped nails. The rest of him is, and always has been, decidedly masculine. He is one of those people who are naturally muscular, even without working out—thighs like tree trunks, calves thick and sturdy. I look at his legs now. Are they thinner, already wasting away?

"Dad, did you know you have lady feet?"

He lifts his head from his pillow, stares down. "What? I do?"

He says it with alarm, as if he's just acquired these feet, as if they are part of whatever ails him.

I laugh. "I mean, you've always had them, I just never noticed."

"I don't have lady feet."

"They're very soft too. Do you use a pumice stone in the shower?"

"A what?"

"I'm teasing you."

I gather all the nail clippings and dispose of them in the bathroom trash can.

"You ready for some lunch?" I ask him.

"It's lunchtime?"

It's just after eleven. "Close enough," I say.

I am used to this, the structuring of days around mealtimes.

"Okay then."

I help him sit, then turn so his legs are off the bed, feet touching the floor. The wheelchair is parked in position. I stand in front of him, grab onto his wrists. His hands clutch my wrists in return.

"One, two, three," I say.

The effort is mostly mine. My lower back complains, but I try to smile. My dad would never want to burden me.

I have broken a sweat by the time he is upright. I help him turn ninety degrees, his feet shuffling an inch at a time. The whole process, a process I would perform myself within seconds, takes about five minutes. It's excruciating, reminiscent of watching Grace trying to put on a shirt herself and sticking her arm through the neck hole repeatedly, or watching Liv stab the same piece of elbow macaroni with a fork, unable to get it.

"Okay, Dad, now fall back."

I think of the patience I've had to acquire as a mother, ushering the girls through the mundanity of this impossible life. Perhaps I have been in training for exactly this moment with my dad as he prepares to leave that life. I am grateful for my ability to do this, but devastated it needs to be done.

~

The three of us eat lunch at the kitchen table. Then the morning repeats itself—he falls asleep, Merry does the dishes, I wheel him to bed, I lie with him. I assume the same routine will repeat for dinner. I don't know how Merry is going to stay sane through this. I, at least, have Elijah.

Dad sleeps until four o'clock in the afternoon. I get dressed in a black skirt that I brought for the express purpose of Elijah pushing it up around my waist to fuck me. I'm wearing a black lace bra and matching panties, which I had to retrieve from the farthest corner of my underwear drawer at home. They must be a few years old, an impulse buy, a past attempt to bring back the elusive spark in my marriage. The tags were still on. At the last minute, I decide to take off the panties. I used to hear of women going commando and thought that was absurd. I was convinced no woman did this, that it was a myth created by the porn industry. But, I decide, Katrina is a woman who likes to feel free in every possible way.

I spritz myself with perfume, put earrings in my ears. It's been so long since I've worn earrings that I basically have to repierce my lobes. I dab the blood with a square of toilet paper.

"Well, don't you look nice," Merry says when she sees me, her face lit up. We both need a reminder that life keeps going, that there is a world beyond the walls of this house, a world worth dressing up for.

"Thank you," I say.

"You're going out with Prisha again?"

I nod. "Yeah. I'll stay at her place. She has the most amazing apartment downtown. Did I tell you about it? The views!"

I stop myself, knowing I'm doing what every liar does—saying too much, sharing extraneous details, speaking in exclamation marks.

"That sounds nice."

"I'll come back by noon or so tomorrow, hang with you guys for a little bit before I drive back home."

"Okay," she says. "Thank you. It means a lot to have you here."

She looks like she might cry. I go to her, hug her. Her body is stiff in response, but she pats my back awkwardly.

"You need anything before I head out?"

She shakes her head.

"If you ever want to come with me, for a drink or something . . ."

I'm offering because I know she'll decline.

"No, no. I don't feel right being away from him. You have fun."

Dad is sitting at the table again, staring at the whiteboard.

"It says Nicole is here today," he says to the empty space in front of him.

I go to him, put my hands on his shoulders, peek around so he can see my face.

"Boo," I say. "Here I am."

He looks surprised, which no longer surprises me.

"When did you get here?" he asks.

I go through the usual question-and-answer routine, then give him a kiss on the cheek.

"I love you, Dad. I'll see you tomorrow."

"Love ya, Nikki."

~

I stand before Elijah's apartment door and take a deep breath. Here I am again. Or here Katrina is again. I knock.

"Hey, you," he says when he opens the door.

His apartment smells like a restaurant. He is cooking. I didn't know this was in his repertoire of skills. When is the last time Kyle cooked for me? I cannot remember. He picks up takeout for us on occasion, though I am almost always the one who bears the burden of calling the restaurant or clicking through the online ordering system. Kyle may have cooked a Valentine's Day or birthday dinner for me before we were married, back when we lived in our crappy apartment near UCLA. We used to celebrate Valentine's Day, something I've forgotten until just this moment. Now, we acknowledge the day only for the girls' benefit.

I linger in Elijah's doorway, and he pulls me toward him, his arm around my waist, hand cupping my ass. We kiss, stumble inside, fall onto his couch, me on top of him. He is already hard.

"What are you making me, Chef?" I ask him.

Both his hands are on my ass now, grabbing.

"Curry," he says between fast breaths. Then: "God, this skirt is hot."

He does as I want him to do—he pushes it up around my waist. That's when he discovers that I'm not wearing underwear.

"My god, woman."

His long fingers reach around to the front of me, caressing before they slip inside. I am wet, ready.

"Is the curry spicy?" I whisper into his ear.

"Not as spicy as you," he whispers back.

I unbutton his jeans, pull them off, do the same with his boxers. I use my teeth to open the condom wrapper. I put him inside me, and his head falls back, eyes closed as he moans. There is nothing better than this, I think—the power of pleasuring.

I come twice on top of him before he flips me over. I come again as he does. His body collapses on top of mine.

"Jesus," he says.

"You're religious?"

He laughs.

"I better not be, because you are sinful," he says.

You have no idea.

He pushes himself off me, and I sit up. I'm wearing my bra, my skirt still bunched up around my waist.

"Well, I've worked up an appetite," he says. "You?"

I nod. "Seriously, though, is the curry spicy?"

"Just a little," he says. "I took you for a woman who likes some spice. Was I wrong?"

I do not like spice. I am a boring, basic white woman with a completely unadventurous palate. Katrina, I decide, will be different.

"You are not wrong," I say.

He stands, still naked. I watch the muscles of his ass contract and release as he walks. He returns to the couch with a plate in each hand, piled high with rice and an orangey-yellow curry. I can't help but stare at his penis, flaccid now but still larger than Kyle's is when fully erect. It makes me feel immature to take note of such a thing.

"Thai coconut curry," he says.

He sits next to me, and we eat, plates in our laps. It is spicier than I'd like, my lips burning almost immediately, but I say, "Mmm," reminding myself that this is what I want—a life less bland.

"I missed you this week," he says.

"I missed you too."

"I was thinking that with all the texting, I still don't know so many things about you," he says.

You have no idea, I think again.

"What do you want to know?"

"The usual things. Where you grew up. If you like your parents. Your hobbies. I mean, do you *have* hobbies? How do I not know this?"

I do not have hobbies. I take care of children all day. I have no idea who I am anymore. That's why I'm here.

"Well, I grew up in Daly City," I say, figuring I will try out occasional truths, see how they feel.

"You did? You're a Bay Area girl?"

"I am."

"You still have family up here?"

I nod. Suddenly, my throat constricts until it feels like it is the circumference of a drinking straw. I am about to cry.

"Hey," he says, putting his plate on the coffee table and then placing one hand on my thigh, the other on my shoulder. "Hey, hey, it's okay."

The tears just come. There is no stopping them. I am in the grip of a grief that does not give me the courtesy of a fair warning.

"I'm sorry," I say.

He takes my plate from me, puts it next to his. He uses the pad of his thumb to wipe the tears from under my eyes. He stares at me, his eyes scanning mine, back and forth, trying to decipher the reason for this unexpected display of emotion.

"Don't apologize."

I try to imagine Kyle saying these words, Kyle wiping my tears with his thumb, Kyle putting comforting hands on my body, Kyle touching me in a way that considers my feelings instead of his own motivations for attention.

"It's just that . . ."

He waits, still staring. Has Kyle ever looked into the belly of the beast that is me? Has he ever *not* looked away?

"My dad is dying."

I was not expecting to share this, but there it is.

191

I had hoped the tears would abate with this confession, but they just come harder. I am sobbing while sitting on the couch of my lover with my skirt bunched up around my waist, my breasts heaving in the uncomfortable cups of this lacy bra. Elijah pulls me into his naked body, holds me there with a force that is off putting in its unfamiliarity at first, but then soothing. With him I feel something I didn't know I wanted to feel with another person—relief.

He rocks me back and forth like I would do with Grace or Liv. He doesn't say anything, not for several moments, what feels like hours. He is not bothered by my emotion. He is not scared of it. He is welcoming, desiring even.

"I'm here," he says, finally.

That's it. Not "It's going to be okay" or "Don't cry." Just "I'm here."

"Thank you," I manage.

He doesn't ask questions, doesn't inquire about what ails my dad or how much time he has left. I am thankful for this. I do not want to answer these questions.

"Let's go to bed," he says.

It's not even eight o'clock, but I say, "Okay."

He pulls me up from the couch, and I put my skirt back in its proper position. He lifts me, my weight nothing to him. I wrap my arms around his neck, my legs around his torso. I rest my head in the space between his ear and his shoulder. One of his hands strokes my back.

He lays me down on his bed, pulls my skirt off me. Just as I'm wondering if he wants sex again, just as I'm starting to feel disappointed by this, he goes to the other room, returns with my overnight bag. I have brought a nightie with me, another item retrieved from the back of the drawer at home, another item that had a tag still attached.

"Can I get you anything? Water?"

"Please," I say.

He goes to the kitchen, returns with a tall glass of water. I drink.

"I bet you weren't expecting this for tonight," I say, a bit embarrassed by myself. If I'm honest, though, it's felt good to cry. I do not regret it.

"Tonight has actually surpassed my expectations."

I raise my eyebrows.

"Like I told you, I wanted to learn more about you. And now I have."

He gets into bed next to me, still naked. I turn on my side, pull my knees into my chest. He presses his chest to my back, wraps his arms around the whole of me. I usually have to make an effort to fall asleep—breathing deeply, counting sheep. This night requires no effort, though. Within seconds, my eyelids feel heavy. I am at peace. I am safe. My body can rest.

Chapter 15

ROSE

October 13, 1984

Dear Diary,

I did it. I applied to all the PhD programs on my list. I finished the forms at the library and let Nicole put them in the mailbox outside the post office. She was giddy at the responsibility, and I was giddy for all my own reasons.

I play this mental game:

If I didn't have Nicole, and I got into one of the programs, would I leave Rob?

Maybe.

Divorce isn't as taboo as it once was.

Fact: By 1889, the United States had the highest divorce rate in the world.

I do have Nicole, though.

A list of things she has needed from me today:

- Help getting out of bed in the morning (she could do it herself, but claims she is too scared)

- Help taking off her overnight diaper and pajamas

- Help putting on her clothes, socks, and shoes

- Hairdressing services

- Breakfast

- Breakfast #2 (after the first attempt was rejected)

- Help wiping her butt after going potty

- Help pulling up her underwear

- Help finding the crayons

- Help cleaning up the crayons upon dropping the box

- Help wiping the tears shed over the aforementioned incident

- Help wiping boogers (lots of wiping in motherhood)

- A hug and kiss on the cheek

- A playmate to tend to the baby dolls and "feed" them pretend milk from plastic bottles

- A snack

- Another snack

- Comfort after falling on her tricycle

- A Band-Aid for her injured knee that is not really injured

- Help clipping back hair that fell into her face

- A cup of apple juice

- Accompaniment on the potty (said she was scared)

- Lunch

- Expression of funny faces for several minutes to elicit laughter

- Fifteen minutes of pre-nap lullaby singing

And we are just at the midway point of the day.
She gets to have so many needs.
I get to have none.
Mothers are expected to sacrifice all, and do so calmly and contentedly.
Adrienne Rich in *Of Woman Born*: "What kind of love is this, which means always to be for others, never for ourselves?"

Maria McIntosh, describing the ideal wife and mother in 1850: "She must learn to control herself, to subdue her own passions; she must set her children an example of meekness and equanimity . . . Never let her manifest irritated feeling, or give utterance to an angry expression."

Sometimes I wonder this terrible thing: Do I regret motherhood?

I love Nicole, I do. But it appears impossible for both my love for her and my love for myself to coexist.

One must go.

I do not regret Nicole. But yes, I regret motherhood. These are different things.

Motherhood, like marriage, has become an institution of female subjugation. Its demands require women to abandon all else, to give all to the children, with nothing left for themselves or the outside world (which is just fine with the patriarchy, of course).

Motherhood didn't used to come with such demands. They are by design.

It's no surprise that in the 1920s, just as women were cropping their hair short and exercising their newly won right to vote, researchers were urging mothers to return home and pay attention to the emerging field of child development. It's funny— women are told that they are biologically wired to mother, that they are naturally capable in a way men never could be (which seems like a compliment, but is really a designation of duty), yet they are also told that they need guidance, that they must constantly study ways to be better at their "natural" vocation.

Similarly, *parent* first gained popularity as a verb in 1970, right at the same time women were taking off their aprons, taking the pill, and fighting for equal rights. This new verb imposed on them a task, something that required their devoted action. They were called to *parent*.

With all the social pressure on mothering, it's no wonder that mothers began to show signs of distress.

In 1957, E. E. LeMasters wrote "Parenthood as Crisis," which states that 83 percent of new mothers and fathers in his study were in "severe" crisis. He chalked this up to being confined to the home without usual social outlets or time and space to pursue personal interests.

Another quote from *Of Woman Born* by Adrienne Rich: "My children cause me the most exquisite suffering of which I have any experience. It is the suffering of ambivalence: the murderous alternation between bitter resentment and raw-edged nerves, and blissful gratification and tenderness."

The ambivalence is profound.

I fear if I get into one of the programs, I will resent Nicole for being the reason I cannot go.

What is better for Nicole? To know her mother pursued a dream? Or to know her mother gave up all to parent?

My own mother is the model of martyrdom. Many mothers are.

My own mother dropped out of college and married my father. She will never admit to any regret, but I wonder.

I thought I had transcended what she never did. I went to college. And here I am, a housewife, a stay-at-home mother, just as she was.

Would I be in this quandary if I had seen my mother pursue her own dreams, if that example had been set? Would I be married? Would I have Nicole?

It's tempting to tell myself I will be doing Nicole a favor if I pursue my studies and my happiness. How easily I can twist things to my benefit! I may be what society says is the worst kind of a woman—a selfish one.

The purpose of applying is not to actually go. Of course, if I get in, I fear I will forget the original purpose. I will want to go. There will be no denying it.

Chapter 16

NICOLE

Merry wants me to interview the prospective caretaker for my dad over Zoom. Kyle is on an important work call, so I have given the girls the iPad, along with their favorite yogurt tubes and banana slices in the shape of a happy face, in hopes that they will be quiet and well behaved.

Usually when I see myself on Zoom, I am so horrified that I select the option that enables me not to view myself, and then, during the call, I google the cost of dermal fillers (insanely expensive). Today, though, I look decent. Could it be possible that Elijah has brought color to my cheeks? Or am I just viewing myself—and the surrounding world— through rose-tinted glasses now that I have a man in my life who adores me for reasons I am no longer interested in questioning?

"Mom, I don't want to eat a FACE," Grace says, expressing horror at the banana slices before her.

She has eaten banana slices in the shape of a happy face many times a week for the past two years.

"Um, okay," I say, taking the plate from her. I will not let this get to me. "How about a heart?"

I rearrange the slices into the shape of a heart and pass it back across the table to her.

"Wow, how did you do that so fast?"

It does not take much to anger or impress a child.

"Mommy is magical," Liv says.

That's a big word for her—*magical*. She knows it because I read them a book called *My Mommy Is Magical*.

"Okay, girls, Mommy has a call, remember?" I say, my voice annoyingly high pitched. Sometimes, it's not just that I hate mothering but also that I hate who I am as a mother. Maybe it's more that than anything.

They turn their attention to the iPad. They are watching a strange retelling of "Cinderella," and one of the characters says, "But your life will be nothing without the prince," and I worry for their future aspirations.

～

The prospective caregiver is named Frank. Merry met him in person and said he seemed "fine," but she felt I should also talk to him before she agreed to have him in their home on a mostly full-time basis.

"I need you to tell me if he seems like the stealing type," she said.

I was surprised when she said the caregiver was a he, and not just any he, but a he with the name Frank. It's hard to picture anything besides a gruff middle-aged man with an expansive waistline. I don't know what such a person would be doing working for a caregiving agency for eighteen bucks an hour.

When he comes onto the screen, he is nothing like what I've pictured. He is not middle aged. He's about my age—fortyish. Which, I guess, might be middle aged, considering life expectancy in the United States is right around eighty. My mind starts to wander, considering whether or not this thing with Elijah is some kind of midlife crisis, exacerbated by my father dying and my daughters annihilating my mental health. Before I can travel too far down that dark and dank rabbit hole, Frank speaks:

"Hello there. You must be Nicole."

He has a southern accent. The surprises keep coming.

After we exchange pleasantries, he says, "The agency thought I would be a good fit. Your dad's not a small guy, ya know? Those four-foot-tall ladies aren't gonna cut it with him."

His laugh is big, hearty. I laugh along with him.

He lifts one of his biceps, flexes. "I work out every day. I can assure you your dad will be in good hands."

He takes it upon himself to show me his hands. They are large and capable looking, which I guess is his point.

He asks if I have any questions for him, so I ask how he got into caregiving. He says he was living at home in his twenties when his mom got cancer, and he took care of her until the end. That experience made him think he wanted to do the same service for others.

"My heart's as big as my hands."

I decide he does not seem like the "stealing type." He seems like the type who will volunteer to be a mall Santa Claus when he gets older.

"I'm assuming they told you what my dad has?" I ask.

I glance up at the girls to see if they are listening to the conversation. They are still enthralled with the Cinderella story. I haven't said anything to them yet about their papa dying. I have been meaning to google tips for having such a conversation.

"They did," Frank says, nodding his head solemnly. "Can't say I'd ever heard of it, but I looked it up online. What a terrible thing. I'm so sorry."

He looks as if he might cry, and I have no idea how someone with such a sensitive constitution can do this job.

"So you can start right away?" I ask.

"I can. Just finished up another job."

I take it that "finished up" means his prior client died. Perhaps it would be a good thing to become so intimately acquainted with death, to be up close with it so often that it loses its power to surprise and devastate.

"That's great. I'll be up there this weekend, so I can meet you in person then. Do you have any questions for me? I want to be the point of contact for you. Meredith is dealing with so much."

"Of course, understood. Just a couple questions for you. Does your dad like music?"

"He does."

"Great, I think it helps them to listen to music."

Them. The dying, he means.

"He likes classic rock mostly. Anything from the sixties."

"Sounds like my type of guy."

"He's most people's type of guy," I say.

Now I feel like I might cry. My throat tightens just like it did when I was with Elijah.

Grace, ever perceptive, looks at me with a level of concern that scares the tears back into their ducts.

"Mommy, what's wrong?" she asks.

I read something a while back that said to validate your children when they correctly identify an emotion in you. So if you're angry and they say, "Why are you angry?" don't say "I'm not angry." Apparently, doing so teaches them not to trust their perceptions, and then they go through life as confused, lost, empty vessels waiting to be preyed upon by ill-intentioned cult leaders who thrive on others' vulnerabilities. It's an interesting concept, but I'm not sure I buy it. Weren't we all raised by parents lying to our faces?

In any case, I don't say "Nothing's wrong," which is what I want to say. Instead, I say, "I'm just a bit sad."

"Is that your little girl?" Frank says as Grace scoots over on the bench seat to be next to me, her little hand patting my back. I do not understand how she can be both an empath and a sociopath.

"Yes, this is Grace," I tell him. "Grace, this is Frank."

Grace does her wave where she flaps her fingers into her palm. Now Liv climbs down from her seat and comes to sit on the other side of me.

"Oh, wow, you've got two of them," Frank says.

He is beaming. Frank would probably be a good dad.

"Yes, this is Liv."

Liv copies her sister's wave.

"Who are you?" Grace says to the screen.

Frank's eyes flick to mine. He is likely trying to decide how to explain his role.

"I'm Frank" is all he says.

"Hi, Frank," Grace says.

"Hi, Frank," Liv parrots.

"Okay, Frank, I'll plan on seeing you this weekend, then," I tell him. "But please call or text if you need anything. You have my number, yes?"

"I do," he says. "Thanks for that. You all have a great day."

I end the call and close my laptop.

"I like Frank," Grace says.

"Me too," I tell her.

～

Elijah and I text throughout the week. He asks what I'm up to on a daily basis, and I lie on a daily basis. I say I am "swamped with work," "in back-to-back meetings," when the reality is that I'm sitting next to Grace while she's on her little potty, whining because "the poo-poo won't come." I say I am headed to the gym when I am really taking the girls to the park yet again. In my defense, I do endure a workout when Grace forces me to sit on the other side of the seesaw from her, pushing us up and down until my thighs burn.

On Thursday afternoon, Grace and Liv jump on the bed as I pack my bag for the weekend, taking tags off more lingerie that's been crumpled up at the back of my underwear drawer. Kyle comes in with a look on his face that immediately makes my insides flip. Something is wrong. I am not going to be able to leave this weekend.

"Hey," he says, his voice weak. This is his sick voice. I am screwed.

Since our fight, we have settled back into a relatively calm complacency that many couples must mistake for contentment. It helps that I'm out of town. It helps that I have Elijah. It helps that Kyle has never wanted to dive beneath the surface of our marriage. He might be storing up all kinds of grievances, like a squirrel with nuts before winter, but he is not one to express his feelings—a previous con that has become a pro. In the end, I will have to introduce the possibility of divorce, and he will say he's shocked.

Kyle flops onto the bed, and Liv jumps on top of him.

"Liv, come on. I'm not feeling good, okay?"

He lifts her up by the armpits, sets her on the bed next to him. He must have pinched her skin or something because she comes to me, her bottom lip trembling, then starts sobbing.

I pick her up because this is what mothers do. They stop whatever the fuck they are doing to make everything okay.

I hold her against my chest, my arms wrapped around her, her legs wrapped around me, her head on my shoulder, big fat tears wetting my neck. I give Kyle a look.

"She's acting. She knows if she does this, you'll coddle her," he says.

A hot flash overtakes me, rolling through my body like a wave. *You're such an asshole,* I think. I've told him before to stop saying things like this, to stop telling the girls to their faces that their emotions are not valid, to stop being so condescending and dismissive. He says I'm too soft with them, and I say he's too hard, and this is just one of several stalemates.

Liv stops crying as I bounce her up and down. Grace comes to me, wraps her arms around my hips.

"I don't want Mommy to leave," Grace says, looking at my partially packed bag.

Liv starts sobbing again.

"I don't want Mommy to leave either," Kyle says.

He is looking at Grace when he says this, not at me. My eyes are full of fury, and he knows it.

"You're sick, Daddy?" Grace asks, going to him now.

Grace is very much into playing doctor, pretending to check heartbeats and administer medicines. For Christmas, I put several boxes of Band-Aids in her stocking so she could tend to our imagined wounds.

She pats his arm and then places her little hand on his forehead.

"Maybe you have a fever," she says.

She's learned about all things medical from YouTube. She was mesmerized by a video featuring a Barbie doll having a C-section. Maybe YouTube isn't all bad. Maybe it will be partially responsible for her future career. Dr. Grace Sanchez. It has a nice ring.

"Are you really sick?" I ask him, doing a horrible job of hiding how inconvenient this is for me.

It's hard to have sympathy. I am always the one who gets sick, rarely Kyle. When the girls were in day care, I was sick approximately twice a month with various colds and stomach ailments. One time, I puked into the cup holder of my car during my evening commute home from work, suddenly overcome with norovirus. There have been two upsides to me staying home with the girls: 1) I no longer have to flog them over many hurdles to get out the door for day care in the morning, and 2) there is much less sickness. It's been months since I've had to force a syringe of antibiotic goop into anyone's mouth.

"Stomach thing," he says. "Probably something I ate."

Which is plausible. He's a big fan of getting DoorDash from questionable fast-food establishments. He does look a bit green around the gills, as my dad would say.

"Poor Daddy," Grace says.

Liv has lifted her head from me to look at her father. Sick people are fascinating spectacles to young children.

"I'll be fine, just need some rest," he says.

This is my cue to usher the girls out of the bedroom. I want to roll my eyes because I know that if I had whatever bug is plaguing him, I would be going about my usual duties, not lying in bed.

"Come on, girls," I say.

They file out of the room in front of me, run ahead to the stairs.

"Should I cancel my trip this weekend?" I ask Kyle.

The idea of not seeing Elijah fills me with intense despair.

"I don't know," he says, wincing as he clutches his stomach.

"Okay, well, I'll need to tell Merry and—"

"Nic, chill," he says. "It's probably just a twenty-four-hour bug. We can figure it out tomorrow."

I hate when he tells me to chill, but I bite my tongue, refrain from my usual admonitions.

"No dinner for you then?" I ask.

He grimaces. "No." He clutches his belly again, making me aware of the extent of his misery.

"I'll bring you some ginger ale," I say, because I'm not a total bitch.

～

After I put the girls to bed, I can hear Kyle vomiting in the master bathroom. It is not looking good for this weekend. I go to the living room, make myself comfortable on the couch, assuming it will be my bed for the night. I text Elijah.

I have bad news.

He replies immediately, as he usually does:

Oh no. What?

I'm not sure I can come up this weekend.

I always thought that phrase "heart sinking" was a melodramatic cliché, but I can really feel something in my chest free-falling.

Him: Nooooooo

My thoughts exactly

Him: Why?

I've got a stomach bug, I think.

Him: Ugh. That sucks. Can I have some chicken soup sent to you?

I imagine that—giving him my address. I imagine him googling it, seeing that I live in a house suitable for a family. With just a little internet sleuthing, he would learn that the house is owned by Kyle and Nicole Sanchez. And the jig, as they say, would be up.

You're sweet, but I'm going to lay off food for the night.

Him: Maybe you'll feel better in the morning

I send the fingers-crossed emoji. He sends back two of the same, then says:

I choose to remain optimistic

Of course you do

Him: What if I come to you? I can take care of you?

I physically shudder at this, imagining him showing up at the front door, Kyle answering.

No, no. I'm a horrible patient. I'm like a sick cat. Just want to find a bush and be alone until I feel better.

Him: Ok. Go get some rest then, Kit-Kat. I hope you feel better

Thank you. I miss you

We trade kissy-face emojis because we continue to be horribly sappy, and then I put my phone on the coffee table and attempt to ignore the sounds of Kyle retching so I can sleep.

~

The next morning, the retching has stopped, but Kyle remains in bed, looking as if death might come for him at any moment. I bring him water and saltine crackers.

"Thanks," he says.

How's my girl doing this morning?

Elijah.
I respond:

Not sure yet. Need to get up and around a bit.

"I'm sorry this messes up your weekend plans," Kyle says.

Illness tends to humble him. He's always sweeter, softer in the twenty-four hours following a minor health crisis.

I shrug. "Not your fault. I'll tell Merry and my dad I'm not coming."

I feel my mood instantly darken, all the pep leaving my step.

"Maybe you can still go," Kyle says.

"Kyle, if you think the girls are going to play calmly on the floor while you rest in bed next to them all weekend, I'm afraid you are sorely mistaken."

"I know that," he says. He is feeling well enough to convey mild irritation with my condescending tone. "I meant you could take the girls with you."

This had not even occurred to me, mostly because including Elijah and my daughters in the same thought process causes my brain to temporarily short-circuit.

"Oh," I say. "I suppose I could."

My mind races as I consider the logistics. Merry and my dad would like to see the girls. It's been so long. Will my dad even remember them? Some of his long-term memory appears to be intact, but who knows? What will I tell the girls about him being in a wheelchair? Is there any conceivable way I could still see Elijah? Would it be possible to enjoy Elijah if I knew my daughters were just a handful of miles away?

"I'll ask Merry what she thinks," I say. "Might be a bit much to have the girls in the house with my dad and Frank."

"Who's Frank?"

I'm reminded that Kyle and I really do not talk to each other about our lives anymore.

"The caregiver."

"The caregiver is named Frank?"

I text Merry:

Looks like Kyle has some food poisoning. What if I brought the girls up with me?

It sometimes takes Merry several hours to respond to a text, but she responds right away this time. I imagine her sitting next to my dad at the kitchen table, passing time on her phone.

Merry: Oh, I bet your dad would love to see them! And me too, of course

I think about how to propose this next part. It's not something I would even consider proposing if Frank wasn't on the scene, but he is. And I need to see Elijah.

Feel free to say no, but would it be too much to ask if you watch the girls overnight so I can visit with Prisha again? It's just that I've had so little time to myself . . .

The self-pitying martyr act is very unbecoming, but it's the only tactic I can think of right now, and it's one Merry, like most women, is familiar with herself.

Merry: Sure! I don't see why not!

It's settled then.

Okay. We'll get on the road soon. Will probably have to make a few stops along the way

And by *a few*, I mean three hundred. This drive is going to be hell. I can barely maintain sanity after an hour in the car with the girls, and this will be several hours. If thoughts of Elijah can sustain me through this, then I need to find a way to continue this affair indefinitely, or at least until the girls have moved out of the house.

Merry: Drive safe!

When I tell Grace and Liv that we are going on a trip to see Papa and Grandma Merry, they both start jumping up and down and screaming "Trip! Trip! Trip!" This enthusiasm is likely to carry us through the first half hour, at which point they will get restless and bored. I charge the iPad and pack an entire duffel bag with snacks, games, and toys from my "emergency stash" (which is basically a box of toys the girls do not know I have that I keep hidden in the master closet for times in which my mental health depends on their entertainment).

I throw together a bag of clothes, pull-ups, stuffed animals, and a multitude of must-have blankets. It's all very rushed and manic. Then I text Elijah:

I think I'm good to come up!

He sends back a party-hat emoji.

Him: I promise to take excellent care of you

You better

~

We leave the house just after ten o'clock in the morning, and the girls are surprisingly well behaved until we hit the Los Angeles County line. At that point, it's about time for lunch, so we do the McDonald's drive-through, and I get them Happy Meals, hoping they live up to their names. They do, thankfully, and then Liv falls asleep. Grace sits with her eyes wide open, resisting the nap, until she finally nods off.

They wake up just as we pass through Santa Barbara. We make a bathroom stop and get ice cream cones. I text Elijah.

Can't wait to see you. Feeling so much better now

Him: So glad to hear it. I want to trace your whole body with my fingertips

212

Just that text is enough to keep me content through the next four hours of driving, which include a chorus of whining, interrupted only by occasional silences when the girls are engaged with something on the iPad.

At five o'clock, I stop at McDonald's again because I really don't care what they eat as long as they eat without complaint. There is still mild complaining with the Happy Meals—Liv says the chicken nuggets are too hot, and Grace says her apple slices are slimy—but they are mostly appreciative of the indulgence.

We get to Daly City just after seven o'clock. They are both beginning to melt down because they are tired. Grace says she has to pee. Liv's pull-up is about to leak. I am starving because all I've eaten is cold french fries, the rejected remains of their meals.

Merry is standing on the front porch. She looks thrilled to see us, and Merry is not normally someone who looks thrilled. We are a reprieve, I'm guessing. We will enable her to deny her current reality for a short, necessary while.

All I've told the girls is that Papa is sick, and Grace said, "Like Daddy?" I told her that he was sicker than Daddy and had to be in bed during the day, but that he was excited to see them. I hope that's true. I hope he remembers their little faces.

"Oh my goodness, look at you big girls," Merry says when we emerge from the car. She goes to Grace and Liv, hugs them with more force than she's ever hugged me with. They are unusually shy until Merry says, "I have cookies!"

Grace says, "Yay!" and both girls follow her inside.

The moment I step into the house, it feels different. There's a noticeably different smell—not bad, necessarily, but nursing-home-ish. Stale, maybe. There are boxes of supplies lining the hallway—rubber gloves (extra large), adult diapers, wipes. As I'm taking stock, Merry is presenting a plate of chocolate chip cookies to the girls, and a voice behind me booms:

"You must be Nicole!"

I turn. Frank, in the flesh. He is shorter than I imagined, a couple of inches shorter than me.

"Frank, hi."

I reach out my hand to shake his, but he gives me a hug instead.

"And you brought the little ones," he says, peeking around me to see the girls shoving cookies into their mouths.

"I did," I say. "Quite the drive."

"I bet! Well, go on in and say hi to your dad. He'll love to see you."

I do as he says, approaching my dad's bedroom with a sense of dread, as if my body knows before my mind that it will be difficult to see what I see.

The king bed has been moved out (to where, I don't know) to make room for a hospital bed, something the hospice team brought a few days ago. My dad is sitting upright in it. His feet are in what look like cushioned booties. It takes me a second to realize that these are to help prevent bedsores on his heels. It takes me another second to realize that he must not be getting out of bed much at all.

"Hey, Dad."

His bed is facing the TV on the opposite wall, so he doesn't see me when I first come in.

"Who's that?" he asks. His voice is quieter than usual, just above a whisper. It's as if whatever is siphoning the strength from his body is also siphoning strength from his vocal cords.

"It's me, Nikki," I say, bracing myself for his confusion.

He turns his head to the side, and I come into his line of sight.

"Nikki! What are you doing here?"

"I came up with the girls, Grace and Liv. Your granddaughters." I have decided I will give him more information than he may need because I cannot handle the pain of his obliviousness.

"Wow," he says.

There is a commode next to his bed. I move it out of the way so I can sit next to him in bed. He smells strange—likely a combination of sweat and pee. Someone comes to bathe him a couple of times a week, and he's in diapers full time now. Smells are inevitable. This must be the source of the nursing-home-ish scent permeating the house.

"What are you watching?" I ask.

The TV is on, but the sound is off. It appears to be some kind of zombie-apocalypse movie.

"I don't know."

"Do you want to watch golf?"

My dad has always liked to watch golf, something that has perplexed Merry and me for years.

"Sure!"

I start to peruse the channel listings and have no idea where to find golf. I ask what I know is a stupid question: "Do you remember what number the golf channel is?"

He furrows his brows and says, "Eighty-three?"

I give it a try, and sure enough, he's right. Then he starts to talk about Phil Mickelson and how he's from San Diego. For a moment, I'm able to pretend that he is my dad, healthy and normal.

Then he says, "When's breakfast?"

"Dad, it's seven o'clock. It's nighttime. We're having dinner soon."

"We are?"

⁓

I leave the room when Frank comes to change Dad's diaper and get him into his wheelchair. Merry has made pesto pasta, garlic bread, and green beans. I put some food on the girls' plates, knowing this is a fool's errand, and then sit with them and Merry at the table. Frank wheels out Dad, who glances around the table, apparently surprised to see all of us. What little hair is left on his balding head is wet, noticeably combed. Sweet Frank.

"Nikki, what are you doing here?" my dad says.

"I came up with the girls," I tell him. I point to each of the girls and say, "Grace and Liv."

The girls stare, slack jawed. I don't know if they've ever seen someone in a wheelchair before. I did not adequately prepare them for this, mostly because I have not figured out how to adequately prepare myself.

"Hi, girls," my dad says.

"Hi, Papa!" Grace says, cheerful. I've never been more thankful for her exuberance.

Frank sits on the couch in the living room, occupied with his phone, while we eat, which is awkward. If I were Merry, I would invite him to join us, but I'm sure she wants the opportunity to forget she has a caregiver in her house. He'll go home after getting Dad in bed for the night.

My dad really can't manage his utensils by himself, but we let him try, his shaky hand maneuvering the fork to the pasta, twirling it once before giving up.

"Want some help, Dad?"

He shrugs like *I suppose I do.*

I feed him, exercising the expertise I've gained from feeding Grace and Liv. I assume Merry usually does this. Or Frank.

Predictably, the girls eat the garlic bread and nothing else, but I tell them they can have ice cream when Merry presents the option. If the girls look back on this phase of life—which they won't, because their brains will not preserve any memories of this time—they will think of it as a happy time, a time when they got to eat a lot of fast food and sugary treats. Perhaps it is a mother's responsibility to foster such blissful ignorance.

As I spoon-feed my dad ice cream, I ask him, "If you could have anything, what would you want?"

I am hoping for one of his rare moments of clarity. I am hoping he will tell us a desire he has for his final days, even though he doesn't know they are his final days.

"If I could have anything?" he asks.

I nod.

He looks around the table. "This," he says.

Just as the tears start welling up in my eyes, he farts loudly, and we all laugh.

～

Merry has placed a full-size mattress on the floor in my bedroom for the girls to sleep on. I change them into their pajamas, which is no small feat because they are overtired and feral. I presume they will awaken me several times during the night. They have never slept side by side like this. I can't imagine it will go well.

"Mommy?" Grace says, as I tuck her in.

"Yes?"

"What's wrong with Papa?"

Children, unlike adults, have no problem asking the difficult questions. They do not yet realize what makes certain questions difficult. They are unrestrained in their curiosity, unburdened by social expectations and niceties.

"Well, he's sick," I say. "Sometimes when people are sick, they have to be in wheelchairs."

Liv looks at me wide eyed. I have no idea if she's following along with this conversation.

"It's hard to hear him," Grace says.

"I know. He's very weak."

"Is he going to die?"

Grace has just started exploring the concept of death, mostly by pointing to bugs on the ground and saying things like "Aww, he died. His battery ran out. I hope he had a good life." I've started googling how to discuss death with young children, and the key, supposedly, is to be very direct and literal. I should not say things like "We lost him" or "He passed away" or "He's in a better place" because all these things are very confusing to a little person. I can already imagine the questions I'd be bombarded with if I tried to use vague language: *You LOST him?*

217

Where is he? How do we find him? Can we visit the better place? Do you have pictures of it on your phone?

"He is going to die," I say, taking Google's advice. I swallow back follow-up statements, attempts to soften what must be a horrific blow.

"Oh" is all she says.

Then: "Where will he go?"

"Well, some believe people go to heaven."

She nods. She seems familiar with the idea of heaven, probably thanks to YouTube.

"Am I going to die?" she asks.

I glance to Liv, who is starting to doze off.

"All living things die. But you will not die for a very, very long time."

Grace starts crying. I'm afraid she'll wake up her sister, but Liv seems undisturbed.

"Are there toys in heaven?" Grace sobs.

I pull her into my body, kiss her soft cheek.

"I think anything you want to be in heaven is in heaven."

The truth is I think heaven is a story mortals tell themselves to keep their fears at bay. But if believing in it makes my children happy, then color me a believer.

Grace takes a deep breath and appears accepting of my answer. I feel like a good mom for a single invigorating moment.

"Can you tell me a story?" she asks.

God, I hate telling stories.

"Okay," I say and make up some nonsense about fairies in a garden with magic paintbrushes.

~

At some point in the night, both girls come into my bed, one on each side of me, causing me to sleep as if I'm wearing a straitjacket. I wake up sweaty and tired but also ecstatic because I get to see Elijah today.

Frank is already here when I come downstairs. Merry is making coffee. I turn on the TV in the living room, put on a show for the girls, then go check on my dad.

I find him sitting on the commode, totally naked. I start to turn away, to give him privacy, but he says, "Oh, hey, Nikki," as if it's not at all weird that I am looking at him as he sits on a toilet.

"Hey, Dad."

Naked, he looks so frail. He's lost so much muscle mass. His formerly thick and sturdy thighs are sinewy and weak.

"When did you get here?"

"Yesterday."

Frank comes in and says, "Oh, yeah, he'll sit there a while. I don't think you can tell when you poop, can you, Rob?"

He claps my dad on the back, as if they are buddies. Dad laughs, as if in agreement that they are buddies.

I leave him be, go to the kitchen table, text Elijah to make myself feel better.

Hey you. You ready for me?

Him: Very ready, indeed. How's your dad?

Elijah knows the routine now—I drive up on Fridays, spend time with my dad, then come to see him. Not everything is a lie.

He's not good. It's just all moving so fast

Him: I'm sorry. I will do my best to make you feel slightly better

I'm counting on that

I go through the motions of the day, sitting with my dad, playing with the girls. Merry seems to enjoy the company, so I don't feel much guilt when we approach the afternoon and I say, "Are you still okay with me staying at Prisha's tonight?"

"Oh, sure. I'll just spoil the girls rotten, won't I?" she says to the girls.

"Where are you going, Mommy?" Grace asks.

"I am going to visit a friend, but I'll be back tomorrow."

"We stay here?" she says in her baby voice, which must mean she feels like a baby, small and vulnerable. I give her a hug.

"Yes. A sleepover with Grandma Merry," I say.

"A sleepover?"

She looks worried, but then her brows unknit, and she smiles mischievously.

"Do we get ice cream?" she asks.

Merry looks to me, and I nod.

"Of course you do," Merry says.

"Ice cream!" Liv says, throwing her arms in the air.

"Ice cream!" Grace shouts.

~

Assured of their joy, I change into a maxi dress, something I bought last year, when Kyle and I were talking about a family trip to Hawaii. I pictured myself walking on the beach, effortlessly sexy, the slits in the side of the dress revealing my tanned-and-toned thighs (I also pictured mermaid waves in my hair, though my hair is stick straight and would never hold such waves). We were about to buy airfare and book a hotel—we were going to splurge for a week at the Grand Wailea—when he got a promotion at work and felt it wouldn't "look good" to immediately take a vacation. I waited for him to resurrect the idea, but he never did.

Once I get in the car, I touch up my makeup and spray myself with perfume. The girls never see me primp. I don't want them to be suspicious. I don't want them to say something to Kyle like "Mommy got so pretty and then went to see her friend." I'm hoping they don't even mention that I left them alone with Merry for the night.

Kyle. I remember that he texted earlier, a "just checking in." He rarely checks in.

I text him:

Hey. All fine here. Hope you're feeling better

Then I put my phone back in my purse and start my drive to Elijah.

~

When Elijah opens the door, he says, "My lady," and gives me a little bow.

"Hello, kind sir," I say.

He closes the door behind me. I lean in to kiss him, but he backs away. "Not so fast," he says.

Is he concerned about my alleged germs? Annoyed for some other reason? He doesn't seem annoyed. He seems up to something.

"I want you to fully relax tonight," he says. "You are not allowed to pleasure me in any way."

"What?"

"Exactly what I said. You drove all this way after feeling sick. I want to take care of you."

He raises an eyebrow, and I know he's not talking about feeding me soup.

I give him a suspicious half smile. "Okay then."

He takes my hand and walks me to the bedroom, where there is soft music playing—something instrumental—and candles are lit. It smells like lavender.

"How about a massage?" he asks.

"I would never say no to that."

Though, actually, I would. For a while, Kyle was into offering massages, mostly because he expected them to lead to sex. I didn't realize that this assumption was in place until he had given me a few massages and they had all led to sex, each time sooner than the last. That's when I started to get annoyed with his "loving offerings" of massages and began to say "No thanks, I'm good" when he asked. When he acted dejected, like his feelings were hurt, I told him that the massages felt calculated, like a means to his desired end instead of an end in themselves. He said, "I thought you liked foreplay. I really can't win," then sulked for days.

I lie back on Elijah's bed, and he is on all fours, hovering over me.

"Do you mind if I blindfold you?" he asks.

Well, this just got interesting.

"Go right ahead."

"It's just that I want you to be able to fully relax, to sink into your body. Sensory deprivation. No distractions."

If he's not careful, I'm going to come just listening to him talk.

He reaches into his nightstand drawer and retrieves a blindfold. I'm just uneasy enough to make a nervous joke: "So you just have blindfolds lying around?"

He laughs. "No. Ordered it yesterday. Thank you, Amazon Prime."

The premeditation of all this has made me wet.

He places the blindfold over my eyes, hooks the straps around my ears.

"I'm going to take off your dress," he says.

"Please do."

"Shhh," he says. "Just rest."

He slips my dress off my shoulders, then shimmies it down my body. Then he reaches under my back to unhook my bra. He slides off my panties, and I'm sure he can see how wet I am, but he doesn't say anything. He doesn't touch me there either, although everything in me is telling him to do just that. I lift my hips, and he gently pushes them back down, which only makes me want him more.

"I'm going to bring you something to eat," he says.

I hear him walk away, and I'm tempted to lift the blindfold to see what he's doing, but decide to play along.

I hear him return, then feel his weight on the bed near me. His breath is near me. He is hovering close to my face.

Something touches my lips. Just barely. I reach for it with my tongue. It's cold, a piece of fruit maybe. He pulls it away, and my tongue chases after it. He laughs softly. Then he brings it back and lets me wrap my lips around it. A strawberry.

There is more after that—grapes, dark chocolate, spoonfuls of sorbet.

"We'll have a full dinner in a bit," he says. "I just wanted to give you a little appe*teaser*."

There is something tickling my belly. I squirm. Is he touching me with a *feather*? I can't help but giggle—over the tickling and the ridiculousness of this.

"Shh," he says.

He stops with the feather, or whatever he's using, and begins to graze my skin with his fingertips, goose bumps following in the wake of his touch. He starts at the soles of my feet, gently stroking each toe. I try to enjoy it, try not to think about the state of my toenails, my cracked heels. He travels up my calves, traverses my knees, lingers on my thighs. I lift my hips again, but he pushes them back down.

His fingertips move over my lower belly, then up to my breasts. My breasts haven't felt like part of my sexual being since I became a mother. Even now, nearly two years out from breastfeeding, I think of them as my retired saggy milk sacs. Elijah reminds me of the beauty they have on their own, detached from the service they provided. They are no longer perky and taut, but they seem to suit him just fine. He dances his fingers around my nipples, cups my breasts, one in each of his hands, massages them gently. They are tender and sore, and for a brief second, I exit the moment and wonder if I'm going to get an ill-timed period all over his sheets.

I forget about that as he makes his way to my shoulders, then down my arms, then back up to my neck. It's nearly impossible for me to lie still as he works his way around my neck and up to my scalp. Every time I start to writhe around, he places his whole hand on my belly until I settle.

How long have I been wearing this blindfold? It could be ten minutes or three hours. I've lost all track of time. I've transcended time completely. Finally, he moves his fingers to my vagina. He strokes softly, seemingly without a next step in mind. I feel the wave of an orgasm approaching, starting way back at the horizon line, then moving toward shore, gaining in size and velocity until it's bigger than any wave I've experienced before. My low, guttural groan increases in pitch until the wave crashes and my head arches back and I let out an *eeee* like a hyena in heat.

I assume he will lower himself on top of me, take his turn, but he doesn't. He resumes massaging me. He reaches inside me—one finger first.

"Is this okay?" he asks.

"Yes."

He puts two fingers inside me. "And this?"

Before I can answer, another wave swells, and I come again.

"What are you doing to me?" I say.

"Shh."

He goes on like this, stroking my body, then using his lips to kiss every inch of me, except for where I want him to kiss. I come again and then again. Four times in total.

"You are insane," I say.

"Are you ready for the blindfold to come off?"

His voice is slow and steady. I'm starting to wonder if he does this professionally, if he's some kind of male prostitute who specializes in making women come without actual sex.

"Yes, take it off," I say.

He lifts it off my eyes and I look up at him. He is smiling, satisfied.

"How was that?" he asks.

"I'm pretty sure you could tell how it was."

"I want to hear you tell me."

"It was . . . ecstasy."

There's a word I never thought I'd say out loud, especially in my forties.

"*Ecstasy* is what I like to hear," he says.

He is still hovering over me, on all fours. He dips his head to gently kiss my mouth. When I look down, I can see the erection in his pants and am impressed he doesn't feel compelled to tend to it (or have me tend to it).

"Are you some kind of sex god?" I ask.

"We didn't have sex."

"Touché," I say. Then: "Are you some kind of erotic massage god?"

He laughs.

"I'm a little bit into tantra."

I sit up, balanced on my elbows. "You're a little bit into tantra."

"I dabble."

"You dabble."

He shrugs.

"I don't wear sarongs and chant or anything. I just like to read about how to please women."

He lies beside me. I swing a leg over him, feeling him hard beneath my thigh. Everything in me wants to pleasure him. I hate that I'm so uncomfortable—guilty, almost—in the role of receiver. Overcome with the need to give, I caress him down there. He places his hand over mine.

"I told you the rules. You don't get to do anything for me today," he says.

I sigh.

"You need to get used to being cared for," he says. "You deserve to be cared for."

Surprise tears come again, just like last time. Except I'm not thinking about my dad. I'm thinking about his words, how true they are, how I've given up on anyone in the world ever expressing such a sentiment to me.

You deserve to be cared for.

"Thank you," I say, still welling up.

He presses down my eyelids with each of his thumbs so that the dam breaks and the tears flow. Then he kisses my cheeks.

"I'm going to make you some dinner."

~

He makes macadamia-crusted mahi-mahi, restaurant quality, along with roasted fingerling potatoes and a salad. I tell him I'm not sure how he's real, and he says he's not sure how I'm real. Mutual awe, borderline bewilderment—this is what all humans should seek in a lover.

We eat at his tiny kitchen table. He asks about my dad, and I tell him the ugly truths. He does not say anything stupid like "Well, he won't suffer much longer" or "Everything will be okay soon." He just listens and nods, behaving the way all women want men to behave.

"Tell me something about you I don't know," he says.

I try to think of something true.

"I used to be a photographer," I say, both embarrassed and surprised that this is the truth that has risen to the surface.

His eyes widen. "Used to?"

"I haven't done it in years."

"Why not?"

I look at my plate, feeling suddenly exposed, uneasy with his eye contact, his desire to truly know me.

"You know, life gets in the way. It's not like I was really good or anything."

Though I was, I think. Once.

"What does that even mean—*good*? Who cares? If you enjoy it, you should do it."

I shrug, still looking at my plate. "Maybe."

"What kind of photography?"

I dare to look up now. "Nature, mostly. Landscapes."

"A creative soul," he says. "I'm not surprised."

"You're not?"

"Of course not. You have that energy."

"That energy?"

"Like, a zest. An appetite for life. A desire to look beneath the surface."

How does he see this?

"I'd love to see some of your work," he says.

I wave him off. "It's literally been years. I don't even have anything on my phone or—"

He holds up both hands in submission. "Hey now, no pressure. You don't have to show me a thing. I'm just saying I'd love to see it. I'd love to see what your eye captures, what your mind thinks should be in a shot. I'd love to hear you talk about what was just outside the frame. That's all."

I try to picture Kyle asking about the intricacies of my photography. The most commentary he ever gave me was to say "That's a nice one." He was never curious about the process. I think he would have rolled his eyes at the idea that there *was* a process.

"You sound like you know a bit about photography yourself," I say.

He smiles. "I dabble."

"Quite the dabbler."

"There are so many interesting things. Can't help but dabble."

We eat in silence for a few minutes, taking the last few bites of our food. Then I work up the nerve to admit something, a confession that's lodged itself in my throat.

"I'm afraid I'm falling for you," I say.

"What's so scary about that?"

He reaches across the table, takes my hands in his.

"Don't worry," he says. "I'm falling for you too."

~

Because I am a terrible person, I don't even think about Merry or the girls until Elijah falls asleep next to me in bed, his beautiful mouth partly open, emitting the softest of snores. Would this adorable snore bother me at some point? What kind of alternate dimension am I in now, exactly?

I reach into my purse for my phone to see two missed calls from Merry and three texts. I break out into a sweat as I unlock my phone and read the texts.

Sorry to bother you. Do the girls have toothbrushes? I know you've mentioned how they need to brush their teeth well.

Then:

I will probably just use one of my extra adult toothbrushes. Okay?

Then:

Never mind, I found theirs! Sorry!

I will my heart to slow as I realize everything is fine. There's nothing wrong. It could have been something, though—a visit to the ER for a broken bone, a child wandering out the front door, now missing. My face hot with shame, my hands shaking, I text Merry:

Weird. I just got your texts and missed calls now. Everything OK?

It's just after nine. She should still be up. The girls should be asleep. Thankfully, she responds right away.

Everything is fine here. The girls are asleep!

The exclamation mark soothes my guilt-ridden soul.

OK, great! Glad to hear! Sorry again! Not sure what happened with my phone!

My relief has resulted in the manic use of four exclamation marks.

I'm going to bed. Hope you're having a nice time with Prisha!

I look next to me at Elijah's sleeping form, the perfection of him.

I am. See you tomorrow.

~

The next morning, I wake up curled into Elijah's body.

"I'm the big *C* and you're the little *c*," he says.

I am not into this metaphor, as it reminds me of teaching Grace her letters. She persists in writing the *C* backward and yells at me when I attempt to correct her.

"Do I keep you too warm at night?" I ask.

His hand is reaching underneath my arm, cupping my breast.

"You are a little heater," he says.

He kisses my ear, sucks on the lobe.

"Hey now," I say. "It's my turn."

I lean back into him until he relents and lies back on the bed. I climb on top of him, one knee on either side of his middle.

"Where's that blindfold?" I ask.

He reaches into his nightstand, throws it to me. I put it on him, feeling both turned on and silly. There is something nice, though, about him not being able to see what I'm doing. He seems so vulnerable, helpless, at my mercy.

I am not nearly as patient as he was with me. I don't have the same ability to pace myself. I start with gentle kisses from his toes up to his lips, but then I get right to putting him in my mouth. He doesn't object. I suppose when it's my turn, it's my rules.

"Do you want me to come?" he asks. I can tell he's close.

"If you want to."

"I'd rather come with you."

"I came so many times yesterday," I say. "The score would be very uneven."

I'm already relenting, though, already positioning myself atop him.

"You need to stop keeping score," he says.

I put him inside me, and within a few minutes, we come together. I collapse on his chest, and we breathe in unison, our bodies moving up and down as one.

"I don't want you to go," he says once we have caught our breath.

I trace each finger of his hand with my fingertip.

"I don't want to go."

"I'm sure you want to see your dad before you drive home, though, right?"

"I do."

"Can I make you breakfast first?"

"I would love that."

~

He makes omelets with a side of potatoes left over from last night's dinner. Watching him cut strawberries for a fruit salad, I'm dumbstruck. I am falling in love with this person who I know so well and also not at all. My self is splitting between a woman who is embarking on something new with him and a woman who is two decades into a life with someone else. How long will it be possible for both identities to exist, to compartmentalize?

"Here you go, my dear," he says. He presents me with my plate and kisses my nose before turning to assemble his own plate.

I suppose I don't have to know how long it will be possible. I just have to know that, at some point, it will not be possible. At some point, the proverbial shit will hit the fan. And I don't know which version of myself will be left standing.

Chapter 17

ROSE

February 10, 1985

Dear Diary,

I just got my first rejection letter. From Harvard.

I must assume that more are on the way.

I feel like a fool to have gotten my hopes up, to have relied on this little kernel of possibility to nourish me.

Now what?

I just finished rereading Kate Chopin's novel *The Awakening*. It's hard to believe it was published in 1899. So revolutionary. I read it for the first time in a literature course as an undergraduate. At the time, I didn't relate to the main character, twenty-eight-year-old wife and mother Edna Pontellier. I do now.

Edna is in a stifling marriage and aches for a fate different from that of other wives, who, as she puts it, "idolized their children, worshipped their husbands, and esteemed it a holy privilege to efface themselves." She believes firmly that "she has a position in the universe as a human being." Like I said, revolutionary.

Edna bucks social conventions by wandering alone in public unescorted, then embarking on an adulterous affair without remorse. She tells her lover she is the possession of no man.

Reminds me of what Audre Lorde said about how we begin to grow weary of self-sacrifice and suffering once we get to know ourselves and our desires intimately.

The book is thrilling until the end, when she commits suicide, convinced this is preferable to living less than a fully human existence.

The book created quite the scandal when it was published. It was condemned universally, banned in Chopin's hometown of Baltimore and elsewhere. The criticism ended Chopin's career and then her life. She committed suicide in 1904, and her work remained in obscurity for more than half a century.

Now it is taught in college literature courses.

Life is stupefying.

Edna drowns herself, which sounds horrifying. If I were to commit suicide (and it does occasionally pass through my mind as a last-resort kind of option), I would drive my car off a bridge. Rob could tell Nicole that it was a car accident, which is probably what it would appear to be anyway. *Lost control of the wheel,* the newspaper article would say.

As should be obvious, I am feeling despondent.

Nicole is calling for me. Just a twenty-minute nap today, a twenty-minute reprieve for me. Considering my thoughts of driving my car off a bridge, it would have been nice to have a bit longer.

Must go.

Chapter 18

NICOLE

I face absolutely zero repercussions following my somewhat-risky trip up north with the girls. They had no complaints about the sleepover with Merry. They asked no questions about my whereabouts. And they said nothing to Kyle about Mommy leaving them. Kyle's stomach bug has passed, and he has been kinder than usual, probably because he enjoyed a weekend by himself in a quiet house. Elijah and I continue to text our way to a deeper connection than I thought possible. My latest daydream is divorcing Kyle and carrying on my relationship with Elijah whenever I don't have the girls. Kyle will blame my desire to separate solely on grief-induced madness, and I will say, "You might be right." That will be the easiest pill for him to swallow. I keep reminding myself that I was daydreaming of leaving Kyle before I even met Elijah. Elijah is just the catalyst.

I have the girls with me for a trip to the grocery store. Once, I overheard a park mom say that she only runs errands without her children, that she counts this as "self-care." I rolled my eyes so hard I thought they would get stuck in the back of my head and I'd see nothing but black for the rest of my life. First of all, how does she have the option to run errands without her children? Second of all, why is the bar so low for maternal self-care? I was most perturbed by the fact that I understood what she was saying. On the rare occasion Kyle watches the girls so I can run errands, it does feel like a luxury. It's like once we become mothers, we are told that any moment that does not involve complete sacrifice in deference to our children is a luxury, something we should count as a blessing. I hated that mom for supporting this narrative. And I hated myself for doing the same.

"Mommy, can I get these?" Grace asks, pointing to a giant container of cheese balls that the manager of this establishment has chosen to place right at the entrance of the store.

"No, Grace. We don't need a vat of cheese balls."

"What's a vat?"

"Hey, why don't you get yourself a little cart?"

Half of parenting is redirection.

Grace goes to the little carts and takes one for herself. Before I had kids, I despised mothers who let their children push these little carts through the aisles. The children were always in the way, and the moms would just chirp "Sorry!" with this laugh that said *I'm just a mom doing my best. Isn't my kid cute?*

I am the annoying mom now. The universe is constantly reprimanding me for my past judgments.

Liv sits in the front of the big cart that I'm pushing. Usually, she's well behaved and giggly in this scenario because she thinks the grocery store is like a ride at Disneyland. Today, though, she is wiggling around and whining. It's a special kind of whine. She might have an ear infection.

Grace likes to be helpful, so I tell her to get bananas. She goes to the bin of single bananas and puts eight of them, one at a time, in her cart. Most of them are already browning, but I don't have the heart or patience to do anything about this.

"Do we need strawberries too?" she asks with enthusiasm.

We always need strawberries.

She picks up a container, but she does it by the top, so the container falls open, and all the strawberries tumble out onto the floor.

She looks at me, and as she takes in my complete annoyance with her mishap, her face transforms from shock at what's happened to utter devastation. There is a precarious moment of silence before she erupts into a wail.

I set aside my annoyance so I can console her and get her to stop wailing.

"It was just an accident," I tell her, stroking her back with my hand. *Please stop making a scene* is what I'm thinking.

She calms down, and I start to put the strawberries back in the container when a guy who works there, some teenage kid, comes over and says, "Don't bother with that. Not like we can sell them now."

As he walks away, I hurl one of the strawberries at his back.

"Mommy!" Grace chastises me.

I miss hitting him, for better or worse, and mutter, "Asshole." It's possible he hears me. His head jerks back slightly, but he doesn't turn around.

Grace and Liv have definitely heard me.

"Asshole!" Grace shrieks.

Now the kid looks at us, as do several others in the vicinity. I give him a tight smile.

With impeccable timing, Liv parrots her sister: "Asshole!"

And that's how the shopping trip goes.

~

I stop by the pediatrician's office on the way home, hoping they can see Liv because I'm quite sure something is going on with her right ear. It's red and crusty, and she keeps putting her pinkie finger in it.

Hey you, how's your day?

Elijah.

The dancing between two worlds has become less exhilarating and more exhausting. I want nothing more than to sit on a park bench and text him back and forth for the next hour, but I cannot, and this constraint makes me more irritable than I already was.

Too busy. You?

The woman at the front desk of the pediatrician's office says she can see Liv in a half hour. I take the girls out into the courtyard of the building, hoping their imaginations will run wild enough to grant me a few minutes of peace.

Him: Busy here too. I notice I like texting you when I'm a bit stressed. You calm me, remind me what's important

"Mommy, be the monster!" Grace yells, just as I sit on the edge of a planter box. She starts to run away from me. "Come get us!"

If I ever go back to working on my résumé, I'm going to put "the Monster" as my most recent job title.

"Grace, not right now," I say.

"Monsta!" Liv shouts.

"Pleeeease," Grace says with her little prayer hands.

"Go look at the pond," I tell them, pointing to a koi pond that should interest them for at least five minutes.

They walk over, and I realize this is a horrible idea.

"Girls, please don't touch the fish!" I yell.

This is why Elijah and I cannot have phone conversations. This is why we cannot FaceTime.

Me: You are the most pleasant distraction for me too

Grace takes off her shoes and socks and steps into the pond.

"Grace, no."

She does not even lift her head to show she's heard me.

"GRACE!"

Him: You are the sexiest woman I've ever met

Liv is now copying her sister, taking off her shoes and socks. She sticks both her hands in the water. They have given me no choice but to intervene.

"Girls, I said NO. STOP."

I grab Grace by the arm, harder than necessary, maybe harder than I ever have.

"Oww!" she screams, insta-tears flooding her eyes.

She looks at me with the same terror Kyle did when I got in his face and told him not to tell me to calm down.

I am the Monster.

I release her arm, and she wraps her fingers around it, grimacing.

"Mommy hurt Gracie," Liv says.

"Honey, Grace is fine," I tell her. "Right, Grace?"

Grace is still holding her arm, looking at me with what can only be described as betrayal in her eyes.

"You girls weren't listening," I say, explaining myself. "That pond is full of bacteria."

Grace continues sniffling.

"I'm sorry about your arm," I say.

She nods, staring at her feet.

"Can you girls just play nicely?"

Grace nods. Liv copies her.

"I don't want to play," Grace says.

"Okay, then sit. Enjoy the sunshine."

They sit.

As the guilt sets in and I wonder if I've damaged Grace forever, she says, "Mom, what's bacteria?"

I sigh. "It's gross. That's what it is."

Liv places her pinkie finger in her ear. So if it wasn't infected before, it is now.

~

After the requisite half hour, we go back to the pediatrician's office. They are not quite ready for us, so the girls make a game of jumping from one floor tile to the next in the waiting room.

Him: I have plans for you this weekend. I can't wait to see you

It's not always possible for me to respond to Elijah, so I just watch his messages come in, savoring each of them, composing responses in my head. This mental composition makes me feel like my brain has come alive again. The lights are now on in my frontal lobe.

My maternal intuition was right—Liv does have an ear infection. When I was a new mom, I was impressed with this intuition thing. It seemed like magic the way mothers *just knew* things about their babies. Now I consider it somewhat handy in certain situations and burdensome in others. Why do I have to be the one with the intuition? It would be nice if Kyle had some, if he could help carry the responsibility of knowing things.

We stop at the pharmacy to pick up ear drops that cost $200 and antibiotics that cost $3. I do not understand American health care. I rack my brain for what else I need at the pharmacy, knowing full well that I'll remember something essential just as we are parking in the garage back home.

I get a pack of overnight diapers for Liv because it's all I can think of, and we wait in the checkout line, which is more of a gauntlet for parents of young children with its displays of knickknacks and candy.

"Mommy, can we have these?" Grace asks, holding up a pack of Skittles.

"No," I say.

How many times a day do I say no? A thousand?

As they continue asking me to buy things and I continue to say no, my eye catches a pregnancy test box next to a display of Kleenex tissues. It seems to be staring at me, sitting there by its lonesome. I think of my still-achy boobs. Elijah and I use condoms. There are a couple of times we didn't, but he pulled out. And besides, it's not like I'm of fertile age.

I cannot be pregnant. It's just wacky hormones, the joys of being a woman in her forties.

But *what if?*

I grab the test and put it under the pack of diapers. *Just in case,* I tell myself. My period will come any day, and I will feel foolish at the first sight of blood.

But *what if?*

~

It is Wednesday, so Liv's ear infection should be mostly cleared up by tomorrow, meaning I should have no issues driving up north on Friday. I will give Kyle detailed instructions for the ear drops and the antibiotics—both verbally and on a Post-it. I don't see how any marriage between people who have small children can stay interesting when wives have to leave husbands instructions on Post-its.

When we get home, the girls clamor for Kyle's attention, which is fine with me because then I can finally respond to Elijah.

What plans do you have for me?

Him: That's for me to know. If you enjoyed last time, you'll enjoy this

241

I'm in a work meeting and you're making me wet

Him: A work meeting at 5? They need to go easier on my baby

That's OK. You always take my stress away

Kyle comes into the kitchen, Grace behind him, hanging on to the waistband of his sweatpants, Liv behind her, hands on Grace's middle—a little train.

"Choo choo," Kyle says with not enough gusto.

The girls giggle and tell him to take them around the house. He gives me a look like *Can you believe these kids?* He wants me to give him a similar look in return. He wants me to bond with him over our offspring and their torturous demands. We used to do this—lean on each other with parenting, vent about it to each other, commiserate. We stopped doing that when I became a stay-at-home mom, when I stopped feeling like we were equal in any way, when I stopped having any compassion for his parenting fatigue.

At dinner, I review the ear infection medication instructions, and we talk about the plan for the weekend. Kyle will be in charge of taking the girls to a birthday party for one of the neighborhood kids, who is turning four. I cannot stand the kid-birthday-party circuit. It's like every mom is trying to one-up the others—the biggest bounce house, the most elaborate decorations, the cutest party favors. Each party is a thousand-dollar Pinterest board explosion that puts pressure on all the moms (like me) who consider it more than enough to order pizza at Costco, get grocery store cupcakes, and pass out party hats. Kyle has never before taken the girls to a birthday party. This one has a tea party theme. He will want to poke his eyes out with a tea party spork. It's possible his boredom will be offset by the way the mothers in attendance will fawn over him: *It's so sweet of you to bring the girls!* Who fawns over the mothers? Or forget fawning. Who gives the mothers basic thanks?

Sometimes, when I daydream of divorce, I ponder Kyle's next wife. I think I would do a fantastic job selecting her. There should be a dating app based on this concept—**NEXT** LOVE could be the name. I would select a woman who would fawn over Kyle. She would have to be someone with no career ambitions, someone passive and pretty in a girl-next-door way. Ideally, she would have far fewer brain cells than me. Not that I think I'm a genius, but I do think my critical thinking skills have gotten me into trouble with this whole marriage institution. He needs someone who does not desire to dip beneath the surface of daily life, someone who garners her worth from supporting him. There are women like this. I have encountered them at the park and at the birthday parties. They do not aspire to more than wifedom and motherhood. Or if they do, they have repressed that aspiration thoroughly. They seem happy. Maybe they are happy, by their definitions. Who am I to judge their definitions? Mine just happen to be different. Arguably, I am unhappier because of my inability to repress and to accept a certain place in this life. In a way, I envy them, as much as I know I can never be them.

~

"You're still good with taking Friday off?" I ask Kyle.

This is an unusually good family dinner. We are all eating the same thing—well, basically. The girls have spaghetti noodles with butter, and Kyle and I are eating spaghetti with an *arrabbiata* sauce. We are all eating breadsticks. It feels almost . . . harmonious. Grace keeps stabbing Liv in the cheek with a breadstick, but Liv is laughing, so I can live with this.

"Yep. I've got Friday," Kyle says.

I am driving up north early in the day on Friday because I have to go to the mortuary to meet with a woman named Carly who said during our phone conversation that she was looking forward to being there for me in my time of need. I cringed. I wanted to tell her that she did not have to speak in this hushed, saccharine voice, that a normal voice would not offend my sensibilities and lead me to emotionally unravel. I suppose these mortuary people go into any new-client situation tiptoeing, unsure of the level of devastation and the bereaved's ability to talk about things like coffin selection. I am devastated, of course, but I know I must accomplish these tasks—for Merry's sake. This is one instance when I am willing to repress for the common good.

"Mommy's leaving again?" Grace says with her pouty face.

"I'm going to see Papa," I tell her. "Remember?"

She nods solemnly. "Can we go? I want another sleepover with Merry."

I hold my breath, waiting to see if she will say more, but she doesn't.

"Another weekend, sweetie. I have some things to take care of up there," I say. Then, redirecting: "Who wants ice cream?"

~

I leave Orange County at nine o'clock Friday morning, which is an hour later than I planned because of the usual household chaos. I get to Fitzgerald Mortuary in Daly City just in time for my four o'clock appointment with Carly, who is waiting for me in the lobby.

When greeting me, she puts a hand on my shoulder, a hand that says *We are compassionate at Fitzgerald Mortuary.* In her other hand, she is holding a black folio case, which likely contains the paperwork we are going to review. It's all very professional, which I guess is what you want in a mortuary.

She leads me to a small room off the lobby with a gigantic circular wood table and four large chairs, big heavy things upholstered in burgundy leather. She sits opposite me and places a folder on the table between us. On the cover, an older woman is looking into the sky at a bright light. It's unclear if it's the sun or a metaphor for impending death. It's a mystery—is she the dearly departed or the loved one left behind? We may never know.

"So I understand your father has CJD?" Carly says. "I'm so sorry. It's such a terrible disease."

"You've heard of it, then?"

"Fitzgerald is one of the largest mortuaries in the Bay Area. We've heard of almost everything."

My mind wanders to consider the horrific nature of her job. She's consoled people in the wake of myriad cancers, multivehicle crashes, sudden infant death syndrome, freak accidents, bullets to the head, stab wounds. I'm not sure how she seems so calm.

"I'm sure it's a hard job," I say.

"Not as hard as yours."

I almost say "Oh, I don't work," but then realize she's talking about the job I'm doing now, being here, making arrangements for my dad's death, a truly surreal task.

She reviews all the services the mortuary provides—everything from ordering death certificates, publishing an obituary, and obtaining cremation permits (who knew?) to creating in memoriam pamphlets for a funeral service and making jewelry out of ashes. There are brochures for each offering, a smattering of them.

"I understand you are thinking of cremation?"

I nod. Merry said that's what he would want. They had a conversation about it a while back. Kyle and I have never talked about such things at all. We are young enough to be in complete denial of our mortality. In any case, I'm glad my dad would want cremation. I've never liked the idea of a body being buried in the ground. It seems damp and dark and worm-ridden.

"We have a great selection of urns," she says, pulling another brochure from her folio case. "Or you can order something online and bring it to us. We can also place the ashes in multiple urns for your mother or siblings or . . ."

"Stepmom," I say. "No siblings."

"I understand," she says. "It's certainly hard to be doing all this on your own."

I think of Grace and Liv sitting together at a table like this one day, perusing brochures while grieving Kyle or me. I'm glad they have each other.

"We also have a few options for the cremation box," she says.

She shows me the options. The first is an ornate coffin and is priced at $1,100. The second is a slightly less ornate $600 coffin. And the third is a cardboard box that, inexplicably, costs $75. Must be special, death-appropriate cardboard.

"I'm a bit confused," I say. "This box . . . it just burns with him?"

This is possibly the strangest conversation I've ever had.

"Yes," Carly says.

I can hear my dad's laugh—so hearty and full that he starts coughing at the tail end of it, his body desperate for oxygen. *Nikki Bear, you are not paying a thousand bucks for a box that will be set on fire.*

"My dad would want the cardboard one."

She nods, circling that option on her little menu sheet.

"Oh, before I forget, he's going to be in a clinical study. They'll be doing a brain autopsy. You guys can coordinate all that?"

"Of course. We can arrange for the necessary transfers to and from the autopsy facility and notify you when he's back in our care."

For the first time during this odd meeting, I am overcome with the grief that I told myself to leave in the car. There's something about envisioning my dad's body being shuttled to and fro that makes my chest tight.

Carly is likely trained in identifying distress. She passes me a box of Kleenex—I now notice that this little room has three of them.

She confirms that we are not having a formal service. My dad wouldn't want that. Merry and I agreed on inviting his buddies to a celebration of life at the local golf club. We will tell everyone to wear Tommy Bahama shirts. There will be cocktails.

Carly asks if my dad has any jewelry I want them to set aside before the cremation. I think of how he lost his wedding band approximately one month after marrying Merry—they never stopped laughing about that.

"No jewelry," I tell her.

She asks me if he has any metal in his body, as that can cause explosions in the cremation chamber. I tell her about his hip replacement. He had that about five years ago. I hated visiting him in the hospital, seeing him incapacitated. I had no idea then what I'd have to witness later.

"What about clothing? Do you want to save anything he comes in wearing, or would you like us to cremate it with him?"

Lately, my dad is wearing T-shirts with slits cut up the back so they're more like hospital gowns—easier for Merry and Frank to get on and off. I picture his favorite shirts—the Joe's Bar one, the Maui Brewing Company one, the Old Guys Rule one. Even though they have slits cut up the back, I want to save them.

"I'd love if you set his clothes aside."

She makes a note.

I hear my dad again: *Nikki, don't make them keep my tighty-whities.*

I smile. I would share this with Carly, but I already know that when he dies, he will be wearing a diaper.

〜

After the appointment, I sit in my car, staring out the window, for a half hour.

Thinking of you.

Elijah.

I don't even have the presence of mind to respond.

When I've accrued sufficient staring-at-nothing time, I head to see my dad. I've spent the past hour speaking as if he's already dead, so part of me half expects to arrive at the house and find this to be true, Merry standing out front, eyes red, face drawn.

When I get there, my dad is, in fact, still alive, though noticeably closer to being not alive than he was a week ago. The weight loss is startling, his body disappearing before my very eyes. Where do they go, the cells that make a life?

I sit next to him as he sleeps. Merry sits at the foot of the bed, one hand on his ankle.

"He's almost always sleeping now," she says.

"How's his eating?"

She shrugs. "Not great. We're sticking to yogurt, oatmeal, soft stuff."

The muscles he needs to swallow are atrophying like all the other muscles in his body.

Frank comes in from the back deck, where he was taking his dinner break. His face brightens when he sees me, and he says, "Well, howdy ho."

He gives me his assessment, repeating some of what Merry has already told me.

"His spasticity is worse," he says. "See how his muscles are all tight, how his knees and elbows are bent like that? It's common with brain damage."

When I take my dad's hand, it is in a clenched fist. I hold the fist. He stirs.

"Hey, Daddy."

His eyes blink open. It must take a while for me to come into focus, but he eventually says "Hi" in his soft, strained voice.

"I'm going to finish making dinner," Merry says, standing from the bed, giving his leg a pat.

"And I'll give you two some privacy," Frank says.

That leaves just Dad and me.

"You have pretty eyes," he says, looking at me. He's always said I have pretty eyes. As I'm about to thank him, he says, "I see four of them." I'm not sure if he's serious until he laughs, and then I laugh, grateful for his ability to still joke.

I lie next to him, my head on his bony shoulder. He stares up at the ceiling.

"What do you see?" I ask.

Vision issues, even blindness, are common as CJD progresses. It is truly the worst disease I have ever heard of.

"It's raining," he says with a wistful smile.

I don't question him. I just say, "I love rain."

"Me too," he says.

My phone buzzes in my pocket. Elijah, again.

You okay, beautiful?

I put it back in my pocket.

"Dad?"

His eyes don't flick to me. He just keeps staring at the ceiling, at the rain.

"Daddy? I have to tell you something."

He continues staring.

"I'm having an affair," I whisper.

It feels like confession, my dad the all-forgiving priest, a messenger of God on earth.

"Am I a terrible person?"

His mouth opens slightly, but he doesn't respond. Then, a moment later, he whispers something I can't quite hear.

"What did you say?" I lean closer, close enough to smell the musty odor that is his breath, the smell of decay.

His eyes finally shift and meet mine.

"Rose?" he says.

Rose was my mother.

Again, I don't question him. I just say, "Yes?"

"I love you, Rose."

I wonder if he sees her waiting for him in the rain. I don't ask. It doesn't matter.

"I love you, Dad," I say.

~

I wait until after dinner to text Elijah.

> Hey. Sorry. Been such a strange, hard day.

> Him: I've been thinking of you. If you're not up for getting together tomorrow, I understand. I just want to support you however I can

I have received no texts from Kyle, for the record. If I make a thing about this to him, he will say, "I assumed if you wanted to talk, you would text me." He has informed me before that he is "not a mind reader."

> I definitely want to see you. Need to see you. You are a portal back to myself and all that is good in this bizarre life

I may have had too much wine at dinner.

> Him: I can't wait to hold you

> I can't wait to be held

Amid all the lies, that is a truth. I cannot wait to be held.

~

That's what he does the moment I show up at his door—he holds me. He pulls me against his chest, kisses the top of my head, and holds me. I start to cry—not dainty feminine tears but big ugly bawling that I didn't even know I had in me.

"I'm here," he says.

That fact, and my gratitude for it, makes me cry harder.

He does something I would normally consider weird—he lifts me off the ground and cradles me in his arms like I'm his child. He is a large enough man for this to be possible, and it feels right and good. He carries me to the bedroom, places me on the bed. The room is dimly lit by candles—it's a dreary San Francisco day, not much light streaming through the windows. I am overcome with a sudden desire to sleep—not just a nap, but a multiday coma-like event.

"I don't know what's wrong with me," I tell him once I've composed myself.

He lies next to me.

"I do," he says. "Your dad is dying."

I stare at the ceiling, then think of my dad staring at the ceiling, seeing rain. This makes me cry all over again.

He traces the shape of my face with his fingertip.

"I'm sorry. I know you had something planned for us, and—"

He shushes me, just like he did when I was blindfolded.

"Hey, I'm not in any rush. You know that, right? We've got time for all my plans. Today, I just want to be next to you and hold you."

All my plans.

What are all his plans?

Can my life accommodate all his plans?

"I'm sure I'll feel better in a little bit," I say. "It's just like . . . whiplash. Going from seeing my dad like he is to seeing you . . . like you are."

"I bet."

"I don't want to spend our one day together *sobbing*."

"We have many more days together," he says. "I want to be present with the real you, the full you. If that you is sobbing, so be it."

"Why are you so nice?"

"My mama raised me right."

"So with all the assholes I've encountered, I should really blame their mothers? Seems like that's going pretty hard on the mothers."

He laughs, having no idea how much more I could say on this topic.

"Can you tell me something happy?" I ask. "Something about you. Something that has nothing to do with anyone dying."

"I sure can," he says. "I found out today that I passed the bar."

I sit bolt upright. "What? You did?"

He smiles. "I did."

"Oh my god, that's amazing, Elijah. Congratulations."

I hug him, surprising myself with how overjoyed I feel for him. I have become entirely too invested in this whole thing.

"Thank you, thank you," he says.

"We need champagne! We need to go celebrate!"

He laughs at me the way I laugh at Grace and Liv when they are going bananas about something like an Amazon shipment of new markers.

"Slow down," he says. "This might not be the best night for celebrating."

"No, this is the very best night for celebrating. This is the night of the day you found out you passed the bar."

He looks at me skeptically. "You sure you're up for it?"

"I am now."

"It's really fine if we postpone."

"I said I'm up for it. Let's go."

~

My knowledge of celebration-worthy restaurants in San Francisco is limited, so I tell Elijah to pick. He picks a fish house on Pier 39, and we manage to get a table with a view of the bay and Golden Gate Bridge. We start with a bottle of champagne and baked oysters.

"This is my treat," he says, taking his first sip of champagne. "So don't be pulling out your wallet at the end or something crazy like that."

"Whatever you say, Esquire."

He laughs.

We order our entrées—the filet for him, swordfish for me—and then he leans across the table with a serious look on his face.

"Thank you for being here with me," he says.

"Oh, stop. I'm so glad I could be here with you."

"I've been thinking."

I take a sip of champagne that I sense I'll need.

"I want to be more to you," he says.

"More to me?"

"I mean, don't get me wrong—I like what we're doing. I just want it to be known that I really like you. I don't want to just be your Bay Area hookup or whatever."

"Oh," I say, reaching for a piece of bread in the basket, and then using it as one would a stress ball. "That's kind of a crass way of putting it. I wouldn't say you're my Bay Area hookup. That implies I have other area hookups."

I laugh. This is what I do when I'm nervous, when the gravity of a particular moment overwhelms me. Elijah does not laugh.

"I'm not really sure what I am to you. And maybe it's too soon to ask. It's not like we've known each other that long."

"I guess I wasn't really thinking about putting a label on it," I say. It is a line that men usually give women who want more, a line that criticizes the woman's need for definition as a cover for commitment issues. I hate myself for using it.

"I'm just looking for some sense of where you're at, that's all." He's so direct, so honest. It's disarming. "It's selfish, really. I want to know

253

how much I need to protect my heart. If you're not in this with any seriousness, then I need to reel myself in. You know what I'm saying?"

I do know what he is saying, and if I was as direct and honest as him, I would say, *You should protect your heart. I'm a mess. My name isn't even Katrina. Please reel yourself in.*

Instead, though, I say, "I totally get it" and then fail to elaborate on what exactly I get or what I plan to do about it.

"I don't want to put pressure," he says. "But I think I need to know where you see this going. Not tonight. But soon. Next time I see you?"

My bread/stress ball has become gummy from the sweat in my palm. I keep squeezing it.

"Okay, yeah, I understand," I say.

I don't see this going anywhere.

Or rather, I have to divorce my husband before this can go anywhere.

Yes, I have a husband.

And children. Two of them.

My name is Nicole.

Do you still want to know where this is going?

I am getting hot, this conversation throwing off whatever internal systems normally keep me at a reasonable temperature. I take a sip of water, let a cube of ice roll around my mouth.

"I'm sorry," he says. "I've made it weird."

I swallow the ice cube, feel it slide down my throat. I take another sip of water. My body cools.

"No, no, I'm the one who has made it weird," I say. "It is one of my fortes."

He laughs. We are back to laughing.

"Can I ask what you want for your future? Like, in general," I say.

He leans back in his chair, puts his hands behind his head.

"I don't know. I think I'd like to get married. Be a dad someday."

Elijah wants to be a dad.

I am still carrying around the pregnancy test in my purse. I haven't gotten my period, and I haven't peed on the stick. I'm starting to think

I'm not afraid that I am pregnant—I'm afraid that I'm not. Elijah would be thrilled if I were pregnant. I know he would. A pregnancy would force the future I'm too afraid to want. Elijah would be an involved father, the type of father who makes motherhood enjoyable. The girls would love to have a baby in their lives. They would be too young to understand the scandal of it all. Kyle would be appalled, as he should be. Our separation would be inevitable, as it should be.

"I don't want to get married and be a dad *tomorrow*," Elijah clarifies. "Please tell me I haven't ruined the night."

"No, not at all," I say. "I'm the one who asked."

He leans across the table, puts his hands on top of mine.

"Let's not get into all this tonight, okay? Let's just enjoy ourselves."

"Deal," I say. Then, to release the pressure valve, I raise my eyebrows suggestively and say, "I'm particularly looking forward to something sweet back at your place."

"It puts me at ease to know you are a huge dork," he says.

"The hugest."

~

We have sex that night—not the soft, sensual sex of last time, but something more desperate and primal. It's what my body needs, a forceful expulsion of energy. In the morning, we have sex again, this time slower, tender. Kyle's never understood the necessity for different types of sex, the importance of context. He has always wanted the same kind of sex from me, whether I'm wearing a lace nightie or a sweatshirt covered in baby puke. He seems perpetually confused that my needs change, that I have needs at all.

Elijah walks me to my car, and we linger there, as we usually do. I feel compelled to say "I think I love you." The words are right there, swirling around my mouth like the ice cube. Either they will melt away or I will spit them out impulsively. I know, though, that I cannot say these words without repercussions. We are not teenagers.

"Have I scared you off? Will I see you next week?" he asks, his hands on my waist, his cheek pressed against mine, his breath hot on my ear.

I avoid the first question and say, "I think you'll see me."

"You like to leave me guessing."

He takes a bite of my lobe.

"You seem to like the guesswork."

"I have no choice but to withstand it," he says.

He moves his mouth to mine, kisses me, his lips enveloping me. I imagine my whole self being sucked through his lips, into his body, away from reality and all its troubles.

"I really care for you," I say, downgrading the sentiment of what I want to say.

"I really care for you too."

He kisses me again.

"Are you sure you're real?" I ask him.

"Are you sure YOU'RE real?"

"I'm not sure, actually," I say.

He kisses me yet again.

"I should head back to see my dad."

"Of course you should."

"It's always so hard to say goodbye."

"Brutal."

I give him one final kiss, then get in the car.

As I pull away, I start formulating a speech to Kyle, an asking-for-a-divorce speech.

Things haven't been good with us for a while.

What if we're both happier apart?

I want a trial separation, just to see.

Usually, I can predict Kyle's reactions. I know him far better than he knows himself. With this, though, I'm not sure. His ego will not be happy with the rejection. He may lash out. But deep down, I think he will be relieved, whether he admits it or not. Or maybe I'm just telling myself that.

I don't have to mention a thing about Elijah. I just have to keep it about me.

Maybe it's grief.

Maybe we'll separate and I'll change my mind.

But I have to find out.

Please let me find out.

Chapter 19

ROSE

February 14, 1985

Dear Diary,

It is Valentine's Day, and I am full of love for none of the typical reasons.

I got into Cornell! With a scholarship, no less!

The acceptance packet—far more substantial than a letter—came in the mail today. The greatest valentine of all. It said, *Will you be mine?* And I want so badly to say *YES*.

In 1956, *McCall's* ran an article entitled "The Mother Who Ran Away." It became the highest single-issue sale ever. In the 1960s, *Redbook's* editors asked readers to provide them with examples of "Why Young Mothers Feel Trapped," and they received twenty-four thousand replies.

I am not the only one who feels caged.

I am not the only one who daydreams of running away.

On my recent trips to the library, I've been researching family structures across time and culture to understand the true importance of the mother.

In traditional Chinese families, the father's extended family had far more say over child-rearing than the mother in the nuclear family.

Among the Cheyenne, a girl is expected to have a strained relationship with her mother and to go to her aunt for comfort and guidance.

The Zinacantecos of southern Mexico lack a word differentiating parents and children from other social groupings. They simply identify the basic unit of social and personal responsibility as a *house*.

In the Caribbean, children are raised by various people, not just their biological parents. Genetic ties do not reign supreme.

What this tells me is that Western society infuses the mother with importance and meaning (again, to keep women at home and too distracted by their maternal duties to attempt to take power from men).

What this tells me is that children don't *need* a mother in the way we think they do.

I am rationalizing. I know this.

To continue rationalizing:

There *are* women who leave their children. In 1943, Doris Lessing left behind her three-year-old son and one-year-old daughter to pursue her writing career (and given the sheer volume of beautiful work she created, can't one argue that she made a good decision?). It's said that she thought that only if her children didn't have a mother could they really be themselves. Perhaps that's true, and/or perhaps that's her own rationalization.

In her 1962 novel *The Golden Notebook*, the character of Anna (Lessing's alter ego, one can assume) comments on her partner's sense of entitlement to her time and attention and her inability to express her own needs. The only solution she can think of is resignation to her unhappiness.

I have no information on how her children fared without her. But I assume they fared.

Would Nicole be okay without me?

In the basic sense, she would. Rob is nothing but dutiful. He adores her. He will provide for her. He will likely meet another woman. He's handsome and about to be making good money as a dentist. He is a decent man. I have made many mistakes, but choosing him was not one of them.

A couple of nights ago, I asked him, "What if something happened to me? Would you and Nicole be okay?"

He looked at me strangely, rightly so, and said, "Nothing is going to happen to you." He put his hand on top of mine, rubbed it with his thumb. I had to look away so I wouldn't cry.

"I'm worried about you," he said.

I mustered all my strength to lie: "There's nothing to worry about."

Nicole is three. She will have no memories of me. That may be for the best. Rob's new wife will be her mother, for all intents and purposes. Maybe she will do a better job than I have.

I will go. I will be free. I will become a doctor of philosophy. I will have a rich, full life. I will be happy. Or maybe I will go mad. I am a woman on the verge—of madness or bliss? I am willing to risk the madness for a chance at bliss.

When in doubt of my pursuit, I will think of something Germaine Greer said: The best thing I can do for my community and loved ones is to be happy.

~

Rob,

I'm leaving you this diary.

So you understand that it's not your fault. Or Nicole's.

This life is not for me. I wish it was.

I won't return. Even if I have a change of heart, which I don't expect I will, it would be unfair of me to impose myself on your life again.

It's up to you what you tell Nicole.

I'm sorry for hurting you. And her. Though I trust you will protect her from the worst of the hurt.

I'm sorry for who I am, for who I need to be.

You are a good man. I do love you.

PS: I have left a tuna casserole in the fridge.

Part 3

.

Chapter 20

NICOLE

It is Wednesday. I still haven't peed on the stick. I've come to enjoy this little fantasy of a baby in my belly and don't want it to end. It's helping me propel myself toward the conversation I know I need to have with Kyle.

I stare at him across the dinner table as he shovels forkfuls of my Mexican casserole into his mouth. Tonight, I'll do it. I'll tell him I want a divorce. I chickened out Monday and again yesterday. Tonight is the night.

The girls give me a particularly hard time before bed, as if they know my mind is elsewhere and they are intent on bringing my attention back to them. It's possible they sense my anxiety and that fills them with their own anxiety, and the only way they know how to process that is by acting out, refusing to cooperate with the bedtime routine that we've done hundreds of times.

"Come on, girls, I need you to help me out," I say, my voice almost as whiny as theirs.

"What if there's a monster in the closet?" Grace says. She forces her lower lip to quiver.

"Grace, there is no monster in the closet. Do you want to look again?"

Both girls hide behind my legs as I open the closet door. I flip on the light to reveal no monster.

"But what if a monster comes later?" Grace asks.

"Monsta?" Liv says, brows furrowed.

"There are no monsters in this house, remember? This house is full of—"

"Love!" Grace shouts.

That's what I tell them: there are no monsters because this house is full of love. This house is also full of a fair bit of resentment, and they seem to have forgotten that their own mother is the Monster.

"Mommy, where's Ella?" Grace asks.

Ella is one of her dolls. Actually, several of her dolls have gone by Ella at various times. I don't know who the current Ella is.

"I don't know, sweetie. Where did you leave her?"

"I thought she was in here," she says, turning in a circle, scanning the room.

This happens a lot at bedtime—toys and dolls cannot be located. There is an escalation of panic. This is another of Grace's procrastination techniques.

"Grace, we'll find her in the morning, okay? I'm not going up and down the stairs twelve times looking for things."

Grace falls to the floor, as if my attempt to set a firm boundary has delivered a blow to her kneecaps.

"But I *need* her!"

"Why don't you go look in the usual places? You need to keep better track of your things, remember?"

When I look over at Liv, her eyelids are at half mast. Liv has recently become unable to physically function past a certain time. It is a blessing. Grace's ability to summon energy long past the time she should be sleeping is a source of ongoing torture.

"I'm too afraid to go look by myself."

She likes to pull the fear card when she is really just lazy and wants me to find the damn doll.

"I'll go with you, then. I'm not going to do it for you."

She stands, assumes a confident posture that does not align at all with her emotional display of a few moments ago.

I carry Liv, her sweet little face resting on my shoulder, because if I try to leave her alone in their room, I risk a meltdown that will send enough cortisol through her veins to keep her awake for another three hours. Grace walks ahead of us, and I follow her through the living room, then the kitchen, where she finds Ella sitting in the toy baby stroller. She cradles the doll in her arms, says, "Hello, my darling. Ready for bed?" in this adoring voice. Perhaps I'm not doing so badly at mothering if she believes this is how moms interact with their babies. Then again, she may just be imitating a YouTube video.

With Ella safely secured, I wrestle them into their pajamas and brush their teeth, then start book-reading time. A few pages into the first book about a giraffe who learns to dance, Grace protests:

"I don't like this story."

Books have become much like snacks—often rejected for no good reason.

I give her other options, and she selects a Berenstain Bears book in which the cubs have a bad case of the "gimmies" and their dolt of a father makes it worse by giving them whatever they want.

Halfway through the book, Grace protests again:

"I don't like this one either."

"Grace, I think you're just procrastinating," I say in my calm voice, though I can feel my blood pressure rising and my body getting hot.

"I am not!" She hates when I tell her she's procrastinating, though I'm not even sure she knows what it means.

Liv starts crying upon hearing her sister upset—dramatic sobbing that is characteristic of her being overtired.

"Liv, shut up!" Grace says.

"Grace!" I yell.

Liv is now hysterical. I pull her from bed, bounce her in my arms.

"Liv is a baby! Liv is a baby!" Grace says.

"Grace, stop," I tell her, giving her my don't-fuck-with-me eyes. The expected sweat has now come out of every pore in my body, and I feel like I could fry an egg on my forehead.

"I *hate* you," Grace says.

She's recently into the word *hate*. She wields it like a weapon.

Liv starts to settle, and I place her back in her bed. Grace, however, is a demon.

"I'm not going to bed," she says, sitting up, arms folded across her chest.

I hate you, I think. I want to be allowed to be as childish as her, to wield my own verbal weapons. Instead, I take my rage and impulsively crouch down and pound my fist into the floor, forgetting that just beneath the carpet is a cement foundation.

"Fuck," I say, too startled by my pain to control my language.

That—the *fuck* and my obvious pain—transforms Grace back into an empathic future health-care professional.

"Are you okay, Mommy?" she asks in her sweetest voice.

Liv is now wide eyed and full-on sucking her thumb, which is not something she has done in months. I have traumatized her.

I clutch my hand against my chest, slowly moving the fingers. Nothing is broken. There will likely be a bruise along the pinky side of my fist, a weeklong reminder of when I momentarily lost my mind.

"I'm okay," I say, my teeth chattering from stress or shock or the rapid cooling of the sweat coating my body. "Now can we please go to bed?"

There is zero protest. I cover them each with their blankets and wish them sweet dreams. They do not call for me after I close their door. There is not a single peep. Perhaps I need to nearly break my hand every night. I have scared them into submission, much like I did with the primal-screaming incident. I should write a book about my parenting techniques.

～

Kyle is sitting in bed, legs outstretched, one ankle crossed over the other.

"Rough one, huh?" he says, eyes on the TV. He loves watching *Dateline*, which makes me wonder sometimes if he's planning on killing me. I mean, if things got *really* bad.

"Rough one." I shake out my hand, grimacing at the return of sensation. Kyle does not comment on this.

I inhale as deeply as I can, feeling my heart rate escalate as I catapult myself into this next life-changing moment.

"Why don't you ever help?" I ask.

"Huh?" he says, taking his eyes off the TV.

"You can hear us in there, right? Why don't you ever help?"

"Babe, I know you've got it handled."

I am supposed to take this as a compliment. I am supposed to be charmed.

"I don't have it handled," I say. "Like, ever."

He sighs. "Babe—"

I interrupt, not wanting to hear how I'm being dramatic. "We need to talk."

He lifts the remotes, turns off the TV.

"Okay?"

His tone is resigned, like he's just waiting for me to lay into him with my grievances.

As I'm about to say the words—*I want a divorce*—my phone starts blaring, the ringer on at full blast because I forgot to turn down the volume after the girls watched YouTube over dinner (the iPad was out of battery because Kyle neglected to plug it in). I'm so startled that I drop it while attempting to take it out of my pocket. It slides across the wood floor, face up so I can see that the caller is Merry. She doesn't usually call, especially at night like this, so I have to answer.

"Is everything okay?"

There is a pause and then the sound of sniffling. She is crying.

"Mer, what's wrong?"

My dad is dead, I think. *His heart gave out. His spirit gave up. He is gone.*

"He's okay," she says.

I sit on the bed, dizzy from attempts to keep up with my fluctuating emotional states.

"I mean, not *okay*. But he's stable," she says. "It's just . . ."

"What? What is it?"

More sniffling.

"The hospice nurse came today. She said he's moving close to a comatose state."

Her voice cracks on the word *comatose*. It is as if I can hear her very being collapsing.

"Okay," I say. "Okay."

A terrible word for the situation—*okay*. Nothing is okay.

"I asked her how long he has. I mean, you were just here this weekend. I don't want you coming up if he has time. I just don't know. She doesn't know. It could be days. A week. Two weeks."

"I'll come up."

There is no thought in the matter. I must be there. I could not live with myself if I wasn't there.

My eyes flick to Kyle. He looks frightened, and I'm overcome with a dormant love for him. His fear makes him look like a little boy.

"I'll get a flight first thing in the morning," I say. "I can bring the girls or . . ."

Kyle shakes his head, mouths, "I'll watch them."

"I'll be there," I tell Merry. I am about to say "Tell Dad to wait for me," but I stop myself. I don't want to burden him with my desires. If he needs to go, he should go. But I like to think he will wait for me.

~

I book a flight from Orange County to San Francisco for the next morning at seven o'clock. Kyle is in crisis mode. He thrives in this mode, this mode that allows for the practical action and problem-solving that I despise in most of our marital conversations. *Don't fix it, just listen to me*—the wife's lament.

"I don't know how long I'll be gone," I say.

"It's okay. The girls will be fine with me. I can take a little time off work. Or just let them watch a lot of YouTube."

"No judgment," I say, though all I've done lately is judge.

Kyle and I may not be "meant to be," whatever that even means, but he's not an awful human being. I, on the other hand, may be.

I pack a suitcase while Kyle keeps watching TV. I don't know how long I'll be gone, so I pack about half my entire closet. It is surreal to think that when I return, when I unpack this suitcase, my dad will be dead.

By the time I get in bed, Kyle is already asleep, snoring away. I gently push on his back so he rolls on his side. I text Elijah:

My dad is going downhill. I'm flying up tomorrow

He responds immediately because his generation is never without their phones. I am old enough to wrestle with such an attachment.

I'm so sorry. How can I be there for you? Can I send food to your mom's place?

My mom's place. I haven't told him that my mom died, that I have a stepmom. There is so much he doesn't know.

That's sweet. Let me get up there and see what's going on first

There are three dots for a while, and I wonder what paragraph-length text he's composing. The dots go away and then reappear momentarily before his words appear:

I think I love you

271

There it is. The words I have both longed and feared to hear. My body thrums with ecstatic energy. If I listen to my body, his love for me is a good thing. My head tells me it's all much more complicated. He adds more:

Sorry. It's not the right time to say that. I just felt . . . verklempt.

I smile.

Verklempt? Nice word choice.

Him: Yes. Verklempt. I do love you though. And I want to be there for you however I can

I respond with something thrilling, words that put me at the top of a roller coaster, soaring down through the breeze, not knowing if I'll crash into the ground or rise up into the sky again:

I think I love you too

~

When I see my dad, I sigh with relief. Things are not as dire as I'd envisioned. He is still here, still him. I lie next to him in bed, take comfort in his warmth. His eyes remain closed, but his lips turn upward in a small smile. Merry says he doesn't open his eyes much anymore.

He is more contracted than he was just a few days ago, curled into himself, almost into a fetal position. I play the role of big spoon, my body wrapped around his. It is a role I never thought I'd play.

He is so, so thin. It's no wonder they call it a wasting disease. I stare at his legs, mere sticks now. With all the surrounding flesh gone, the bones are all that remain, smaller than I ever thought possible. I place my palm on his femur, marveling. Where did his flesh *go*?

His breathing is fast and shallow. There is an oxygen machine now, emitting rhythmic whooshing sounds. Merry says his heart rate has been increasing, which the hospice nurse said happens near the end. His heart is literally racing to get enough blood to his vital organs. The body is programmed for survival. It will make all kinds of adjustments to carry on.

~

Frank comes to the house with jars of baby food, several varieties of Gerber. My dad is subsisting on food my daughters are too old to eat. I trade spots with Merry, watch as she attempts to spoon-feed my dad, deliver minuscule portions into the small opening he is able to make with the slight parting of his lips. It is excruciating to witness.

"I'll be right back," I say, finding it impossible to stay.

There's a knock at the front door, and I answer it. A thirtysomething woman in navy blue scrubs is standing there with an overstuffed bag over one shoulder and a clipboard in her hands. She frees up one hand and sticks it out to me.

"Hi," she says. "I'm Becky, the hospice nurse."

"Oh, hi," I say.

"Are you Rob's daughter?"

I like that she refers to him by name, that she knows his name without consulting her clipboard.

"I am. Nicole."

I open the door to give her a wider berth, and she comes in. She is bouncy and energetic, and I want her cheerfulness to be contagious. I follow her to my dad's room, where Merry is still spoon-feeding him.

"Hi, Meredith," Becky says. She is good with names. I wonder how many visits she has per day with the dying and their agonized families. I wonder how she remains so perky.

"I know you said to consider not feeding him," Merry says to Becky, guilt all over her face. "I just . . . can't."

Becky gives her a thin smile and puts a hand on her shoulder. "It's okay. These last days are as much about your comfort as they are about his."

"Wait, why should we stop feeding him?" I ask. Merry hasn't told me this.

Becky goes to my dad, places a thermometer in his mouth.

"Well, there's the risk of aspiration pneumonia because he's having trouble swallowing," she says. "But at this stage, it is what it is."

She pries open my dad's eyes, points a little flashlight into them.

"His eyes are fixed and not responding to light."

"What does that mean?" I ask.

"He's likely going blind."

Merry's face falls, and she starts to cry, her shoulders heaving. I go to her, hold her, let her put her weight into me.

"Can he hear us?" I ask.

"Yes," Becky says without hesitation. "Hearing is the first sense we gain in the womb and the last we lose."

If he can hear us, does he comprehend that he's dying? He appears so calm. I like to think he does comprehend and that he has come to acceptance and peace. It is the rest of us who suffer.

"I can't be here," Merry says before leaving the room.

I follow her to the kitchen. She falls to her knees, hanging on to the edge of the granite counter. She weeps. I crouch next to her, my own tears coming.

"I don't know who I'll be without him," she says.

He has been the sun she's revolved around all these years. Movies glamorize this as the ultimate form of love, something to aspire to. I see the dark side.

"You don't have to know that right now," I tell her.

We stay like that on the floor until Becky comes into the kitchen and says, "Okay, all set. I'll be back tomorrow."

I stand. "Is there anything we should be doing for him?"

"You're doing it," she says brightly. "Just be with him. He knows you're here. He can hear you. Talk to him."

~

As soon as she leaves, I heed her advice. I go to my dad. Frank has elevated the back of the bed so he's sitting up.

"I was going to bring him into the other room for dinner," Frank says. "Merry likes that."

He's wheeled over the Hoyer lift, a manual hydraulic lift that looks like a giant version of that arcade game where you maneuver a claw to grasp a toy. With the Hoyer lift, the "claw" connects to a sling that's placed under my dad's body. With a push of a button, he can be lifted out of bed and placed in his wheelchair.

"Can I just have a minute with him?" I ask.

Frank says, "Absolutely!" and quickly makes himself scarce.

I sit next to my dad, his eyes still closed. He is wearing his navy blue Wave Rider T-shirt, a favorite, cut up the back like all his shirts now.

My face is inches from his. I see up close the definition of his cheekbones.

"You look like a runway model," I tell him.

We've always preferred levity in times of crisis.

"Daddy," I say, leaning in close to his ear, my lips already quivering. "You've been such a good dad. You know that, right? I love you so much."

His lips part as if he may want to say something back, his usual "Love ya," perhaps. But no sound comes. I stare at his mouth, which is slightly agape, notice that his bottom front teeth are chipped, something I'd never noticed before. He's always been a chronic nail-biter. When I was a teenager, he let me paint his nails pink in an attempt to help him quit.

"I hope it doesn't hurt you when they use this lift thing," I say. "I'm sure you just want to rest in bed."

He gives a barely perceptible shake of his head, as if rejecting the notion that he is at all bothered by the lift or anything else that's happening to him. He's never been one to admit struggle.

When Frank returns, I help him slide the sling under my dad's body—no easy feat. When he's securely latched to the lift, I watch as Frank operates the machine, my dad's body slowly levitating off the bed, his knees pulled into his chest. Suspended in the air, he looks like a baby in a blanket held in the stork's beak. He looks as if he is about to be delivered, and maybe he is. Maybe that's what death is—a delivery.

~

I admit it is nice to have him at the dinner table, even if he sits in silence. I remember what the hospice nurse said about him being able to hear.

"You know what one of my favorite dad memories is?" I say to Merry.

She has made us plates of chicken and rice, but she is just pushing her food around her plate with her fork, creating labyrinths through the rice.

"Hmm?" she asks, not looking up.

"Remember when he was in his running phase?" I ask.

It was when I was eleven or twelve, that awkward transition between child and teenager, between thinking your parents are cool and thinking they are absolutely mortifying. My dad had become something of a runner, signing up for local 5Ks. I vacillated between standing on the sidelines, cheering him on, and staying as far away from the races as possible, worried someone from school would see me with him while he was wearing his dorky sweatband and matching athletic socks.

"I do remember," Merry says with a wistful smile. "He was in the best shape of his life then."

During my freshman year of high school, he signed up for the San Francisco Marathon. He'd run every morning before the sun came up. I remember the sound of the door closing behind him when he sneaked out in those early hours. When I heard him come back, that served as my alarm telling me to wake up. He'd make breakfast for Merry and me, usually still wearing his running clothes, then shower and get ready for his workday while we ate. I knew it was a big deal, this race, the training and dedication involved. But I was also a new teenager and couldn't be bothered to give many things beyond myself much attention.

"Remember that one morning . . ."

I start laughing before I can even continue, the mental image of the story I'm about to recount triggering instant glee.

Merry looks confused for just a few seconds, and then it clicks for her, and she can't help but laugh too.

"The shorts!" she says.

My dad always wore these short shorts—another reason I didn't want to be seen with him at races. On this one morning, I came into the kitchen while he was making breakfast after his run and found him wearing the shorts inside out, with the hammock-like netting on the outside. At first, I wasn't sure what I was looking at, but then Merry came in behind me and laughed harder than I'd ever heard her laugh. She doubled over, one arm clutching her stomach. It took her a solid five minutes to catch her breath.

"Didn't you realize you had no . . . support . . . down there?" she said, before erupting in laughter again.

"I get dressed in the dark," he protested. "Because I don't want to wake you by turning on the light."

"And I appreciate that almost as much as I appreciate this sight before my eyes," she said.

I laughed along with her. "Did you notice anybody giving you weird looks?" I asked him.

He shrugged. "I don't think so."

Merry and I laughed about that for days. We begged him to wear his shorts inside out for the marathon, told him he would get more enthusiastic cheers from the crowds that way.

"You girls are ridiculous," he said.

I look to Dad's face now and think I see a small smile there. Maybe I'm imagining it.

"I was so proud of you when you ran that marathon, Dad," I say to him.

His head bobs a little, a nod, maybe.

～

After dinner, I wheel him back to his room and help Frank use the lift to get him back into bed.

"His lips are dry. He's probably a bit parched," Frank says.

He brings over what looks like a lollipop, but there's a small sponge at the end where the candy would be. He dips the sponge into the glass of water at Dad's bedside, then places it on Dad's lips. Dad's lips manage to purse around the sponge, giving it enough pressure to extract a tiny amount of water.

Merry comes in. She gives him little kisses on his cheek—five, ten, twenty of them.

"Good night, my love," she says. She strokes his bald head. I stare at the constellations of sunspots on it, start to count them, stop when I get to thirty.

I give him a kiss on his other cheek—just one.

"I'll be right upstairs," I tell him, in case he's wondering, in case he's worried about dying without us nearby.

"I'll be here until the hospice nurse comes," Frank says.

This is the first night a hospice nurse will stand watch through the night. Meaning this is the first night they think he might die.

～

Merry and I go up the stairs together. My legs are heavy. It feels as if I am wearing boots made of concrete.

"The nights are so hard," she says. "I hate thinking of him alone down there."

"He won't be alone tonight."

"Should I be sitting with him all night? Is that what I should do?"

"I think you should get some sleep," I tell her. "Or try to."

She sighs. I walk her to her room, pull back the sheets on her bed, and encourage her to get in. She acquiesces, sitting up straight against the headboard, eyes wide open and alert, the eyes of someone bracing for impact.

"Do you want me to stay in here with you?"

I could sleep next to her, in my dad's spot.

She shakes her head. "No, no. Thank you. You get some sleep too."

"The nurse knows to come get us if—"

"Yes," she says. "I told them."

With that, I go to my room, quite sure I won't be doing any sleeping.

~

Waiting for death is a lot like waiting for birth—health-care providers bustling about, taking vitals, tracking numbers. There is the anticipation, the uncertainty, the mystery. Then eventually, the agony, the gore, the release, the beauty. Nobody can say exactly when he'll die. "When he's ready," they say. They—the doctors—said the same when I was at the end of my pregnancies—"She'll come when she's ready." There is so much surrender required.

I have several text messages waiting for me on my phone—a couple from Kyle, a few from Elijah.

Kyle: Just checking in. How's your dad?

Kyle: Girls are in bed. Hope all is ok there

Elijah: Thinking of you nonstop

Elijah: I can come to you if that would help in any way

Elijah: Even if we just sit in my car and you cry, that's fine with me

I respond to Kyle first:

Things here are heavy. They say he could pass any time now.
Thanks for holding down the fort.

I wait for three dots to tell me he's responding, but there are none. He's probably already asleep, exhausted by the girls. I can't even find it in myself to resent him. Like I've said, Kyle is not an awful human being. He just doesn't love me the way I need to be loved. I had no idea how I needed to be loved until I met Elijah. I was discontented before Elijah, yes. I had a vague sense of "not this" when I contemplated my marriage to Kyle. But there was no proof of something else, something more, being possible. A stronger, more courageous person wouldn't need proof. A stronger, more courageous person would walk away from "not this" into the unknown, trusting in the existence of something more. I think I have demonstrated that I am neither strong nor courageous.

I respond to Elijah:

Actually, that sounds nice. To just sit with you. It's hard to believe anything will make me feel better right now, but you are probably the most likely to succeed

He responds immediately, as he always does, never giving me even a moment to doubt his care for me.

You just tell me where to be and I will do everything in my power to make you feel momentarily better. And if that's not possible, I'll just hold you

My eyes well up with tears at his words, at his kindness, at how undeserving I am of it.

How do you always know the exact right thing to say?

Him: I think we just have one of those special connections, when the things that are most natural for me to say are the things that you naturally want to hear

There are two conflicting viewpoints in the zeitgeist. One states that true love should be easy. The other states that true love takes hard work. My marriage has been predicated on the latter. My relationship with Elijah, whatever it is and whatever it will be, is predicated on the former.

There's a park just down the street from the house. When I was a teenager, I used to sneak out at night and meet my high school boyfriend there. He'd bring a blanket, and we'd make out on the grass, the moon casting what felt like a spotlight just on us. It was romantic, sweet.

I can't have Elijah come to the house, for obvious reasons. But I could have him meet me at the park.

I'm going to get some fresh air soon. There's a park near here. Do you want to meet me there?

He doesn't ask any questions, doesn't imply that he finds this idea strange in the slightest. He just says:

You got it

I send him the address.
He asks:

Can I bring anything for you?

Yes. Bring a blanket

Chapter 21

THERESE

They send a woman named Margot to come get me. It seems a bit excessive—I could have driven myself—but I suppose they've deemed me a flight risk. After all, I've already tried to leave my life (in a sense). They have every right to think I'll do it again.

Margot is about six feet tall, with the shoulders of a swimmer who specializes in the breaststroke. She has uncannily good posture. If she holds her head any higher, she might tip backward.

"Are you ready?" Her voice is as gruff as her appearance suggests it would be.

I am standing in front of my house, a large suitcase and a small duffel bag at my feet. I am ready, practically speaking. I will never be ready otherwise.

Margot doesn't wait for me to answer anyway. She picks up my suitcase, which must weigh forty pounds but looks to weigh five pounds in her impressively capable hands. The sleeves of her shirt stretch across her flexed biceps as she takes the suitcase to the car and tosses it into the back of the white van as if it's a child's backpack.

All this reminds me of that show *Intervention*, when they escort the addict to a rehab facility—always in a white van—before cutting to ninety days later when the addict is clean and sober, carrying a healthy amount of extra weight, face glowing, full of hope for the future. Occasionally, right before the credits roll, text on screen reveals a relapse, an overdose, a death. I wonder what the final on-screen text of my episode would say.

Margot opens the side door of the van, and I climb inside. I hug my duffel bag against my chest as if it is one of my children. I cannot think too much of them, or I will sob.

Margot puts the key in the ignition, and the van comes to life. This is really happening.

"Last chance. Forgetting anything?" Margot asks.

I'm leaving my family behind, so I'm forgetting everything.

"Therese?" she says when I don't reply.

"No," I say. "I'm good." A bald-faced lie.

～

The first ten minutes of the drive are silent, which is just fine with me. We aren't going far. It's the only place of its kind in the country (so far), and it just so happens to be forty-five minutes from where I live. It could be a coincidence, or it could be that my area has an extra-high concentration of insane women.

"You doing okay back there?" Margot says.

Her voice is softer now, perhaps because she has captured the target (me) and successfully strapped me into the vehicle. I am en route and she can relax. Her job is nearly done.

"Are any of the women who have been in this seat okay?" I ask.

She meets my eyes in the rearview mirror, smiles.

"Good point," she says. "You are definitely one of the calmer ones, so I suppose I was hoping you were okay."

I try to imagine how the other women behave. I assume there are lots of tears, perhaps pained moaning. Some may kick and scream. Such effortful expression seems futile, though. Very simply, what would be the point?

"I guess I've surrendered to this," I say.

"They say that's the first step in healing."

"How many steps come after that one?"

"Don't know. You'd have to ask a healed person."

She exits the freeway, and I stare out the window as we approach what will be my home for the next few months.

"Do people leave this place healed?" I ask.

"I wouldn't know. I only see them going in. But I'm told the success rate is very high."

"How do they measure success?"

"You have a lot of questions. Someone in there can answer," she says, pointing ahead.

The van makes its way up a long, narrow driveway, then parks in one of three spots. There's a sign atop two posts on the expansive green lawn in front of the facility that says:

WELCOME
Center of Maternal Evolution

It feels like an aggressive demand: COME! I imagine all the women, mothers like me, heeding the demand, walking as if entranced to the doors of this place that promises to make them better.

Margot hops out of the van, opens my door for me, and then goes around to the back to get my suitcase.

"You ready?" she asks.

She needs to stop asking me this.

I follow behind her as we make our way to the entrance, where a plump, round woman in khaki pants stands with her hands neatly clasped in front of her, an eager smile on her face. She is waiting to greet me.

This is really happening.

"Hello!" the round woman says. Her excitement startles me.

Margot sets my suitcase next to me and says, "Well, good luck," then salutes me and returns to the van.

Everything in me wants to run after her, to beg her to take me home. Why did I agree to come—to COME!—to this place?

I take a deep breath, remind myself that I owe my loved ones this, an admittance of my insanity, a willingness to improve and return a new person. Or not a new person, but the person I was before I became the one I am now. Regression is considered a bad thing for children—a six-year-old suddenly peeing the bed, a two-year-old waking two times a night after sleeping through for months, a five-year-old babbling like a baby. But for adults, regression can be desirable.

I just want my wife back.

Every woman here has probably heard those words.

"Therese? I'm Phoebe," the round woman says, "and I'm so excited to wel*come* you." The effortful overemphasis on the *come* makes me embarrassed for her.

"Hi," I say.

"What do you say we go inside?"

Chapter 22

NICOLE

Elijah is waiting for me at the park, leaning against a light post, the hood of a jacket pulled over his head.

"Hey, you," he says when he sees me coming. He holds out his arms, welcoming me into an embrace that I happily receive.

It's not a typical hug with a five-second duration. It is an encapsulation. His body seems to absorb mine, along with all the troubles it contains within. I do not want to let go. Thirty seconds pass, a minute. I wait for the muscles in his arms to relax as he pulls away, but they remain tight and tense, committed to holding me for however long I need, possibly forever. I cry, not about my dad but about the fact that I have someone in my life who is willing to hold me like this, someone who is honored to hold me like this.

"Thank you," I mumble into his ear. My lips settle on the warm skin of his neck.

"You don't need to thank me."

"Yes I do. If I didn't, it would be like saying that this type of thing is normal—driving to a random park at night, shivering in the cold, giving whatever bodily warmth you have to someone else."

"It's my pleasure," he says.

I am the one to release his hold, to drop my arms at my side, because I sense he never will. Kyle will never hold me like this, with such generosity of spirit. It's just not in his relational wheelhouse. We adapt to the partners we have, adjust expectations so diligently that we forget what we even desire.

He bends down to retrieve a folded blanket at his feet, holds it out to me.

"I brought the warmest one I have," he says.

I shake it out onto the grass; then I lie flat, staring at the black sky. It is too cloudy to see any stars tonight—typical for Daly City. He lies next to me, takes my hand in his, his thumb stroking each of my knuckles.

"He's really dying," I say.

He squeezes my hand.

"I'm sorry."

"Have you ever seen someone dying?"

"Nope."

"It's terrible."

"I can only imagine."

I appreciate that he says that instead of "I can't imagine." I hate when people say "I can't imagine" in response to someone's tragedy. *You can imagine,* I want to say. *You just don't want to.*

"Nobody talks about this, the process of it. People just die behind closed doors, and the rest of the world thinks it's this neat, tidy experience. But it's fucking brutal."

He doesn't say anything, just squeezes my hand again.

"And I guess I have it easy in that this disease is so fast moving. Some people watch someone die over the course of months, years."

"I don't think you have it easy. I imagine your mind can't even catch up with reality most days."

"There you go again—saying the exact right thing. It's like you're in my brain," I say.

"Maybe I am. Maybe I'm part of a special government program investigating mind-reading technology."

"Well, if that's the case, the program is a booming success."

Neither of us says anything for a few minutes.

"Is there anything I can do for you?" he asks.

"You're doing it."

Here I am, with this real *connection* with this person who was supposed to be just a fling, a one-night departure from my real life. It doesn't make any sense. Or rather, it makes as much sense as a one-in-a-million brain disease.

"My life is a mess," I tell him.

"Everyone's life is a mess."

"Maybe, but mine is egregiously messy."

My real name isn't Katrina.

I'm married. I'm going to get a divorce. For you.

I have a pregnancy test in my purse. I have a fantasy that I'm carrying your baby.

The confessions sit poised on the tip of my tongue.

I am too afraid of the response, too afraid of his shock and horror, too afraid of his abandonment. My psyche cannot handle Elijah exiting my life right now. The confessions will have to wait.

"I don't mind your mess," he says.

That's because you only know the half of it.

"You are a unicorn of a human being."

He turns his face toward mine, kisses my cheek. "So are you."

∼

We stay cuddled on the blanket for an hour before I say, "I should get back." I've been keeping an eye on my phone, terrified to get a text from Merry that says, Where are you? It's time. I would tell her I was just out for a walk. She wouldn't ask questions or even care. But I would hate myself if I missed his last breath, if I wasn't there with him then.

Elijah takes my hands, helps me stand. Then he picks up the blanket, folds it, stuffs it under his arm.

"I'll wait to hear from you," he says. "Just know I'm thinking of you during all this. Constantly."

I rest my forehead against his chest, then turn my head so my ear is pressed against him. I can hear his heart beating, a slow, steady, relaxed beat.

"It's just so weird. I won't have a dad soon."

He kisses the top of my head. "You'll always have a dad."

~

He offers to drive me home, but I insist on walking. He doesn't push. The house is quiet when I get back, except for the sound of the oxygen machine. I close the door quietly behind me, go to my room, and get into bed in an attempt to trick my body into sleeping. It doesn't work.

When I see daybreak outside the window, I go downstairs. The overnight hospice nurse is sitting in a chair at Dad's bedside, holding his wrist in her hand, taking his pulse.

"Hi," I whisper. "How is he?"

"He's comfortable."

We exchange names. Hers is Tianna.

"His respirations are fast—about thirty per minute."

I have no idea how fast that is, have never considered the pace of my own respirations, another bodily function I have taken for granted.

"I want to start giving him Ativan to help with any panicky feeling he may get from breathing so fast," she says. "I'll need his wife to approve first."

Just as she says that, Merry walks in, the bags under her eyes even more pronounced than yesterday. She's wearing a robe, her arms wrapped around her middle as if she's hugging herself.

"What do you need my approval for?"

Tianna explains the Ativan. Merry agrees. We follow Tianna's instructions—bring a shot glass from the kitchen. It says "Acapulco" on it, something Merry says they got on a cruise. Tianna shows us how to dissolve the pills in three drops of water in the glass. Then she sucks up the murky liquid with a syringe and places it in my dad's mouth. She massages his throat to help the medicine go down. It takes a few minutes, but she manages to empty the syringe.

"You can give that to him every hour. I'll put a note in his chart for the next nurse."

She places a hand against his forehead. "He's a bit warm."

She takes his temperature—99.8.

"It's common for patients to spike a fever." She hands us two blue latex gloves. "Take these and fill them with ice cubes."

I do as she says. She ties off the gloves and places the makeshift ice packs against his cheeks.

"You can also fill gloves with water and place them in the freezer."

This Tianna has all kinds of tricks. She's also balled up some of Dad's socks and placed them in his hands to keep him from clenching his fists shut so tightly.

~

We spend much of the day sitting and waiting. I watch his chest rise and fall, wondering with each breath if it will be his last. Blood starts to pool in his calves. His nail beds start to turn purple. His blood pressure hovers around sixty over forty, his heart rate around one hundred. Merry records his vitals every hour, filling up lines in a notebook that she's designated for this purpose. I know why she's doing it—for some sense of control, however illusory. I remember when I was in labor with Grace and I did the same, recording each contraction in a notebook—the time it occurred, the duration, the pain level. It was something to occupy my brain on the verge of this monumental event that I couldn't begin to process.

When Tianna's shift ends, Nurse Becky comes. She turns my dad on his side to inspect the pressure sore on his tailbone. I saw it yesterday when the nurse was changing his diaper; it was purple-red and angry. In just twenty-four hours, it has worsened considerably. It is a crater of black. One quick glance, and my stomach clenches. I cannot look again. Becky replaces a bandage with a sigh.

"Should I turn his head?" I ask.

His left ear is black from the pressure of his lying on his side for two days.

"You don't need to," she says. "It's fine."

I imagine her thoughts: *He is dying. He will be dead soon. The state of his ear is inconsequential.*

We continue to give him water via the sponge lollipops. It helps us feel like we are caring for him, doing something important. It is all we can do, besides sitting with him, placing our hands on his body. But this, the placing of hands, is more for our own benefit than his. I will my hands to remember the feel of him, though this current version of his body is so unlike the one I grew up touching and holding.

Kyle texts to check in, and I tell him what the hospice people continue to tell me:

It could be any time . . .

Him: You doing ok?

I can't remember the last time Kyle inquired about how I was doing. I can't remember the last time he showed interest in my mental state, my thoughts, my feelings.

I'm hanging in there. It's all so surreal

Him: Ya

He tells me the girls are fine. He got them Happy Meals for dinner.

Don't worry—I'll remember to brush their teeth

Bless him for not making me ask.

Thank you. I hope they go easy on you at bedtime

Him: They will. They know I can't handle them like you can

I want to say *I can't handle them either! You just have to try harder!* But I don't want to get into it, so I just say:

I'll text tomorrow. Night.

I sit by my dad's side until one o'clock in the morning. The new overnight hospice nurse, Ingrid, sits in a chair next to me, alert and focused. She is older than the others who have passed through—in her fifties. She has an accent, something Nordic.

"You can get some sleep," she says. It's only when she says this that I realize I've started to drift off. Merry went up to bed a couple of hours ago.

"I just don't want to miss . . . it."

She gives me a smile that seems to pity me a little. "Sometimes, they wait until you leave the room to die. Sometimes, they want to be alone."

"They do?"

She nods. "It's quite common."

"Why?"

She shrugs. "I think the transition is a very personal thing. He might not want you to see his life leave him. He might want to protect you. He might think it would be too painful for you."

"It wouldn't be."

She shrugs again. "I'm only guessing."

Of course she is. How could any of us pretend to know?

"You'll call us if anything changes?" I ask.

Lying in bed, even if just for a few hours, does sound good. My body is tired.

"Of course."

I give my dad a kiss on his cheek, whisper, "I'm going to get some rest, Dad. I love you. I'll be back soon."

That way, he knows I'm stepping out. If he wants to die alone, he can. If he wants to wait for me to return, he can.

"Do you think he can still hear me?" I ask.

Again, how could she know for sure? I am desperate for her omniscience.

"I think so." She must know that's what I want to hear. I am grateful.

∼

I go upstairs and get into bed with Merry. She stirs lightly. I wonder if she thinks, for a split second, that I am Dad, coming to bed late.

"Oh, it's you," she says groggily, taking me in.

"Can I sleep with you tonight?"

I feel like a child asking this.

"Okay."

I get under the sheets on my dad's side of the bed. I reach my arm over to touch Merry's arm, and I fall asleep just like that.

∼

Merry's cell rings just before four o'clock. She has the ringer on high. It nearly gives me a heart attack.

"Hello?" she says, already sitting up straight, then swinging her legs over the side of the bed.

"I think it's time," the voice says.

Ingrid.

Merry and I go downstairs, holding onto each other for comfort and balance. I have never felt my heart beat so hard, vibrating my rib cage, preparing my body for the unprecedented experience I am about to have.

When we enter the room, Ingrid is bent over Dad, her stethoscope pressed to his chest.

"I'm sorry," she says. "I saw him take one big gasping breath, and I thought there would be at least one more after that, but it was just that one."

"He's gone?" Merry asks, her voice at a pitch I have never heard before.

"I'm so sorry," Ingrid says.

Sorry that he is gone, or sorry that we did not see him take his last breath, I'm not sure which.

She continues listening to his chest, just to be sure, but does not amend her original conclusion.

Looking at my dad now, I realize that the state he was in the last couple of days was not as corpse-like as I thought. This right here is a corpse. The life is gone. His skin is ashen. His mouth gapes open. His eyes are a quarter open. Ingrid goes to him, closes his mouth for him, gently presses down his eyelids.

"Oh, Daddy," I say, the pitch of my own voice startling me. I sound like someone in shock, someone who has lost a loved one suddenly and without warning, not someone who has been preparing for this event. It's blatantly obvious that there is no way to prepare for death. Shock is inevitable.

Merry strokes his bald head with her hand. I grasp his arm. It's so cold.

Ingrid has tears in her eyes. Despite her years of doing this, she is still moved.

"I can feel your love for him," she says.

I watch a tear roll down her cheek. She doesn't swipe it away. She lets it free-fall from her face. She puts her hand on my shoulder, leaves it there, steadying me as my body is racked with sobs.

"Would you like me to call the mortuary?" she asks. "It usually takes them an hour or two to come, so you will still have time with him."

I look to Merry. She meets my eyes but appears helpless, unsure, incapable of making any decision at all.

"Yes, you can call them," I say.

Ingrid nods and then steps into the hallway. I hear her on the phone with them, reporting the time of death, confirming the address. The mortuary has a team of people on standby for predawn calls like these. There is a whole world I know nothing about.

∿

There is a knock at the door an hour later. I open it to find a man in a black suit with a clipboard in his hands. If I didn't know better, I would think him a Jehovah's Witness.

"Hello, ma'am. I'm with Fitzgerald Mortuary. I am so sorry for your loss."

"Thank you," I say, opening the door for him. That's when I see that he has a woman with him, also in a black suit, standing a few steps behind. She follows him inside.

"My condolences," she says with a respectful bow.

They have me sign some papers, then go to my dad's room and confer among themselves quietly. I'm sure they are discussing his size—he's still a large man, even with the weight loss—and wondering how they will negotiate the steps out front. After their brief conference, they return outside. I look out the window as they unload a stretcher from the back of their white van. I see another stretcher inside. I wonder if they make multiple stops, if there are certain days with more deaths than others, certain times of day that are common for people to leave the world.

Merry and I wait in the living room while they put Dad on the stretcher. We can't watch. When they emerge, he is enclosed in a black velvet body bag. I hold the door open for them.

"Thank you," the man says. "Again, we are so sorry for your loss."

They walk slowly down the steps, the man in front, the woman in back. I can't watch that either, can't bear the thought of them tripping, my dad's body falling to the cement. I just stare at the van, wait for them to make it there. They do. They slide him inside and shut the doors. The man takes off his suit jacket as he walks to the driver's side door. He has a tattoo of barbed wire encircling his upper arm. It bothers me for some irrational reason. I don't want my father driven away by a dude with a barbed wire tattoo.

When I turn around, I expect to see Merry, but she isn't there.

"Merry?" I call.

I find her in Dad's room, stripping the hospital bed.

"Hey," I say.

She doesn't look up, just keeps bustling about, now making piles of all the hospice supplies on the floor.

"I want this stuff out of here," she says.

She unplugs the oxygen machine, wraps the cord around her hands in a tight circle, then rolls the machine into the hallway.

"Okay," I say. What else is there to say? "I'll get a couple trash bags."

We use one trash bag for actual trash, the other for items we plan to donate to nursing homes—diapers, gloves, bandages. I don't know why she wants to do this *right now*, but I can tell it's making her feel better. At the very least it's forcing pent-up energy out of her body, freeing her.

After a couple of hours, we have everything organized. Merry sends an email to the hospice company, tells them she needs them to pick up their equipment as soon as possible.

"All right," she says, hands on hips, her face covered in a thin sheen of sweat, "that's done."

I suggest we eat some breakfast, and she looks at me like she's never heard of breakfast before.

"I'll make us some coffee and toast," I say, "something easy."

She agrees, reluctantly. We sit at the kitchen table, sipping our coffee, taking small bites of our toast. At seven, there is a knock at the door, and I briefly fantasize about it being the mortuary people, saying my dad came to life in the back of the van and is miraculously healed.

The mind is capable of crazy things.

But it's just Frank. He's here for his workday. Nobody from the hospice company has told him Dad died.

"Morning!" he says with his usual joviality.

His face falls when he takes in our faces. We must look completely wrecked.

"Oh no," he says.

He goes to my dad's room, then comes back.

"No," he says.

I nod. He comes to us, his arms outstretched, with the clear intention to take us both in. Merry and I allow this. Frank's arms are thick, and his body is warm, and it is just what we need.

"I'm so sorry," he says, pulling away from the embrace after a few moments. His eyes are wet with tears. He is shocked too. Even the professionals are not spared.

Merry asks him to help her wheel the hospital bed into the hallway. It is not a logical task to insist upon. The hospice company said they would come tomorrow or the day after to take away all the equipment. Merry must feel the need to make progress of some kind, any kind. Frank does not question her. I've found most men are also comforted by progress making, especially in times of unfixable despair.

I sit on the couch.

This is the first time I'm sitting on a couch without my father being alive, I think.

How many of these types of thoughts will I have in the coming days?

This is the first shower I've taken as someone without a living father.

This is the first dinner I've eaten without my father on earth.

This is the first time I've had sex since my father died.

Life has been cleaved into before and after. I feel as if I am standing at the precipice of a great unknown.

He died

I send this text to Elijah and then to Kyle.
Elijah responds first:

Oh, sweetheart

It is the first time he has used this term of endearment with me. My dad has died, and I am someone's sweetheart.

Him: I knew it was coming, but my heart still breaks for you

The idea of his heart breaking on my behalf makes me sob in the same way I did when Ingrid said my dad had taken his last breath. I start crying again, my body summoning tears from some unknown reservoir of pain after all the usual wells have been drained dry.

I knew it was coming too and yet I feel completely caught off guard

Him: Of course you do. You've never not had your father so there would have been no way to be ready for such a reality

Kind, eloquent Elijah. He is too good hearted to be a lawyer. I need to tell him this in a hopefully not-so-distant future when I am able to laugh again.

I can't believe it's reality. I just don't believe it

Him: There is no rush to believe. Give yourself time

Bask in the denial. That's what he's advising. Linger in this stage of grief. The others may be even more arduous.

Him: Can I do anything? What do you need right now?

I have no idea.

Him: Do you want to meet at the park tonight?

I don't know if I do, can't seem to get a grasp on anything at all in this moment, but I respond anyway:

OK.

Him: I'll meet you there at the same time. And if you change your mind, that's okay too.

Thank you. You're so good to me

He sends me three red hearts in return.

~

Kyle responds ten minutes later. I am lying flat on the couch. Merry and Frank are still busy moving various things into the hallway from what will forever be known as the room where my dad died.

Him: Ugh, how you holding up?

Not well

Him: How's Merry?

We're both having a hard time

Him: I wish there was something I could do

There is, I want to say. *You could say tender things like Elijah. You could offer to fly up with the girls and hold me.*

Him: Should I send flowers?

Is he asking me for guidance on etiquette? Requesting my help with an appropriate gift in this situation? Is there no time I can be free from being his wife?

I don't know, Kyle. Why don't you google how to be thoughtful after a father-in-law dies?

Him: OK. I'm sorry. I don't know what to say

Don't say anything then. I'm used to that

Him: Nic, come on. I'm sorry. You know I'm terrible with things like this

Things like this? Like death? I don't think anyone is good at death, Kyle.

Him: Look, I'm obviously fucking up here. I'll call you later if that's ok?

I don't respond. Maybe if he calls later, I'll just blurt it out once and for all: I want a divorce.

~

Tears come again when Frank leaves. It's strange that he has been part of this deeply profound part of my life and I will never see him again. I don't even know his last name. I could ask him for his contact information, but I think we both know that any ongoing correspondence is unlikely. I will miss the essence of him, but will want to distance myself from the memories he elicits.

"Take good care of yourself," he says before walking down the front steps, steps last traveled by the mortuary workers who took my father away.

"You too."

~

Back inside, I find Merry in the walk-in closet of the room where my dad died. It is a closet they've always used for storage. She is standing on her tippy-toes, reaching for a giant box on the top shelf.

"Need help?" I ask.

I'm a few inches taller than her. She doesn't admit to needing my assistance, but doesn't protest when I pull down the box for her.

"What is this?" I ask.

It's a cardboard box, formerly white and now yellow. It weighs at least twenty pounds. I place it on a table that was the makeshift hospice-supplies table until Merry completely cleared it earlier.

"Photos," she says. "We should pull out some good ones of him. I'll want to do a slideshow at the memorial service. Do you know how to do that?"

I carefully take her wrists with my hands and turn her toward me. I look into her sad, tired, frantic eyes and say, "Merry, we don't have to do this *right now*."

Her eyes dart away from mine, unable to keep focus.

"I know, I know. I just want to."

She instructs me to pull down the other boxes in the closet, five in total. She removes all the contents, begins making piles on the floor.

"Are you hungry?" she asks when all the boxes are emptied.

It's just about five o'clock. We didn't think to eat lunch.

"I am," I say, perplexed by the stubbornness of my appetite at a time like this. My dad has died, my world has tilted on its axis, and my stomach continues to growl, reminding me of the necessity of life going on.

"I'll make some pasta," she says. "You stay here, start looking through photos."

I don't particularly feel like bringing on more tears, but I comply anyway. I sit in the chair next to where my dad's hospital bed used to be and open a forest green leather album. There are photos of my dad as a twentysomething. *Quite a strapping young man,* I would tease him if he were here. *Is* he still here in some way? I'd be lying if I said I hadn't googled theories on what happens when people die. Many believe there is a window of time when a person who has died is still lingering, preparing to transition to the other realm. *It's like checking out of one hotel and into another.* Someone wrote that in an article I read online. I like that idea.

I flip through the album. There are photos of my dad with my mother, Rose, the woman who carried me and gave birth to me and then died when I was too young to formulate any lasting memory of her. I wonder if there is any truth to the idea of dead people reuniting on "the other side." I wonder if my dad is with her now, if they are hugging and laughing and dancing a jig.

I doubt Merry would want any photos of my dad with his first wife at the memorial, so I close the album and move to place it back in one of the piles on the floor. When I do that, though, something slides out of it. It's a black-and-white composition notebook. It literally falls into my lap, and I can't help but think my dad is, in fact, here.

I open it.

September 16, 1984

Dear Diary,
Ha. Dear Diary. Look at me, acting like an eleven-year-old schoolgirl. I didn't even keep a diary when I

was an eleven-year-old schoolgirl. It never occurred to me to keep a diary until just now, at age twenty-eight. They say necessity is the mother of invention, but I think motherhood is the necessity of invention. My thoughts have to go somewhere.

A few paragraphs in, it becomes clear that this is my mother's journal, Rose's journal, started in 1984, just months before she died. I start to flip through the notebook and realize it's mostly blank. There are only five entries, the date of the last one being February 1985, right before the accident.

I read.

And read.

And read.

> Rob,
> I'm leaving you this diary.
> So you understand that it's not your fault.
> Or Nicole's.
> This life is not for me. I wish it was.

I stand from the chair, my instinct to run, go somewhere, do something. The journal falls to the floor. I have to sit again. I feel like I have vertigo, like I may pass out or throw up or both.

Merry comes into the room, saying, "Should I make a salad?"

When she sees my face, the color leaves hers.

"Nicole, what's wrong?"

Her eyes go to the floor, to the journal.

Does she know? Has she always known?

"Oh," she says.

And then I know that she knows, that she has always known.

She comes toward me. "Nicole, I'm so sorry. I can explain," she says. "He saved it because he was going to tell you and—"

"Why?" It is the only word that will come.

I stand, the room still spinning around me, my legs wobbly. *Noodle legs,* my dad used to say after his runs. My feet don't feel like my own, but I will them to move anyway.

I leave the room and then the house, grabbing the car keys on the console table on the way out. Merry's voice is behind me, sounding like it's coming from underwater: "Nicole!"

But I keep going.

I will drive to Elijah. I can't wait for him to come to the park later. I need to see him now.

My father is dead.

My mother never was.

My father is dead.

My mother might not be.

Elijah will think I've lost it. But he will hold me anyway. That's what I need. That's what any of us need. To be held.

Chapter 23

THERESE

The inside of COME looks like a hotel lobby. It's possible this place used to be a hotel. Or an apartment building. There are no people in sight, aside from a young woman at the front desk who is wearing a headset and currently talking to someone, saying, "We will have a bed available next week."

Too-chipper Phoebe leads me to a small office off the reception area. She sits on one side of a desk, and I sit on the other.

"So I'm the new-client coordinator here at COME," she says. "We just have a few paperwork things to get out of the way, and then I'll give you a tour of the facility."

She is in the wrong career. She should be working on a Disney cruise.

I cross and recross my legs, tap my foot on the floor.

"Are you nervous?" she asks, glancing at my foot.

I force myself to stop with the tapping.

"Sorry."

She furrows her brows. "Oh, don't be sorry. Women are altogether too apologetic for feelings that are quite valid. Everyone is a bit nervous on their first day."

I want to punch this woman in the face.

"So you know the name policy then?" she says, looking at something on her computer screen.

"Yes, though I can't say I really understand it."

She reestablishes eye contact with me and says, "We refrain from using real names here, for the protection of everyone's identities."

"Protection?"

She's talking like we're in a government witness protection program.

She leans across the desk, as if sharing a secret.

"Some women want to reemerge into their real lives with nobody knowing they were here."

"Their real lives."

"Not that this isn't real life," she stammers. "Their post-COME lives is what I mean."

"Post-COME," I say, finding it impossible not to giggle like a dirty-minded teenager. She is straight faced. I doubt Phoebe was ever a dirty-minded teenager. She probably tattled on those kids.

"I see you've selected Therese."

"I was told to use my middle name, and that's my middle name."

"Oh, brilliant! Some women don't use their middle names, but choose whatever they like. We'd have so many Anns and Maries if everyone used their middle name, you know?"

She laughs heartily. This is what makes Phoebe laugh.

When I don't say anything, she goes on: "Therese is a *beautiful* name! It sounds very French!"

"It is very French."

"Well, I *love* it. Everyone here will love it!"

She says this like it's a compliment that's supposed to make me blush. I had nothing to do with my middle name.

"How many women are here?"

"Right now, we're at twenty," she says. "We have intentions to expand, but we want to do so mindfully. Our pilot program included ten women, and it was such a success."

"They're doing well now, those ten women?"

She nods emphatically.

"*Thriving*," she says. "Truly!"

"And most women are here because they were . . . struggling?"

The emphatic nodding continues.

"Yes, struggling. With a variety of things in a variety of ways. The modern world asks so much of women, you know?"

She doesn't blink.

"We see so much here. Marital troubles, childcare challenges, career realignments, mental breakdowns, grief and loss, addictions and other coping mechanisms—eating disorders, alcoholism, obsessive cleaning, affairs."

She holds steady eye contact throughout the list, careful not to convey any judgment of what's brought me here. She knows what brought me here. I assume there is a whole file with my name on it.

"It's amazing how similar we are, though, at our cores, regardless of our 'issues.'"

She uses air quotes when she says *issues*.

"We really take a holistic approach to helping women get back on track. Group therapy, one-on-one therapy, yoga therapy, art therapy . . ."

"Lots of therapy."

She smiles tightly, her thin lips barely visible.

"I promise you'll find it immensely fulfilling."

This is a tall order. Have I ever found anything immensely fulfilling?

She starts to stand. "Are you ready for the tour?"

~

As she shows me around, it is obvious that, yes, this used to be a hotel. There is a large dining area that must have been a banquet room before. There is a gym. Ground floor conference rooms have been transformed into group therapy rooms and yoga studios. Hotel staff offices are now reserved for individual therapy sessions.

"We have four therapists on staff, with five clients each," Phoebe says. "You have been matched with Crystal, who you're just going to *love*."

Her eyes go big. She nearly squeals.

"Crystal is in a session right now, but you'll meet her tomorrow."

We take an elevator to the third floor.

"Your room is on our top floor," she says.

I follow her down the hallway until she stops in front of one of the doors. In place of a room number, there is a little plaque that says YOU HAVE THE POWER TO HEAL YOUR LIFE.

"Here we are," she says.

Inside, the bathroom is right off the door, and then a short hallway leads to a main room with two double beds. I'm surprised to find a woman sitting on one of the beds, knees pulled to her chest, paperback book in hand.

"Marie, this is Therese," Phoebe says.

"Hello," Marie says, looking up briefly before returning to her book.

She has dark-brown hair, almost black, cut short, and she's wearing tortoiseshell glasses. She's very thin, her arms and legs long and gangly. I try to see the title of the book she's reading, but can't. She seems like the type to casually read Nietzsche. She doesn't bother even faking a smile.

"I think you two will be great roommates," Phoebe says.

"I didn't realize I'd have a roommate," I say.

"Oh yes! I thought you knew. We have some single rooms, but your sponsor elected the double."

By "sponsor," she means husband. And by "elected the double," she means he's frugal, which is accurate.

"I'm not excited about it either," Marie says, which makes me like her.

"I'll leave you two to get acquainted. You'll hear the dinner bell at five thirty," Phoebe says before pulling the door shut behind her.

I sit on my bed and wait to see if Marie will speak. She does not.

"How long have you been here?" I ask.

She answers without looking up: "Two days."

I wonder if she arrived in this state of apparent despair or if two days have done this to her.

I proceed to unpack once I realize there will be no conversation.

An hour later, at precisely five thirty, a bell rings. Dinner.

Marie sighs.

"I don't know why they do dinner so early. We're without our children for once. You'd think they could treat us to an adult mealtime."

I smile. Marie and I will be friends, whether she likes it or not.

Chapter 24

NICOLE

I put my dad's keys into his Ford Escape, a car I've never seen anyone drive but him. He's had it for years. Before this one, he had another Ford Escape, the same color—gray. Was he loyal, or did he just hate change? Is there a difference?

I drive several blocks away and then pull over to text Elijah. I don't even know how to get to his place from here, so I put his address into the app that will lead the way.

Can I come over? I've got my dad's car

Him: Of course. But I can come to you. Is everything ok?

No.

Him: Are you sure you should be driving?

No. But I am. Should be there in a half hour

Him: Please drive safe

I've never understood that request—*please drive safe.* Who intends to drive recklessly? Accidents are usually just that—accidents. They are not the result of someone failing to remind someone to drive safe, or someone failing to obey that command.

I drive the 280 into downtown, soothed by the calm female voice telling me what turns to make. And then I am at Elijah's apartment building.

I'm here. Can we just go for a drive?

For whatever reason, the thought of getting out of the car and ascending several floors to the one that is his sounds too daunting, as if I might collapse in the elevator for a security guard to find me.

Him: Ok, be right down

He appears at my car window a few minutes later. I can tell by the concerned look on his face that I must appear as unhinged as I feel. He goes around to the passenger's side, and I unlock the door for him, then return my shaky hands to ten and two on the steering wheel. I have a flashback of my dad teaching me to drive: *They say ten and two, but I'm a fan of eleven and two myself, sometimes just one hand on twelve if I'm feeling dangerous.*

"Do you want me to drive?" he asks.

That would be the wise thing, but my body feels welded to the seat.

"No, that's okay. You can navigate."

He nods slowly, a reluctant nod. "Where are we going?"

"I was thinking Half Moon Bay. That's a nice drive, isn't it?"

Am I speaking faster than usual? I think I might be. I tell myself to slow down, to sound more normal, to not worry Elijah, the man I may leave my husband for.

"Sure," he says. "Half Moon Bay."

His words are careful and measured, like the words of a hostage negotiator speaking with a lunatic wielding a gun.

My dad used to take me to Half Moon Bay. He liked to look at the birds. Half Moon Bay is home to over 20 percent of all North American bird species. At least, that's what he told me. I don't want to google it and find out he was wrong or exaggerating or whatever. We would spend hours at Pescadero Marsh or Pillar Point Marsh. He would point out the birds, tell me their names. I would pretend to make mental notes, though the names never settled into my memory.

It's nighttime. We won't see any birds. It doesn't make any logical sense to go to Half Moon Bay *now*. Elijah knows this, which is why he's talking to me like I'm an insane person.

We take the 101 to the 380 to the 280. We do not speak until we turn onto CA-35, the highway that leads into the bay.

"Do you want to tell me what's going on in that head of yours?" he asks.

"My dad died today."

I know this is not news to him. I just feel the need to confirm it aloud for myself. It's strange that in a handful of hours, I will say, "My dad died yesterday." Then, "My dad died last week." Then: last month, last year, a few years ago. At some point, the time frame will become irrelevant. It will just be *My dad died.* Or *My dad is dead.* At some point, I will reach an age when this fact will not be interpreted by others as any kind of tragedy. Perhaps I'm already at that age. I am not a child or a teenager or a college student who has lost her dad. I am a woman in her forties. My dad was in his sixties. He was "elderly." I am his only child. His death, the tragedy of it, is unique to me, and that is the loneliest feeling in the world.

"I was going through some photos," I say. "And I found this journal."

I start to feel dizzy. My vision goes blurry.

"Kat?"

Kat.

Kat.

Who is Kat?

He yells it now: "Kat!"

And then I see why he is yelling. We are veering off the highway. Or I am, I guess. I am the one holding the steering wheel.

I hear my dad's voice: *Look at all the trees, Nikki Bear.*

And then all goes black.

Chapter 25

THERESE

I am two weeks into my time at COME. It's more of a retreat than a rehab center, and I want to tell whoever is in charge that they could make a boatload of money with a slight change in their marketing strategy:

Now: You are broken. Let us fix you.

New: The world is broken. Let us love you.

Everything is very structured and predictable, a salve to any anxious nervous system. There are two "betterment activities" each day.

On Mondays, we have restorative yoga, which is basically just lying on the floor in various stretches, as well as one-on-one therapy. My therapist, Crystal, is fine, I guess. She wears a quartz crystal around her neck, and I cannot tell if this is ironic or not. She is at least ten years younger than me and wears combat boots with pink laces. One side of her head is shaved. The hair on the other side is dyed pink and combed into a wave every day. I am skeptical of her ability to heal me in any real way, but she is kind, and I must comply with these sessions to get out of this place. We haven't really delved into any of the heavy stuff yet—I'm sure that's coming. She has been focused on how I'm settling in and has started to ask me about my stresses as a mother and wife. Layers of the onion, as they say.

On Tuesdays, we have a "Mastering Mothering" class, which is mostly about how to manage our emotions so that we can then help our children emotionally regulate themselves. Everything in this place is about emotional regulation. Deep breathing is the key to calming the vagus nerve, which runs through the body and touches every organ system and is, apparently, the key to everything. They should really call it the Vagus Nerve Institute.

We also have group therapy on Tuesdays, during which we talk about how we miss our children, but also love having some respite. At least one person breaks down in tears every time. It's often this woman, Sheila, who was sent here by her husband after she refused to get out of bed for thirteen days straight. She continues to insist that she is not depressed, just very tired.

It's during group therapy that I learn the various reasons people are here.

Alexis and Jennifer became full-blown alcoholics in their first years of motherhood. Once, while grocery shopping in the middle of the day, Alexis was so drunk that she left her two-year-old daughter in the cart and proceeded to drive home, only realizing once she'd gotten home and unpacked the groceries that her daughter was missing. Jennifer drank a bottle of wine while sharing a bath with her four-year-old and, when she went to get out, slipped and hit her head on the tub's faucet. She lay bleeding and unconscious on the tile floor, her daughter likely screaming in terror, until her husband found her. There is significant worry about the trauma experienced by the children in both of these incidents.

Catherine's mother died of cancer, and she simply lost the ability to do anything but put her three children in front of the TV for seven hours a day. Raquel told her husband she was ill so she could stay in the basement bedroom for a few days. She so enjoyed the reprieve from her parenting duties that she fabricated fibromyalgia, which led her husband to hire a nanny. Then her husband caught her in the basement doing an online aerobics class, seemingly pain-free, and that was that.

Serena left her family—including four children under the age of eight—to be with a man in Argentina who she'd met on a dating app for married people. After he scammed her out of all the money in the checking account she shared with her husband, she came back home. Her husband took out a second mortgage on their house to send her to COME.

Nobody has had my exact situation. They've had bits and pieces of my situation—marriage issues, death and grief, affairs—but not the whole shebang. Crystal and I have only begun to scratch the surface of the whole shebang. It's a surface I'd much rather ignore until the nuclear death of the sun.

On Wednesdays, we have restorative yoga in the mornings and "Live Out Loud" scream sessions in the afternoons. During these sessions, we all gather in the courtyard and scream. It's surprisingly therapeutic.

On Thursdays, there's more one-on-one therapy and a yoga flow class in the evening. At the very least, I am getting quite flexible.

On Fridays, there's more group therapy and then a "Laugh It Off" session where we all gather in the courtyard and laugh hysterically. This would be much better if we were all high, but drugs are frowned upon here.

On Saturdays, we do a nature hike, which is really just a walk through the hills across the street from the property, and a half-hour guided meditation (during which I fall asleep, despite getting nine hours of blissful sleep at night). "Your body is recovering from long-term deprivation on multiple levels." That's what Crystal said, which felt so validating that I wanted to cry.

On Sundays, we have a free-dance class with this woman named Marcella who always shows up in three-inch black heels and a red flamenco dress. She encourages us to move our bodies in whatever ways feel good, and for most of us, that means flailing about, limbs akimbo, like Elaine in *Seinfeld*. They should really combine this with the laughing session—two birds, one stone. We also do letter writing on

Sundays, which is very similar to the "making amends" bit of Alcoholics Anonymous. They tell us the letters are just for us and we don't have to send them, but there is also subtle encouragement to send them. My letters have been lame so far—staccato sentences that read like something written by a five-year-old. *I feel sad. I feel shame. I have regrets. I'm sorry.* Crystal says this represents my reluctance to tap into the enormity of my emotions.

My roommate, Marie, has warmed to me, which infuses me with satisfaction. Crystal says this means I am too reliant on external validation. I say I am a woman; I have been conditioned this way.

Marie's story would horrify people in the outside world, but nobody bats an eye at it here. Like me, she stopped working (she'd held a fairly high-up position in the finance world) to care for her children—twin boys.

"Having twins, that did me in," she told me on the night of our initial confessional. This was last week. We each sat against our respective headboards, not daring to look at each other, as we traded our truths.

"I really only wanted one," she said. "And I wasn't even sure about one. I had all the typical worries about how a child would change my life. Then I got two of them."

She considered terminating one of the fetuses—such a thing is possible—but there were risks involved for the other fetus, and she didn't think she could live with herself if that baby also died.

"How old are they now?" I asked.

"Three."

"Such a hard age."

"Aren't they all hard?"

"God, I hope not."

One day, while her architect husband was working in his home office, she told him she was stepping out to run an errand, and she just didn't come back. *For two weeks.* Actually, she didn't even come back after two weeks. Instead, she finally responded to her husband's frantic texts to say, simply, "I'm fine. I'm at a hotel in Seattle." He came to get her and then brought her immediately here.

"So you haven't seen your boys since you left for . . . the errand?"

She shook her head.

"Do you miss them?"

She looked at me then. "Do you want me to be honest?"

"I do."

She shrugged. "I don't know. I know they're doing okay, maybe better without me. I like having time to myself. I'm not sure I ever should have been a mother."

Many of the women here say things like "Maybe I'm not cut out for this" and "I love my kids, but I hate raising them." The therapists assure all of us that maternal ambivalence is normal, that we would all be better off if it was more socially acceptable to admit to its existence.

"Do you miss yours?" she asked me.

I sensed she wanted me to say something similar to what she had, but that wouldn't have been true for me.

"I do."

~

It is Monday, and I am sitting in Crystal's office. I know who her other four clients are, and I like to think I am her favorite. I suppose she would say that's me craving external validation again, so I don't inquire about whatever hierarchy of favorites she may or may not have.

"You look good," she says. "More rested, maybe."

"You think?"

She nods.

"Does that mean you're going to start going harder on me with the therapy?"

She laughs. "Just to be clear, my intention is never to go hard on you. But yes, I do feel like you're ready to start exploring some things a bit more."

Exploring some things. She'd warned me of this in our last session. "Sounds terrifying."

She laughs again. "It might be, just a little. But that's normal. We can pull back at any time."

I shove my hands under my thighs, clutching myself, bracing for whatever conversation she has in store. There are so many topics to choose from. She must have an extensive checklist in the binder that's on her lap. I imagine her spinning a wheel, making a game of the disaster that is my life.

"I know most people start at the beginning," she says, "but I was thinking we could start at the end."

"The end?"

"Why don't you take me back to the day of the accident, and then we'll go from there."

Chapter 26

NICOLE

I am in a hospital bed. I am wearing a gown. I have an IV hooked up to a clear plastic bag of unknown fluids. The room is dim—overhead lights off, curtains on the window drawn. There is light in the cracks around the window, though. It is daytime.

My body hurts. My right leg is in a cast, but it's not my leg that hurts so much as my midsection. It aches with each breath.

"Well, look who's up," a voice says.

It hurts to turn my head. It doesn't turn as much as I'd like, but I see a woman, a nurse, coming toward me. She goes to the little computer station next to my bed, types something in.

"I told your husband you'd be up today," she says. "I'm Jocelyn, your nurse."

"Hi," I say.

"Your husband will be back soon. He just stepped out for a bit."

"What happened?"

"You don't remember?"

Do I? When I close my eyes, I see the car, my dad's car, barreling toward a tree.

"A car accident?"

She nods. Her eyes go wide. "A big one," she says. "It's amazing you had such minor injuries."

Whatever injuries I have do not feel minor.

"You broke your leg, just below the knee. A few cracked ribs. No internal bleeding, though. No head injury. We had you sedated to run a few tests. The doctors say it's a bit of a miracle."

"Oh" is all I can say.

"You must have someone looking out for you." She tilts her head upward, toward the heavens, toward the angels she believes in. I remember that my dad is dead, and this fact startles me as if it's one I've just learned.

I close my eyes again, see Elijah's face right before we make impact. Pure terror.

"Is Elijah okay?"

"Hmm?"

"Elijah?"

Her brows furrow. "Sorry, love, who's that?"

"The man who was in the car. In the passenger's seat."

She looks puzzled. One of the machines next to me beeps louder, probably alerting her to the sudden increase in my heart rate and blood pressure.

"You were alone, sweetie," she says.

She is my age, so the *sweetie* feels condescending.

"No, there was a man with me."

How bad was the accident? Was he wearing his seat belt? I have horrific visions of him being ejected from the car, of his body lying on the side of the road. Who would know to look for him there? Nobody in my life knew he existed. They could have easily identified me by the car. The license plate would be attached to my dad's name. A phone call would go to his phone. Merry would answer. They would know to look for me, but not Elijah.

Jocelyn, who is beginning to irritate me, is still looking at me like I'm nuts when Kyle walks in. He has more stubble on his face than I've ever seen on him. He is a ritualistic shaver. The facial hair suits him. Perhaps we could give our marriage one last go, with him sporting a beard. He would have to forgive me for Elijah, though. How could he ever forgive me?

"You're awake," Kyle says, rushing to my side. He sits on the edge of the bed next to me. Has he ever been this happy to see me before?

"Hi," I say.

My head feels like it is full of cotton candy, a big pink puff of it.

"God, you had all of us so worried." He takes out his phone. "I gotta text Merry."

He types a quick message, then looks at me again, scanning my eyes with intent, like he really wants to see me. Has he ever looked at me like this before?

"I'll give you two some time," Jocelyn says before leaving and pulling the door shut behind her.

"We'll have to call the girls when you're up to it," he says.

The girls. Who is with them if Kyle is here?

"We all flew up here. They're with Merry," he says, as if reading my mind. Has he ever successfully read my mind? I sure as hell have wanted him to, have considered that a mark of true love.

What if I just don't ask about Elijah? What if I just pretend the affair never happened? Could I live with myself knowing that Elijah may be dead off the side of Highway 35? I think of how close he is with his mother, how tormented she must be not hearing from him, her mama's boy.

"Kyle," I say. When I swallow, it feels as if a giant navel orange is sliding down my throat, attempting to block what is coming next. "There was a man with me in the car."

He looks at me, and I watch his face transform from confusion to tentative anger.

"What?"

His voice is still calm. He is hoping I don't mean what I mean.

"There was a man. In the passenger's seat."

"Who?"

I swallow what feels like another navel orange. "Elijah Baker."

"Who?"

He is shaking his head now, shaking off the reality I am presenting to him.

"Elijah Baker. I met him when I was up here."

I let the words hang. I don't want to have to say it: *We were having an affair.* I wait for him to come to the conclusion himself. It is agonizing.

"What are you talking about?"

"I was involved with a man here. Elijah Baker. He was in the car. I just needed to go for a drive after my dad died, and . . ."

I'm about to tell him about the journal I found, but then don't want to get into it. Has Merry already told him about that?

"Honey, are you sure you're thinking clearly right now? Nobody said anything about another person in the car."

I start to cry. "What if he's on the side of the road? Did they look?"

He puts his hand on my leg, and that's when I know he doesn't believe me. If he did, he wouldn't want to be within ten feet of me.

I touch my belly.

"I could be pregnant. Am I pregnant? Is the baby okay?"

"Nic, slow down. You're not pregnant. They've done a ton of blood work and tests. You thought you were *pregnant?*"

Did I? Nothing is making sense.

"You need to find out about Elijah. He could be on the side of the road," I repeat.

"Honey, look, I'll contact the police department and ask whoever was on the scene, but I think it's more important that we ask the doctors about your head."

Jocelyn just said they checked my head, though. *A bit of a miracle.*

"Wait, do you have my phone?" I ask.

"Your phone? I don't know where—"

"Or log into our Verizon account on your phone. You'll see his number in there."

"Whose number?"

"Elijah Baker's," I say. "Maybe he's at a different hospital or something. I need to try to call him."

"Nic, look, I think you're mistaken, okay? But if you want me to try the police department, I will."

That will have to do. For now.

"Okay," I say. "Call them."

He looks dumbfounded. "Really?"

I guess he thought I was going to say, "Never mind, you're probably right, I'm mistaken."

I'm not mistaken, though.

"Please," I say. "Please call them."

He sighs heavily, then takes out his phone. He googles, then lifts the phone to his ear.

"Hi, yes. My wife was in a car accident last night, and I'm wondering if I can talk to the officer that was on the scene first."

He looks at me like *Happy now?* I just stare at him, waiting for information.

"Sure, I can hold."

He sighs again. If there's one thing Kyle can't stand, it's making a fool of himself. I'm sure he thinks I'm forcing him to do exactly that.

"Yes, hi," he says after a few moments. He stands from the bed, starts pacing.

"Right, the accident on Highway 35. My wife just woke up from some fairly heavy sedation, and she's saying there was a man in the car with her."

"Okay, yes. That's what I told her."

He looks at me like *I told you so.*

"Ask him to please drive by, to look around the area, to make sure. There was a man with me. Elijah Baker."

Kyle tilts his head back, looks at the ceiling, seemingly in agony.

"She's asking if you can go by the scene and make sure someone else isn't there," he says.

There is an "Uh-huh" and an "Okay" and a "Thanks," and then he ends the call.

"He said it's on his patrol route so he's happy to look, but he's quite sure nobody else was in the car, honey."

He has called me *honey* three times since walking into the room. It may be more times than he's called me *honey* in the entirety of our marriage.

"Okay," I say. "Thanks."

I'm not settled, though.

"You were alone, hon."

Hon.

I shake my head.

"Give me your phone," I say.

"Why?"

He looks distrusting.

"Just give it to me."

He acquiesces. I google Elijah's name, just as I've done before. I find the image of him from the LinkedIn page.

"That's him," I say, turning the phone to Kyle.

He leans in, squints.

"Log in to the Verizon account. You'll see his number. We've called, texted . . . for weeks now."

I never thought I'd be here, not trying to hide my affair but instead trying to prove its existence.

Kyle takes back his phone, taps the Verizon app, logs in, humors me.

"Here," he says, handing it back to me.

I tap the link to the records associated with my phone number. I've worried about Kyle doing this, about him sensing my distance and investigating, coming face to face with the reality of my betrayal. I knew if it got to that point, I would have no defense. I would have only weak apologies, perhaps relief.

I look for Elijah's number, his 415 area code.

It's not there, though.

There is one 415 number, repeated a few times. Merry.

I look up, and Kyle is staring down at me. "Well?"

"Something's wrong," I say.

"I agree."

"No, I mean . . . something's really wrong."

"Again, I agree."

He seems suddenly exhausted.

"You have LinkedIn, right? Message him there. See if he's okay. Tell him I'm in the hospital."

There's a knock at the door. It opens to reveal a woman bringing me a tray of plastic-wrapped food.

"Lunch!" she says.

As she arranges the tray in front of me, I feel Kyle's eyes boring into me. He thinks I am deranged.

Am I deranged?

"I'm going to the nurses' station," he says. "I think we should talk to your doctor."

Completely deranged, that's what he thinks.

He leaves, and I unwrap the turkey sandwich. It's the saddest sandwich I've ever seen—dry deli meat accompanied by a single piece of wilted lettuce and a mealy tomato slice. It makes me think of my dad again, of the rubbery chicken they served him that day I took him to the hospital.

I take a bite of the sandwich because I'm starving, wash it down with a sip of apple juice. The apple juice makes me think of the girls. What has Kyle told them? Are they worried? Scared? When they are older, will Kyle tell them the truth? *Mommy was having an affair with a man named Elijah Baker, and they got in an accident . . .*

I guess he would have to come to terms with that truth first.

Maybe I'll have to be the one to tell them. Or not. Maybe my dad had it right. Maybe there are certain things children should never know.

My head still cotton-candy-like, I doze off after lunch despite all efforts to stay awake and figure out this Elijah thing. When I wake, the light around the window is gone. The clock on the wall says seven o'clock. Somehow, I have slept seven hours.

"Hey," Kyle says.

I startle, had no idea he was here. He is sitting in a chair just out of my peripheral vision. I turn to him.

"Hi," I say.

"How you feeling?"

"Groggy."

"They said you'll feel the sedation effects for a day or so. You've been through a lot."

"I feel like you've been through more. This all seems like a dream to me."

"It seems like a dream to me too," he says. "Or nightmare, rather."

I shift, sit up straighter in bed, my back sore and creaky.

"You hungry?" he asks. "They came by with dinner, but I didn't want to wake you."

He juts his chin in the direction of the door, where my dinner tray is pushed up against the wall.

"Not particularly hungry," I say. "Can I talk to the girls?"

"I told them you'd talk to them tomorrow. Probably best to wait until you're a little more back to normal."

"They're okay, though?"

"Yes. They know you were in a car accident, but I didn't give them details. I told them you're okay and the doctors just want to keep you for a little while."

They are too young to understand the seriousness of anything, and this is a blessing.

Kyle comes to the bed, sits on the edge of it, his hand on my leg.

"So I did what you asked," he says. "I messaged this Elijah Baker. On LinkedIn."

My heart starts thudding away.

"Did he respond? Is he okay?"

"Do you want to see?" he asks.

My hands are shaking as I take the phone from him. He has the LinkedIn message thread displayed, ready for me.

Kyle's message:

Hello, Elijah. This may be the strangest message you ever receive. My wife is in the hospital after a car accident just outside Half Moon Bay yesterday. She said that you were in the passenger's seat of her car and insisted I message you. Do you mind replying, even if it's just to say this is crazy? Thank you.

Elijah's message:

Hey man. Wow. That's wild. I definitely was not in a car accident yesterday or anywhere near Half Moon Bay yesterday. I'm at a conference in Phoenix actually. It could be another Elijah Baker. Not me, man. Sorry.

I take a closer look at the photo. It is definitely my Elijah Baker. He's trying to cover it up. He doesn't want Kyle to know about us. But at least he's okay, I guess.

"Happy?" Kyle says, peering over.

I shake my head. "He's lying."

"Nic, this is getting insane. He's not lying. There was nobody in your car."

I add a message to the thread:

Elijah, it's me. Katrina. Kat. I told Kyle everything so you don't have to pretend. He thinks I'm nuts. Just please confirm you're okay. I don't have my phone. You may be trying to text me. This is all a mess . . .

Kyle looks at what I'm writing, then looks at me.

"Katrina?" he says.

"It's such a long story . . ."

He does one of his heavy sighs. "Look, I talked to the doctors. Convinced them to do another scan of your brain to make sure nothing is going on."

His phone dings with an incoming message. We both stare at the screen. It's Elijah.

Katrina? You mean from the bar a while back? I remember the name. Dude, I have no idea what you're talking about though. We talked for a half hour and then I left to meet my girlfriend for dinner. Not sure what the confusion is, but wish you well. Peace.

I just shake my head. This doesn't make any sense. Is he breaking things off? Ghosting me or whatever the young people call it?

"Hon, look at me," Kyle says.

I do.

"The doctors said they'll do another scan before discharge tomorrow. But they said there were no abnormalities on the first scan. They think perhaps this is more of a . . . psychological issue."

"What?"

"You've been under so much stress," he says.

"A psychological issue?"

He puts a hand on my shoulder.

"Don't worry, okay? We're going to get you some help."

Chapter 27

THERESE

I am in week 3. I have confessed all to Crystal, and she has done a remarkable job of maintaining a poker face and convincing me that she is not horrified with who I am as a person. Then again, I'm assuming she knew most of my story before I arrived at COME and had time to recover from any initial shock.

It is Thursday, and in this one-on-one session, Kyle will be making an appearance. I am dreading this. I haven't seen him since Margot escorted me from our home. We've talked on the phone, which is always awkward and makes me feel like an inmate calling from prison. It's clear he doesn't know what to say to me, and I don't know what to say to him. I am ashamed, and he is terrified of me. His wife, the nutcase.

Usually, I sit on the middle cushion of the couch in Crystal's office, but today I sit on the far-right cushion in anticipation of Kyle's presence.

"Remember, he's probably nervous too. I'm here to help the two of you, okay?" Crystal says.

Before I can respond, there's a knock at the door, and when Crystal opens it, Kyle is there with ever-smiling Phoebe. He is a deer in headlights. His hair is longer than usual, borderline disheveled, and he still has the facial hair he had when I was in the hospital. He puts a hand to his beard. I give him a meek smile, a cautious peace offering. He returns the same.

"You must be Kyle," Crystal says to him.

His eyes are on me when he says, "Yeah."

"Have a great session!" Phoebe says with too much enthusiasm before going on her way.

Crystal leads Kyle to the couch, and he sits on the far-left cushion, as I thought he would. Crystal watches this initial interaction, likely noting that we have not made any physical contact. Hands are not reaching for each other; bodies are not colliding into one another.

"So," Crystal says with a long exhale. "I know we have a lot to get into, and it's my hope that both of you will leave here a bit less uneasy after our hour together."

Out of the corner of my eye, I see Kyle nod as he presses his palms to his thighs.

"Let's jump right in and talk about the elephant in the room," Crystal says. "The Delusion."

That's what we've been calling the Elijah situation—the Delusion. She has been careful not to call me delusional, though I was and may always be.

"Kyle, I'm sure this was a big shock to you, and I'm curious what your thoughts are now that you've had some time to process this."

He groans. Audibly.

"My thoughts?" he says, seemingly bewildered by what's being asked of him.

"Yes. How did you feel when you understood that your wife was having this imagined affair?"

He lets out a long sigh. "Well, confused at first. Then angry. I mean, I know the affair wasn't *real*, but this whole . . . delusion, as you call it . . . was still a betrayal."

Crystal squints at him—her inquisitive therapist stare.

"How so?"

"She was obsessed with this guy. I've read the texts."

Apparently, the whole time I thought I was texting Elijah, I was just texting myself, texts Kyle has since perused. I have never been so humiliated.

"And beyond that, there's just this disbelief. Like, how did her mind *do* this? She was staying at the freaking Hilton and thought she was in this guy's apartment?"

Yes, that's what I did, which explains Liv finding that hotel key card in my purse. The charges were all there on our credit card: the nights spent at the Hilton, meals out—the breakfast spot I thought I went to with Elijah, the Chinese takeout, the Pier 39 fish house. The amount of money spent suggests I purchased enough for two people. Again, humiliated.

"Okay, let's take the two things separately. First, her obsession—as you said—with Elijah."

Crystal glances at me, as if to check if I am okay with where this is going. I am. She and I have already gone here in our sessions.

"Do you want to share with Kyle some of the things we've discussed?" Crystal asks me.

I nod, reluctantly, and dare to turn my head to look at Kyle. He turns to me. His eyes are both sad and infuriated. I have never seen him like this.

"I think Elijah represented something to me," I say, my voice soft and cautious.

Kyle just stares.

"Like, he was this ideal man. He was this escape from reality."

"And this imagined ideal speaks to a lot of what she felt was missing in her life," Crystal says. She nods at me, signals to me to continue.

"I wasn't feeling seen. I wasn't feeling tended to or cared for. I hated losing my job. I felt put in this position at home with the girls, and you didn't seem to get it. You didn't seem curious about what was going on with me. You just seemed . . . annoyed."

"I was annoyed," he says. Honest, at least.

"Why were you annoyed?" Crystal asks.

He turns away from me to Crystal.

"Nobody said she had to stay home forever. This was a temporary thing. I thought she liked doing the mom stuff. She's not the only one who didn't feel . . . *tended to*."

"He's talking about sex," I say to Crystal, crossing my arms over my chest.

"It's not just sex," Kyle says. "It's connection. That's how we connect."

"That's how *you* connect."

Crystal puts up both hands, telling us to pause.

"Ultimately, what I'm seeing here is a communication breakdown," she says. "There wasn't an open and honest discussion of needs, for both of you. You were both expecting a lot of mind reading."

"Shouldn't your partner be able to read your mind?" I ask. "We've been together since college, for god's sake."

"I wish our partners could do that. Alas, they are human."

She smiles, but I do not find this amusing.

"We'll come back to this—the communication breakdown," she says. "But I also want to talk about the other half of what you said, Kyle, which is you questioning how your wife's mind could do this."

"I've never heard of anything like this," he says. "This can't be common."

Crystal squints at him again.

"Common? Maybe not. We would classify this as a dissociative disorder. From a psychological perspective, considering all the factors, it's understandable."

"Understandable?" He nearly spits the word.

"Hear me out," Crystal says, showing him her palms again. "Grief is an incredibly powerful force. Your wife was grieving the impending loss of her father—we call that anticipatory grief. She was grieving a loss of self in her role as mother and wife."

I glance at him to confirm that, yes, he is rolling his eyes.

"I think she was grieving the marriage, the ideals she harbored about how two people should support and be with each other."

I don't have to look at him to know that his eyes are still rolling.

"Then there's the grief related to her mother. I see that as directly contributing to the accident," Crystal says. "It's a lot of grief, Kyle. And the human mind is amazingly self-protective. It will do fascinating things to protect us, to shield us from pain."

"Okay," Kyle says. He presses fingertips into his temples. "I get that she was going through a lot. I'm not really sure what to say."

Crystal turns to me, begging me with her eyes to chime in: "I know you've talked to me about the shame you feel from this."

"Shame, yeah," I say. "I mean, I'm basically reaffirming the stereotype of the batshit-crazy woman. That's how he sees me now."

I glance at Kyle, and his face says *Pretty much*.

"I think it's important for us to push through this stereotype," Crystal says. "In my opinion, society doesn't exactly support maternal mental health or maternal . . . anything. Women, particularly mothers, have the deck stacked against them. And we can get into all the reasons for that another time, but I just want to reiterate that your wife's experience is, like I said, understandable. The way things have . . . manifested . . . is unique, but your wife is not crazy. If we are going to make any progress, we need to start there."

I expect Kyle to scoff, but he is silent.

"For what it's worth, I think both of you see this as this terrible thing that's happened, but I don't," Crystal says. "I think this has broken open your lives in a very necessary way. If it hadn't been this, specifically, it would have been something else. Things wouldn't have continued as they were, not with all that was going on."

When Kyle is silent, Crystal says, "Does any of that resonate with you?"

He sighs, again. "I guess. But I still maintain that I've never heard of anything like this. People go through all kinds of stress and *this* doesn't happen."

"Okay, what's beneath that disbelief?"

"Beneath?" he says. He does not know therapy-speak.

"Meaning we can't just stay stuck in disbelief. There's something beneath that, something deeper that's gnawing at you. For example, do these events make you worry that this will happen again? Are you fearful? Angry?"

"Yes," Kyle says. "All of that."

Crystal nods and turns to me. "You're fearful, too, right?"

I clear my throat. "Yes. I don't trust myself. I'm just as perplexed as he is at how this happened. It's not like I've ever had something like this happen before."

"So you're both afraid. You're both having a hard time trusting the future."

I nod, and Kyle nods too.

"Good, that's an honest admission. You don't have to know the future right now. Trust of self and others can take time to rebuild. What *I* trust is that you two will figure it out."

I look at Kyle just as he looks at me. His eyes look doubtful, and I do not blame him.

～

At the end of the session, we hug awkwardly, his hand patting my back twice, as if I'm a buddy on his softball team. Crystal says we will schedule another joint session soon. I walk him to the reception area and ask him how the girls are doing. He says they are doing fine but they miss me.

"They do?" I ask.

"Are you serious?" he asks. He really does think I'm batshit crazy. "Of course they miss you."

～

I go back to my room to find Marie moving clothes from her drawers to a suitcase that's open on the bed.

"What's going on?" I ask.

"I'm leaving. Patrick said he's had enough of this, doesn't think it's helping."

Patrick is her husband. They've just started having joint sessions like the one Kyle and I just had.

"So you're just going back home?"

"No," she says, not looking up at me. "I'm going to rent an apartment nearby. Patrick will have custody of the boys. I'll visit sometimes."

I try to hide my shock.

"Okay," I say. It's all I can manage.

She looks up. "I know it's awful of me."

I don't know what to say. I do think it's awful—not that *she's* awful, but that it's awful it has to be this way.

She sits on the edge of her bed.

"It occurred to me that I'm basically your mother," she says.

I've told Marie my whole story—all the ugly little bits.

"No," I say on impulse. Though as I think about it, she is right. She is resigning from motherhood, not as completely as my mother did, but a resignation just the same.

Crystal and I have talked some about my mother. I'm sure we'll discuss her more in coming sessions. Crystal has given me space to admit my anger at my dad (and Merry) for keeping the truth from me. She's enabled me to come around to see my dad's deception as an attempt to protect me from pain. He was a papa bear that way. He wouldn't have ever wanted me to feel abandoned.

"Deception of self or others can have the sweetest intentions," Crystal said. "Not that the intention makes it less painful . . . but it's important to hold both feelings—the pain of being lied to and the gratitude for his desire to care for you."

My eyes welled up when she said that. Hers did too.

I have this fear that I *am* my mother. The whole thing with Elijah was an escape, just a different kind than hers. Crystal asked me if I envied what she'd done in running away. And I don't. I pity her. She missed out—on me.

"You attempted to escape without ever really leaving," Crystal said. "It's much different from what she did."

"Maybe."

"But for forgiveness to be possible—and it's totally up to you if you want to seek that within yourself—you may need to have compassion for what she did."

I scoffed. "I don't think I'll ever get there."

But now, looking at Marie, at the anguish in her face, I think maybe I will get there. Or close to there.

"You're not awful," I tell Marie. "Life is just . . . hard."

She smiles. "Well, that's true."

"I'd like to keep in touch, if you want," I say.

"Really?" She looks surprised. Perhaps she was expecting me to shun her.

"Of course."

She goes to her nightstand, scribbles something on a piece of paper—a phone number and a name: Amber.

"So that's your name," I say, finding it funny that neither of us has cared to inquire about the other's real name until now. We've been content pretending all this time.

"Amber Marie," she says.

"Nice to meet you, Amber," I say. "I'm Nicole."

Chapter 28

NICOLE

The recommended stay at COME is ninety days, just like at centers for recovery from alcoholism and other addictions. Apparently, ninety days is the agreed-upon time it takes to establish meaningful change. Apparently, a self can be reinvented in ninety days.

I'm not so sure I feel reinvented. I am still me. But now, at day 90, I feel, well, less likely to invent an entire person. I've started taking a low-dose antidepressant. I've gotten my hormones under control thanks to the very same birth control pill I took in my twenties. With therapy and time and space to myself, I am calmer, saner. I am someone who says things like "I feel very in my body."

I am ready to go home.

Well, not home, exactly.

Kyle has come in for multiple sessions—once a week since that first one. We have discussed the state of our marriage and come to the agreement to stay separated for now. Crystal says that with any type of infidelity or breach of trust, the old relationship must die. It must be grieved. And then both parties must decide if a new relationship will emerge. "To paraphrase Esther Perel," she said, "many of us will have multiple marriages in our lives. Some of us will have them with the same person."

Crystal is a big fan of Esther Perel.

Kyle and I are still grieving. There is so much we don't know yet, so much we are still understanding about why we chose each other twenty years ago, how we strayed from each other over all these years, what's possible in all the years yet to come. Kyle has said, "I don't get why you're unhappy. I'm the same guy I was when we first met. I haven't changed." To that, I said, "But I have."

It was Kyle's idea to lease a condo for me. We perused listings when he visited and selected a unit just a few blocks from our family home. We both use the word *temporary* when describing this arrangement. He says, "until you get on your feet," and I say, "to set myself up for success." It's only nine hundred square feet, but there are two bedrooms—one for me, one for the girls when they visit.

The girls.

Starting in week 4, I got phone privileges and was allowed to FaceTime them a few times a week. I cried each time. I have not seen them in person or touched their skin for three months, and I feel a clenching in my chest when I think about this. Kyle assures me they are doing well. They are back in day care five days a week. I don't know how we're affording all this—the condo lease, day care, my recovery bills. Kyle says not to worry. I assume Merry is helping. She doesn't know the Elijah component of my breakdown, but she knows enough. She checks in often. She's in the midst of her own "process," as Crystal would say. She goes to a grief group once a week and has taken up tai chi, which is incredibly random in the best way possible. She has dinner with Jim and Alice several nights a week. She is trying to feel better. It is a herculean effort. I admire it. Some people just give up, resign themselves to misery.

The girls think I am still recovering from the accident, which isn't completely false. When we FaceTime, they always ask, "Are you feeling better, Mommy?" and press their snot-filled noses to the screen, so close that every other part of their faces blurs. "Better and better," I tell them every time, and they cheer.

Everyone says kids are resilient. I think it's more that they are less attached than adults to any definition of *normal*, more accepting of the cards dealt to them because they have so little knowledge of other possible hands. Their mother was in an accident. She was not well. She had to be away to heal. She is "better and better." She is coming home. This is what they know. I wonder if I'll ever tell them the whole truth, or if I'll keep it from them, like my dad kept truths from me. I cannot judge him now. I find myself standing here in shoes similar to his, and I cannot say for certain I will walk a different path.

∼

There is no formal ceremony to send me off, but everyone at COME signs an oversize card with their well wishes. Phoebe does an exit interview with me in which she says, "I'm not supposed to say this, but you are one of my favorites." I assume she says this to everyone, but then she starts dabbing her eyes with a tissue, and I'm left to wonder.

Crystal brings me flowers and carries my bag as we make our way to the front of the building, where Kyle is waiting in the car. It's not goodbye with Crystal. She has a private practice a few miles away and will remain my therapist on an outpatient basis, thank god.

"Call or text if you need to," she says, giving me a hug. "I mean it."

I nod, unable to manage words because I can feel my throat tightening. This place has made me a *feeler* and I have mixed *feelings* about this.

Kyle puts my bag in the back seat and opens my door for me.

"You ready?" he asks.

"I have no idea."

Crystal leans in: "She's ready."

∼

We decide I'll reunite with the girls at the house, then talk to them about the condo situation. The tentative plan is for Kyle and me to each keep the girls for two days at a time, though we will take turns with day care drop-offs and pickups so we each see them every day. In our minds, it seems like a rather idyllic, albeit unconventional, arrangement. We each get time with the girls, time to show up as our very best parental selves, and we each get time alone to indulge our nonparental selves. I'm sure reality will be less idyllic than what we envision, but I am cautiously optimistic, which Crystal says is progress.

~

When we pull into the driveway, I see Merry in the window, likely the lookout for the girls. Kyle said she wanted to be here for my homecoming. I can hear the girls squealing before I even get to the front door, and I start to cry the happiest tears I have ever cried. Merry opens the door, and they barrel toward me, a flurry of limbs and wild hair. They launch their bodies at mine, and I stumble backward, sit on my butt, then lie flat on my back, face to the sky. The girls jump on top of me, and Kyle says, "Girls! Careful!" but they do not care. They will not be pleased until every inch of their bodies is in contact with mine. I kiss their faces—not just their lips but also their cheeks and noses and foreheads and chins and eyelids and earlobes. They breathe hard and say, "Mommy, Mommy, Mommy," their hearts beating like hummingbird wings.

I do not move. I stay still. I let them confirm for themselves that I am here, that I am back. I breathe deeply, in a way that would make everyone at COME proud, and I start to feel their breathing match mine, our bodies moving up and down in unison.

"It appears you all missed each other," Merry says finally, and we laugh, Grace and Liv giggling in the hysterical, almost maniacal way people do when whatever they fear does not come to pass, when the boogeyman is not in the closet, when the ghost is not under the bed, when the sound in the kitchen turns out to be nothing.

They did not think I would be back.

I am back.

I am back.

I am back.

Chapter 29

NICOLE

Six months later

"Mommy? Mommy? Mommy?"

The girls are back to summoning me every sixty seconds. The one summoning me in this particular moment is Liv. We are in the midst of the never-dull, usually agonizing Morning Routine as I try to get them out the door for day care by eight o'clock so I can get back home for a work call at eight thirty.

Michelle Kwan called a week after I left COME to say the ad agency had signed a new client and would love to have me back. I didn't even try to play it cool; I just said, "Yes!" before she could finish explaining the opportunity (which is designing advertising materials for a brand of silicone patches that people—mostly women—stick on their faces to diminish the appearance of wrinkles). I'll do thirty hours per week and see how it goes. I'm considering a little side business—photographing weddings, babies. Yes, I see the irony in memorializing others' familial bliss, but there's good money to be had, and I'm determined to pay back Merry whatever ungodly sum we owe for her support over these past several months. Crystal has been encouraging me to return to photographing ocean waves and rock formations in Joshua Tree. She says motherhood is inherently hard because of all its practical demands and ongoing sacrifices, but that the real sorrow for most women is not in what they must give to their children, but in what they lose in themselves.

"Mommy?" Liv says, tugging on my sleeve.

The pleas for my attention don't bother me like they used to. If my blood pressure rises, the increase is marginal. I no longer feel as if I'm close to a stroke every time my children whine. My nervous system has been rejiggered. Crystal uses this bucket analogy. She says when I came to COME, I had a very small bucket, meaning I was quick to get "filled up" by life's stresses and then overwhelmed by all that was spilling over, essentially drowning me. Now my bucket is much larger. I can, in a sense, carry more.

"Mommy?" Liv says. "I have accident."

Liv is three now and has gotten much better with her words. We are in the process of transitioning her out of pull-ups and into undies during the day (I am quite content to leave her in pull-ups at night until she is a teenager if it means I do not have to change sheets at 2 a.m.). There are, of course, accidents, usually right as we are trying to get out the door in the morning.

I put down my phone—I've been checking work email—and comfort her.

"Oh, it's okay, sweetie," I say, taking a deep breath. I have become quite skilled at deep breaths, breaths that make a slow, round-trip journey through my nose to my belly and back.

It's okay, sweetie, I tell myself. Crystal says I need to work on self-compassion, comforting my inner child. This still feels silly, but I try.

"Mommy, I'm still hungry," Grace says, standing before me with slumped shoulders and a pouty face.

"You are? I asked if you wanted more cereal, remember? We're done with breakfast now."

One of my strategies for making motherhood less taxing is setting clearer boundaries. Kyle was right when he used to say I let the girls control me. They were the puppeteers, me the puppet. Crystal assures me that establishing rules for the household gives everyone a sense of safety and security. "Clear is kind," she's said again and again. My first successful boundary has been around mealtimes—I decide when, where, and what we eat. The end.

Of course, the girls don't always love my rules.

"But I'm huuuungry," Grace says, letting her head fall to her chest in a dramatic display of defeat.

When I first returned from COME, the girls were overly affectionate and well behaved—little angels. They were constantly snuggling me and asking me if I was feeling okay. Grace insisted on bringing me water and snacks at regular intervals. Liv routinely stuck Band-Aids to every exposed area of skin on my body. It was, in a word, unnerving. I feared that my three-month absence had completely traumatized them and found myself longing for occasional demonic behavior to assure me we were returning to some semblance of normal.

After about five days, the demonic behavior began to return, along with a touch of the irritability I told myself I'd never feel again. Crystal says it's okay to feel agitated by motherhood. She says the difficult parts of motherhood will not become magically easy, but with my larger bucket, I'll have an easier time managing them. Or that's the theory. So far, it's held true.

"It's so weird. I have two favorite things," I told Crystal in our session yesterday. "One is spending time with my girls, and the other is *not* spending time with my girls."

She laughed. "That's maternal ambivalence."

"Do you therapists have a name for everything?"

"We try."

"I guess the fact that it has a name means it's not that unusual."

"Exactly," she said. "Have you heard that Jane Lazarre quote?"

"Who's Jane Lazarre?"

"A writer. She said that ambivalence is pretty much guaranteed and even natural in motherhood."

"Do you therapists collect tidbits of information like this in a secret online forum or what?"

She smiled. "That's actually a brilliant idea."

∼

When Grace continues to whine and I feel myself getting impatient, I take another deep breath. I remind her again, calmly, that we are done with breakfast.

"What I can do is make an Eggo waffle as a snack for you to eat in the car," I say. "But we do have to get going."

Grace sighs. "Fine."

She is four, which I hope is better than three. I talked to a mom at the playground the other day who has twin four-year-olds, and she referred to this stage as "the Fucking Fours," so we'll see. I like this park mom. Her name is Gabby, and I have identified her as a potential friend. Crystal wants me to work on friendships—as in having them. Crystal wants a lot from me.

"I want Eggo too!" Liv says as I place her still-chubby little legs in the holes of a clean pair of underwear.

"Okay, little one," I tell her.

I put two waffles in the toaster as Grace starts whining again. She is sitting on the floor, putting on her shoes. I buy only slip-on shoes, nothing with buckles or shoelaces. I consider this an act of self-preservation.

She throws one of the shoes across the floor. I take yet another deep breath. *It's okay, sweetie.*

"What is it, lovebug?" I ask her.

"I think my feet growed," she says. "These shoes feel weird."

Someone on Twitter wrote, "Nobody has more grievances than a toddler on the way out the door." So I'm not alone in my Morning Routine angst, though I do feel like Grace and Liv are particularly challenging. Crystal says it's a type of separation anxiety, and she didn't have to explain why my girls would feel more intense separation anxiety right now. Bedtime is also grueling—even more so than before. Some nights, I let both of them sleep in bed with me to avoid the Hour of Despair. It's another act of self-preservation for me, and necessary comfort for them. At some point, there will be a rule about sleeping, but for now, our bodies need each other.

I help Grace find a more suitable pair of shoes, which are, of course, the exact same size as the other ones. She approves. I grab the Eggo waffles, lift Liv into my arms, and head for the door.

"Do we go to Daddy's today?" Grace asks, still lingering behind.

She asks this every day, noticeably anxious about the schedule, the back-and-forth.

"He's picking you up at school today, but he's bringing you home here. You'll go to his house tomorrow night."

She sighs.

I put Liv down so I can hug Grace. The girls and I hug all the time now. As I said, our bodies need each other. It's like we are reconfirming each other's presence—*You're here, right? Are you here?*—on a daily basis.

"I know it's hard sometimes," I say to her.

For today, that little validation is what it takes to get her to follow me out the door.

After drop-off, I rush back home only to discover that my eight-thirty call has been moved to noon. I check my phone, tend to neglected texts. There is one from Kyle, asking if we are on for tomorrow. We are hiring a babysitter so we can go out on one of our prescribed dates. We schedule these outings every two weeks in an attempt to connect. So much remains uncertain. There is the basic question: Do we like each other? We haven't had sex, and I feel no desire to do so. Kyle says he feels desire, but when pressed, he admits it's a more generalized desire, not specific to me. I take no offense at this; the radical honesty is refreshing.

I told him we feel more like comrades in arms than anything, bonded by the battles we've survived so far. He didn't disagree, but said, "Aren't all married people with kids like that?"

I never feel particularly excited about our dates, but I don't dread them either. We usually talk about the kids, despite promising not to. We might not have anything else to discuss anymore. Maybe that's okay.

On our last outing, I suggested that he might want to try a dating app, to see if he feels something with someone else. His eyebrows shot up to his hairline, and he laughed it off, but there was a twinkle of intrigue, of hope, in his eyes. I want him, and us, to be happy—with each other or apart. He asked if I wanted to try a dating app, and I guffawed. I cannot imagine dating, cannot imagine presenting myself to a stranger—"So I'm less than a year out from a complete psychotic break. What's your story?"

Yes, we're on! Meet you there at 5?

There being the new local brewpub we both want to try. He texts back a thumbs-up.

There's a text from Merry too.

Emailed you some photos from the memorial, FYI

We had Dad's memorial service at the golf club last month, his "One-in-a-Million Celebration of Life," as we called it. Merry wanted to wait for me to be "in a good place" before doing the service, and I appreciated that. I told her I felt bad for delaying her closure, and she said, "Oh, Nicole, how could I ever have *closure?*" And I know what she means now that the memorial service has come and gone. There was no closure. The event was nice, a type of container we attempted to construct to hold the experience of Dad's death. But we both know it will never be fully contained. It will run like a river through the rest of our lives.

It still shocks me that he's gone. I'll think of something I want to tell him and then remember, *Holy shit, my dad is dead.* The other day, Merry texted me from his phone, and when I saw his name pop up, I thought for a brief second that he was still alive.

> Hi. It occurred to me to look at what your dad had in the Notes app of his phone. Thought you might want to see too. Here it is

Then she pasted random notes he'd made—a reminder for his next oil change, a list of restaurants with good coupon deals, golf scores for the past three years, a list of Christmas-gift ideas. Next to my name for the Christmas-gift list, he had "bonsai tree," and I have no idea why, but I do know I will buy myself a bonsai tree.

~

When I log on to my work computer, Jill messages me to say hi. It's been good to be in touch with her again. As part of my mission to have friends, I plan a lunch date with Jill once a month. Last month, she told me she's pregnant, after all these years touting the benefits of her child-free lifestyle. "We had a profound change of heart," she said by means of explanation, and I tried to maintain a neutral expression on my face though I was laughing like a mischievous teenager inside. I have evolved in some ways but not others. I wanted to tell her that she was in for a profound change of *life*, but I knew nothing I could say would adequately prepare her. The adjustment will be alarming, and I'll be there for her as she, like all mothers, undertakes the yearslong process of coming to terms with just how alarming it is.

> Jill: Michelle Kwan is on a rampage today

We love gossiping about Michelle Kwan.

Already? It's not even 9

Jill: She's been emailing since 6

Oh god

Jill doesn't know about Elijah, but she knows I went to a "recovery center" to get help with "stress." She wasn't surprised. Her exact words: "You were seeming a little unhinged." She says I seem less unhinged now. Maybe one day she'll get the full story, but that day will not be anytime soon.

Jill: So . . . give any more thought to sending the email?

Ah yes, the email.

In explaining my "stress," I told Jill about the shock of my mother's existence. And yesterday, I confessed to her, after first confessing to Crystal, that I've been considering reaching out to her.

I googled "Rose Fournier" a couple of weeks ago, and there she was, alive and well on the internet. I'd googled her in years past, when I thought she was dead and was just curious if the World Wide Web contained any information about her, but I'd always typed "Rose Larson" and gotten no helpful results. I didn't know she'd kept her maiden name until I read the now-infamous journal. Crystal condoned the googling. She'd never believed me when I claimed I didn't care to know anything about my mother. "Your curiosity is natural," she said. "There is healing to be had there."

According to the internet, Rose Fournier recently retired from teaching feminist theory (surprise, surprise) at Cornell. The blurb about her retirement said she was moving back to California to "enjoy some much-needed sunshine." There was a photo of her. It looked like me, just with one of those app aging filters applied. I remember what my dad used to say—"spitting image."

The retirement announcement included a link to her website, which featured various publications of hers, along with video clips of her lecturing. Her voice is deeper than mine, more authoritative. We share so many mannerisms—head tilts, hand gestures. In one of the clips, she's speaking from a stage, and she paces the length of it, her stride so similar to my own. I watched that clip over and over and didn't realize until the fourth viewing that my hands were shaking.

I think of maternal ambivalence, of how my mother felt it, like so many others. But unlike so many others, she decided the scales tipped toward the side of abandoning her role completely. I wonder if she's had regrets, if she ever wanted to contact me. Or when she left, perhaps the ambivalence vanished as she embraced the life she truly wanted. When it comes to liberation from oppression (and I do believe my mother felt oppressed), there are those classic words of advice: don't look back. Perhaps my mother heeded that advice, steadfastly.

I've been in touch with Amber from COME. I thought she would have regrets. I thought she would look back. But no. Exactly as she planned, she got her own apartment and rarely sees her boys. She visits with them for a handful of hours a couple of weekends a month, and that's it.

"Not every woman is cut out for motherhood," she said to me, with a confidence and conviction in her voice that I hadn't heard at COME. "We're told we are, that it's part of our DNA, but that's just not true. And we need to talk about this before women sign on for something they're told will fulfill them. We do all women a disservice by silencing women like me."

"Women like you are the threat, though," I said. "If more women embraced your thinking, if more women opted out, the human race would be in trouble."

She laughed. "The human race is in trouble as it is."

When I asked her if she's happy, she said she's happier than ever, that she finally feels like herself again. In my efforts to not judge her, I have thought over and over again of my mother. In efforts to forgive my mother, I have thought over and over of Amber.

Me: Ugh. I started to type it out and . . . I just don't know

Jill, like Crystal, says she doesn't have an opinion on whether I should or should not contact my mother. "Only you know," they both said. They have more trust in my intuition than I do.

Jill: If you're not sure, wait. You'll know

Will I? I don't know. But thank you

Jill: Sorry, gotta go. Kwan is calling about the headline options I provided for this stupid brochure

Godspeed

This is the short, pitiful draft in progress:

Dear Rose,

This is your daughter, Nicole. My father died and I found the journal you kept all those years ago . . .

I don't know what to write after this.

Would you like to talk on the phone sometime?

Do you want to meet over Zoom?

Where in California are you? Should we do lunch?

Do I even want contact with her? She has never wanted contact
with me all these years. Am I after something else? If I'm honest, perhaps
I just want her to know I know. *You couldn't hide forever!* Perhaps I'm
hoping that will torment her. Perhaps I long for an apology. Perhaps
I long for her remorse, if just to prove to myself that staying in the
trenches of motherhood, despite all temptation to go AWOL, is worth
it. Perhaps I long for this more than I long for an actual relationship.
Perhaps when Crystal said, "There is healing to be had there," she
wasn't implying healing via reaching out to my mother, but healing via
reaching within myself.

It's a busy workday. I stop only to make myself a sandwich and
enjoy the silence of my home. It was uncomfortable at first, the silence.
After all, what mother ever gets quiet time alone in her own home? I'm
ashamed of my needs at times, embarrassed by my privilege.

Before I know it, it's four o'clock, and I hear Kyle open the front
door, the girls calling, "Mommy!" Kyle says, "Give her a few minutes
to wrap up work, okay?" but they do not listen. Their feet are loud
and fast on the wood floor, and then they are standing before me. I
feel the ambivalence in my body—the joy of seeing their little faces,
the annoyance at an earlier-than-expected end to my workday. I am
learning to carry both. There is room for both.

Grace is holding out a picture she drew at school—two stick figures
that have only heads, a line for their bodies, and feet. No arms. She says
one is me and one is her. Liv is shouting over her that she did not have
an accident all day. I transform my face into one displaying enthusiastic
joy and watch their faces do the same in response. We are, the three of
us, wide eyed and ecstatic.

"Mommy done?" Liv asks, looking at my open laptop.

"Almost," I say as I stand and pick her up. She wraps her legs
around my middle.

"I want to koala too," Grace says. We have recently made *koala* into a verb.

I put down Liv and lift Grace. She is heavier, and my back aches, but I know someday soon they will be too big for me to hold, and I'll feel an ache of a different kind. I have to wonder how much of suffering is rooted in shortsightedness. These moments with them are fleeting, so fleeting.

"Girls! Let Mom finish!" Kyle shouts, looking out for my sanity in ways he never did before. "Come here!"

I put Grace down, and she says, "Mom, I can do a pirouette!"

She shows me, and Liv copies her, and they turn in circles toward the door as Kyle yells for them again.

"Okay, tiny dancers, go with Daddy. I'll be right out."

They obey. It is only when they are gone that I realize I've been holding my breath. I am still working on relaxing into the ambivalence.

I exhale as I sit and turn back to my laptop, stare at the draft of my email to Rose Fournier. I move my cursor over the words, highlight them.

I inhale.

I hit Delete.

The girls erupt into laughter, and I rise from my chair, compelled to discover the origin of such glee.

I close my laptop.

I do not need to write to my mother. Not today, anyway.

Today, I do not have answers or resolutions, but I do not require any. Today, I am sure of nothing except that I have everything I need.

Acknowledgments

Writing a book starts as a solitary endeavor and ends as a team effort. I'm so grateful for my team.

Thank you to Carey Nelson Burch Leo for playing matchmaker and introducing me to Margaret Riley King, agent extraordinaire. Margaret, thank you for your steadfast belief in this book. Sophie Cudd and Meagan Irby, thank you for your parts in ushering this book along.

Thank you to Norton for allowing me to use quotes from Adrienne Rich's *Of Woman Born*.

Thank you to Amazon Publishing and Lake Union Publishing for embracing me with open arms. Danielle Marshall, thank you for seeing my vision for this book and for my career as a whole. Huge thanks to Nancy Holmes, Carmen Johnson, Jen Bentham, and everyone at Amazon/Lake Union who helped escort this book across the finish line.

Let it be known—Jenna Free is one of the best editors in all the land. I usually dread edits, but hers made so much sense. It's amazing when people can see inside your brain, understand what you're trying to do, and guide you accordingly. Thank you to Annie S., whose copyediting skills blew my mind. I like to think I have a firm grasp of the English language, and then a good copyeditor humbles me.

There are many works of fiction and nonfiction that inspired me as I wrote this book. I want to thank a few of the authors of those books— Amanda Montei, Darcy Lockman, Minna Dubin, Rachel Cusk, Rachel

Yoder, Sheila Heti. I must also give credit to the late Nora Ephron for the apt description of children as grenades.

Last, thank you to my daughter, Mya, my little grenade who has blown my heart wide open. Motherhood isn't always easy, but loving her is. I am the luckiest.

About the Author

Photo © 2022 Ashley Hooper

Author Kim Hooper was born in Los Angeles and has worked as an advertising copywriter for twenty years. She holds a bachelor's degree in communications from the University of California San Diego and a master's in professional writing from the University of Southern California. *Woman on the Verge* is her seventh novel. Hooper's most popular previous titles include *No Hiding in Boise* and *People Who Knew Me*, which is also a podcast series. The *Wall Street Journal* describes her work as "refreshingly raw and honest." Hooper lives in south Orange County with her daughter and a collection of pets—and adores them all. When not writing, the author enjoys running, doing yoga, or reading a good book.